THE
LAUGHTER
OF DEAD
KINGS

WILLIAM MORROW

An Imprint of HarperCollins *Publishers*

ELIZABETH PETERS

THE LAUGHTER OF DEAD KINGS

THE LAUGHTER OF DEAD KINGS. Copyright © 2008 by MPM Manor, Inc. All rights reserved. Printed in the United States of America. No part of this book may be used or reproduced in any manner whatsoever without written permission except in the case of brief quotations embodied in critical articles and reviews. For information address HarperCollins Publishers, 10 East 53rd Street, New York, NY 10022.

HarperCollins books may be purchased for educational, business, or sales promotional use. For information please write: Special Markets Department, HarperCollins Publishers, 10 East 53rd Street, New York, NY 10022.

FIRST EDITION

Library of Congress Cataloging-in-Publication Data has been applied for.

ISBN 978-0-06-124624-1

08 09 10 11 12 WBC/RRD 10 9 8 7 6 5 4 3 2 1

to Roxie Walker

Foreword

Recently I discussed, with several mystery writer friends, the problem of what we sometimes call "the current now." One of my series is set in real time; the characters age appropriately with each passing year and with each volume. The Vicky series, and those of many of my friends, don't work that way. Vicky made her first appearance in 1973. She was not yet thirty. The most recent volume was published in 1994, more than twenty years later, but Vicky had aged only a few years. She's still in her early thirties, although the world in which she lives has changed a great deal. The Cold War has ended, the horror in Iraq is under way, the Internet has its tentacles into everybody's lives, and people go around with cell phones glued to their ears.

So how do we writers explain the inconsistencies and anachronisms? We don't. We can't. So please don't bother writing to point them out to me, ignore them as I have, and place yourself in the "current now." To quote my friend Margaret Maron, to whom I owe that phrase and other excellent advice, "Isn't it fun being God in our separate universes, where we can command the sun to stand still, and it does?"

THE
LAUGHTER
OF DEAD
KINGS

ONE

I cover my ears, I close my eyes,
Still I hear your voice, and it's tellin' me lies . . .

My singing doesn't inspire thousands of fans to emit screams of delight, but I was a trifle hurt when my dog jumped up with a howl and streaked for the stairs. Usually he likes my singing. He's the only one who does like my singing. Otherwise his hearing is pretty good.

John was coming down the stairs. He halted Caesar's headlong rush with a peremptory order—something I've never succeeded in doing—and sauntered toward me.

I hadn't seen him for two weeks. My toes went numb. He was wearing a blue shirt that matched his eyes and those of the Siamese cat draped over his shoulder. One of his hands supported Clara's front end, his long fingers as elegantly shaped as the small seal-brown paws they held. Clara had not cared much for John at first, but he had set out to win her feline heart (the alternative being bites and scratches) and he had succeeded, with the aid of frequent offerings of chicken. They looked sensational together. He looked sensational.

So I said grumpily, "Right on cue. Why can't you come in the front door like normal people instead of climbing up to my bedroom window?"

"It brings back such fond memories."

Memories of the time when Interpol and a variety of competing crooks had been looking for him and the art treasures he had made off with. He was now a respectable antiquities dealer, if I could believe him. Which I probably shouldn't. Tellin' me lies had been one of his favorite activities.

I picked up the grubby wad of white yarn and the crochet hook precariously attached to it, which I had dropped onto my lap, and pretended to study it. Playing it cool, so as not to be beguiled by the winsome smile and melting blue eyes. Damn him, he hadn't showed up for two damned weeks. London is less than two hours from Munich by air. I should know, I'd made the trip often enough. Thanks to an indulgent boss I could get away from my job at the museum more easily than John could get away from his antiques business. Or so he claimed. Tellin' me lies?

"So how's business?" I inquired.

No answer. A thud and a loud Siamese complaint made me look up. Clara was on her feet—at HIS feet, glaring at him, and John was . . . not glaring . . . staring at me with a look of glazed disbelief. No, not at me. At the misshapen object I held.

"What is it?" he croaked.

"You needn't be so rude," I said defensively. "It's a baby cap. I'm not very good at crochet, but I'll figure it out eventually."

2

John staggered to the nearest chair and collapsed into it. He was white as a sheet, a lot whiter than the mangled little cap, which had suffered from Clara's occasional attempts to play with it.

"What the hell is the matter with you?" I demanded. "Bob—you know, my brother Bob—his new wife is expecting her first and I thought it would be a nice gesture if I . . . if I . . ."

He let out a long gasp of air, and then it hit me. Like a sock in the solar plexus.

"Aaah," I said. "Aha. Sometimes I am so slow. Is that what you thought? That *is* what you thought! Not only that I was about to become a mummy but that I—wait a minute, it's coming, I'll get it eventually—that I had got myself pregnant in order to trap you into unholy wedlock. And the very idea made you sick! You low-down skunk! You son of a bitch! I'll bet your mother has been hinting for months, 'Watch out for that worthless trollop, she'll try to—'"

"Vicky!" His voice is usually a mellifluous tenor, but he can out-shout me when he has to, and believe me, he had to. He jumped up and came toward me. I threw the baby cap, complete with crochet hook, at him. He ducked. The ball of yarn rolled off the couch and Clara went in pursuit. John grabbed me by the shoulders.

"Stop yelling and listen to me."

"You did, didn't you? Believe it."

"Believe what? That you'd be dim enough to pull an antiquated stunt like that one? Never in my wildest fantasies. But you must admit my initial impression was justified by the evidence available to me at the time."

"Stop talking like a lawyer. It wasn't what you thought, it was your reaction. The very idea terrified you. You looked as if you were about to pass out."

"Yes."

I was gearing up for a loud, satisfying fight, but that quiet-voiced confession took the wind out of my sails. The best I could come up with was a feeble "So you admit it."

"I may be all the things you called me and more, but I'm not so complacent as to be blind to the consequences of my own misdeeds. Bloody hell, Vicky, I'm terrified all the time! Admittedly I'm one of the world's most flagrant cowards, but I'm also afraid for you. There are a lot of people in the big bad world who hate my guts and who harbor grudges." The words came spilling out, his face was flushed and his fingers bit into my skin. "When we agreed to be together, I tried to talk you out of it. I put you in danger simply by associating with you. But as you pointed out with considerable eloquence, you were an adult and it was your choice. You convinced me against my better judgment, and the few remaining shreds of my conscience. How do you suppose I felt, for one ghastly moment, when I thought there might be another hostage to fortune, a helpless, totally vulnerable, completely innocent potential victim of my various sins? The people I'm referring to wouldn't feel the slightest compunction about using a child to get back at me—and you."

I felt like a low-down skunk.

"I'm sorry," I mumbled. "I blew up without stopping to think. There are a few people who hold grudges against me, too."

"Quite a few." He managed to smile.

"Well. It's okay."

"I'm sorry. For . . . everything."

I knew what he meant, and I didn't dare go down that road, even in my own mind. I stood up, leaving him sitting with his hands limp in his lap, looking uncharacteristically helpless, and rescued the pitiful remnants of my attempt at domesticity from Clara. By the time I had untangled the yarn from under chairs and around legs of tables, John was at the cupboard mixing drinks. I didn't blame him. Tossing the pathetic wad of yarn into a wastebasket, I accepted the glass he handed me.

"I'm sorry for what I said about your mother." At least I had run out of breath before I started calling her names. Jen and I would never be best friends, and in my not so humble opinion she was too possessive about her baby boy, but rudeness is rudeness, even when it's true.

John shrugged. "She's the reason I haven't been in touch recently. No, it's not what you think; I had to pop down to Cornwall and deal with a little emergency there. Someone broke into the house."

"How terrible," I exclaimed, with only a moderate amount of hypocrisy. I pitied the burglar who ran into Jen unless he was armed to the teeth.

"She wasn't hurt, or even frightened. You know her."

"Oh, yes."

"She wasn't aware a break-in had occurred until she took it into her head to do a spot of housecleaning, and ventured into the attic."

My first, and thus far last, visit to the family homestead had been a well-meaning attempt on John's part to get his mother used to me, or at least the idea of me. John had once told me: "You wouldn't like her. She wouldn't like you either." But when I first met Jen, on what could be called neutral territory, I had found her mildly amusing and perfectly pleasant.

That was before she found out who I was—or rather, what I was, in relation to John.

When he suggested we spend a few days in Cornwall, giving Jen a chance to know me better, I thought, what the hell, why not give it a try? I did try, I really did. I even bought a dress. It was an inoffensive shade of green with a demure neckline and a skirt that reached to mid-calf. I put pink polish on my nails and bought a matching lipstick. I had my hair done. I looked, as John was unwise enough to remark, like an ingénue in a forties musical.

Bear in mind, if you please, that I didn't regard Jen as a threat. I had realized early on that John's feelings about his mother were a mixture of exasperation and tolerant affection. He'd go his own sweet way no matter what she said or thought. What I hadn't realized was that Jen refused to accept that.

They say Americans are suckers for antiquity. I suppose we are; we don't have many houses that are over three hundred years old. This one had all the right stuff—gateposts with shapeless heraldic beasts on top, heavy wrought-iron gates, a winding drive overhung by gloomy trees, a circular carriage drive. The house itself was like a caricature of a Gothic novel's cover: the original, rather elegant stone facade, now smeared with lichen and thick with ivy, had inappropriate towers on either end and, of all things, crenellations. I wondered somewhat hysterically if there was an Ornamental Hermit lurking in the grounds.

It had been raining and drizzling all day; clouds hung low and dark over the house and fog twined around the towers. I wouldn't have been at all surprised if Jen had ordered up the weather. The front door opened as we approached and there she stood, like the evil housekeeper in one of those novels: robed all in black, leaning on a black, silver-headed cane. I felt pretty sure the cane was a prop; she had been brisk as a cricket during that Egyptian cruise, and there hadn't been a single long black robe in her wardrobe.

We had tea in the Small Drawing Room (you could hear the capital letters when Jen pronounced the words). I had expected it to be served by an Aged Retainer (sorry about the capitals, they are contagious). I guess Jen couldn't rake one up, but the maid wore an apron and a ruffly white cap pinned on top of her head. John sat there looking bland while Jen and I made conversation. I was so afraid of saying the wrong thing I let her do most of the talking. It was all about the distinguished family tree and general worth of the Tregarth family. She summed it up by remarking, "There has never been a dishonest or dishonorable Tregarth." I choked on my iced biscuit.

After tea Jen showed me round the entire place, making sure I realized that this wasn't just a house, it was the Family Mansion, reeking with the sort of history and tradition a Colonial from the American corn belt could never appreciate. I knew what she was doing, and I didn't appreciate it much, but as we paced along corridor after corridor and climbed stair after endless stair, my mounting annoyance had another cause. The place was an anachronism, a gigantic white elephant. I wouldn't be in the business I'm in if I didn't appreciate historical values, but one has to draw the line somewhere; in some cases the old has to make way for the new. This place was quaint but not unique, picturesque but useless for any practical purpose. It was costing John a small fortune to keep it from falling down around Jen's ears. He had once remarked in a rare moment of pique that he'd have torn the house down and sold the land if it had not been for Jen.

"The storerooms are in the attic, if you remember," John went on. "She got something of a shock when she saw what had been done— every box and chest opened, the contents strewn around. She rang up the local constable and got him out to inspect the wreckage. After she'd ranted at him for a while, he informed her there wasn't much he could do. As far as she could tell nothing was missing—certainly nothing of any value, since nothing of value had been there. We don't keep the family jewels in the attic."

"I didn't know you had any family jewels."

"A metaphorical statement," John said, looking shifty. "The point is that there was nothing worth stealing. And no useful clues. She couldn't even be sure when the break-in occurred."

"Still," I said, getting interested, "it's frightening to find out that you are vulnerable to any casual intruder. How did the non-thief get in?"

"My dear girl, you've seen the place; there are twenty doors and a hundred windows on the ground floor alone, and three separate sets of staircases. She's a sound sleeper and her room is at the front of the house."

"Doesn't that suggest that the intruder knew the layout of the house? He wouldn't go tramping past the door of her room."

"Don't get carried away, Sherlock. One can't arrive at any sensible deductions from the evidence at hand. The most likely theory is that some local youth was dared by his friends to see whether he could get into the house and out again without being caught. Stupid, I know, but that's youth for you. Jen is regarded as a mixture of lady of the manor and local witch. A challenge, in other words."

He sipped his drink, and I said righteously, "That's a very cavalier attitude for a dutiful son. She oughtn't be there by herself, in that large isolated house."

"I've tried to persuade her to move to London," John said. "She won't hear of it. Honestly, Vicky, she's perfectly all right. We don't breed serial killers in that part of the world, and any miserable sinner she might come across would be in more danger than she would. She takes her cane to bed with her. There's a pound of lead under that silver head."

I wandered to the window and looked out. Everything was gray—gray skies, gray streets, gray houses, little boxes all in a line, their flower beds and shrubs and other brave attempts at individuality dulled by the weather. I have to have a house and yard on account of my oversized Doberman, and this suburb, outside the city center of Munich, was the best I could afford. It was okay. I spend my working hours surrounded by medieval and Renaissance art, I don't need more of it at home.

The silence lengthened, broken only by the purring of Clara and the heavy breathing of Caesar. I said, without turning, "Something has happened, hasn't it?"

"I told you—"

"Not Jen. Something else."

He started to stand up and let out a yelp as Clara dug her claws into him. I took the empty glass from his hand and refilled it. Another sign, if I had needed one. As a rule it took him a lot longer to get through a drink.

"You overreacted," I said. "Okay, so did I, but not for the same reason. You wouldn't have gone into panic mode if you hadn't been recently, and forcibly, reminded that you are, as you put it, of interest to several unpleasant persons. Who's after you now? What have you done?"

"Nothing! Not a damned illegal thing. That's the truth, believe it or not."

I did believe it. Not because of the candid gaze of those cornflower-blue eyes—John could lie his way into heaven—but because of the note of indignation in his voice. Like that of a burglar who has been charged with breaking into a house when he has a perfect alibi because he was actually robbing a bank at the time.

"Schmidt is coming for dinner," I said. "He'll be thrilled to see you."

The reaction wasn't flagrant, just a blink and the tiniest of pauses before he replied. "How nice. I hope my unexpected presence won't leave you short of food. I can run out to the shops if you like."

Maybe I was imagining things. Whether or not, pursuing the

subject wouldn't get me any further. "He's bringing food from his favorite deli. There'll be enough for a regiment. You know Schmidt."

"Know and love. What's the little rascal been up to lately?"

Actually, it had been several weeks since I'd set eyes on my boss. I had missed him. Herr Doktor Anton Z. Schmidt, director of the National Museum in Munich, is one of the top men in his field. What makes him so much fun to be around is that he has some decidedly nonacademic interests, from American country music, which he sings in an off-key baritone and a hideous accent, to his latest passion, *Lord of the Rings* collectibles. He has all the action figures, all the swords, Gimli's axe, and the One Ring, which he wears on a chain around his fat neck. He also harbors the delusion that he is a great detective and that I am his loyal sidekick. Together, Schmidt is wont to declaim, we have solved many crimes and brought innumerable villains to justice. Allowing for Schmidt's habit of exaggeration, there was some truth in the assertion. Despite my best efforts I had been unable to keep him out of several of my encounters with the criminal element—most of them, I should add, instigated by John.

"He's been on vacation," I said.

"Where?"

"I don't know. He was very mysterious about it—winks and chuckles and so on. He could have been anywhere—in New Zealand, single-handedly reenacting the battle of the Pelennor Fields, or in Nashville at the Grand Ole Opry, or at the Spy Museum in Washington, you know how he is about spies."

John said, "Mmm."

Clara had decided to forgive him and was settled on his lap, shedding all over his elegant tweeds. Caesar was drooling on his knee, hoping for the tidbits that in his experience often accompanied glasses of liquid.

"When is Schmidt due?" he asked.

"Not for a few hours."

"Well, then . . ." He dislodged Clara, claw by claw, and came toward me.

"Oh, no," I said, backing up. "I refuse to be distracted."

"Is that the latest euphemism? Very ladylike." He scooped me up and started for the stairs. I'm almost as tall as he is, and although he is in extremely fit condition he only made it halfway up the stairs before he had to stop. He put me down and collapsed onto the step next to me, panting, and we both started to laugh, and the need for distraction came over me like a tornado. It had been two long weeks.

John sat watching me while I bustled around the living room, plumping pillows and trying to scrape Clara's hairs off the sofa cushions.

"Why this sudden burst of domesticity?" he asked. "Schmidt will sprinkle cigar ashes and spill beer over everything as soon as he settles in."

"He's bringing a guest."

Another of those slight but meaningful pauses. "Oh? Who?"

"He didn't say. From the frequency of his chuckles I suspect it's a lady. A female, anyhow."

I paused for a quick look in the mirror over the couch. Some of my guests have complained that it is a trifle high for them, but I'm almost six feet tall and whose mirror is it, anyhow? Actually, I hate being tall. It's okay if you want to be a fashion model or a basketball pro, but being tall and blond and well-rounded (as I like to put it) can be detrimental to an academic career. Some people still cling to the delusion that a female-shaped female can't possibly have a functioning brain.

I tucked a few loose strands of hair into the bun at the nape of my neck, checked to make sure my makeup was on straight and grimaced at my reflection. For whom was I primping, anyhow? Schmidt's postulated lady friend?

John glanced casually at his watch. "I think I'll take Caesar out for a quick run before they arrive."

"It's still raining."

"Misting. Normal weather where I come from."

Moving with his deceptively casual stride, he almost made it to the door before I caught hold of him.

"All right, that's enough. Sit down in that chair and tell me what's wrong."

Caesar began barking indignantly. He's not awfully bright but he was smart enough to put two and two together: somebody had been about to take him for a walk and somebody else had interfered. The sheer volume of his protest almost drowned out another sound. The doorbell.

"That can't be Schmidt yet," I exclaimed. "He's never on time."

The doorbell went on ringing. It sounded almost as frantic as Caesar. John put his head in his hands.

"Too late," he moaned.

"Who is it?" I shouted over the cacophony. A longish list of dangerous names unrolled in my head. "Max? Blenkiron? Interpol? Scotland Yard?"

"Worse," said John, in a voice of doom. "Shut up, Caesar."

Caesar did. In the comparative silence the sound of the doorbell was replaced by rhythmic pounding. John got up and went to the door.

The forty-watt bulb on the porch illumined the form of a man, his black hair shining with damp. Shadows obscured his features, but I saw enough to identify him. Relief left me limp.

"Feisal? Is that you? Why didn't John tell me you were coming?" And why, I thought, was he so appalled at the idea of your coming? Feisal wasn't an enemy, he was a friend, a really good friend, who had risked life, limb and reputation to keep me safe during our latest escapade in Egypt.

John caught Caesar by the collar and dragged him out of the way so that Feisal could come in. Now that I saw his face clearly I knew this was not a social call, a happy surprise for Vicky. He is a handsome guy, with those hawklike classic Arab features, long fuzzy eyelashes, and a complexion the color of a caffe latte. Only now it was more latte than coffee, and the lines that framed his mouth looked as if they had been carved by a chisel. I didn't ask any more questions. Why bother, I wasn't getting answers anyhow. Wordlessly I gestured Feisal to a chair.

"I'd offer you a drink," I began, groping for a steadying cliché. "But you don't. Drink. Alcohol."

"I do," said John, "thank God."

He filled three glasses—vodka and tonic for me and for him and plain tonic for Feisal.

"Start talking," he said curtly.

I stared at him. "You mean you don't know what this is about either?"

"No. Dire hints, hysterical groans, a demand that I meet him here—immediately, if not sooner. Talk fast, Feisal. Schmidt will be here before long."

"Schmidt!" Galvanized, Feisal sprang to his feet. "Oh, Lord, no. Not Schmidt. Why didn't you tell me he was coming? I've got to get out of here!"

"I didn't know until it was too late," John said. "You've got approximately three-quarters of an hour to put us in the picture and then make a run for it, or compose yourself and behave normally. If

I'd been able I'd have headed you off, but alas, it was not to be. Do we want Vicky in on this?"

"She's in on it," I said, folding my arms in a decisive manner.

Feisal nodded gloomily. "May I smoke?"

I shoved an ashtray at him. "I thought you'd quit."

"I had. Until day before yesterday."

"Get on with it," John said.

"I'm going to tell you what happened, as it was told to me by the man on the spot. I wasn't there. As Inspector of Antiquities for all Upper Egypt I have a huge territory to cover, and I'm short on personnel, and—"

"We know all that," John said impatiently. "Don't make excuses until you've told us what you're accused of doing."

Ali looked up at the sun, glanced at his watch for verification, and sighed. Over an hour before he and the other guards could kick the tourists out of the Valley of the Kings and go home. He unscrewed the top of his water bottle and drank. It was a day like any other day, hot and dusty and dry. The fabled burial ground of the great pharaohs of ancient Egypt held no charm for him; it was just a job, one he had held for more than ten years.

The mobs of visitors had diminished somewhat, but there were still hundreds of them crowding the pathways of the Valley, kicking up dust, chattering in a dozen languages. A group of Japanese visitors passed him, clustering round the flag held high by their guide. Like little chickens, Ali thought, scampering after the mother hen, afraid to leave her side. He didn't know which was worse, the little chickens or the Germans, who kept wandering off and poking into places where they weren't supposed to go, or the French, who went around with their hairy legs bare and their bodies indecently exposed.

He didn't hate any of them. He just didn't like them much, any of them. At least the Americans tipped well. Better than the British, who haggled over every pound.

The tomb he guarded was locked, as it often was, but that hadn't prevented people from trying to bribe him to let them in. One fat-faced American had offered him a hundred Egyptian pounds—two months' pay for him, the price of an inexpensive dinner for the American. God knew he could have used the money. But it would have cost him his job to break the rules, especially with this tomb. It was too conspicuous, right on the main path, the most famous tomb in the Valley.

He leaned back and closed his eyes. The babble of voices faded; and then a sound brought him wide awake. He sat up and stared.

Coming toward him was a black SUV, horn blaring, warning pedestrians off the road. It had to be an official vehicle, no others were allowed in the Valley. It was followed by two other cars, and behind them was an object that made Ali's eyes open even wider. It was as big as a tour bus, but it wasn't a bus; it was a van, painted white and covered with writing in some language that definitely wasn't Arabic. Memory stirred and Ali invoked his god. He'd seen a van like that before. What was it doing here now? Why hadn't he been told?

The cavalcade pulled to a stop in front of the tomb. Men in black uniforms got out of the sedans and fanned out, forming a cordon around the entrance. The doors of the SUV opened. A man got out and strode briskly toward Ali. He was bearded and wore horn-rimmed glasses. Another, younger, man followed him. He carried a worn briefcase.

"You the fellow in charge?" the older man barked. "Jump to it. Get that gate open. We haven't much time."

"But," Ali stuttered. "But—"

"Oh, for God's sake. Weren't you notified we would be here?"

Ali's blank stare was apparently answer enough; the man turned to his younger companion and said something in an undertone. Ali caught the words "typical Egyptian efficiency."

"Well, we're here now," the bearded man went on. "I am Dr. Henry Manchester of the British Institute of Technoarchaeology. I presume you would like to see my authorization. Yes, yes, quite proper."

He snapped his fingers. The younger man fumbled in his brief-case and pulled out a paper, which he handed to Manchester, who handed it to Ali. "I don't suppose you read English, but you should recognize the signature."

Ali prided himself on his knowledge of English but knew better than to express his resentment. The document looked impressive. The Supreme Council of Antiquities, Office of the Secretary General. It was signed by the Great Man himself. Not that Ali had ever received a letter from the Great Man, but he had met him once, just after his appointment to the post, when he made a tour of the major sites. Perhaps "met" wasn't the precise word; but the Great Man had nodded graciously in his general direction.

"Yes, I see," he said slowly. "But I cannot—"

"Put in a call to the Supreme Council, then," the Englishman said impatiently. "Only make it fast."

Oh, yes, Ali thought. Telephone the Supreme Council. This is Ali, you remember me, the guard from the Valley of the Kings. Put me through to Dr. Khifaya right away . . .

"No," he said. "The paper is in order."

"I should think so. Now don't delay me any longer, we were held up at the bridge and are short on time. Never mind the key, I have one."

He pushed past Ali and went down the stairs.

From that point on things moved so fast Ali couldn't have stopped them if he had wanted to. The back doors of the van opened. Inside was a bewildering medley of machinery—cables, tubes, shapes of plastic and metal. Several men in crisp white dungarees jumped out and followed the two Englishmen down the stairs. Ali looked around for help—advice—reassurance. A small crowd had gathered, tourists gaping and speculating, and several of his fellow guards, kept at a distance by the men in black uniforms. After a moment he went down the stairs and along the corridor into the tomb chamber. He let out a faint cry of protest when he saw that the glass covering the stone sarcophagus had been set aside. The white-garbed men were in the process of lifting the lid of the gilded coffin inside the big stone box. From the coffin base they removed a long, rigid platform covered by dusty fabric. Moving quickly but with care, the bearers maneuvered their burden through the narrow space and out of the room.

By this time interest and curiosity had replaced Ali's initial concern. Yes, it was like the last time. The van wasn't the same—the other one had been larger—but from what he could tell, the equipment inside was similar. Only this time there were no journalists or television crews. He'd seen himself on television when they showed the program—just a fleeting glimpse, but he'd bought a tape and played that part over and over. Maybe they had got it wrong the first time and had to come back and do it again? That made sense. They wouldn't want to admit a mistake, so they had arranged for this to be done without publicity and advance notice.

Finding himself alone in the burial chamber, he went back along the corridor and up the stairs. They had put the litter and its contents into the van and closed the doors. Machinery was humming and sputtering. There were beeping noises and people talking. He squatted down and lit a cigarette and waited and thought about . . .

him. How did he like being dragged out of what he had hoped would be his final resting place, stared at by impious strangers, discussed as if he were a piece of wood? He had been an infidel, a pagan, but once he had been human and he had been faithful to his own gods in his time.

The sun was low above the cliffs when the doors at the back of the van opened again. The shrouded shape was lifted out and carried back into the tomb.

"You have been very helpful," the Englishman said. He smiled for the first time, and Ali saw the glint of a gold tooth or filling. "I shall mention you to Dr. Khifaya. Here."

Ali took the folded paper but he didn't look at it until after the men had piled back into their vehicles and driven off. Then he unfolded the banknote. His lip curled. Ten miserable Egyptian pounds.

Englishmen.

I don't get it," I said. "Why the consternation? Nobody told you in advance, but maybe this was a sudden decision and they tried to get in touch with you and couldn't because you were out in the desert or something. Or maybe . . ."

My voice trailed off. The two of them sat there staring fixedly at me. "Oh, Lord," I said.

"She's a little slow this evening," John explained, nodding at Feisal. "Be patient with her. What did you do after Ali informed you of the—er—visit?"

"Went into the tomb." Feisal removed a crumpled white handkerchief from his pocket and mopped his brow. "At first sight everything looked normal. But I had a feeling . . . One of *those* feelings. It was unlikely, verging on impossible, that I wouldn't have been notified in advance. I'd have ordered Ali to leave, but I couldn't lift the coffin lid by myself, it's too heavy. We managed to shift it just enough to get a look inside. The poor devil is in pieces, you know, they've got the various parts laid out on a sand table, padded all round with cotton wool and covered with a sort of heavy blanket. At first glance it looked normal. But when I folded the blanket back from where his head was supposed to be, it wasn't there. He was gone. Not so much as a stray bone left."

"King Tut?" I gasped. "They stole King Tut?"

Two

John's only reaction was a lifted eyebrow. He'd seen it coming. I had a feeling that he wished he'd thought of it himself.

"But why?" I asked. "Why on earth would anyone want a beat-up, dried-up old corpse?"

"We'll get to that in due course," John said. "First things first. Who else knows about this, Feisal?"

"Who knows he's missing, you mean? Only Ali and I. We managed to get everything back in place. Actually, I can't swear that his legs weren't still there, we couldn't reach down that far, but . . ."

"Ick," I said.

"It's a safe assumption that if they took the rest they'd have made a clean sweep," John said. "They had plenty of time. Will Ali keep his mouth shut?"

Feisal laughed bitterly. "Damn right he will. He'll lose his job for sure and probably end up in prison. In the cell next to mine."

"Come on now," I protested. "It wasn't your fault. You weren't even there."

"The Supreme Council will want a scapegoat, and it happened in my jurisdiction. My God, Vicky, Tutankhamon is a symbol, a legend, a unique historical treasure. The media will go crazy. There will be jokes on late-night talk shows and criticism from every museum and institution in the world, and they'll all say Egypt has a hell of a nerve asking us to give its antiquities back when it lets a bunch of crooks walk off with the most famous pharaoh in history."

"Hmmm." John rubbed his chin. "I'm afraid you're right. It would definitely embarrass the government."

"Embarrass!" Feisal flung up his hands. "Embarrass is when you spill a drink into the ambassador's wife's lap. This is shame, disgrace, heads rolling right and left. But if I could get him back . . ." He turned to John; his long, flexible hands went out in a gesture of appeal.

Him, not it, I thought. He kept talking about that battered mummy as if it were alive. Well, but it—he—had been alive, once upon a time. Not an inanimate object like a coffin or a statue, an actual, living human being, a king, incredibly preserved for an incredible length of time. I began to get a glimmering of why Feisal was so frantic. Imagine someone making off with the bones of George Washington. And he'd only been dead two hundred years.

"We'll help if we can," I said, wondering how.

"You aren't keeping up, Vicky," John said. He leaned back and crossed his ankles, the picture of ease. "You think I was responsible, Feisal. That's why you dashed over here, to ask me to give it—"

"Him."

"Sorry. *Him* back."

"Please?"

"For Pete's sake, Feisal," I said. "That's crazy."

"Not really," John said pensively. "It's the sort of thing I might have done in my younger and giddier days, for the sake of the challenge. The operation was well planned. They chose a time when you'd be elsewhere, waited till late in the day when the guards would be tired and anxious to leave, moved fast and with arrogant authority. Your friend Ali was in no position to stop them. It's probably lucky for him he didn't try. I don't like the sound of those chaps in the black uniforms." John brooded, thinking it over. "A setup familiar to Ali from a previous occasion: proper documentation— even a key to the tomb. A copy of that wouldn't be difficult to obtain. He couldn't confirm, you were out of cell-phone reach even if he had had access to one, and he'd never have got through to the Supreme Council. The equipment was fake, of course. Ali wouldn't know the difference, any more than I would, so long as it looked impressive. They shoved it—er, him—into the van, moved him off the sand tray into another sort of container, sat around for half an hour making interesting technical noises—laughing their heads off, I don't doubt—and then took the empty tray back in. Or maybe . . . Maybe they had a duplicate of the tray ready. That way they wouldn't have to move those fragile bones. Yes, that's how I would have done it. Only . . ." He leaned forward, hands clasped and eyes intent on his friend. "Only I didn't, Feisal. Aside from the fact that I wouldn't pull a filthy stunt like that on you, I was in London and I can prove it."

A knot under my breastbone loosened. I hadn't believed it—not really—but I hadn't laid eyes on him for two weeks, and the modus operandi, as we sleuths say, was reminiscent of some of his deals.

"Your gang," Feisal began, only half convinced.

"I don't have a bloody gang! Gangs are composed primarily of extremely stupid, dishonest individuals who are for sale to the highest bidder. I learned from painful experience I couldn't trust anyone except myself. That's why I—"

"John," I said sharply.

"Oh, right." He glanced at his watch. "I need to know a lot more about this, but as Vicky so rightly reminded me, we're running out of time. Can you be the charming, debonair guest with Schmidt and his girlfriend? He mustn't get wind of this."

"Allah forbid that he should," Feisal said. He looked a little more . . . well, no, not more cheerful. A little less haggard. "I'd better go. Schmidt has an unfortunate effect on my nerves, which are already shaky. Call me after he's left."

"Where are you staying?" I asked.

Feisal looked blank. "I don't know. I came straight from the airport."

From the street outside came the familiar squeal of abused tires. I knew that sound. "Oh, my God, it's Schmidt," I exclaimed. "He's early. What are we going to do?"

Thoroughly rattled, Feisal bolted for the door. Caesar followed, barking helpfully.

"Upstairs," John ordered. "Second door on the right."

Feisal didn't stop moving, he spun in a circle and ran toward the stairs. John picked up his briefcase and thrust it at him. "Lock the door. We'll tell you when the coast is clear. And don't make a noise!"

Feisal stopped halfway up the stairs. "What if I have to—"

"Improvise," said John through his teeth. The doorbell rang. Caesar barked. Feisal let out a faint scream and fled.

"Deep breath, Vicky," John said. "Once more into the breach, dear friends. Into the mouth of death, into the jaws of hell . . . Or is it the other way round? I'll get the door, shall I?"

Still incapable of speech or movement, I nodded. It will be all right, I told myself. Just keep Schmidt amused and unwitting for a few hours. I should be able to do that.

John flung the door open with what had been intended to be a jovial greeting. It ended in a catch of breath, and then I also saw the woman with Schmidt. His new girlfriend. Suzi Umphenour.

That wasn't her real name. It was the name by which I had known her when she was a fellow passenger on the ill-fated *Queen of the Nile* during my last trip to Egypt—our most recent criminal investigation, as Schmidt called it. My assignment had been to identify a notorious thief who was purportedly about to rob the Cairo Museum. Suzi played the silly society matron from Tennessee with such panache that I probably should have suspected it was a caricature; but I had had other things on my mind and I didn't find out who—or what—she really was until after the grisly affair was over and I encountered her again in a certain office in the U.S. Embassy in Cairo. Her precise affiliation had never been made clear. Interpol? Some set of initials? CIA, NSA, BFAE?

I might have known Schmidt would take up with her. He had described her as "a fine figure of a woman." That's been the story of my life: if something can go wrong, it will. Of all the people in the universe, the last one I wanted to see on a night like this was a woman who worked for an organization that tracked crooks. FBI, BFE, DAR, AA, PETA?

All that and more swirled around my befogged brain as I stood frozen.

"Surprise!" Schmidt shrieked. "A night of surprises, is it? John, my friend, how good to see you! You remember Suzi? She is my surprise!"

"And a very pleasant surprise," said John, making a valiant effort. "Do come in. Let me take your coats."

Schmidt was loaded down with parcels. "I take them to the kitchen," he announced.

I followed him. Compared with Suzi, Schmidt was the lesser of two evils. "These in the refrigerator," he announced, suiting the action to the words. "These on . . ." He looked down into the hopeful face of Caesar. "On the high shelf. And here is wine."

I took the bottle he handed me. "I didn't know you and Suzi were an item."

Schmidt smirked. "I don't tell you everything, Vicky. Yes, we have been friends for some time. Good friends."

If he giggles, I thought, I'll hit him with this bottle.

Schmidt struck a pose, hand on hip, chin lifted. "You have not told me how well I look."

I hadn't really looked at him. Same old Schmidt, five feet six standing on tiptoe, round as an orange and rosy as an apple, bristly white mustache . . . Wait a minute. Not white—brown. Rich, decisive brown. If I hadn't been so bemused by Suzi I would have seen it immediately. Other details began to penetrate. The cheeks weren't quite as plump or florid, the stomach had retreated behind what appeared to be a solid barrier of some kind.

"You dyed your mustache," I said.

"Not dyed; brought out the natural color," said Schmidt indignantly. "It is a special formula designed for prematurely gray individuals. Is that all you see?" He thumped his stomach, winced, and went on, "I have lost twenty pounds. I am fitter than most men half my age. Would you like to see my pecs?"

"Good God, no! I mean . . ." This new development almost made me forget Feisal, the missing mummy, and gimlet-brained Suzi, who must not, MUST NOT get wind of either of the former. "You look great," I mumbled. "Was that where you were? At a fat . . . uh, I mean, a spa?"

"A scientific health clinic," Schmidt corrected. "In Switzerland." Selecting a knife from the rack above the counter, he sliced cheese and apples onto a plate. (Apples? Schmidt?) "Come, we must join our friends. Er—I would appreciate it if you would not mention the clinic to Suzi."

From the look of relief on John's face I deduced he had found conversation heavy going. Catching my eye, he supplied me with a drink. It was mostly tonic, I discovered with regret. He was right, though; we needed to keep our wits about us.

For the next half hour Schmidt did most of the talking. My God, it was boring. Calories, saturated and unsaturated fats, carbs, the glycemic index, the food pyramid, the ratio of this to that and that to whatever peppered his speech. Red wine was mentioned, and so was dark chocolate. There wasn't a food fad, scientific or pseudo, Schmidt had missed. John listened in open fascination. His gaze kept moving from the plate of sliced apples to Schmidt's bright-brown mustache to the bottle of wine. (Red wine, of course.) I watched Suzi.

As a Southern belle she had affected masses of blond hair, a toothy grin, and a well-developed, ostentatiously displayed figure. The last time I had seen her, at the embassy, she had worn a tailored suit, very businesslike. Only the grin had been familiar. It was still in evidence, but her hair was short and there were glints of silver in its sandy waves. I wondered how old she was. Over forty, under sixty? It's hard to tell these days. Her trim figure suggested she worked out regularly. Tonight she was casually dressed in jeans and T-shirt, the latter loose enough to be discreet but tight enough to make Schmidt's eyes keep wandering back to her chest. There was no doubt in my mind that Schmidt's interest was romantic, not professional. But what about her?

I tried to remember the details of that last conversation I had

had with Suzi. They were foggy. I'd been somewhat upset, or, to be more accurate, mad as hell. When I agreed to go on that damned cruise I had been assured that the anonymous officials who sent me would have an equally anonymous agent on board who'd come to my rescue in case there was trouble. There was plenty of trouble, and Suzi had screwed up. It wasn't entirely her fault, and most of my fury had been directed at her bosses, whoever they were. Anonymous. I hate those people—FBI, CIA, all of them. They are so obsessed with security, it supersedes everything else, including the welfare of the people they are supposed to be protecting. They don't even talk to one another.

Whatever Suzi's precise affiliation might be, it had to have something to do with art and antiquities fraud, otherwise she wouldn't have been on that cruise. "Sir John Smythe" was still a subject of interest to several European governments, not to mention Interpol. My connection with that notorious crook was well documented. Suzi might not know that Smythe and John Tregarth, respectable dealer in legitimate antiquities, were one and the same, but at the very end of that interview she had said something . . . No, she hadn't actually said anything, she had just looked as if . . .

Catching the notorious Sir John Smythe would be a feather in any agent's cap. Was Suzi trying to get to John through me and to me through Schmidt? Or was I reading too much into a look, an imagined hint? Why couldn't she have taken a fancy to Schmidt? I couldn't visualize him as anything but my cute little, crazy little roly-poly pal, but that was no reason to suppose he wouldn't appeal romantically to a woman. *Chacun à son goût.* He was funny, charming, brilliant, and, bless his heart, starving himself into relative—I said relative—fitness. Losing a little weight certainly wouldn't do him any harm. But if Suzi broke his susceptible heart I would murder her.

What with eating and drinking and listening to Schmidt babble on about fitness we got through the evening. I kept trying to think of ways to draw Suzi out about her work without indicating why I had a personal interest. "Any unusual cases lately?" (a question that made John bite his lip and roll his eyes heavenward) elicited only a toothier grin and a bland "Nothing I can talk about."

As a rule I have to kick Schmidt out while he's still chattering, or put him to bed on the sofa if he has had too much to drink. That night he was the one who announced it was time to end our delightful evening. The look he gave Suzi was, as they say, meaningful. She gave him one back, and rose obediently to her feet. They did not linger over their farewells.

I stood by the door until I heard Schmidt gun the engine and roar away. Then I turned very slowly to face John.

"I need something," I croaked. "I don't know what, but I need it bad."

"You've had enough to drink, smoking is unhealthy, and we've no time for—what was the word?—distraction."

"Damn it, I think you're actually enjoying this!"

"I am enjoying the fact that thus far no one has tried to shoot me, stab me, or hit me. Let's get Feisal . . . Ah, there he is."

"I watched from the window, saw them leave." Feisal edged cautiously down the stairs. "Who was the woman?"

John and I exchanged glances. "That isn't immediately relevant," John said. "I expect Feisal is hungry. He hasn't dined."

"Nor lunched, nor, as far as I can recall, breakfasted," Feisal said.

We settled down around the kitchen table and the remains of Schmidt's bounty. Though he had stuck strictly to his diet, he hadn't stinted the rest of us; Feisal tucked into a sandwich of goose pâté and dark bread.

"So what do we do now?" he asked. His eyes, big and soft and brown, were fixed on John with a look of touching hope.

"Well . . ." John loves being appealed to. He leaned back, steepling his fingers like Sherlock Holmes. "The first step is damage control. You did all you could to prevent discovery, but you had better get back to Luxor as soon as possible and make sure Ali doesn't crack under pressure. Keep the tomb closed. You have the authority to do that, I presume."

"Unless I'm overruled by a direct order from the SCA."

"Another reason why you must be on the spot. It's likely that the thieves will contact someone—you, the Supreme Council, or the press."

Feisal choked. I leaped up, ready to apply the Heimlich maneuver, but he managed to swallow. "Why would they do that?" he gasped.

"That depends on their reason for the theft," John said. "Which is the most interesting part of the entire business. Offhand, four possible motives occur to me. One, the perpetrators were funded by a private collector whose tastes are, shall we say, extremely bizarre. Should that be the case, they and their client won't communicate with anyone. The second possibility is that they are holding the mummy for ransom. I expect certain parties would be willing to pay a tidy sum for its safe return, and for keeping the whole business quiet. In which case they will contact the SCA directly; there will not be any publicity, but you, my friend, will be on the spot."

"What's the third?" I asked, knowing John was dying to be prompted.

"Political. Embarrassing the government, nationally and/or internationally."

Feisal put the remains of his sandwich down on the table. He looked sick. John didn't have to spell it out; if that was the motive, the thieves would want publicity, the more the better.

"That's weak," I said. "It might make Mubarak and company look silly, but it wouldn't do them any real harm. The U.S. isn't going to cut off aid on account of a mislaid mummy, and it wouldn't give any real leverage to the various parties that would like to overthrow the government—of whom, I presume, there are quite a number."

"There always are," Feisal said. "Ranging from radical Islamists who want a theocratic state to liberals who want genuinely democratic elections, freedom of speech, and all those nice things. Vicky's right. A scandal over a missing antiquity, even one as important as Tutankhamon, isn't enough to start a revolution."

He reached for his sandwich and encountered instead the large head of Caesar. Caesar swallowed and slunk under the table.

"That dog is getting out of hand," John said. "You don't discipline him properly. To return to the subject under discussion—your point is well taken, logically speaking, but would-be revolutionaries aren't always logical. However, I am inclined to believe that my fourth motive is the most likely."

He waited for somebody to ask him what it was. I had already played stooge once. I got up and made Feisal another sandwich. The silence lengthened, broken only by the sound of a large dog under the table licking its lips.

"Personal enmity," John said. "Someone is out to get you or your boss."

"It can't be me," Feisal protested. "I'm not that important. This was a big, expensive operation. I don't have enemies—at least not rich enemies."

"I can think of one—" I bit my tongue. Feisal didn't need any more negative thoughts.

"We're still a long way from listing names," John said. "It's late, and I want Feisal on a plane to Cairo tomorrow."

"Aren't you coming with me?" Feisal asked.

"I can't do anything from that end."

"But—" Feisal began.

John raised a finger, like a schoolmaster enjoining silence. "This is how it stands. We don't know what these people are likely to do next. Our only hope at the moment is damage control, to whatever extent that is possible. Your position is that you knew nothing in advance about the visit, you assumed when you learned of it that it was legitimate, and that you have no reason to suspect anything is wrong. You did not inspect the tomb or look in the sarcophagus. Neither did Ali. Notify me at once if you hear anything from anybody. That includes seemingly idle rumors and casual remarks from observers who might have noticed the route that damned van took. It would be nice to know where it went and when it disappeared off the radar, but it might be risky to ask direct questions."

Feisal muttered something. I didn't understand the words, but they sounded profane.

"In the meantime, I'll see what I can do from my end," John went on. "There are only a few organizations in my—er—former profession that have the means and the motives to pull off such a stunt. I need to send out feelers, see if there are any rumors starting to circulate."

"This could be an entirely new group," I suggested.

"Try to say something encouraging," Feisal muttered.

"The encouraging aspect is that an act this preposterous will have repercussions," John said. "There are connections, overt and covert, between the legitimate antiquities market and the illegal underground. I won't give you examples—"

"No, don't," I said. "I see what you're saying, and I'll bet I can say it faster. The word will get around. People will talk. The network will operate the way networks do."

"I could have said it better," John remarked. "But in essence that's it. I'll start networking (dreadful word), and I can best do that in London."

"I'm going with you," I said.

John obviously didn't trust Feisal to do what he was told, so we personally escorted him to the airport in time to catch an afternoon flight to Cairo. I had spent the morning at the museum, arranging for my leave of absence. I was prepared to point out to Schmidt that he owed me, after his four frivolous weeks at a fat farm, but to my surprise he didn't even ask where I was going. He didn't have to. Thanks to the miracles of modern communication the little rascal could locate me wherever I was, by any one of a dozen different ways. Sometimes I yearn for the good old days of the Pony Express. By the time you got the news of someone's imminent demise the person was dead and buried. And by the time your response arrived, the survivors had put off their mourning and were getting on with their lives.

"Enjoy yourself," Schmidt said, standing on tiptoe so he could pat me on the head. "You are not looking your best, Vicky. You need a rest."

So I wasn't looking my best, was I? Compared to whom? I sulked out and located Karl the janitor, who had a crush on Caesar, and who was thrilled at the prospect of looking after him while I was gone. Schmidt was not particularly thrilled at the prospect of dropping by my house daily to check on Clara, but I knew I could count on him to do it when he remarked, "Suzi will be glad to help. She is very fond of cats."

So Suzi was going to be around for a while. I hadn't noticed any bonding going on between Suzi and Clara. In fact, Clara had made rather a point of trying to climb onto Suzi's lap, which, as any cat person knows, is intended to be annoying rather than affectionate. A nasty new suspicion slid into my nasty suspicious mind. I didn't say anything to Schmidt—what would have been the point—but I raced home and spent a frantic hour going through files and drawers to make sure I hadn't left anything incriminating lying around. Since I wasn't sure what might be incriminating, it was a somewhat futile procedure. When I mentioned my worries to John, he shrugged.

"There is no way one can defend oneself from a difficulty which is undefined and may not even exist. And don't mention Suzi to Feisal. It hasn't occurred to him to ask who Schmidt's ladylove is, and I'd just as soon he remained ignorant."

"I wish I were," I grumbled. "What do you suppose she's after?"

"Schmidt, perhaps." He turned back to the computer. I slammed the drawer I had been searching.

"You aren't leaving any incriminating e-mails on that thing, are you?"

"What do you take me for? Finish packing. We haven't much time."

Packing was another undefined difficulty, since I didn't know how long I'd be gone or where I was going. John and I were planning to catch the first available flight to London after we got Feisal on his way; but after London, who knew where the quest would take us?

Probably someplace I didn't want to go.

I made a final call to the museum, to leave last-minute instructions with my new secretary: "Don't call me, I'll call you, and if you give my number to someone who doesn't already have it I will Take

Steps." Gerda, my former nemesis, had left to get married; I wondered if she was reading her new hubbie's mail the way she had pried into mine. Her replacement didn't open my mail, but his inhuman efficiency was almost as irritating. I had a feeling he thought he could do my job better than I did and was out to prove it. (I wasn't worried; Schmidt likes me best.)

We made it to MUC with no time to spare and escorted Feisal to Hall C for his EgyptAir flight. Instead of proceeding through security, he stood shuffling his feet and shifting his briefcase from hand to hand.

"There's something I have to tell you."

John groaned. "Worse than what you've already told us?"

"No. I hope not. I mean . . ." His long lashes fell, and his high cheekbones turned a shade darker. "I'm in love."

"Oh," I said blankly. "Who—"

"For God's sake!" John's voice rose over mine. "What—"

"It's not just my job I stand to lose." Feisal grabbed my hand and squeezed it. "I'll lose her too, if I'm disgraced and discredited. You understand, Vicky. You won't let me down, will you?"

His big soulful brown eyes would have melted the heart of a dried-up mummy. "Of course not," I said, squeezing back. "Who—"

"Stop that," John said through his teeth. "Get going, Feisal, or you'll miss your flight."

"If she loves him she'll stick by him whatever happens," I said, as we watched Feisal proceed on his way.

"Is that a promise?" John inquired.

I decided to ignore that one. "I wonder who—"

"Does it matter?" John took my arm. "We needn't be at our gate for another hour or so; I'll buy you a coffee."

British Air leaves from a different hall in the same terminal.

John and I hadn't been able to get adjoining seats, and since I hadn't brought anything to read I made him stop at a bookstall, despite his sneers about lowbrow literature.

"I suppose you always travel with a copy of Plato in the original Greek," I countered, browsing the racks of magazines and newspapers. The latest issue of *Der Stern* caught my eye. "Hey," I said, picking it up. "Isn't that Dr. Khifaya on the cover?"

"So it is. Wonder what he's done to make the cover of *Der Stern?*"

He had been photographed at Giza, leaning casually against a column, with a couple of pyramids in the background. He bore a certain resemblance to Feisal—the same strong features and thick black hair and tall athletic body, the latter set off by neatly creased khakis and a matching jacket covered with pockets, the kind worn by photographers and a few archaeologists, and tourists trying to look like one of either group. Dr. Ashraf Khifaya, the secretary general of the Supreme Council of Antiquities, didn't have to try. Though remarkably young for that high post, which he had held for less than a year, he had excavated at practically every site in Egypt.

"The usual," I said. "Asking for Nefertiti back. He's been picketing the Altes Museum in Berlin off and on for weeks, but this time he says he's going to bring along a few friends. I wonder what . . ."

I paid for the magazine and went on reading, guided by John's hand on my elbow. Most of the material was familiar. German and Egyptian scholars had been arguing about the beautiful bust of Nefertiti ever since it went on exhibit in Berlin back in the 1920s. The Egyptians had a point. Some of the other antiquities they wanted back, like the Rosetta Stone, had been found and appropriated before the foundation of the Egyptian Antiquities Organization, as it was once called. By 1912, when Nefertiti had turned up in a German dig, the laws governing the division of finds were strict: the Egyptians kept pretty much whatever they pleased, especially unique items, and the rest was divided between the Cairo Museum and the excavators. Somehow or other, Nefertiti had been included in the objects handed over to the excavators. It was hard to understand how anyone, even an inexperienced inspector, could have failed to claim her. Like Tutankhamon, the life-sized painted bust is unique, and unlike poor old Tut, it is outstandingly beautiful.

John steered me into a chair; when he returned with two cups of coffee I had finished the article.

"I wonder if he'll really do it," I said.

"Bring a brass band and some dancing girls to help him picket the museum?" John chuckled. "I hope so."

"Wouldn't the cops run him in?"

"He'd love that. Excellent publicity."

"I'm surprised you never tried to steal her," I said.

"Nefertiti?" John looked pensive. "I might have had a stab at it if anyone had offered me enough. I didn't steal things for myself, you know," he added self-righteously.

"The important word in that sentence is not 'myself,' but 'steal,'" I pointed out, and closed the magazine. "He is a good-looking guy, isn't he? Is it only a coincidence that this—um—business happened soon after he took over? Speaking of people who have made enemies—"

"We weren't."

"Then let's. I trust you didn't point out to Feisal that there is a certain multimillionaire who might hold a grudge against him. He was instrumental in foiling Blenkiron's plan to steal Tetisheri's tomb paintings. And if we're talking about collectors with bizarre tastes—"

"Blenkiron's name does come to mind," John agreed. "Though the word exotic is more accurate than bizarre. The paintings were beautiful. Tut isn't. Anyhow, you and I and Schmidt did our share of the foiling."

"Is that supposed to be a happy thought?"

"I can't believe Blenkiron is responsible for this. He collects art objects, not curiosities, and if he were the sort of man to hold a grudge, he wouldn't focus on Feisal. However, you have raised a point I hadn't considered—the timing. What do you know about Khifaya's background?"

"Not much," I admitted. "When I spoke of making enemies, I was thinking about his position rather than his personal history. His predecessor made a huge point of demanding that foreign museums and collectors return Egypt's stolen antiquities, and Khifaya seems to be intent on carrying on the good work."

" 'Stolen' isn't strictly accurate in some cases," John said. "The Rosetta Stone—"

"I know more than I need to know about the Rosetta Stone. But you, of all people, can't deny that a number of museums and private collectors have objects whose provenance is dubious."

"I take leave to resent that implication," John said primly. "Why do you keep wandering off the subject? All I said was that Khifaya's background might bear investigation."

"A nasty divorce? Hey, is he married?"

"Don't be frivolous." John glanced at his watch and rose. "Let's go."

"It's a good picture. If we go to Egypt, maybe I can get him to autograph it. 'To dear Vicky, my biggest fan.' "

John's lip curled in one of his elegant sneers.

"He's even handsomer than Feisal. Or," I said, struck by a new and inspiring thought, "maybe he'll let me be one of his friends next time he pickets the museum."

Content to be towed by a masterful hand on my arm (so I could go on admiring the picture of my new crush), I didn't take note of where we were going until we arrived at the gate.

"Hey," I said, digging in my heels. "This is the wrong flight. It's not going to London."

"Neither are we." He had timed it perfectly; the last passengers were lined up. He handed over our boarding passes and propelled me forward.

"Why are we going to Rome? When did you change plans? Why didn't you tell me?"

"I didn't change plans."

"But you told Feisal—"

"No, I didn't."

"Yes, you . . ." Now that I thought back on his reference to London, he hadn't actually said we were going there. "Damn it, I don't want to go to Rome. Please don't tell me you mean to confer with Pietro and whatsername and the other crooks you were working with when we first met."

"All in the past, my dear, the distant past. In point of fact I hope to confer with someone at the Vatican. Here's your seat."

He went on to find his, leaving me in a frenzy of speculation. Someone at the Vatican. Not the pope. Surely not the pope. Not John.

I had ample time for reflection during the flight. Unfortunately, all I could do was go over and over the same ground, like a cat chasing its tail, getting nowhere. Not one cat, several of them, a random feline ballet, interwoven and endless. Suzi. Rome. Tutankhamon. Why in heaven's name would anybody steal Tutankhamon? Why would anybody want to steal it . . . him? What would you do with him once you had him? You couldn't stick him away in an attic or a closet, he'd require . . . What does a mummy require? Controlled temperature, sterile atmosphere, room service?

I jerked awake from a dream that featured an air-conditioned suite in the best hotel in Cairo, and Tutankhamon laid out on a Posturepedic mattress surrounded by harem beauties in white nurses' uniforms.

I had planned to intercept John when he passed my seat, but everybody was pushing and shoving and I didn't catch up with him until I reached the baggage area.

"Not the pope," I said.

"I beg your pardon?" He raised one eyebrow, in that maddening way of his.

"All right, not the pope. Who? And if you say 'Who what?' I will lie down on the floor and kick and scream."

"Not here, someone will trample you underfoot." He turned and ran a seemingly casual eye over the passengers who were shoving and pushing as they waited for the belt to deliver their luggage. Nothing unusual about them that I could see: the young mother shepherding two darling kiddies who were beating at each other with stuffed bunnies; the self-important business types yelling into their cell phones; two priests in black cassocks; a pair of twenty-somethings, nationality indeterminate, wound round each other like pretzels; a little gray-haired lady wearing sunglasses and carrying an enormous purse . . . Nobody brandishing an UZI or a deadly vial of shampoo.

"Nobody could have followed us onto that plane," I declared. "I didn't even know we were taking it."

"Precisely."

By the time we got through passport and customs it was late evening and I was starved. I informed John of this.

He didn't even respond with a raised eyebrow. Taking me by the arm, he hustled me out of the airport, past a line of waiting taxis.

Pausing by an anonymous dark sedan, he opened the back door, shoved me in, and followed me.

"What—" I began.

"Quiet," said my beloved. Leaning forward, he pressed a knuckle into the back of the driver's neck.

"Albatross," he said.

"Ancient mariner," replied the driver, and giggled. The car pulled smoothly away from the curb.

"Oh, for God's sake," I said. "How paranoid can you get?"

"Just because you're paranoid doesn't mean—"

"I am familiar with the reference."

"This is Enrico."

"How do you know?" The man was as anonymous as the vehicle. He wore one of those chauffeur-type peaked caps, which would have made it difficult to see his face even if it hadn't been dark and he hadn't been looking forward.

"I'd know that giggle anywhere," said John.

Enrico obligingly produced another giggle and a polite *"Buona sera, signorina."*

John turned to look out the back window. Apparently he was satisfied by what he saw, or didn't see; after a while he returned his attention to me.

"You may now finish your question," he said graciously.

I refused to give him the satisfaction of asking the obvious. Obviously he had set this up before we left Munich, at the same time he had changed our reservations. Obviously the driver was one of his old acquaintances. Obviously he was deathly afraid of being followed, which meant—obviously—that he had reason to suspect he would be followed.

"Never mind," I muttered.

A chilly silence ensued. At least it was silent in the backseat. Enrico began crooning in an off-key falsetto. It took me a while to recognize the tune: one of Cherubino's arias from *The Marriage of Figaro*. I joined in, hoping to annoy John. He is an excellent musician with well-nigh perfect pitch, which cannot be said of me. Except for twitching a bit when Enrico and I tried for a high note and missed, he did not react. Enrico told me I had a beautiful voice. We sang more Mozart, all the way into Rome, at which point I looked out the side window and tried to figure out where we were going, since I was damned if I was going to ask John.

The narrow streets of Trastevere gave me the clue. When we stopped in front of a small hotel I said, "Well, well, here we are again. I'm surprised the cops haven't closed this place down. If you are representative of its customary clientele—"

"Shut up and get out," John snarled.

It hadn't changed a bit. The same quiet, rather elegant lobby, the same creaky lift, and, of course, the same room. The same heavy off-white drapes, the same cozy little sitting area, with a red plush love seat and low table, the same bathroom. The same bed.

"You didn't even let me say good night to Enrico," I said, seating myself on the red plush and crossing my legs.

John tossed his suitcase onto the bed and began unpacking.

"I'm hungry," I said.

John stiffened, gave me a piercing look, and then relaxed. "You're always hungry. Call room service. You remember the procedure, I trust?"

That and a lot of other things, I thought, as I picked up the phone. John had brought me here after the end of our Roman escapade—if I may use such a light-hearted word to describe a scenario that included murder, attempted murder (of me), grand theft, fraud, another murder, attempted seduction (of me), and a spectacular nervous breakdown (not me). The hotel didn't have a restaurant; if a guest wanted anything, from a gourmet meal to a piano, he called the front desk and asked for it—and got it. On the occasion of my first stay I had requested medical supplies and copious quantities of booze, in addition to food. The booze was for me. My nerves were in terrible shape. The medical supplies were for John, who had incurred a number of well-deserved injuries. He'd been one of the gang initially and had come over to my side only because . . . Well, to make a long story short, by the time we left the hotel next day I was inclined to believe he had repented of his evil deeds and learned to care deeply for me. At least I believed it until the next time we met . . .

With a sigh, I picked up the phone. "What do you want to eat?" I asked.

"Give it to me." John took the telephone. "You don't know anything about wine."

"I know I want lots of it."

The wine arrived almost at once. It was red. The waiter slithered silently out; John sat down next to me and raised his glass. "Cheers."

"Is it the pope?"

"I knew you were going to say that," John remarked with satisfaction. "That's one of the reasons why I love you. Your bull-headed one-track mind. No, dear, it isn't His Holiness. I don't move in such exalted circles."

"Shouldn't you check to see whether Feisal has called?" I held out my empty glass.

"And I love the way you leap from one non sequitur to another. He's barely had time to reach Cairo. Anything from Schmidt?"

I hadn't bothered to turn my cell phone on after we landed, since I didn't particularly want to hear from anybody, especially Schmidt. When I did so, I found not one but three text messages from him.

Schmidt adores texting. He adores every new gadget until the next one comes along.

"Clara bit Suzi," I reported.

"Good for Clara."

"The damn woman has the run of my house. What do you suppose she—"

"Suzi is an unknown quantity and the least of our worries at the moment. She can't have any knowledge of—shall we refer to it henceforth as Feisal's loss?"

"She'd taken up with Schmidt before it happened," I conceded.

"Anything else?"

"Just the usual. Oh, there's the waiter. Good. I'm—"

"Starved. I know." John went to the door and opened it. The hallway outside was discreetly dim, but I made out a cheering sight—a cart loaded with serving dishes. The waiter was an undersized youth possessed of an oversized mustache; grunting with effort, he propelled the cart forward.

John let him get all the way into the room before he moved. The boy let out a shriek as his arm was yanked back and up. The gun he had been holding hit the floor with a thud.

THREE

D on't just sit there, do something," John gasped. His pris-
oner was squirming and writhing and directing ineffectual blows at John's midriff.

"Hit him," I suggested.

"That would be unkind and unnecessary," said a fourth party.

He stood in the doorway, pretty nearly filling it. His mustache
was even larger than the boy's. His gun was bigger too.

"*Idiota,*" he remarked, addressing the boy.

"*Scusi, Papa,*" said the boy. He kept swinging at John, who had
shifted his grip and was holding the kid out at arm's length. The
mustache hung by a thread, or rather, a hair, and the face now visible to my wondering eyes was spotted with pimples.

"Let him go, you big bully," I said.

"Damn it," said John.

"Let us compose ourselves," said the newcomer, in a fruity baritone. "Sir John, I beg you will release my incompetent offspring.

Giuseppe, sit down and behave yourself. Signorina, my compliments."

John dropped Giuseppe and gestured pointedly at the gun the big man held. "The atmosphere of cordiality would be improved if you would put that away, Bernardo, old chap."

"Certainly. It was only meant to get your attention."

"It did that," I said, watching Bernardo stow the gun away in one pocket. He scooped up the weapon his son had dropped, and shoved it into another pocket. They did not improve the hang of his coat.

Bernardo chuckled. "You haven't taken to carrying a weapon, have you?" he inquired of John.

John took his empty hands out of his own pockets. "How much did you pay Enrico?" he asked.

"You do him a grave injustice. It was not necessary for me to bribe him. Your arrival was noted and reported. Signorina." He bowed gracefully. "May I offer you a glass of wine?"

"Only if you're paying for it."

This sally produced a shout of laughter. "Ah, she is witty as well as beautiful! I get it, as you say in America! Then may I beg that you will offer me a glass?"

I was beginning to like Bernardo. He was about John's height, and about twice his breadth, especially through the chest and shoulders. He had an outdoorsman's finely lined skin, eyebrows almost as oversized as his mustache, and a head of black hair so impeccably smooth it looked like a designer toupee. He bared a set of expensively capped teeth, and took a chair opposite me.

At his father's request, Giuseppe produced another glass and we all settled down round the table. Giuseppe kept rubbing his wrist and shooting malevolent glances at John.

"None for him," said Bernardo, indicating his son. "He does not deserve any. How true it is, your English saying, that one should never send a boy to do the work of a man. The mustache, as I tried to tell him, was a mistake."

"Why did you send him, then?" I asked curiously.

"He must learn sometime. To your health, signorina. And to yours, my dear old friend."

John acknowledged the salute with a sour smile. "What do you want, Bernardo?"

"Simple." The big man put his empty glass on the table and leaned forward. "I want in on the deal."

After our uninvited guests had taken their leave, John made sure the door was locked. "If you had bothered to close the door while I was subduing the incompetent offspring, Bernardo wouldn't have got in."

"He'd have got in one way or another," I said, lifting covers. "Anyhow, what was the harm? He was very nice. Veal scaloppini? Tomato-and-mozzarella salad? Osso buco?"

"Don't overdo it, Vicky."

He wasn't talking about the food. Abandoning my attempt at positive reinforcement, I went to him and put my arms round his neck. "As Bernardo might say, I do get it, John. He's heard about—er— Feisal's bereavement, and if he knows, so do a lot of other people. But he doesn't know who pulled it off."

"He thinks I did. What he was offering, in case you missed it, was to act as middleman in helping me dispose of it."

"It wasn't so much an offer as a demand," I mused. "At least we know he wasn't the one who stole Tut."

"Splendid," John said sourly. "We can cross one name off the endless list. I didn't suppose he was; he's never been known to oper- ate outside western Europe."

47

I couldn't think offhand of anything positive to say about that. I carried my filled plate to the table.

"Eat something. Your blood sugar is probably low. Good Lord, listen to me. I sound like Schmidt."

"Don't mention his name. You might conjure him up, like a helpful elf."

I looked up. He was watching me, his mouth curved in a smile. "I don't deserve you," he said softly.

"I was under the impression that you did."

"I didn't do it, Vicky."

"That's what this is all about, isn't it?" I put my fork down. "That's why you're so nobly intent on tracking down the real thieves. Not for Feisal's sake, but because you realized you'd be the prime suspect. No wonder! It's precisely the sort of insane operation you once specialized in. Like the time you tried to build Camelot in the back pasture."

John wandered over to the cart and busied himself removing covers and shifting plates around. "Jen would be deeply offended to hear you refer to the grounds of our stately manor as a pasture. You are, of course, correct."

"And the time you tried to pose as an archaeologist so you could dig up a cache of buried treasure and—"

"Make off with the loot," John said with a reminiscent smile. "You don't know the half of it, darling. Did I ever tell you about—"

"I don't want to hear about it. I want to hear about Bernardo. How did he find out?"

"He did rather avoid answering that question, didn't he?" John joined me on the settee. Bending over, he inspected the underside of the table.

"What are you looking for?" I asked. "Oh my God. Did he put—"

"There was one under the shelf of the cart." John took it out of his pocket, dropped it onto the floor, and stamped on it. "I was watching his hands, and I don't think he managed to get another under the table."

"What about the phone?"

"Bernardo didn't know we were here until we were. Here, that is to say."

"He seems like a civilized sort of guy," I said, trying to look on the bright side. "No threats, no intimidation."

"Aren't you forgetting those large guns? Believe me, love, he will turn very uncivilized when he realizes I'm not going to cut him in, for the simple reason that I can't. At the moment, thanks to my quick thinking and incessant talking, he thinks we are in the first stage of negotiation."

"How long can you keep it up?" I asked, remembering those large guns.

"Not long enough, I fear."

"Why don't you try telling him the truth?"

"Good heavens," said John, eyes widening. "What a novel idea. Because, you ingenuous young woman, he wouldn't believe me. For some reason I have great difficulty convincing people of my veracity."

The night passed without incident. John slept like a log, and as I tossed and turned I remembered another of the quotations he was fond of repeating: "The worse a man is, the more profound his slumber; for if he had a conscience he would not be a villain." However, I felt a little easier in my mind now that I had (finally!) figured out what was driving him. If he were only going through the motions, pretending to be unwitting, he wouldn't go to so much trouble.

Or would he? What if this trip had another motive? An excuse to get in touch with one of the other people involved in the theft, perhaps? In order to pass on instructions or receive a progress report? Communication by almost any other means could be intercepted. Hell, our government is listening in on half the world, and if they can do it, anybody can.

"Damn," I said loudly. John grunted and turned over.

I finally got to sleep. Fifteen minutes later, or so it seemed, I was aroused by John, who was wearing one of his swishiest dressing gowns. "Didn't you sleep well?" he asked solicitously, offering me a cup of coffee. Room service had come and gone, presumably without firearms.

I growled and snatched the cup. He stood watching me, tapping his foot, until I had finished the first cup and was halfway through the second. "Sorry to rush you," he said, "but our appointment is at ten. Pop into the shower, why don't you, and then we'll have breakfast out."

He followed me into the bathroom and helpfully adjusted the shower. Having reached a state of relative alertness by then, I expected he would join me. Instead he murmured softly, "We didn't say anything last night that would put Bernardo on his guard, but from now on watch what you say. In fact, I would prefer that you say nothing except yes and no."

"What—"

"Just keep quiet and listen. Cram all your vital belongings into that dreadful backpack of yours. Leave everything that is not absolutely essential. We won't be returning to the hotel after our appointment."

"Okay."

Both of John's eyebrows rose in a look of exaggerated surprise. "No argument? No questions?"

"I'm not exactly stupid, you know."

"I do know. I'd kiss you if you weren't so wet." He handed me a towel and left the room.

We had brief but silent arguments over some of the items I considered essential. I lost most of them. He was right, damn him. Trust is not a conspicuous characteristic of evildoers. Bernardo would assume John had been lying through his teeth and that he would bolt if he got a chance. Finding our personal possessions still in situ might delay him temporarily.

I had hoped to scrounge another cup of coffee, but by the time we got through sorting things and gesticulating at each other, the hour of our appointment was upon us. Conspicuously sans luggage, we left the hotel and strolled to the corner, where John hailed a taxi.

He couldn't have selected a more conspicuous spot for a rendezvous. The via della Conciliazione runs from Vatican Square to the bridge. It is lined with souvenir shops and cafés and it is always packed with people, tour buses, and taxis, and it echoes with the roaring of engines and the curses of drivers stuck in traffic. The soaring dome of Saint Peter's rose pearly white against an azure sky, remote and eternal amid the hubbub.

The man we were to meet was waiting for us at a table outside one of the cafés. He wore a black cassock and a black biretta. Being on good terms with God (or his local representative) makes a man healthy and wise, if not wealthy; he had plump rosy cheeks, an expression of innocent amiability, and a pair of the shrewdest dark eyes I had ever beheld. He greeted John with a fond Italian embrace, hugs and kisses on both cheeks, and me with a bow and a smile. He didn't look surprised to see me, and John did not introduce us.

I tucked into a hearty breakfast of pane and jam and butter and lots more coffee, while the other two conversed. My Italian is pretty good, but the Roman dialect isn't easy to follow, especially when it is spoken at top speed and when the ambient noise level is high. As every spy and would-be spy knows, the safest place for a meeting is not on a lonely heath but in the middle of a crowd. Even if you are followed, the other guy can't get close enough to overhear anything without practically sitting on your lap.

I still had a couple of chunks of bread to go when John tossed a suspiciously large roll of money onto the table and got to his feet. I'd been expecting him to move fast when he did move (as I kept telling him, I'm not stupid) so I crammed bread into my mouth with one hand, grabbed my backpack with the other, and let him tow me out into the middle of the via della Conciliazione. Brakes squealed and drivers waxed profane, and an alert taxi driver came to a shuddering stop. A final glance over my shoulder showed Monsignor Anonymous nodding and waving like a plump puppet, and a weedy youth shaking his fist at the air.

"Well done," said John breathlessly. In response to the driver's question, he said, "Cavalieri Hilton. Double fare if you make it in less than twenty minutes."

"You have just signed our death warrant," I said, remembering how Romans drive even when they lack monetary incentives.

"I am trying to avoid doing precisely that" was the reply. "Did you spot Giuseppe?"

"Uh-huh. He blended in nicely with the other slouching teenagers, but he really ought to do something about that acne. Bernardo must be short-handed. The kid isn't up to this sort of thing."

"Be fair. Few people would be."

The walls of Vatican City passed in a jerky blur, and I stopped trying to carry on a conversation and concentrated on holding on. We made it in less than twenty minutes; it took less than thirty seconds to leave the first taxi and get into another. This time our destination was the airport.

"Where to now?" I inquired, getting a firm grip on the armrest. "Munich? London? Egypt? Kathmandu? What do I get if I guess right? A new wardrobe, maybe?"

John was staring out the back window, watching the taxis that had left the rank after us peel off or pass. He turned back to me with a sigh and brushed a lock of hair away from his forehead. "Vicky, in case it hasn't dawned on you yet, I haven't had time to think, much less explain. The truth is—well, the truth is I miscalculated. I didn't expect the word would spread so quickly. All I'm trying to do at the moment is keep one step ahead of people like Bernardo."

"Okay," I said, recognizing the tone. "But I would appreciate hearing any ideas that may be floating around in your pretty head."

John gave me a sour look, and then an equally sour laugh. "Our hoped-for destination is London. It is now imperative that I start working my contacts. I daren't do it on anything but a secure line, and the only line I'm sure of is the one in my office."

No new wardrobe, then. I kept clothes and other necessities in John's London flat. "Makes sense. So what was the point of meeting Monsignor Anonymous?"

"He's in charge of relics and other human remains, including mummies, at the Vatican museums. I wanted to know if they had suffered any losses recently."

"Very ingenious," I said. "Had they?"

John shook his head morosely. "It was a far-out theory, but I rather hoped it was accurate. An insane collector, who could be counted on to keep mum, would give us some breathing room."

"So no missing saints' skulls?"

"He says not."

"Goodness gracious me, don't you trust a holy man?"

"The Vatican administration, as distinct from the papacy, is a business organization, Vicky, with all the characteristics of any other such group. They are efficient, secretive and cynical—or, as they prefer to call it, realistic. Luis's passion for dried-up bits of people has led him once or twice into dubious transactions. I can't prove it—nor would I bother to do so—but he knows that I know, and that gives me a certain hold over him. I'm pretty sure he was telling the truth when he said nothing has gone missing, and that he'd inform me if anything of interest came on the market."

"So he hasn't heard about Tut."

"Unfortunately," said John, "the mere fact that I inquired about petrified people aroused his curiosity. It was inevitable but unavoidable. However, I'm hoping that of all the mummies in all the museums in the world he won't think of that one unless he hears of it from another source. In which case he will get in touch with me, because he will assume, like everyone else, that I'm the thief."

John claims he is not superstitious, but when you come right down to it, who isn't? We tend to interpret good luck as a good omen. He cheered up when we managed to get the last two seats on a flight to London leaving in half an hour. They were first-class seats, and I thought I saw him hold his breath when he handed over his credit card.

"Must be nice to be rich," I remarked.

"I wouldn't know," John said. "Setting up shop in London cost a bundle, and that damned white elephant in Cornwall is draining me dry. Oh, well, carpe diem."

First class, I was sorry to learn, isn't that classy anymore. The drinks were free, but the food consisted of soggy salad and tasteless sandwiches. By the time we got through customs and passport control at Heathrow, I found myself a bit peckish. Before I could mention this, John said, "I'm not taking you out to dinner. Don't tell me there isn't something edible in that backpack of yours. I've never known you to travel without a stash of food."

"I want a regular meal," I whined.

"Vicky," said John, in the patient voice that makes me want to throw a temper tantrum, "it's too late to get a reservation at an acceptable restaurant. Every hour that passes before I begin my inquiries is an hour lost."

"If you are suggesting that one miserable hour may mean the difference between life and death—"

"It's an uncertain world, my dear. There's sure to be something in the fridge."

We took the tube from Heathrow. John offered to carry my backpack. I haughtily refused. I do really dumb things sometimes. The damn thing weighed a ton. I wondered what I'd tossed into it during my last-minute frenzy. There were a few odds and ends of food—a chocolate bar, an apple—but pride forbade that I should search for them.

It wasn't that late. When we came out of the Marylebone Station there were plenty of people around, and—I noticed—several perfectly acceptable restaurants open for business. John relieved me of my backpack, so the only alternative to trotting docilely after him was to throw a temper tantrum in front of one of the perfectly acceptable restaurants.

The street he graced with his presence was off the Edgware Road, in a residential area without a restaurant in sight, acceptable or otherwise. The lift was working, thank heaven. It doesn't always. By the time we reached his door I was ready to sink my teeth into moldy cheese, stale bread, or anything else that might lurk in the depths of his pantry.

Old habits die hard; John still enters a room as if he expects an assassin to be lurking within. Standing well back, he gave the door a shove and reached around for the light switch before peering cautiously into the room.

"Oh my goodness," I said, looking past him.

Drawers stood open, pillows had been tossed onto the floor, and several books toppled from shelves. Through the door that led to the bedroom I caught a shadowy glimpse of comparable chaos.

"Stay back," John ordered, barring the door with an outflung arm.

"If anybody was here, he'd be pointing a gun at us by now."

"I am in no mood for one of your arguments. Do as I say."

He made sure I would by giving me a shove, and then slid into the room. I heard him moving around, heard the click of light switches, and finally he said, "You can come in. Close the door."

One of the many reasons why John and I do not cohabit is that he is as neat as a finicky maiden lady and I am not. On closer inspection his living room didn't look all that bad—no worse than mine on most days, after I have returned from work to find Clara and Caesar had been whiling away the lonely hours by knocking various objects off various surfaces. The sofa cushions had been pulled out and replaced, in a haphazard sort of way. I straightened them and plumped up one of the pillows, which was lying flat instead of being artistically propped up against the arm. ("You don't sit on them," John had once raged, "you look at them.") Like everything John owns, it was beautiful—a fragment of Chinese embroidery in shimmering shades of gold and turquoise and scarlet. I replaced a few other items and made my way to the door of the room John used as an office. In addition to the desk and a few file cabinets, it contained a couple of straight chairs and a narrow sofa bed. Presumably this was where Jen slept when she visited. It had not been designed to inspire a prolonged stay.

John sat at the desk, pecking away at the keyboard of his computer. Images came and went on the screen.

"Did he get into your files?" I asked.

"No." John closed the file he was inspecting before I could get a look at it. "Not that he could; everything of importance is protected. But it looks as if he didn't even try. That's odd."

"Depends on what he was after."

John followed me into the bedroom. The drawers of the bureau stood half open. The mattress was half off the bed, sheets and blankets tumbled around it. I studied one of the drawers, sacred to John's meticulously folded handkerchiefs. They were now in a tumbled heap. I considered refolding them and decided I wouldn't.

"What are you doing?" John demanded.

I closed the drawer. "I'm about to investigate the kitchen. Who knows what havoc has been wrought there?"

When John joined me I was sitting at the kitchen counter digging into a light repast of Brie and smoked oysters and crackers and a few other odds and ends.

"I threw out the grapes," I informed him.

"Don't talk with your mouth full. What was wrong with the grapes?"

I swallowed. "They looked tired. The apples are withery and the bananas have gone dark brown. You don't eat enough fresh fruit and vegetables."

"I have heard enough about healthy eating habits to last me, thank you." He dug into the Brie, which was nice and runny. "Anything missing out here?"

"Don't talk with your mouth full. Not that I could see. He investigated all the cupboards, even the fridge. Spilled a bottle of milk."

"I don't suppose you mopped it up," John said, without hope. "What could he have been looking for in the fridge?"

"The family jewels, maybe?"

"I told you, we don't have any." John smeared Brie on a cracker. Not many people can chew and look thoughtful at the same time, but he could. "He dug into every drawer and looked under the mattress and the sofa cushions."

Not to be outdone in the deductive process, I chimed in. "He was looking for something relatively small and portable, something that would lie flat under a mattress or a pile of hankies."

"I do not hide stolen antiquities under my sofa cushions or in my bureau drawers, if that's what you are implying."

"My, my, aren't we sensitive."

He had finished the Brie. I snatched the remains of the smoked oysters. "I agree, you wouldn't be that stupid."

"Even if I possessed stolen antiquities."

"Even if you did. One thing for sure—he wasn't looking for King Tut."

John let out a choking sound. "Sorry. I had a sudden insane image. If this were a horror film, there'd have been a withered hand under the handkerchiefs, a leg or two among the sofa cushions and Tut's head glaring out of the cupboard between tins of baked beans and tuna."

"He couldn't glare, his eyes have been poked out."

John grimaced. "Did you have to say that? And how do you know?"

"I looked him up at the museum. There are dozens of photos and X-rays. Back in 1926, when Howard Carter put him back in his coffin, he still had eyelids and a little skullcap thingie on his head, and lots of beads and gold bits on his chest—part of an ornamental collar that was so stuck in hardened resin, Carter decided not to try to remove it. In 1968, when a specialist X-rayed him, the skullcap was missing, and so were the pieces of the collar, along with the ribs that had lain under it. And the eyes were just empty sockets."

The photographs had struck me not as horrible but as pathetic. The shriveled skin was stretched tight over his bones and his teeth were exposed by shrunken lips, not in the menacing grin of film-dom mummies but in a smile that looked almost shy. He had only been eighteen years old when he died.

Damn it, I thought, I refuse to feel sorry for a three-thousand-year-old corpse. And damn Feisal for infecting me with his senti-mental nonsense.

John was thinking along more practical lines. "That eliminates one motive for stealing the mummy. There was nothing of value left on it."

"No. His penis was missing too."

"Enough about bloody Tutankhamon!" John sprang to his feet.

Men are so touchy about that particular part of their anatomy. Tactfully I changed the subject. "Are you going to call the cops and report a break-in?"

"What would be the point? Nothing seems to be missing, no bodily assault occurred. I hate to trouble the overworked Metro-politan Police with such a petty crime."

"They could look for fingerprints."

"Nobody leaves fingerprints these days," John said gloomily. "Thanks to television and films, even the dullest miscreant knows enough to wear gloves. The hell with it. I'm too tired to think straight. I'll make the bed if you clear up the remains of the food."

He did look tired. "I'll even mop up the spilled milk," I offered. "Unless your daily is due tomorrow."

"I don't have a daily, or even a fortnightly."

"Are you economizing or just suspicious-minded?"

"Both."

I had to use a brush to loosen some of the dried-on milk. It had been there for at least twenty-four hours, if I was any judge. I don't have many long-lasting spills. Caesar takes care of them immediately if they are edible, and sometimes if they aren't.

The sound of low voices woke me from a dream that featured the head of Tutankhamon gibbering at me and demanding to know what I had done with his penis. John was already up and dressed; I dragged myself out of bed and into the shower.

John was alone when I joined him in the kitchen. Accepting a cup of coffee, I asked, "Who was here?"

"The super, as you would call him. He denies having seen any suspicious characters, or of having lent someone a key."

"Well, he wouldn't admit it, would he? Someone must have had a key. The lock wasn't forced."

"An expert could have picked it," said John, in the tone of one who knows whereof he speaks.

We breakfasted on coffee and stale bread and headed out. The Closed sign hung at the shop door, but it wasn't locked, and the lights inside were on. John's assistant manager was sitting at the desk at the back of the showroom, his head bent over an object in his hands.

"Hi, Alan," I said.

Alan let out a little shriek and dropped the object he was holding. "Must you creep up on a person like that?" he complained. "I didn't hear you coming."

"Too absorbed in your artistry?" John inquired. "I told you not to bring your sewing to work."

"Hi, Alan," I said.

"Vicky!" He sprang to his feet. "Do forgive me. John so dominates his surroundings, one fails to notice more attractive objects."

Superficially he resembled John—fair hair, slim build, and that indefinable air of superiority produced by a public school education. At close range one couldn't have mistaken one for the other. To put it as nicely as possible, Alan was a watered-down version of John, paler, slighter, less well defined, as if he was trying to imitate his boss and not doing it very successfully.

"What are you making?" I asked.

It was obviously a hat—large, broad-brimmed, with a white plume drooping dispiritedly over one side. Alan was polite enough to avoid making a sarcastic remark about my dumb question. He picked up the hat and pushed the plume up. It fell over again. "It's for the reenactment," he explained. "I'm a Cavalier."

"Of course," I said. "It's the Roundheads and the Cavaliers this time? Cromwell and the head of King Charles?"

"Don't show off," John snapped. "Or encourage him. Of all the childish occupations in the world, reenacting old battles is the silliest."

"I'd offer to help," I said, as Alan pushed the plume up again and watched it slowly subside. "But I can't sew either. May I suggest superglue?"

Alan pursed his lips. "It isn't authentic, but it's a very bright idea. Thanks."

"I hate to interrupt," John said, raising both eyebrows, "but might I venture to inquire whether anything of interest has transpired in my absence? Anything in the way of vulgar business, that is?"

"A couple of messages about the Egyptian piece. They're on your computer."

"I don't know how to thank you." John stalked into the office. Alan made a face at his back. "What's new in dear old München?"

"Not much." I followed John into the office. He was already at the computer and into his e-mail.

"Anything from . . . him?" I asked.

"Mmmm," said John, staring at the screen.

I leaned over his shoulder. Feisal had written a nice chatty letter, full of irrelevant gossip about what was going on in Luxor. It ended with fondest regards and the hope that we'd be able to pay him a visit in the not too distant future.

"So we can assume that everything is okay so far?" I asked.

"Mmmm," said John.

"Do you want me to go away?"

"Mmmm."

He shifted position so that I couldn't read the screen. I took the hint. The bells over the door jangled as I entered the showroom. Alan looked up. "Would you mind demonstrating an inordinate interest in the amber necklace?" he hissed.

A woman of what is known as "a certain age" had sidled in. What I could see of her hair, under her enormous hat, was an odd shade of grayish blue. The hat was eye-catching: bright scarlet, with a floppy brim that drooped down over her brow, leaving only nose and mouth exposed. Seeing me, she stopped just inside the door.

"Oh," she said.

Alan advanced, smiling winsomely. "Come to have another look at the necklace?" he asked. "I put it aside for you, but I'm afraid you'll have to come to a decision shortly. This lady is also interested."

"Oh," said the hat. "No. I, um . . . Thank you."

The door closed after her. Alan shook his head. "One does meet the most peculiar people in this business."

"What's so exciting about the necklace?" I asked, leaning over the case of jewelry. "It's just rough chunks of amber."

"According to our esteemed chief, it came from a fifth-century Viking hoard. He's got the papers to prove it."

"I'm sure he does."

"Some people," Alan rattled on, "buy not for the intrinsic value or the artistry of the piece concerned; they focus on specific periods or areas."

I stopped listening, since he was telling me stuff I already knew or didn't care about. "This is nice," I said, moving along the length of the case.

"Which?" Alan leaned over the case. "Oh, that. I'd forgot you were an authority on antique jewelry. Would you like to have a closer look?"

He fished out a bunch of keys, unlocked the case, and placed the pendant carefully on my outstretched palm. It was silver filigree set with roughly cut turquoise, with loops at the top so that it could be hung on a chain or cord.

"Turkoman," I said. "It's not that old; late nineteenth century, probably."

"Show-off," Alan said agreeably. He replaced the piece and locked the case again. "Darling, since you and the boss are here, would you mind if I popped out for a coffee?"

"Not if you bring one back for me."

He waved his way out. The office door remained uncompromisingly closed.

I amused myself by wandering around the showroom. Some of the objects on display had been there as long as I could remember: a study in black chalk of an elephant, purportedly by Rembrandt (I had my doubts), a stunning *Entombment of Christ* in walnut polished to satiny smoothness (fifteenth-century German), and a bronze Chinese ceremonial vessel of some sort (not my field). One new object occupied a pedestal in the center of the room. I was gaping at it when John emerged from the office.

"Where on earth did you get this?" I asked.

"Do I detect a note of accusation in your voice?" After a quick but comprehensive survey of the showroom, he came to stand beside me. "It's been in the family for years. I am reduced, tragically, to selling off our treasures."

It *was* a treasure—a small alabaster head, with the distinctive elongated cranium of an Amarna princess. Eighteenth Dynasty Egypt is not my period either, but artifacts of that quality are memorable; they don't come on the market often. The lips were delicately tinted and the musculature of the face sketched in by an expert hand.

"How many years has it been in the family? Four?"

"Your skepticism cuts me to the quick. It was purchased in Egypt quite legitimately in 1892. I have the original bill of sale, and several dated documents describing it."

I turned to meet his placid blue gaze. "So you do have family jewels."

"A few. Where—"

"And they aren't in the attic or your hankie drawer."

"No. Do stop asking irrelevant questions. I want to talk to you before Alan comes back. Where is he, by the way?"

"Gone for coffee."

"That usually takes quite a while. Still, I will be brief. Amid the plethora of trivia that constitutes my correspondence, there were a few interesting items."

"From your former business associates?"

"One or two. Indicating, in the most tactful fashion, that they were presently at loose ends and would be pleased to act as middlemen in any transactions that might be pending."

"Competitors of Bernardo? Or Monsignor Anonymous?"

"I beg your pardon?"

"Don't try that icy stare on me. You didn't go all the way to Rome to ask about thefts from a place like the Vatican, and you didn't hand over that wad of money for information about relics. Why can't you tell me the truth?"

"I paid you the compliment of assuming you would prefer to work it out for yourself." He put a long arm round my shoulders and leaned toward me.

"Don't try that either." I turned my head away. John planted a kiss on my cheek and removed his arm.

"Assuming that you are on the level, which I am prepared to do for the time being," I began.

"How can you doubt me?" John asked in hurt tones.

"Easily. Assuming that, I presume you are attempting to work out which organizations are capable of pulling off a job like the one in question. In the process you are weeding out people like Bernardo, who wouldn't have tried to cut themselves in if they were already in, so to speak. May I add that your method of eliminating such individuals strikes me as somewhat hazardous?"

John shrugged. "Not really. Persons of that ilk don't take drastic action until they have tried and failed to achieve their ends through simpler methods. You don't suppose I would have taken you to Rome if I had anticipated danger?"

The door opened. Alan edged in, juggling several paper cups. "Thoughtful little me, I brought one for each of you. I expect to be reimbursed, naturally. My salary isn't large enough to promote generosity."

"Take it out of petty cash," John said. "Plus a generous tip, of course."

They sneered genteelly at each other; John gestured, and I followed him back into the office.

"Why are you so nasty to him?" I asked, easing the cap off my coffee.

"He's a nasty little man," John said, his lip curling. "I doubt he has a moral scruple in his head."

"So why did you hire him?"

"Vicky, you have the greatest gift for idle curiosity of anyone I've ever met. He's some sort of cousin—I have hundreds of them. He wormed his way into Jen's good graces and asked her help in finding a nice gentlemanly job. He's good with computers and he knows something about art and antiques. I need someone to look after the shop when I'm away, which is a great deal of the time: attending auctions, running down leads, responding to would-be sellers and so on. I know he's untrustworthy, so I keep a close eye on him."

"Always expect the worst, then you are never disappointed?"

"Or deceived. I trust that satisfies your curiosity. I haven't opened the post yet. Why don't you check your messages while I do so?"

"I didn't think anybody wrote letters these days," I said, fishing in my backpack.

"Jen does," John said morosely. He waved an envelope at me—I noticed it had a coat of arms emblazoned on the backside—and ripped it open with the air of a man who knows he is going to be hanged and decides he may as well get it over with. "She wants me to pay her a visit."

"Fat chance," I said. I picked up Jen's envelope and examined the coat of arms. It was divided into four sections—quartered, I think is the term. One contained a shapeless blob, roughly square in shape and gray in color, another a dagger or sword; the third had several fleurs-de-lis and the fourth a couple of leopards or lions standing up on their hind feet. The royal arms of England and/or France? I

wouldn't have put it past Jen to claim a relationship with either and/
or both.

While I tried to figure out the Latin motto, John went methodi-
cally through the rest of the post. It appeared to be the usual sort of
thing—brochures, catalogs, and, of course, bills.

"Well?" he inquired.

"Well what? Oh, Schmidt." I returned to my backpack and located my cell phone.

"Put it on speaker," John suggested, leaning back in his chair
and picking up his cup. "I can hardly wait to hear whether Clara
has attacked Suzi again."

She had. Schmidt rambled on about that for a while; the message ended with a reproachful "Where are you? You have not returned my calls. Why do you not return them? You know I worry."

"I'm surprised he hasn't figured out how to track you," John remarked.

"Shh." The second message was more of the same. The third . . .
I clutched the phone with a suddenly sweaty hand and John sat up
straight.

"Where are you?" Schmidt's voice was so choked I barely recognized it. "Vicky, I need you. Something terrible has happened. You
must call me at once. The number—"

"I know the number," I groaned. "And that one, and that one . . .
Schmidt, for God's sake tell me what's wrong."

"He can't hear you," John pointed out.

The other numbers he had given me were those of his office at
the museum, his home, and my house. At least he wasn't in a
hospital—or in jail. Neither one of which, knowing Schmidt as I
knew him, would have surprised me.

I tried his cell phone first. It rang and went on ringing. I was about to try the office when Schmidt's voice fell like music on my ears. "Vicky! At last! Why have you not—"

"You sound all choked up. Where are you?"

"In a café. You remember it; we were here together, one rainy day, when you wept on my shoulder and bared your heart to me."

"You're eating," I said, watching John's eyebrow go up. I remembered that café well. There wasn't a thing on the menu that wasn't covered in whipped cream. "Schmidt, what's the matter? Have you gone off your diet?"

A sound of Schmidt being throttled would have alarmed me had I not known he was swallowing a large bite of something. Something with schlag all over it, I did not doubt. "I have gone off my diet, yes. Why should I torture myself? I am too old, too fat, too disgusting—" Another gulp.

"She's ditched him," John mouthed.

"Oh, no," I mouthed back. Aloud I said, "Schmidt, darling, you are not disgusting. Nor any of those other things. Tell Vicky."

He proceeded to do so, at some length. Chocolate and whipped cream perked him up; indignation replaced his woe. "She did not even have the courage to tell me to my face. She wrote a note. I will read it to you."

"You don't have to—"

"But I will. *Noch einmal, bitte.*" The last addressed, I assumed, to the waiter. "She says I am a wonderful man and she does not deserve me. It is the past and the future, not the present, that separates us."

"Uh-oh," said John.

"What?" Schmidt yelled. "Who is that? What did he say?"

"It's just me, Schmidt," John said, taking the phone. "Sorry, I couldn't help overhearing."

Schmidt assured him, between mouthfuls, that there was no need to apologize, and proceeded to repeat the whole sad story. "So," he concluded, "in such a case as this, a man needs to be distracted and to have his friends by his side. I am coming to see you. I have already my ticket. You will not be put out by me, I will stay at the Savoy. Until tonight, my dear friends."

I grabbed the phone from John, who appeared to be temporarily paralyzed; but it was too late. Schmidt had hung up.

"I'll call him back," I said, fumbling. "Tell him we aren't here."

"But we are. And he knows we are. How does he know?"

"I didn't tell him. Really. Maybe he just assumed we were going to London."

"Maybe. I'd suggest we run for it, but that would be cruel, even for me."

"Yeah," I said, visualizing Schmidt's round pink face slowly sagging as the phone in the flat rang and rang and rang and nobody answered.

"Let us try, for once, to stick to the point. Why did Suzi decide to jilt Schmidt, and why now?" John raised an admonitory finger and declaimed, "Is there a clue, perchance, in that cryptic reference to yesterday and tomorrow?"

"Hmm. What you want me to say is that Suzi may have got wind of the—er—of Feisal's deprivation. That would fit the clue; it happened in the past and if she's on the case she's warning him that the future may be unpleasant for him or somebody close to him."

John shook his head. "Too many assumptions. Besides, your theory gives her credit for an extraordinary degree of altruism. If she's after it—him—and I am the principal suspect, sticking close to Schmidt would be her best lead."

"Too many assumptions," I said meanly.

"Isn't that what you would do?"

"Not if I really cared about him. Using the man you love to trap his friend would be a lousy thing to do. Sure, I'd use any means possible to trap a child abuser or serial killer, but this is just a miserable missing mummy."

"What a hopeless sentimentalist you are. She's a professional, Vicky, and a damn good one. People in her business don't allow personal feelings to interfere with their chance of promotion."

"Well, then, it doesn't make sense. Unless you have some bright ideas."

"At the moment my mind is a black hole. Why don't you go for a walk, or help Alan dust? I do have a business to run."

"Something interesting?" I asked, as he picked up one of the letters he had discarded.

"Might be. It's from a Miss Eleanor Fitz-Rogers, who claims to have a collection of pre-Columbian artifacts inherited from her father that she's considering selling. Elderly spinster ladies," said John with a faraway look, "are my favorite source."

"Because they are easily swindled?"

"You are obviously not well acquainted with elderly spinster ladies. The important thing is that the collection probably dates from a period when exporting antiquities was perfectly legal." His eyes went back to the letter. "Definitely worth following up. I think I'll give her a ring."

"Not my field," I said, and left.

Alan was sitting behind the desk at the back of the room reading a magazine. Seeing me, he whipped it into a drawer, but not before I had got a look at the cover, which featured a trio of *Star Wars* storm troopers. Evidently Alan was into fantasy as well as historical reenactment.

"Business isn't what I'd call brisk," I observed.

"This isn't Marks and Sparks, duckie. We aren't trying to attract the sort of people who shop at Alfie's."

There was that sneer again. Personally, I am very fond of Alfie's, which is an antiques market just up (or down, depending on which way you are going) the street. However, many of the dealers focus on twentieth-century stuff and what is known in the trade as collectibles. Known to John as junk.

"It takes time to build the kind of clientele we want," Alan went on. "Museums, serious collectors, specialists. We notify them when we acquire a piece we believe will be of interest to them, and if the object is valuable enough, we'll deliver it for inspection."

I was familiar with the process, since I am sometimes called in to evaluate and authenticate an object that's being considered for the museum. I nodded. "Are you still accepting bank transfers and checks?"

Alan gave me a wry smile. "Oh, you heard about that little scam."

"I've heard of several." The most outrageous, which had happened only a few years earlier, involved a gang that had rented a chic apartment near the Grand Canal in Venice. Dealers from London, Frankfurt, and Amsterdam had delivered paintings worth more than a million pounds to a charming, elegantly dressed gentleman in exchange for a receipt and the promise of a bank transfer next day. The bank transfer never arrived, and (I like this touch) the check for the apartment bounced.

"It served the suckers right," I said.

"That sort of transaction used to be standard practice, Vicky. In part it's because people in this business like to think of themselves as gentlemen, dealing with gentlemen." Alan shook his head. "Unbelievably naive. Fine art and rare antiquities have become big business.

Paintings are selling for incredible sums at auction galleries, and the black market is flourishing. I might accept a wire transfer from the Metropolitan Museum, but not from anyone or anything less well known."

"Interesting. Well, thanks for the lecture."

"I didn't mean to sound patronizing."

"That's okay. Art scams aren't my field."

Which was not strictly true. My long association with John in his Mr. Hyde (i.e., Sir John Smythe) persona had taught me more than I really wanted to know about the illegal aspects of the trade. Take forgeries, for instance. Laymen innocently assume that any museum curator knows how to spot a fake, but I wouldn't swear to anything unless it was in my own limited field, and sometimes not even then. So-called critics talk learnedly about brushstrokes and technique, but the only sure way of detecting a fraud is through scientific analysis—such as the use of pigments which weren't known before the twentieth century in a purportedly sixteenth-century painting. As for flat-out theft, the security systems in many museums can be circumvented by anybody with a pair of pliers or a nail file—or enough money to bribe a guard. As John had once remarked, the fancier a gadget, the greater the likelihood it will break down at the wrong time. He preferred to deal directly with venal human beings.

It was all very depressing.

I said, "I'm going out for a breath of air."

I wandered slowly along the street, looking in windows and thinking vaguely about lunch. There was an open-air market not far away; I decided to check it out and maybe pick up a few healthful fruits and vegetables for the flat. I hadn't gone far when a car pulled to the curb and a voice called, "Miss? Excuse me, miss?" At the window I made out a large piece of paper that appeared to be a map, with the top of a bald head visible over it. Some poor lost soul wanting directions, I assumed.

The sun was bright, the pavement (as they call it in England) was busy with pedestrians. Helpful little me, I was within a few feet of the car when an arm went round me and pulled me back. The car took off with a screech of rubber, barely missing a taxi.

Four

"oddamn it," said John. "What do you think you're doing?"

"I was just . . . Ow. That hurts. What do you think *you're* doing?"

His grip relaxed. I rubbed my ribs.

"Saving you from a fate worse than death. Again. Have you no sense of self-preservation?"

The suspect vehicle had vanished. "I don't suppose you got the license number," I said, trying to catch my breath. It was beginning to dawn on me that I had just had a narrow escape.

"I was otherwise occupied. A futile procedure in any case; the vehicle was probably hired, and tracing a license number isn't easy unless you're a copper. Did you get a look at him?"

"No," I said, resisting his attempt to lead me back to the shop. "He was hiding behind a map. Naturally I assumed . . . Give me a break, John, I had no reason to suppose anybody was after me. What made *you* suppose that?"

"My general operating principle—always expect the worst. Hasn't it dawned on you that you are my weak point?"

He paid me the compliment of not spelling it out in detail. The attempt had been so blatant that it might well have succeeded by virtue of its sheer unexpectedness. A few seconds of shock and confusion on the part of bystanders, and they'd have had me inside the vehicle and away. And once they, whoever the hell they were, had a hostage, they could get anything they wanted from John. I remembered seeing someone in the backseat. Maybe more than one.

A few passersby had stopped to stare. John kept tugging at me and I kept resisting. One Good Samaritan, a little man with a brushy mustache and horn-rimmed glasses, cleared his throat. "Miss, is this person annoying you?"

John turned to give him a furious look. I was tempted to say yes, but his nobility demanded a kinder response. "No, we're just having a little domestic disagreement," I said. "He wants to go one way and I want to go another. But it's very kind of you to ask. You are the sort of citizen who makes this country great."

The little man marched off, preening himself, and John said under his breath, "Come back inside."

"I was going to the market," I explained. "Which is where I'm going now. With you by my side, my hero, who would dare interfere with me? Stop glowering before some other chivalrous soul decides to come to my rescue."

The corners of John's mouth twitched. "You win, as usual. I doubt they'll try it again so soon. Give me your word, for what that's worth, that you won't venture out alone from now on."

I love street markets. I still retain the delusion that produce is fresh from the local farm, even though I know most of it is imported from faraway places with strange-sounding names. Some of the stalls had lovely veggies, lettuce and tomatoes and bananas and artichokes, some sold baked goods and bottled fruit juices, coffee, chocolate, and so on. I had a feeling I wasn't going to be allowed out for a while, so I loaded up as for a siege. "We need butter for the artichokes," I remarked.

"I've got all I can carry," said John. One hand was empty, but I saw his point.

When we got back to the shop, Alan was lounging in the doorway. "Everything okay?" he asked.

"Why should you suppose otherwise?" I inquired.

"No reason." Alan gave John an odd look. "Do you want me to stick around? I have a date, but I can cancel it."

"Take the rest of the day off," John said. "And don't forget your hat."

After Alan had stalked out we retired to the office, and I spread out a few edibles on the desk. John condescended to accept an apple.

"Spare me the lecture," I said. "I realize I have to alter my behavior. I just wish I knew what the hell is going on. Is everybody after us?"

"Three, by the latest count. Bernardo and Company, the chap in the car just now, and the spinster lady in Kent."

It took me a minute to remember. "Oh, the lady with the pre-Columbian collection. You called her?"

"She was a baritone." John studied the apple distastefully and put it down on the desk. "Said she had a cold."

"And?" I prompted.

"She suggested I call on her at the earliest opportunity. Today, if feasible. Gave me directions to her remote manor house deep in the country."

"Oh. Was that what alerted you to my peril?"

"I suppose so." John rubbed his forehead. "Perhaps it was the mental bond between us, the marriage of true minds, et cetera."

"Right."

"And the fact, brought home to me by the baritone, that some individual or group here in England is already on our trail. That we need to be on our guard every bloody second of every day."

"You'd like me to butt out of this, wouldn't you?" I said, responding not so much to his words as to his tone of voice.

"It's too late for that, Vicky." He put his head in his hands.

"We could have a spectacular public fight," I suggested. "Declare to the world that we have split up and that we loathe each other."

John lowered his hands and gave me a feeble grin. "You have the most unusual ways of trying to cheer me up. Believe me, I thought of that. There are two problems. First, that we wouldn't be believed. Second, that the lads and lasses who are after me would assume you'd be more than happy to coopcrate with them for the sake of revenge."

"Okay," I said briskly. "So what do we do now?"

"Leave town. As soon as possible."

"What about Schmidt?"

"That's our next problem. He didn't tell you what time he'll arrive?"

"No. I could call him back."

"There's not a chance we could get on a plane before tonight. Anyhow, I think we need to have a little chat with Schmidt. It's too much of a coincidence that Suzi should decide to break off with him at this precise time. We'll hole up in the flat, wait for him to ring, and then go to see him at the Savoy. If he makes it that far."

Leaving me with that encouraging thought, he turned back to the computer. "Nothing of significance," he reported, after checking his e-mail. "You had better see if Schmidt has been in touch again."

Once again I found myself yearning for the good old days when letters and telephone calls (with no call-waiting, no voice mail, no answering machines) were the only means of communication, bar the occasional telegram. There was nothing new from Schmidt. By the time I finished reading chatty notes from a few friends, John was brooding over his cell phone.

"Feisal is beginning to sound a trifle nervous," he remarked, and read the message aloud.

" 'Looking forward to seeing you. I have much to tell you, much to show you. Let me know the time of your arrival.' "

"Perhaps you had better reassure him."

"At the moment I can't think of any news that would do that." He began poking at the buttons, pronouncing the words as he wrote them. " 'Hope to have plans made by tomorrow. Let's keep your news for a surprise, shall we?' "

"You both have a somewhat telegraphic style," I remarked. "I take it you haven't gone in for instant messaging?"

"We have to assume that all our means of communication are compromised. How I loathe modern technology," he added petulantly. "Every new so-called advance in communication is only a new way of eavesdropping."

Before I could voice my hearty agreement the bell at the shop door jangled. John stood up. "Stay here," he ordered, and went out.

Naturally I went to the door and looked into the shop. The potential customers looked harmless enough: two middle-aged women wearing twin sets and pearls. John advanced on them, exuding charm; in response to his question, "May I be of assistance?" one of them chirped, "Just browsing."

"By all means," said John. He retreated to the desk at the back of the showroom and sat down.

The women—Mabel and Allie, as they referred to each other—looked at every painting and every artifact, asking questions and requesting prices. They were free with their comments. "Two hundred pounds for that? It's quite ugly, you know."

They were at it for almost an hour, obviously killing time, with no intention of buying anything. John answered their questions fully and courteously, but without moving from his chair. After they left I ventured out of the office.

"I suppose you get a lot of that," I said.

"Oh, yes. Most of the drop-in customers are 'just having a look round.' But one never knows when a live one may turn up. Come here and sit down. We close in another three-quarters of an hour."

He didn't seem inclined toward conversation, so I opened a drawer looking for the magazine Alan had been reading. It wasn't there. But something else was.

"I thought you never carried—"

"It's a toy. Good enough to fool most people, though, wouldn't you say?"

"Modern technology," I murmured, staring at the deadly black shape.

"Life in the metropolis," said John, "is increasingly hazardous, especially for innocent merchants. I've had this ever since an acquaintance of mine up the road was robbed at gunpoint a few months ago. They beat him rather badly and got away with two diamond rings."

He picked up a pile of papers from the in-box and began going through them. An occasional grimace suggested that some of them were bills.

One other customer showed up just before closing time. The

drawer was open and John's hand was on the fake Beretta before the bell stopped jangling. It was a man this time, sturdily built and bearded, wearing a turban.

"I am in the market," he said, in the accents of Whitechapel, "for African textiles."

"I'm afraid we have nothing of that sort," John said. "Try Alfie's."

"I have been there," said the bearded man, standing his ground.

"There's a place around the corner that specializes in African crafts," John said, gripping the barrel of the gun so hard his knuckles went white. "Marks and—uh—Markham and Wilson. Turn right when you leave, and right again at the next intersection. You can't miss it."

"Thank you." The beard opened in a smile. "You are most helpful."

The bell jangled. John let out his breath and relaxed his grip. "That's it. Get your gear while I close up."

John unlocked the door of the flat. "No one's been here."

"The old thread-in-the-doorframe gimmick," I said, watching it float to the floor.

"Simple but generally efficacious. However, just to be on the safe side . . ." He cast a searching glance round the room, went into the bedroom and study and did the same, and preceded me into the kitchen.

"All clear," he said.

I put the groceries away and then settled down to watch telly and wait for Schmidt to call. John, who professes to despise popular culture, retreated into the study, his nose in the air. In a way I didn't blame him for avoiding what has become an exercise in despondency (the news) and/or idiocy (most sitcoms), but I find it relaxing. I had a bag of crisps in one hand and a beer in the other and was switching from channel to channel when I caught something that made me spill the crisps.

"John," I yelled. "Get in here. Quick!"

He shot through the door. Seeing me bolt upright and unthreatened, he was about to expostulate when I gestured at the screen. "Look. It's him!"

I recognized the background: the facade of the Altes Museum in Berlin. In the foreground Dr. Ashraf Khifaya, secretary general of the Supreme Council of Antiquities, in full glorious color, was being interviewed by a BBC reporter. He was wearing a pristine pith helmet and carrying a huge sign that read, in English, German, and Arabic: "Let Nefertiti come home." Other newspersons surrounded him. He looked like a particularly gorgeous Hollywood star playing an adventurous archaeologist. The bullwhip would appear any second. In the background a long line of black-robed women paced slowly along the sidewalk, accompanied by the slow throb of drums.

"No dancing girls," John said critically.

"This is better. Solemn and dramatic."

"I ask only for what is ours," Khifaya declaimed, in excellent English with just enough accent to sound exotic. "After years of exploitation . . ."

They cut him off in mid-spiel; no news item is worth more than a few minutes. In keeping with their declared policy of presenting both sides, the cameras switched to a man sitting behind a desk.

"It's him," I squealed.

"He," said John.

"Shh."

"This is a free country," said the man behind the desk in clipped tones. "If the distinguished secretary general chooses to make an exhibition of himself, that is his privilege. Thank you."

"So Nefertiti is not going home?" asked a blond female, twinkling at the camera.

"You have received a press release on the position of the museum. It has not changed. Thank you."

"So the feud continues," said the blonde, with a merry laugh.

She was replaced by an equally blond starlet answering questions about her upcoming divorce. John grabbed the remote and switched off the set.

"You recognized him, didn't you?" I demanded. "Not Khifaya, the second guy."

"I presume he is the director of the museum."

"Assistant director. It was Jan Perlmutter. You remember—the guy that stole the Trojan Gold out from under our noses."

"Your nose."

"Oh, come on, you were in on the hunt too. So we picked the wrong grave. I still don't know how Perlmutter figured out which was the right one."

"Ah, yes, it's coming back to me." John began collecting scattered crisps. "My guess would be that he winkled the information out of your chum, the little old woodcarver. I got the distinct impression that the old chap knew more than he was telling you. Didn't you ever ask?"

"There wasn't time. I fled with my tail between my legs and Herr Müller had left Garmisch to stay with his sister. I meant to get in touch with him, but a few weeks later I got a note from the sister telling me he had died."

I still felt a little guilty about not making more of an effort to find out how the old fellow was doing. I had grown fond of him and I had thought he was fond of me. Had he been holding out on me? If so, it was surely because he feared that for me knowledge might be dangerous. As it definitely had been. He might have meant to tell me more if he hadn't died suddenly . . . It was irrelevant now.

"If you mean did I ask Perlmutter how he figured it out, the answer is a loud profane no," I went on. "I haven't spoken to the skunk since then."

"I didn't recognize him," John admitted. "He's losing his hair." He ran a gentle hand over his own shining locks.

"Serves him right," I said vindictively. "That discovery put him on the high road to promotion and left me looking like an idiot."

"If it's any consolation, he didn't look very happy."

"He didn't, did he? He's finding out that being a museum big shot isn't all rich donors and fine art. Hey—why don't you check the Net and see if there are any stories about the siege of the museum?"

"Sure to be," said John. "Every other piece of trivia is."

Reuters and the German newspapers had stories, with lots of photographs, mostly of Khifaya. His good looks, his showmanship, and most of all that pith helmet had a visual impact as impressive as that of any celebrity. He spoke with eloquence and passion and an occasional winning touch of humor. I could have sworn there were tears in those big dark eyes when he appealed to the world for justice.

"You're drooling," John said nastily, and switched to what he referred to as the Egyptology blogs. They were full of Khifaya too. I pulled up a chair, shoved John over, and began reading some of the comments. Opinion was divided. Some thought Egypt's claim should be honored, some had accepted the museum's statement that the famous bust was too fragile to be moved. Then I got distracted by other items. They ranged from the soberly professional to the utterly loony. Debates raged about everything from the construction of the

Great Pyramid to the age of the Sphinx, and ignorance of the subject didn't prevent people from voicing their ideas.

A word caught my eye and I stopped John as he was about to scroll down.

The word was "mummy."

It took a few minutes to pick up the thread of the discussion, which had apparently been going on for a while. Somebody had found Queen Hatshepsut—again—and somebody else said no, it couldn't be she, because she was another mummy in another tomb, identified only by a number that didn't strike an immediate chord, and somebody else declared that mummy number two was Nefertiti or maybe her daughter.

"I could get hooked on this," I said, fascinated. "Look at that sketch of mummy number two. She's copied it straight off the Berlin head."

"The world is full of fanatics," said John. "At least they aren't talking about—"

My cell phone rang. I snatched it up.

"I am here," said a doleful voice. "Shall I come there?"

"No," John said loudly.

"Schmidt, are you all right?" I said.

"No. I am in deep distress. I am coming—"

"Stay where you are." John grabbed the phone. "The Savoy?"

"*Aber natürlich.* I always stay at the Savoy when I am in London. I am well known here, and they—"

"We are coming to you," I said, retrieving the phone. "Stay put, Schmidt. We'll be there in half an hour."

"*Sehr gut.* I will buy you dinner."

A long sigh followed. I hung up in the middle of it.

"You had better change," John said, eyeing my jeans and T-shirt critically.

"Don't they have a grill, or someplace less formal than the main dining room?"

"There is no informal dining spot at the Savoy. Change. And hurry. Schmidt isn't known for his patience."

He skinned off his jeans and shirt as he spoke. By the time I had located a pair of respectable pants and a top without a rude saying printed on it he was knotting his tie.

"The Royal Marines?" I asked, studying the pattern of stripes.

"First Gloucestershire Regiment."

"You ought to be ashamed of yourself."

"My dear girl, there is no law against wearing a regimental tie." He began transferring various items from the jacket he had worn that day into the pockets of an elegant wool-and-silk navy blazer. The last item was the fake gun. Toy or not, it was heavy enough to make the pocket sag. He studied the effect in the mirror, frowned, and transferred the gun to an inside breast pocket.

"How about getting me one of those?" I asked.

"You move around too much. Try getting one of these through airport security and you will discover that nobody finds it amusing."

The Savoy was one of the numerous (read: expensive) places in London to which John had never taken me. I took to it right away— the circular drive set back from the Strand, the top-hatted serf who leaped to open the door of the taxi, the beautifully appointed lobby. Schmidt was waiting, arms open. He hugged me and would have hugged John if John hadn't been ready for him, and announced he had been able to wangle a table in the grill. It must have been a big deal. John looked impressed.

While Schmidt pored over the menu I studied him with mounting concern. His color was fine and he certainly hadn't lost any more weight, but there was something . . . His eyes kept shifting.

He babbled, not with his usual manic enthusiasm, but as if he were talking at random to keep his mind off other things.

Finally I said, "Okay, Schmidt, that's enough. Get it off your chest. That's what we're here for."

Schmidt took out a large handkerchief and pressed it to his face. "I do not want to talk about it. Later, perhaps. Not here. I do not wish to weep in public. Distract me. Tell me about yourselves, what you are doing. How is the business? Any new objects of interest?"

"There's a rather nice *Entombment of Christ* by one of the fifteenth-century German wood-carvers," I said. "But don't expect you'll be offered a discount. He always ups the prices for friends."

Schmidt broke into a loud peal of laughter. "Very good, very good. I will go to the shop tomorrow to have a look."

I opened my mouth and got a sharp kick on the ankle.

"By all means," John said. "How long do you intend to stay, Schmidt?"

"I do not wish to interfere with your plans," Schmidt said.

"They are flexible," said John, in what had to be the understatement of the year. I felt sure he still intended to get out of town next day, without telling Schmidt. Not a good idea, I thought. That would leave Schmidt on the loose in London, thoroughly and (from his point of view) legitimately mad as hell at us. I had learned not to underestimate my boss. He'd be on our trail as soon as he learned we had vanished from his ken. The idea of having his rotund and conspicuous person following us to Egypt made me very uneasy. Supposing, that is, that we were going to Egypt.

Observing my knitted brows, Schmidt said, "You are not worrying about Clara, I hope. I have made certain she will be looked after."

"Good," I said absently.

I think we had an excellent meal, though I can't remember what

I ate. New and alarming ideas kept popping into my head. John had made rather a point of making sure Schmidt stayed off the streets. Was the old boy in danger? And if so, from whom? And if so, why? And if so, we couldn't leave him unprotected.

I came back to the real world to hear John and Schmidt chatting about the Victoria and Albert Museum.

"I have not been there for some time," said Schmidt, dabbing daintily at his mustache. "I would like to have another look at the armor collection. Vicky, you will join me, I hope? You too are welcome, John, though I suppose you will be busy with the shop."

"I thought you were coming by to look at the *Entombment*," John said.

"Another day, perhaps."

Schmidt insisted on escorting us to the door. "So," he said, "tomorrow at nine, Vicky, for breakfast, and then the Victoria and Albert."

He stood waving and blowing kisses as the taxi pulled away.

"Did you get the impression that I am not wanted tomorrow?" John asked.

"I got a lot of impressions, none of which makes any sense. I am beginning to think—"

"Not now. That is to say," John amended, "you are of course free to think all you like, but let's not discuss it now."

So I confined myself to staring out the window. London is one of my favorite cities. I used to feel safe there, even after the suicide attack in the Underground and the foiled bombings. Terrorist attacks are as random as tornadoes, I told myself; they are, unhappily, as likely in New York and Madrid as in the Middle East. But that morning I had come close to being yanked into a car by people who were after me, Vicky Bliss, not any anonymous victim. One would suppose I had become accustomed to it during my long acquaintance with John, but take it from me, you never get used to that sort of extremely personal interest.

John made a quick tour of the flat before settling down on the sofa and gesturing me to join him.

"Still thinking?" he inquired.

"Yes. No. I think we ought to let Schmidt in on the whole thing."

His only response was a raised eyebrow. I had marshaled my arguments, so I plunged on.

"Schmidt has a lot of contacts. He knows everybody. You keep denigrating him with adjectives like old and little, but if it hadn't been for Schmidt, our Egyptian venture last year wouldn't have ended so well. Hell's bells, he was the deus ex machina the whole time, dragging us out of one hairy situation after another. He may strike you as a comedic figure—"

"He is a comedic figure. That's one of the things that makes him so effective. People underestimate him. But I," said John, "am learning not to do so. Believe it or not, I was considering the same idea. The only thing that deters me is the fact that I am rather fond of the old—sorry—the dear chap. I don't want to see him hurt."

"Do you think I do? But he's an adult, John, even if he is fat and—oh, hell—not as young as he used to be. I haven't the right to make decisions for him, and neither do you. His male ego has already taken a blow, from that bitch Suzi. Maybe he'd rather risk his life than his self-esteem. Maybe you'll feel the same way when you're his age."

John reached for my hand. "Don't cry."

"I'm not crying," I said snuffily.

"You had *me* on the verge of tears," John said, handing me a handkerchief. (He always has one.) "And you've convinced me. God knows I'd rather have Schmidt on our side than against us."

"Furthermore . . . Oh. You agree? So what's the plan?"

"You meet him at the Savoy as promised, enjoy a hearty breakfast, hop in a cab, and head for Heathrow. I'll meet you there. International terminal, half past ten."

I had more or less expected it. "What'll I tell Schmidt?"

"If I know Schmidt, all you need say is that we are off on another thrilling adventure and that I will fill him in on the details in due course. You have sworn an oath of secrecy," said John, warming to the theme, "and dare not divulge the plans of the mastermind. (That's me.) We are all in deadly peril until we arrive at our destination, at which time he will be formally inducted into the cabal. We might have a little ceremony, handing out disguises and masks and the like."

John employed silliness as a defensive weapon. It was contagious—to such an extent that when he asked if I felt like a snack I declined in favor of another variety of amusement.

Schmidt's reaction to the change of plan wasn't what I had expected or John had predicted. When I told the cabdriver we wanted to go to Heathrow instead of the V and A, he looked as if he had just been informed of the death of a close friend.

"So, you are on the run," he said, his brows knit. "Again."

"*We* are on the run," I corrected. "What's the matter, Schmidt? I thought you enjoyed adventures."

"Yes, yes," Schmidt said testily. "But why did you not tell me? How can I set off for—for some unknown destination without my luggage?"

He had the most important things—his passport—and his laptop, encased in elegant leather. I doubted that he would have been allowed to take it into the museum, but there was no point in bringing that up since we weren't going there anyhow. He wasn't much worse off than I. I had crammed a change of underwear and a toothbrush into my backpack. Sooner or later somebody was going to have to buy me a new wardrobe. I hoped it would be Schmidt. He was more generous than John.

Reasonably enough, Schmidt wanted to know where we were headed. And why. John's speech, which I repeated almost verbatim, didn't improve his mood. After announcing that he would ask no further questions, he relapsed into sullen silence, arms folded and lower lip outthrust. That wasn't like Schmidt, and if I hadn't been so preoccupied with other worries, I might have wondered what was up. Not that it would have mattered in the end.

John was waiting for us, boarding passes in hand. Schmidt snatched one of them.

"Berlin," he said flatly.

"Berlin?" I said, on a rising note.

"We've just time for a coffee," said John, taking Schmidt's arm.

He stuck as close to Schmidt as a long-lost brother, through security, and even into the Gents. When we boarded, I was relegated to a seat between two strangers while John snuggled up next to Schmidt several rows forward.

Always expect the worst; then you are never disappointed. Always prepare for the worst; then you are never caught off guard. It was one of John's basic rules of operation, but I felt sure that in this case he was overdoing it. Schmidt was acting strangely, but it was inconceivable that the old (oops) boy was up to no good.

I hadn't brought anything to read, so after perusing the in-flight magazine and deciding which Hermès scarves I would have selected if anybody had offered to buy me a few, I tried to figure out why we were going to Berlin. I hoped we weren't headed for a meeting with a German version of Bernardo. A German version of Monsignor Anonymous? Somebody connected with the museum? Maybe I could make myself a sign and join the picket line. If it didn't accomplish anything else it would annoy the hell out of Perlmutter, especially if I could get on television. Ah well, I thought, mine not to reason why, mine but to follow blindly where the mastermind led. I might as well be married. Love, honor and especially obey.

There was no hired car waiting outside the terminal, but the hotel to which the taxi delivered us bore a certain resemblance to the one in Rome—in a quiet neighborhood, small, unobtrusive. The desk clerk did not indicate recognition of John, but after he had consulted with the manager we were given a suite, with two bedrooms, which strongly suggested hanky-panky past if not present. We showed ourselves up; within a few minutes a waiter arrived with a bottle of wine.

Schmidt had managed to get into the bathroom unescorted. When he came out he looked unenthusiastically at the wine.

"A pleasant little Merlot," John said. "You prefer red wine, I believe."

"I would rather have beer."

"Certainly." John picked up the telephone. "A small snack, perhaps? What would you like?"

"Nothing."

"Come on, Schmidt," I said, genuinely alarmed. "It's past time for lunch. I feel sure they can supply anything you want."

Impassive as a mustachioed Buddha, Schmidt stared off into space. John ordered, more or less at random, and sat back, arms folded.

"The time has come," said he, in measured tones. "To tell all."

Schmidt muttered something.

"What?" I said.

"You don't have to tell me anything."

"Your absolute trust and loyalty touches me to the depths of my heart," said John, placing his hand on the approximate location of that organ. "It is because I feel the same for you that I want you to know the truth, the whole truth, and nothing but—"

"Cut that out," I said irritably. "This is what happened, Schmidt. Three days ago . . ."

John kept trying to interrupt, but I was in no mood for his rhetorical embroidery. I made it simple and as short as the complexities allowed. Schmidt transferred his fixed stare to me; his eyes got wider and his mouth fell open.

"Tut?" he gasped. "They have stolen King Tut?"

"And they think I did it. They," John explained, "being an indeterminate but measurable number of individuals involved in my erstwhile profession."

"Crooks," I translated.

A gurgling sound emerged from Schmidt's open mouth.

"I am innocent, Schmidt," John intoned. "Innocent as a new-laid—"

I poked him in the ribs. "This is no time for levity."

"I wasn't being levitous," John said indignantly. Returning his candid blue gaze to Schmidt, he went on, "I am appealing to you, Schmidt. For old times' sake, and because you are the wisest, most courageous ally I could ever want. Will you—can you—help me to clear my name?"

Schmidt sat down on the sofa and burst into tears.

He's very sentimental, is our Schmidt, but these tears weren't a gentle trickle from an overflowing heart, they were a flood, a torrent that soaked the ends of his mustache and wandered around the creases in his cheeks until they found their way to his chin and poured off.

I went to him and tried to put my arm around him; he fended me off with a frantic flapping of hands.

"No, do not be nice to me. I do not deserve it. I have betrayed you!"

FIVE

The scene ended on that dramatic note, because the waiter turned up with our order. Sobbing, Schmidt fled into the bedroom. John gestured to me to open the door, and flattened himself against the wall, prepared, I assumed, to defend me from pistol-packing waiters. This one had thinning gray hair and an expansive stomach. If he was a member of a gang, the gang must be pretty hard up. John indicated he need not linger; he gave me a genteel leer and took himself off.

Hearing the door close, Schmidt made a tentative appearance. Everything drooped—mouth, mustache, both chins.

"Can you ever forgive me?" he whimpered.

I gave him a big hug. John said, "Have a beer."

It was probably the beer, not the hug, that did the trick.

"I will not weep again," Schmidt announced after a long swig. "I will show the stiff upper lip. And I will bare my chest."

John gallantly resisted that one. I joined Schmidt in a beer and

John had a glass of wine. Health fanatics be damned, there's nothing like a little alcohol to relieve stress and create a cozy atmosphere. The beer and the prospect of clearing his conscience did wonders; Schmidt was himself again, his cheeks pink and his eyes candid.

"Suzi put you up to this," I prompted.

"I will tell it," said Schmidt, manfully squaring his shoulders. "We were in your house, to look after Clara, as I promised. Clara did not want Suzi to look after her. She growled and spat and was rude. So I went to get her food and while I was doing that, Suzi went into your bedroom. When I found her there I was shocked— shocked! And then she told me. That a valuable, unique antiquity had been stolen from Egypt, and that you, John, were the principal suspect."

He looked hopefully at John, who promptly provided him with another beer. "She didn't tell you what antiquity," he said. It was not a question; Schmidt's drop-jaw astonishment had been proof that Tut had not been mentioned.

"She said she was not at liberty to do so. *Natürlich,* I thought of the great statues in the museum, Khafre and Menkaure, and the golden coffin and mask, the fabulous jewels. Who would bother to steal a dried-up ugly mummy?"

"But now I understand why you are under suspicion. The caper has your trademark, *nicht wahr?* She knows who you are, John—who you were. She has not told her superiors, because she wants the credit of bringing you to justice."

"So that's it," I said. "Before we left Egypt last time, I had a hunch she had fingered John but that she wasn't blowing the whistle because she liked us and was sorry for us."

"And because at that point she couldn't prove anything," said John.

"Right. God, what a sucker I am!"

"You trust people," John said. "It is a serious character flaw which I have endeavored without success to correct. So, Schmidt, when she asked you to play spy, you agreed."

Schmidt hung his head. "I was a besotted old fool. But, my friends, I swear to you that I agreed only because I knew I would find proof of your innocence. I will find it! And I will hurl it in her face!"

"So that pitiful story about Suzi breaking up with you was pure fiction?" I inquired.

"She told me what to say," Schmidt admitted. "But it was my performance that convinced you, is that not so?"

"It convinced Vicky," John said. "She trusts people. Especially her friends."

"But you do not." Schmidt gave him a reproachful look. "You made sure to be at my side every minute, so I could not text to her. Vicky—I would not have done it anyhow. From the moment I saw you again I was in agony, torn between friendship and—er—"

"Lust," John suggested.

Lips pursed, Schmidt considered the noun. "Yes, yes, that was part of it. But only part. I loved her. She made me laugh."

"Suzi?" I said. She hadn't struck me as the funniest lady in the cabaret.

Schmidt blushed. "Private jokes, you understand. And she said that I did not owe you loyalty, John, because you had deceived me and lied to Vicky. But now I know she pretended to care for me only because she wanted to lay you by the heels. I have learned my lesson. Never again will I succumb to the lure of the flesh. The marriage of true minds, mutual respect, common interests, they will be my guiding principles."

"Quite," John said. "Go on. What other orders did she give you?"

"To report to her at once if you left London."

"But you didn't," I said.

"No. No, I have told you—"

"They'll track us down before long," John said. "But it may take a little time. What else, Schmidt?"

"Only to pass on any information about your recent activities, persons you had contacted, but—"

"But you didn't," John said, with a curl of his lip. "Can I believe that?"

Schmidt wilted, and I said, "Lay off, John. I believe you, Schmidt."

"So do I," John said. The curl of his lip turned into a smile.

The declaration of faith cheered Schmidt enough to awaken his appetite; he started lifting covers, and browsed among the varied dishes while, at his suggestion, we gave him a rundown of our recent activities. Schmidt didn't say much because his mouth was full, but he nodded and rolled his eyes and made inarticulate noises indicative of amazement, concern, and interest. Finally he sat back, wiped his chin, and opened another beer.

"*Also,*" he said. "Let us summarize. Feisal (poor Feisal!) is holding the fort in Luxor. The Supreme Council has not yet learned of the theft. Several dangerous persons have learned of it—Bernardo in Rome and at least one unknown party in London. They, however, are not the persons who committed the theft. Suzi has also found out. The dissemination of information seems random, but is it? Is there a pattern? A single source, *vielleicht?*"

"Very good, Schmidt," I said. "If we knew the answer to that, we would be well on the way to learning not only the motive for the theft but the identity of the real thieves."

"Possibly," said Schmidt. He steepled his fingers and peered at me over them. I recognized the Sherlock Holmes persona. Well, he was entitled, bless his heart. I remained respectfully silent and, for a wonder, so did John.

"You seem to have considered most of the possible motives," Schmidt resumed. "The most likely would seem to be simple greed. Ransom, to be precise. But if that is the case, why has not the Egyptian government or the Supreme Council been approached?"

"How do we know they haven't been?" John asked.

"I was about to make that point," Schmidt said, giving John a Holmes-to-Watson look. "They would have good reason to remain silent."

"No, but surely their first move would be to make sure he was missing," I argued. "Tut, I mean. Feisal is sounding nervous, but not as frantic as he surely would be if somebody from the SCA had demanded entry into the tomb."

"This is all idle speculation," Schmidt grumbled. "There is one way to find out for sure whether the secretary general of the SCA has received a ransom note. We will ask him."

What Schmidt meant was "I will ask him." He claimed to be a dear personal friend of Khifaya. He thought he was a dear personal friend of everybody he'd ever met, but his connections and his reputation did give him an edge when it came to extracting information. I offered, out of the goodness of my heart, to approach Khifaya by joining the picket line at the museum. Schmidt thought this was a fine idea. He would carry a sign too. However, we were doomed to disappointment. Khifaya had left Berlin.

Hovering over his laptop, Schmidt continued to search the more esoteric reaches of the World Wide Web, from one of which he had retrieved that information. Khifaya was no longer an item of current interest, but his name turned up in a lot of places, including his

Web site. So did Tutankhamon's, although he didn't have his own Web site.

"Nothing relevant to our inquiries," Schmidt announced, rolling the *r*. "We must proceed forthwith to Egypt."

"In hot pursuit of Khifaya?" I asked hopefully.

"Has anyone a better suggestion?" Schmidt demanded.

John put down the wurst on which he had been nibbling. "I wondered when someone would ask me."

"Consider yourself asked," I said, investigating the cheese selection.

"I had several reasons for coming to Berlin," John said. "The notion of joining the picket line had its charm, but I also hoped I might hear from an old acquaintance."

"Another crook?" I inquired. "I don't mean to sound critical, but you've already got one gang in Rome and another in London after you. Why can't you leave bad enough alone?"

"I agree," said Schmidt, reaching for the last slice of Gouda. "Now let us organize ourselves. First, you should communicate with Feisal. Who can tell what may have transpired within the last few hours?"

"I suppose that makes sense," John admitted. "Perhaps I'll risk a telephone call."

Feisal answered on the first ring. "Where are you?" he demanded.

"On our way," said John. "We saw your boss on the telly the other night. He seems to be having a jolly good time harassing the Berlin museum."

"He's back. In Cairo. I," said Feisal pointedly, "am in Luxor. When will you join me?"

Schmidt reached for the phone. John turned his back, clutching it protectively, and I hissed, "Don't say anything, Schmidt."

"But I would like—"

"We're saving you for a surprise."

John rang off. "So far so good, one may deduce. He wasn't actually screaming. I told him we'd try to get a flight first thing tomorrow."

"No, we cannot do that," said Schmidt. "In the evening, *vielleicht*. In the morning I am going to picket at the museum. Yes, yes, I know, Dr. Khifaya has left, but some of his students may still be there, and if they are not—well, I will be even more visible, will I not? Perhaps I will lie down on the pavement and be arrested."

"You want to make Perlmutter squirm," I said, torn between amusement and consternation.

"*Warum nicht?* He has made me squirm, allowing me to dig up that grave in full public view when he knew nothing was there! Also, I would like to question him, subtly and slyly, as is my method. Has either of you bothered to ascertain whether museums and legitimate collectors have heard the rumors?"

"I haven't had time," John said defensively.

"Tsk, tsk," said Schmidt. (He is the only person I've ever met who pronounces each separate consonant.) "Not even the British Museum? The Keeper, I believe, is a distant—"

"Very distant. He wouldn't know me from Adam."

"Leave it to me, then." Schmidt glanced at his watch and rose. "We must hurry. There is much to do."

"What precisely do you have in mind?" I asked, expecting the worst.

"Shopping, of course. I do not have with me so much as a toothbrush."

"The concierge," John began.

"The concierge cannot purchase for me clothing. *Heiliger Gott,* I cannot go to Egypt with only one suit and no pajamas, no dressing gown, no—"

"Can I come too?" I asked hopefully.

"Aber natürlich." Schmidt beamed at me.

He trotted into his room to put his laptop away and, as he put it, "tidy myself as much as is possible." John gave me a critical look and began, "Vicky, you aren't going to let him—"

"Buy me a new wardrobe? Damn right. Don't you see, he's trying to make up for mistrusting us. I bet he'll buy you a new suit too if you're nice."

"Not under any circumstances whatever."

I gave him a quick kiss. "You're just sulking because you aren't the mastermind anymore."

Schmidt was well known in all the right shops. One genuflecting merchant promised to have the pants of three white linen suits shortened and delivered to the hotel by eight the next morning. Another supplied various items of haberdashery, from socks to nightshirts. I put my foot down when Schmidt tried to lure me into an elegant boutique, and led the way to Gesundbrunnencenter, where I picked up jeans and a couple of shirts. Schmidt went off, sulking, while I was in the dressing room, and came back with several bags, which he pressed into the unwilling grasp of John.

"We have almost finished," he announced. "Another stop and then we will go to dinner."

One look in the window of the establishment to which the taxi delivered us was enough to confirm my suspicions. There was a single garment on display: a nightgown which appeared to have been spun by spiders. It glimmered like a dragonfly's wings, semitransparent, shot with pearly threads.

"They're closed," I said, trying not to sound disappointed. A woman of my height doesn't go forth in lace and chiffon, but as Schmidt well knew, I have a weakness for sexy nightgowns.

"Trudi will open for me," Schmidt said. "She expects us."

He pushed a discreetly concealed button. A light went on inside; a curtain was drawn aside, an eye peered out, a cry of rapture echoed, and the door was flung wide. Schmidt rushed into the outspread arms of a well-endowed blonde wearing a negligee trimmed with crystals, cascading ruffles, and God knows what else.

He and John sat at a marble-topped desk sipping champagne while Trudi thrust intimate garments into the dressing room to which I had been led. None of them had anything so vulgar as a price tag, which was in itself a sign that I couldn't have afforded so much as a hanky. I was determined to behave myself, but that damned nightgown, which Trudi removed from the show window, was too much.

Ideas of sensuality vary from culture to culture and era to era, but an excessive display of skin can be—well—excessive. (Especially when, as is only too often the case these days, the skin covers vast expanses of wobbly flesh.) It isn't so much what you show as how you show it. Victorian gents used to get short of breath when a lady bared an ankle, and the ancient Egyptians knew what they were doing when they draped queens and noblewomen in transparent linen. I wanted that nightgown. It moved with me, graceful as a cloud. I wanted it really badly.

I'll pay him back, I told myself.

I joined Schmidt in a glass of champagne (another glass, in his case) and Trudi presented him with a pale pink, gold-handled bag with tissue paper billowing out the top.

"Many many thanks for your courtesy, *Liebchen*," said Schmidt, handing the bag to John. "Put it on my account."

The taxi she had called pulled up as we exited; we waited until
we heard the chains rattle and the locks click; and I thought, Account? How come Schmidt had an account at a shop that specialized in hideously expensive lady's underwear? How many other
women had been beneficiaries of his largesse? And what business
was it of mine?

When I unpacked Trudi's bag later that night, I found not only
the nightgown but a matching negligee and a selection of bras and
panties. They all looked as if they had come from the spiders'
workshop—and they were all my size. Either Schmidt had a trained
eye or he had been rummaging around in my bureau drawers.

If I had been true to my principles I would have marched into
Schmidt's room and handed them back, with a dignified refusal. I
couldn't resist trying a few things on, though, and the nightie inspired John to quote several of the Restoration poets. It inspired
more than that. That night I didn't dream about Tutankhamon.

A thunderous pounding on the door woke me. I groaned and sat
up. The flow of dragonfly wings all about me made me con-
fine my response to a mild "What do you want, Schmidt?"

"It is time to get up," Schmidt yelled. "We must be at the museum in one hour. There is coffee. Shall I bring it there to you?"

John had pulled the sheet over his face, but that offer got him up
and out of bed. I put on the negligee that matched the nightgown
and wafted my way to the door.

"Ooh, that is very nice," said Schmidt, inspecting me.

"You look very natty yourself," I mumbled. "You got your suits,
I see."

"Oh, yes, I can always depend on Friedrich. Have your breakfast. There are eggs and wurst, hot rolls and jam, cheese and ham."

"What, no caviar?" said John, emerging.

Schmidt reached for the telephone. "I was joking," John said hastily.

Schmidt had already eaten breakfast, but he kept us company, nibbling on various odds and ends until we finished, and then shooed us into the bedroom, demanding that we hurry. When we came back, Schmidt was on his knees putting the finishing touches on an enormous banner. In passionate German it besought the return of Nefertiti.

"Is that a bedsheet?" I asked.

"Yes, I could not find paper large enough," said Schmidt, working away with his purple Magic Marker. "I will pay for it, of course." He added a few words.

"You can't say that about Perlmutter," I objected.

"I wish to get his attention." Schmidt rose stiffly to his feet. "Oh, and by the way, I have made reservations for us on the evening flight to Cairo. You should telephone to Feisal and tell him we arrive at ten forty-five."

"I think I'd better wait to see whether you two get out of jail in time," John said.

Meekly we followed Schmidt to the lift. "You're enjoying this, aren't you?" I asked John.

"I'm beginning to. There is something to be said for being a foot soldier instead of an officer. Whatever happens, it won't be my fault."

"What about your friend?"

John shrugged. "I'll see if I can get in touch later. This is bound to be one of Schmidt's more memorable performances. I wouldn't miss it for the world."

There were no pickets in evidence. The handsome classical facade of the museum faced onto a circle with a fountain in the center.

The sidewalk was wide enough for half a dozen people walking abreast—or, as it turned out, for two people holding Schmidt's banner. I took one end and Schmidt the other.

"The center sags," Schmidt said. "John—"

"Oh, no," said John, retreating.

"Do we start walking or stand in front of the stairs?" I asked.

"We wait." Schmidt consulted his wristwatch. "He said he would be here. Where— Ah!"

The green van that screeched to a stop had the logo of a local television channel. A man wearing dark glasses and carrying a camera got out.

"*Verzeihen Sie, Herr Professor.* Sorry I couldn't get the whole crew, there's a warehouse fire in Dahlen."

"We must do the best we can," Schmidt replied. "Ernhardt Flugschaften—my assistant, Fräulein Doktor Victoria Bliss. Now, Ernhardt, go back ten feet; we will come marching toward you, carrying the banner and shouting our slogan."

"What is our slogan?" I asked, holding my end of the banner high.

"Or perhaps we should sing," said Schmidt, who obviously hadn't come up with a slogan. "What is the Egyptian national anthem?"

"Damned if I know."

Inspiration came to Schmidt. He let out a bellow that made me and Ernhardt jump. *"Wahrheit! Freiheit! Gerechtigkeit!"*

I couldn't see what freedom had to do with it, unless it was our freedom from jail, but I joined in at the top of my lungs. "Truth! Freedom! Justice!" It had a great rhythm, and it rhymed, too. Grinning, Ernhardt backed away, filming as he went. From a safe distance near the railings, John looked on, hands in his jacket pockets. We were beginning to attract an audience—not only the people who had had to jump out of our way and remained to shake their fists at us, but several museum guards.

"Wahrheit!" we shouted. *"Freiheit!"*

The nearest of the guards cleared his throat noisily. *"Herr Doktor—entshuldigen Sie—"*

He jumped back as Schmidt barreled down on him without stopping or veering aside. *"Ach, Überwald, mein alter Freund! Ihre Familie ist gesund?"*

"Ja, vielen Dank, Herr Doktor—aber—aber . . ." We made a right about-face, not too smartly, since I wasn't expecting it, and bore down on Überwald again. "You cannot do this! It is *verboten. Bitte . . ."*

We passed him at a brisk walk and Schmidt handed him a card. "Announce me to Herr Doktor Perlmutter."

Schmidt knew everybody. Guards at the museum, shopkeepers, restaurant owners, journalists; he probably knew the name of the guy who picked up the trash, and the names and ages of all the guy's kids. He had a memory like the proverbial pachyderm and he had often proved his claim that he never forgot a face. We weren't going to get arrested. Everybody knew Schmidt.

It took several trips back and forth to arrange the interview with Perlmutter. He wanted us to come to his office and Schmidt insisted he come down to us. Schmidt handed another of the guards a wad of money and told him to go get food, lots of food, any sort of food, not only for us but—with an expansive gesture at our growing audience—"for all our friends here."

Before long we were joined by several people who didn't know what we were marching about but who wanted to get on television. The rest of them sat down on the steps to watch. John remained aloof. The chorus swelled. *"Wahrheit! Freiheit! Gerechtigkeit!"*

Jan Perlmutter tried to make an unobtrusive appearance, but Schmidt was on the lookout and saw him cowering behind one of the columns. Alerted by Schmidt, Ernhardt got an excellent shot of the huge classical columns and Perlmutter peeking nervously out. Chortling, Schmidt handed his end of the banner to me and trotted up the steps, waving and calling. I passed the banner on to a couple of volunteers and followed.

Wrenching himself free of Schmidt's fond grasp, Jan tried to maintain his dignity. "I am surprised to see you here, Vicky."

I had once had an old-fashioned crush on Jan, who resembled a gorgeous young saint in one of my favorite paintings. Alas, the magic was gone. Not only did I have a new crush, but Jan was no longer gorgeous. The hawklike features had sagged, the crisp curls were silvery pale instead of bright gold, and they had retreated so far that his forehead looked like a mountain massif topped with snow. He turned his back on Ernhardt, who was climbing the stairs, filming industriously, and hissed, "Tell him to stop! Schmidt, come inside at once. Have you not made a sufficient spectacle of yourself?"

Schmidt nodded judiciously. "Perhaps so. Come, Vicky, John. Ernhardt, my thanks, and best wishes to Erma."

Jan led the way to his office, moving at a clip that left our admirers behind. Settling himself at his desk, he demanded rather piteously, "Why have you done this to me, Schmidt?"

Schmidt said, *"Wahrheit! Freiheit!"* and offered Jan a sausage in a bun.

"Spite," said Jan, ignoring the sausage. "Revenge. This is not worthy of you. It is not my fault if you were not clever enough to find the gold of Troy."

Schmidt started to eat the hot dog, to use that term loosely, so I took it upon myself to reply. "How did you do it?"

Schmidt swallowed. "That is in the past," he said, with a dismissive wave of his hand. "We are here in the cause of truth, freedom—"

"What will it take to make you go away?" Jan demanded.

". . . and justice," said Schmidt. He put the bun down, leaving a smear of mustard on the polished desk. Jan snatched a tissue from his pocket and wiped it off. "The Egyptians ask only that Nefertiti be lent to them for a special exhibit. Why can you not agree?"

"The bust is too fragile—"

"Bah," said Schmidt. "Special packing, a private airplane. The Egyptians have sent equally delicate objects abroad."

"They won't give her back," Jan burst out. He leaned forward, hands tightly clasped. "They will refuse to return her, claiming, as they have always done, that she was stolen. And what will happen to her there? The Cairo Museum is a disaster, overcrowded, filthy, vulnerable to theft. Without climate controls, even air-conditioning, objects are deteriorating by the minute. All over Egypt there are tombs, temples, precious monuments falling to pieces. We have rescued Nefertiti! She is part of our heritage too, she belongs to the world!"

It was the old familiar argument, made by all the looters. Where would the Elgin Marbles be today if they had remained on the Parthenon? What would have happened to the Pergamum Altar if it hadn't been "rescued" from what is now Turkey by a German expedition? Would the Rosetta Stone have ended up in a Cairene house foundation if the French hadn't recognized its worth? There are usually two sides to every argument, and this side had its merits.

So did the other side.

"The new museum, where they plan to exhibit her, will have all the amenities," I said. "They're doing the best they can, Jan. Egypt has too much stuff. The world ought to be helping preserve that heritage, instead of wasting money on wars."

"Stuff," Jan muttered. He passed his hand over his forehead. "Your proposition is noble, but it will never happen, Vicky. All we can do is save what we can."

"And how far would you go," Schmidt asked, "to save what you can?"

Jan stiffened. "What are you implying, Schmidt?"

"There are rumors," Schmidt began.

Jan didn't bite. Schmidt went on, "That the museum has objects acquired under dubious circumstances."

"Oh, that. The same is said of almost every museum in the world. Laws have changed. What is now illegal was once perfectly proper."

"So if you were offered a unique artifact you would refuse unless you were certain of its provenance?"

If that was Schmidt's idea of subtle, sly questioning, it missed the target. Jan actually laughed. "Certainly. And now, Schmidt, if you have nothing more to say . . ."

He hadn't asked us to sit down. The desk was a barricade and a symbol of authority and superiority. Leaving us standing constituted a strong hint that we should go away.

"Where are your manners?" John asked. "Here, Vicky, take this chair. Schmidt . . ."

"Who the devil are you?" Jan demanded.

"You did not give me time to make introductions," Schmidt said. "Mr. John Tregarth, a colleague of mine and a well-known art dealer."

"I believe I have heard of you," Jan admitted. "A colleague?"

"Friend," John said modestly. "You might call me an amicus curiae."

"On which side? As a dealer in antiquities, surely you realize the importance of protecting precious articles."

"Not exactly," I said. "He realizes the importance of making money from them."

"Hmmm." Jan studied John's impassive face. "I cannot recall

that we have ever purchased anything from you. Yet you look somewhat familiar . . ."

"We've never met," John said. It was true; he had made a point
of staying out of Jan's way during the Trojan Gold fiasco. He went
on, "I have recently acquired a few Egyptian pieces in which the museum might be interested."

"You might send us photographs," Jan said. "Assuming, of course,
that their provenance is impeccable."

"I assure you, it is."

"We would never consider purchasing an object that had not
been legally acquired."

He smirked at Schmidt and gave John a warm smile. John
smiled warmly back.

Though we assured him it wasn't necessary, Jan summoned a
guard to escort us out of the museum. This indication of mis-
trust offended Schmidt, who insisted on stopping by to say hello to
Nefertiti.

I had seen her many times, but I never tired of it. The photographs don't do her justice. The tall, distinctive blue crown that
hides her hair, the delicately tinted face and smiling lips, the long
throat and lifted chin . . . Even the missing eye didn't detract from
her beauty. I could see why the Egyptians wanted her back. If
Tutankhamon is the most famous of all Egyptian symbols, Nefertiti
runs him a close second—and she's much nicer to look at.

Schmidt paid her the tribute of a long sigh, and then let himself
be led away.

The audience had dispersed, and our banner had disappeared—
thrown into a trash can, I supposed.

"Time for lunch," said Schmidt. "There is a restaurant—"

"You just ate four hot dogs," I protested.

"We may as well feed him," John said. "He's more amenable to suggestion when he's eating."

The restaurant was crowded and noisy. The perfect setting, as all spies know, for a private conversation.

"So what suggestion?" Schmidt demanded. "Perlmutter gave nothing away, the sly dog, but you did well, John, to form a bond with him."

"Thank you," John said humbly.

"Do you really have objects of museum quality? Why was I not given a chance to see them?"

"Because our collections don't include ancient Egyptian material," I said.

"How did you acquire them?" Schmidt demanded.

"Quite legitimately, I assure you."

"Aha," said Schmidt. "From—"

"Irrelevant and immaterial," John said. "They should serve as a means of maintaining amicable relations with Perlmutter, however. On a completely unrelated subject, isn't it time you were in touch with Suzi?"

Schmidt choked on the bite of food he had just ingested. Then he mumbled, "Yes, you are right. I was told—asked—to report every day, whether I had news or not."

"Maybe there's a message from her," I suggested.

"No, she would not message me, for fear you might intercept it. She is very careful." Schmidt dug out his cell phone. "What shall I say to her?"

John had obviously given the matter some thought. "That we're in Berlin." He waved away Schmidt's incipient protest. "If she hasn't found out through her sources, someone is bound to see you on the evening news."

"I had not thought of that." Schmidt looked crestfallen.

"No harm done. Tell her we mean to stay a few more days and that you have high hopes of catching me in the act of negotiating with one of my gang."

Schmidt chuckled. His pudgy little fingers were already punching buttons. "Gang, yes, that is good. What else shall I say?"

"Love and kisses," I suggested.

Schmidt made a face, but complied.

I hadn't indulged in wurst in a bun, so I made a hearty lunch. I know it sounds as if I eat all the time, but traveling with John means I never know when the next meal will be available.

"Are we actually going to Egypt, or is this another evasive technique?" I asked. "Not that I expect a truthful answer."

John raised an eyebrow. "I cannot imagine why you should say that. The fact is we don't seem to be getting anywhere from this end, so perhaps it's time we started looking for him. I think he's still in Egypt."

"He? Oh—him. Why?"

"Consider the logistical difficulties of getting him out of the country. How would you transport a six-foot-long object through ordinary channels? One might posit such methods as a boat at a Red Sea port, or a hired aircraft landing in the desert, but why go to all that trouble when he could just be tucked away someplace handy, ready to be returned upon payment of ransom?"

"That makes very good sense," said Schmidt.

John smiled modestly. "There is also the difficulty of getting him away from the Luxor area. As I recall, one can't go far in any direction without encountering a security checkpoint. Vehicles usually have to wait to join a police-escorted convoy. I can think of several ways around the checkpoint problem, but we may as well start from the assumption that they won't have gone far." John glanced at his watch. "We'd better get back to the hotel and start packing."

"Then I must have a suitcase," Schmidt said, brightening at the prospect of more shopping.

We didn't take the first taxi. I wondered when the bad guys were going to figure out people were on to this maneuver, and have the kidnapper drive the second cab.

KaDeWe, Berlin's equivalent of Harrods, was not the right place to take Schmidt. He bought each of us a suitcase (genuine leather), and John a watch (a Rolex), and me a scarf (Hermès), and in the toy department, an exact replica of Princess Leia's pistol.

"You'll never get that through security," I said.

"I will place it in my checked baggage. A present for my godchild, you see. Shall I get one for you too?"

"Well . . ."

"Two godchildren," said Schmidt. "And perhaps the sword of Aragorn for each."

The swords were four feet long. We talked him out of them.

We got back to the hotel with time to spare. I put all my new presents, including Leia's gun, in my new suitcase and checked to make sure I hadn't overlooked anything. John had already finished packing and left the bedroom. When I went out into the sitting room, he wasn't there.

Six

He wasn't anywhere in the suite. Schmidt, still packing things I hadn't even seen him acquire, interrupted his off-key rendering of "Night Train to Memphis" long enough to deny seeing or hearing him.

"Stay here," I said, through clenched teeth. "I mean it, Schmidt; don't stir from this room until I come back."

Had I been a nice person I would have been wringing my hands and working myself into a frenzy of concern. However, cold reason reminded me that there had been no sound of a disturbance, not even a stray gunshot. He must have left of his own accord, on his own well-shod feet, for his own reasons. Which he had not bothered to confide to me.

The lift was located in a hallway just off the lobby. I wasn't quite furious enough to come barreling out of it shouting threats; peering cautiously round a potted palm, I saw two people standing by the outer door engaged in earnest conversation. One of them was John, smiling and urbane, not a hair on his head ruffled. The other person was shaped like Schmidt, short and rounded, but she was obviously female, and to judge from her attire, no longer young: a dark print dress that reached to mid-calf, sensible laced shoes, and a scarf that covered her hair. She carried an oversized purse and a cloth shopping bag. I couldn't see her face, since she had her back to me.

I stayed where I was, ears pricked. Only soft murmurs were audible. When I finally caught a phrase it was uninformative: *"Auf Widersehen,"* from John. A throaty chuckle from the hausfrau was her only answer. John sprang to open the door for her, and out she marched, purse swinging.

I emerged from behind the greenery. John's reaction to my appearance was a smile and a reminder that we were running late.

"So whose fault is that?" I inquired, as he bowed me into the lift. "Why didn't you tell me you had an appointment with your contact?"

John put his arm round me and turned me to face him. "Were you worried?" he asked tenderly.

"I was furious."

"So I assumed." He removed his arm. "I did tell you earlier today that I meant to get in touch."

"Who is she? She didn't look like a crook."

"The most successful crooks don't." John looked smug. "However, in this case the word 'crook' does not apply. She's one of the most respected antiquities dealers in Berlin. She wasn't keen on being seen in public with me, so she agreed to drop by here for a brief consultation."

"I was under the impression that you were also a respectable antiquities dealer. Why was she unwilling to meet you in public? Aha— wait, let me guess. She's heard a thing or two."

"Very good," John said patronizingly. He rapped on the door of the suite. Schmidt must have been standing right behind the door. It was flung open. There stood Schmidt, pointing Princess Leia's pistol at us.

"God be thanked, you are safe!" he exclaimed.

"I can't imagine why you should suppose we wouldn't be," John said. "But I appreciate your concern, Schmidt. Have you finished packing?"

"Yes, yes, only the pistol. Where—"

"All in due time," John said. "Where's your bag, Vicky?"

"Oh, are you going to carry it for me? How gallant."

I ended up carrying the thing myself, since, after watching Schmidt drag his bulging suitcase toward the door, John decided he needed assistance more than I.

"What on earth have you got in here?" John demanded.

Schmidt looked self-conscious. "A few odds and ends. Necessities. What—"

John refused to talk until we were in the taxi on our way to wherever. Leaning back, hands folded, he said, "Instead of answering a string of questions, I shall expound briefly on the most recent developments. I didn't mention my appointment because it was a last-minute arrangement, and I knew it wouldn't take long. Helga's reluctance to meet me was a strong indication that she'd heard something of interest, but I wanted more information than that and I didn't want to discuss it on a line that might no longer be secure."

"You think Suzi—" Schmidt clapped his hand over his mouth.

"No names," John said. "It's possible, yes."

"And Hel——— the other, it is—er—the one on Ludwigkirch-platz?"

"You know her, of course," John said.

"*Aber natürlich.* One of the most—"

John cut him off. "She and several other important independent dealers had been notified of a recent theft. No details, only that it was an Egyptian antiquity of considerable value. She was asked to communicate immediately with the Supreme Council of Antiquities if she were approached by anyone offering such an object for sale. Or," he added, after a slight pause, "if she were approached by me."

"Hmmm," said Schmidt.

"Hmmm indeed," I agreed. "That's strange. Why the SCA and not Interpol? And why mention your name?"

"She asked me the same questions," John said. "My current reputation in the trade is impeccable. At least it was, up until now. Given the context, the mere mention of my name is enough to arouse certain doubts. I wouldn't be the first dealer to go wrong."

"You assured her of your innocence, I presume," I said.

"No problem," John said smugly. "I simply said I had heard rumors as well, and since I meant to be in Berlin anyhow, I was curious to know what, if anything, she had heard. I was shocked—shocked!—when she said my name had been mentioned. My distress moved her so much, she promised to let me know if anyone contacted her about the antiquity."

"In other words, you put on one of your better performances," I said.

"Butter would have melted in my mouth." He sobered. "It's more than odd, Vicky, it's inexplicable. The—er—missing object is not the sort of thing people like her would handle even if it had been legally acquired, which, as the message made clear, it was not."

"Perhaps it is not so inexplicable," said Schmidt, frowning.

"What do you mean?" John asked sharply.

"Only that your once impeccable reputation is now being sullied," Schmidt said in surprise. "As you have said, it is not unheard of that a dealer should succumb to temptation, if offered a prize of great value."

"Very few dealers, I daresay, would be tempted by—by something like that," John said. "How the bloody hell would one dispose of it?"

Schmidt made conciliatory noises. John had come close to losing his temper, which was unusual. And I had begun to wonder. Most dealers wouldn't know how to handle a bizarre object like a famous mummy. But if anybody would . . .

Need I say that our tickets to Cairo were first class? I love traveling with Schmidt.

Schmidt had arranged for us to be met at the airport by a courier, who accepted a wad of money and our passports from Schmidt and went off to get our visas. He came back with the visas, and a wheelchair, into which Schmidt settled himself.

"Are you okay?" I asked.

"Yes, yes. There is a special line for the handicapped." Schmidt winked, and then let his face fall into lines of bravely controlled pain.

"He's gotten worse," I whispered to John. "Is there nothing to which the man will not stoop?"

"I certainly hope not. I've used the wheelchair method myself—bewigged, bandaged, and/or dribbling in a senile fashion—but so far Schmidt has lived up to my fondest expectations."

Trailed by a small procession carrying our luggage, we proceeded to and, thanks to the wheelchair, handily through passport control. Beyond the security area, people lined the barrier waiting for arriving passengers. Foremost among them was a familiar form.

John said, "I'd better go on ahead and warn . . . Oops. Too late."

Schmidt had already spotted Feisal. He let out a genial bellow and began waving. Until that moment Feisal had not spotted Schmidt. His expression was that of the hero in a horror film who has just seen the monster lurching toward him.

Schmidt jumped up and embraced Feisal. "We wanted to surprise you. Are you surprised?"

Feisal took a deep breath and proved himself to be the man I had always known him to be. "Yes. Yes, I am definitely . . . surprised. Hello, Schmidt. Vicky. Johnny . . ."

"You will come with us to the hotel," Schmidt announced. "We are staying at the Nile Hilton. It is not my favorite hotel in Cairo, but it is convenient to the museum."

Cairo traffic is vicious at all hours. It was well past midnight when we reached the hotel and were shown to our rooms. Schmidt's was a suite, with a balcony looking down on the city. It was a glorious sight by night, glittering like a jeweled robe, with the Nile running through like a shining snake. I was admiring the view when Schmidt summoned me.

"Come, come, this is no time for nostalgia. We must have a council of war."

Feisal sank down onto the sofa and fixed John with a baleful stare. "He knows. You told him. Why did you tell him?"

Tempted though I was to have John take the blame, fairness demanded that I own up. "It was my idea, Feisal." The stare moved to me. "Uh—that is—both our ideas."

"And why not?" Schmidt demanded. "Have I not proved my quality? Are we not like the four musketeers, one for all and all for one?"

"I want to be d'Artagnan," I said.

Schmidt chuckled. "But it is I who am the greatest swordsman in Europe, *nicht wahr?*"

"You only challenge people to duels when you're drunk, Schmidt."

"That is not true," said Schmidt, who honestly believed his statement. "Sit down, Vicky, sit down. We will have beer and talk."

"There is no beer," Feisal mumbled. "The hotel doesn't—"

"There will be beer," said Schmidt.

And sure enough, there was.

Busy guzzling, Schmidt allowed John and me to fill Feisal in on what we had discovered. Feisal failed to react to our encounters with the criminal underworld except to mutter "Serves you right"; but when I told him about Suzi he let out a few resounding Arabic oaths. I assumed they were swear words, not only from the tone, but from the fact that Schmidt, who can swear in a dozen languages, shrank back and stared sadly into his empty glass.

"Don't be mad at Schmidt," I said.

"I have repented," said Schmidt hollowly.

"What's more," said John, "Schmidt is now our spy in the enemy camp. A double agent, no less."

"Hmmm." Feisal nodded grudgingly. "But that's bad news. I remember her. Did you ever figure out exactly who she's working for?"

"I'm betting on Interpol," I said. "Some special branch dealing with art fraud. Feisal, she can't prove anything. Not yet."

"Somebody is spreading the word," John summarized. "Selectively and secretly. If we knew why—"

"I take it you haven't a clue," Feisal said, sipping water.

Schmidt said nothing, so loudly we all turned to look at him.

"Well?" John demanded.

"What? Oh." Schmidt tapped his forehead. "An idea or two is bubbling in my head. But it is too early to speak of them. We need more information. I would like to examine the scene of the crime and question the witnesses."

"You mean the tomb?" Feisal's eyes widened. "Do you think that's a wise move? Surely we don't want to draw attention to it."

"I agree with Schmidt," John said. "So far we've been on the defensive, waiting to see what other people are going to do. I can't see that it's getting us anywhere." He smiled angelically. "I also have an idea or two bubbling round in my head."

Feisal looked sick.

Schmidt got on the phone with his unfortunate courier, whom he had apparently rousted out of bed, and instructed him to get us all on a flight to Luxor the next morning. The courier's protests were shouted down by Schmidt. "Yes, yes, I know it will be difficult, but you can do it. Employ whatever means are necessary."

I hope that meant bribery instead of threats and intimidation. Schmidt's new, self-appointed role as mastermind had gone to his head.

Feisal got heavily to his feet. "I'll ring you in the morning. Good night, all."

"Maasalama," said Schmidt, bright-eyed as a little bird.

He opened another bottle of Stella. He offered me one; I shook my head. "It's after two A.M., Schmidt. I'm going to bed. Don't call me, I'll call you."

I was aroused, only too soon, by the phone. "Breakfast is here," said Schmidt. "Hurry. Our flight is at ten."

"What time is it?" I croaked.

He had already hung up. I fumbled for my watch. Half past seven.

I was beginning to hate traveling with Schmidt.

We hadn't heard from Feisal, and Schmidt waxed critical. "He does not answer his mobile. He is not in the hotel. Where is he? Why did you not ask where he was going last night?"

I had had enough coffee to be fully awake, but not enough to put me in a pleasant mood. "You didn't ask him either. It's none of our business where he went. Maybe he spent the night with his girl-friend."

"What girlfriend? Who?"

"I didn't ask," I snarled. "That's none of our business either."

"Calm yourself, Schmidt," John said. "If he misses the plane he'll follow as soon as he can."

We were almost ready to leave when Feisal finally called. Schmidt ordered him to meet us at the airport and shooed us out the door.

The car he had ordered was waiting. While Schmidt settled the hotel bill, I said to John, "I vote you take over as mastermind. Schmidt is getting worse and worse. What was the point of our staying at a hotel near the museum if we didn't go to the museum?"

John shrugged.

It took over an hour to get to the airport. There was no sign of Feisal outside the terminal. Only local EgyptAir flights use the do-mestic terminal, but the place was bustling; porters snatching at luggage, in the hope of picking up a little baksheesh; travelers of all nationalities in all sorts of clothing: conservative Muslim ladies tented in black, students in jeans bent under the weight of bulging backpacks, a couple of dignitaries in flowing white robes and head-cloths, a little old lady with her nose in a guidebook, uniformed se-curity guards . . .

"Mr. John Tregarth?"

There were two of them. They wore ordinary business suits, not uniforms, but John took an involuntary step back. The two moved closer.

"Yes," John said warily.

"You will please to come with us."

Schmidt and I were included in the invitation. The two men were perfectly courteous, they just ignored our questions and smiled politely when we protested. Schmidt's blood was up. He clenched his fists and began muttering about truth, freedom, and justice.

"Never mind, Schmidt," John said.

"You will not resist?" Schmidt demanded fiercely.

"Refuse a courteous invitation?" John inquired, eyebrow lifting.

"But if they are enemies, like the man in Rome—"

"I think not. There are only two of them and they don't appear to be armed. If this were an attempted kidnapping they wouldn't have selected a place where there are so many people about, including a number of policemen. The air of confidence displayed by these affable gentlemen implies that they are acting in an official capacity."

"Oh, damn," I said. "Are we being arrested?"

"Taken in for questioning," John corrected.

Our escorts raised no objection when John collected a few porters to bring our luggage. Still smiling those bland smiles, they led the way to a long black limo. When one of them opened the door I saw Feisal inside. He was just sitting there, hunched over and looking like a scolded puppy. There was no one else in the car except the driver.

Schmidt, John, and I joined Feisal in the tonneau. One of the men got in front with the driver. The other took the seat facing us.

"I presume you know no more about this than we," John said.

Feisal shook his head. "I'm sorry," he muttered. "I couldn't warn you."

"We have no reason to fear," Schmidt said loudly. "We have done nothing wrong."

Feisal's expression brought home to me, more clearly than the articles I had read or the stories I had heard, that we were not in a country where a man was presumed innocent until proven guilty.

But we were foreign nationals, I told myself, citizens of countries considered to be allies of Egypt. Foreigners might be arrested and accused of espionage in other parts of the Middle East. Surely not here. Not when the U.S. kept pouring in all that lovely money.

Where that might leave Feisal I didn't like to think.

Schmidt asked a few questions of our guard, getting only shrugs and smiles in return. Finally John said softly, "Don't waste your breath, Schmidt. I don't think they understand much English."

"Then we can speak freely," Schmidt exclaimed. "Make plans."

"This would seem to be an occasion for improvisation," John said. He added pointedly, "And for taciturnity."

The long drive took us back over the skyway into central Cairo. The cacophony of traffic reached us even through the closed windows. We were a little cramped in the backseat, thanks to Schmidt's ample sitting area, but the car was very posh, with gray velvet upholstery and an air-conditioning system that ruffled my hair. Schmidt kept quiet, although he looked as if he were about to burst with questions. I occupied myself by studying the man who faced me. His hair was graying and his suit was a little shabby. If he was a member of the secret police, or whatever they might be called, he didn't look very dangerous. Catching my eye, he produced another of those meaningless smiles and looked away.

After a while I began to see a familiar sight or two and I realized we were headed toward the river. We came out on the corniche and joined the line of traffic crossing one of the bridges. Straight ahead, the Cairo Tower raised a pointing finger toward the sky.

Feisal sat up straight. His mouth was set in a tight line.

"What is it?" I whispered.

Feisal shook his head. Oh my God, I thought. He knows where we're headed. One of those horrible prisons, where captives are tortured in secret dungeons.

Feisal ignored my pokes and whispers. I tried to catch John's eye and failed. The car finally pulled up to the curb. Feisal had the door open before the vehicle had come to a complete stop; he flung himself out, staggered, caught himself, and went racing across a paved plaza and into a building that looked as if it housed offices. Bemused and confused, I let John shove me out. Neither of the guards tried to stop us; we pelted after Feisal and found him standing in front of an elevator jabbing at the buttons. Schmidt was too out of breath to speak, but I managed to croak out another "What?" I got no answer. The lift doors opened and we piled in. When the lift stopped on an upper floor, I saw the sign on the door across the way. The truth began to dawn on me. I had caught a glimpse of letters like those on the facade of the building before John hustled me inside.

The room into which the door opened was just an ordinary office, no bars, no Iron Maiden, only desks with secretarial-looking people seated behind them. Feisal, still in the lead, barreled across the room toward an inner door. He moved so fast, the secretaries hadn't a prayer of stopping him.

The inner office was imposing, with big windows and a picture of Mubarak on the wall, and a large table surrounded by sofas and chairs. At one end of the room was a huge desk with a man seated behind it. Feisal launched himself across the desk, sending papers flying like huge snowflakes, and grabbed the man by the throat.

People ran in all directions, in and out of the room, yelling and screaming. A few valiant souls tried to get hold of Feisal, but he shook them off. He was yelling louder than anyone. I caught only the word "son" repeated several times and deduced that Feisal was calling his victim bad names. I glanced at John, who stood watching interestedly. Then I sat down on one of the nice comfortable chairs by the table.

The man Feisal was trying to choke was none other than the secretary general. After a few moments he grabbed Feisal's wrists and broke his hold with a quick, brutal twist.

"Now that you've got that out of your system, why don't you sit down so we can talk sensibly?" he inquired.

He wasn't even out of breath. Feisal lay sprawled across the desk amid a welter of papers, file folders, books, pamphlets, pens, bottles of water, scarabs, several small boxes (brass, wood adorned with mother-of-pearl and turquoise) containing various objects, and a stuffed camel. He was breathing hard, but I decided it was from rage more than from exertion.

Feisal called the secretary general a son of something else. Khifaya grinned. Close up, he was even better-looking than in his photographs. He was wearing a white silk shirt open halfway down his tanned chest and a modest display of jewelry—a heavy gold wristwatch, several rings, and a gold chain round his neck.

"Good morning, Dr. Bliss." The smile hit like a searchlight. I blinked. "Herr Professor Schmidt, Mr. Tregarth. Do make yourselves comfortable. Tea? Coffee?"

He snapped his fingers. A head peered round the door frame, followed shortly thereafter by the accompanying body, that of a young woman wearing a head scarf and a well-cut pantsuit. The secretary general looked inquiringly at me.

"Coffee," I squeaked. "Thank you, Dr. Khifaya."

"Please—call me Ashraf. We are going to be good friends, I hope."

I hoped so too.

Feisal slid off the desk, onto his feet. "You—"

"You are about to repeat yourself, I believe," said my new friend. He picked up a vase containing a single red rosebud. Water had spilled across a corner of the desk and was dripping onto the floor. Ashraf shook his head sadly and handed the vase to another young woman, who began mopping up the water. "Really, Feisal, there was no need to make such a mess."

Hands on his hips, feet braced, Feisal fairly vibrated with indignation. "That was a filthy, low-down trick. We thought we were under arrest!"

"Oh dear. Did you really? Dr. Bliss, please accept my apologies if I inadvertently alarmed you. I assumed Feisal would recognize my car."

"How the hell was I supposed to recognize your car?" Feisal demanded. "I didn't know you rated a limo these days."

"Are you two by any chance related?" John asked.

"Cousins," Feisal muttered, in the same tone in which he would have admitted being kin to a serial killer.

"You never told me that," I said.

"Second cousins."

"Once removed," Ashraf said, with another of those incandescent grins. "He's jealous of my superior rank and resents the fact that my branch of the family is wealthier than his."

Busy hands, most of them female, had collected the scattered objects and supplied trays with coffee and plates of little cakes. Another snap of the fingers sent them scurrying out of the room. Ashraf rose and gestured toward the table.

"Let's start again, shall we? I greatly enjoyed seeing you all on television. Thank you for supporting our cause with such panache."

"I made the sign," Schmidt said, reaching for a sugared cake.

"So I assumed. I have fond memories of our conversation in Turin a few years ago, before I assumed my present position. Did you speak with Dr. Perlmutter?"

"Yes. I am sorry to say he remains obdurate." Schmidt took a bite of the cake. He added thickly, "But we will persevere."

"Indeed. Feisal, you aren't drinking your coffee. Would you prefer tea?"

"I would prefer an apology," Feisal growled. "Or at the very least, an explanation."

"I do apologize for being somewhat peremptory in my invitation, but really, you left me no choice. I have been trying for two days to get in touch with you, but you move round so fast! I didn't learn until this morning that you were in Cairo, and when I telephoned the hotel you had already left for the airport."

The man did have a way with him. Charm oozed from every tooth and every inch of skin. Even Feisal had relaxed, though he still looked wary.

"Why did you want to see us?" I asked.

"Not you, Dr. Bliss—although seeing you is a pleasure. Alas, business must take precedence over pleasure, and I have imperative reasons for wishing to speak with Mr. Tregarth."

I hid my face behind a paper napkin and surreptitiously removed coffee grounds from my teeth. Turkish, aka Egyptian, coffee is half grounds; usually I know when to stop drinking, but Ashraf's sudden attack of candor had caught me off guard. He had been playing games with our nerves and thoroughly enjoying it. John took a careful sip, put his cup down, and met Ashraf's gaze eyeball to eyeball.

"Please feel free to use my first name," John said. "We are going to be good friends, I hope."

Schmidt choked on a bite of cake. Ashraf let out a little sigh of satisfaction.

"I believe I am going to enjoy dealing with you, Mr. Tregarth— John. That is my hope as well. Are you wondering, perhaps, why I was so anxious to get in touch with you?"

"I feel certain you are about to tell me," John said.

"And I feel certain you—all of you—are about to tell me various things."

The two of them watched each other like duelists, eyes locked. I remembered a quotation: "Don't bother watching his eyes, watch the bastard's hands." Good advice under some circumstances, but irrelevant here. Ashraf's hands, lightly clasped, neatly manicured, were empty. He was good, but he was no match for a man who had spent most of his life avoiding dangerous slips of the tongue.

Feisal wasn't as experienced. He started squirming. His forehead was beaded with perspiration. His lips parted. Schmidt, cozily close to Feisal on the sofa, shifted position and cleared his throat loudly.

"Yes, Feisal?" Ashraf asked.

"Nothing."

Ashraf's eyes moved from him to Schmidt, and then to me. So did John's. If I had needed any incentive to keep my big mouth shut, that cold blue stare would have provided it, but I felt as if my brain were about to burst with questions. He knew. The SCA must have received a message, ransom note, threat, whatever, from the thieves. But in that case wouldn't Ashraf have dashed off to Luxor to check on Tut? And wouldn't Feisal have told us if he had? I picked up my cup and swallowed a spoonful of coffee grounds.

Ashraf chuckled. "It appears we have reached a stalemate. Very well; it is my move."

He got up and went to a safe that stood against the wall and punched in a combination. It contained several open compartments filled with ledgers and files, plus a closed compartment, another, internal, safe. Ashraf took a key from his pocket and unlocked it. Inside was a single object—a small box wrapped in heavy brown paper, which Ashraf removed. Returning to his seat, he put the box on the table.

"This was delivered to my flat day before yesterday."

He took his time, carefully folding back the paper, slowly lifting the lid of the cardboard box it enclosed. Inside was another box, this one of wood inlaid with mother-of-pearl. You could find boxes like that in every shop in the suk. It had a rather flimsy brass catch, which Ashraf unfastened. Ashraf moved like a slug, in slow motion, watching John, whose expression of courteous patience didn't change. The hinged lid was lifted, the layer of cotton wool inside was removed. And there it was.

A mummy's hand.

SEVEN

I had only seen mummies and parts of same in movies. We have a few so-called relics in the museum, purchased because of the artistic merits of the reliquaries, which are usually made of precious metals, bejeweled and beautifully carved. I had never closely examined the contents. Seen close up, this fragment of humanity was something of a shock to the system—dried and brown, the fingers slightly flexed. Some of the skin was gone, exposing the finger bones. It could have been a well-made fake, a prop for a movie. But Feisal sprang to his feet and reached for the box.

"Carefully, carefully," Ashraf said. "Don't damage it."

"Him," Feisal whispered. He gazed yearningly at the horrible thing.

Ashraf leaned back, his lips curved in a smile of satisfaction. Thanks to that single pronoun, the cat was doing its damnedest to squirm out of the bag.

"Disgusting," I said, in a feeble attempt to fend off the inevitable.

"Who would send a thing like that? Some sicko, or maybe a publicist for a forthcoming horror film? I suppose there are people who—"

"Don't waste your breath, Vicky," John said. "He's playing games. Feisal, are you sure?"

"Oh, yes. I would know him anywhere." Feisal's voice rose in a cry of distress. "Again he is being dismembered. What part will be next?"

Ashraf retrieved the box and began replacing the wrappings.

"Let us stop playing games, then," he said briskly. "I will place my cards on the table and I expect you to reciprocate. When I first saw this, my reaction was like yours, Vicky. We do get such bizarre communications from time to time; Egypt breeds strange fantasies in certain minds. Then I saw the message that had been enclosed."

He reached in the pocket of his shirt and took out a folded paper, which he handed to John. John read it aloud.

"'If you want the rest of him, it will cost you three million American dollars. You have ten days to collect the money. We will be in touch.'"

"It was not difficult," Ashraf resumed, "to deduce whose hand this might be. No anonymous mummy would be worth so much, and only one of the great kings rested in his tomb, outside the protection afforded by the Royal Mummies room of the museum. I went to my reference books. There are innumerable photographs, many by Harry Burton, who worked with Carter. They had dismembered the mummy in order to remove the jewelry on it. The head, hands, arms, feet, and legs had been detached, the lower legs separated from the upper, the lower arms from the upper arms, and the torso bisected. In an attempt to conceal their sacrilege, the excavators had arranged the body on a sand tray and reattached the feet and hands with resin. You can see traces of the resin at the wrist of this hand."

The cat was prowling around the room lashing its tail. Feisal knew it, but I think he was still clinging to the forlorn hope that Ashraf hadn't discovered his failure to report the theft. The hope didn't last long.

"Why didn't you tell me, Feisal?" Ashraf asked gently.

"I—um—"

"Did you think I would hold you accountable?" He spoke like a father to an erring son.

Feisal could only be jerked around so much. He sat up straight and glared at his cousin. "Damn right I did. I've been trying ever since I found out to get it—him—back. I didn't know until after it happened, they picked a day when I was in Aswan—"

"I know. I spoke to Ali."

"Poor devil," Feisal said feelingly. "It wasn't his fault either, Ashraf. What have you done to him?"

Ashraf's big brown eyes widened. "Promised him immunity and promotion, of course. Good Lord, Feisal, sometimes your naïveté astonishes me. The last thing we want is for Ali to break down and babble. Enough of this. I have an outer office full of people and most of them are wondering why I am spending so much time alone with you lot."

He looked at each of us in turn, enjoying Schmidt's desperate attempt to keep his face noncommittal, and Feisal's quickened breathing. I was biting my lip to keep from yelling at him. Finally he said, "I want to hire you, Mr. Tregarth, to retrieve Tutankhamon."

I had braced myself for an accusation, not an offer. So had Schmidt; he let his breath out in an explosive whoosh. John crossed his legs and smiled.

"Why me?" he asked, his big blue eyes widening.

"Because you and your friends here saved the treasure of Tetish-eri for us."

"Ah," said John.

"The details of that extraordinary business are known only to a few, of which I am one. You received no reward except the thanks of a grateful nation. This time the reward will be worthy of the deed."

"How much?" John asked.

Raised eyebrows indicated Ashraf's disapproval of such crudity. "I am prepared to negotiate. But not here and now. Do you accept?"

"I must consult my associates," John said. "But not here and now. If you and I can come to an agreement, we will proceed to Luxor and begin our investigation."

A timid tap on the door prevented what would probably have been another cute remark from Ashraf and a violent assault from me, on him or John. I wanted to get the hell out of there. Ashraf shouted, "What do you want? I told you to hold my calls." The door opened a crack; taking its cue from him, the voice spoke English.

"Yes, sir, but the minister is on the telephone and the director is here for your appointment, and—"

"We mustn't keep you," John said, rising to his feet.

"When may I expect to hear from you?" Ashraf asked. His smile indicated that although he might have lost this round, he was look-ing forward to the next one.

"Tomorrow."

"Why not tonight? We have no time to waste."

It was a good point, and John didn't really have a good answer. "It may take a while to get in touch with some of my sources."

"Sources," Ashraf repeated thoughtfully.

The ambiguous, suggestive word hung in the air like a hooked fish. John was smart enough not to elaborate, but I noticed he was beginning to perspire.

"Tonight, then," he said, rising. "I'll ring you."

Our departure rather resembled the mad dash of freed prisoners. When we emerged from the building there was the limo waiting at the curb, next to a sign that said "No parking under any circumstances."

Feisal swore and turned as if he were ready to run. John grabbed his arm.

"Your nerves are in frightful shape, Feisal. It's all right. And if it isn't all right, there is not a damned thing we can do about it."

There was only one man in the limo—the driver. Seeing us, he jumped out and opened the back door.

"Where are we going?" I asked.

"Back to the hotel, I suppose." Despite his advice to Feisal, John sounded a trifle rattled. "Do you think we can get our rooms back?"

"Yes, yes." Schmidt whipped out his cell. "I will arrange it. Get in, Vicky."

The vehicle forced its way into the stream of traffic. After a few fraught moments I said, "I want a drink."

"I have vodka and Scotch in my suitcase," Schmidt said.

"And beer."

"*Aber natürlich.* But we can wait until we reach the hotel. It is all arranged."

"*Aber natürlich,*" Feisal echoed. "How the hell do you do it, Schmidt? Never mind, I don't really care how, so long as you do it. *Alhamdullilah!* Much as I hate to admit it, Johnny, you pulled that off rather neatly."

"He was the one pulling the strings. We are doing precisely what he wanted us to do."

Feisal gestured at the driver.

"No problem," John said. "I have a gun pointed at the back of his head."

The driver didn't even twitch. Having made his point, John went on, "He kept us off balance every step of the way, and he knew it. I do wish you three could learn to control your gasps and twitches; you might as well have fallen on your knees and confessed."

"I thought he was going to accuse you," I said.

"He knew I would deny it, and there was no way he could prove anything. This way he has both bases covered. If I am guilty I may be willing to negotiate, cutting out my confederates and saving him money. If I am innocent, I will cooperate in order to preserve my good name and my freedom. He's good," John said grudgingly. "Very good. Did you see how he pounced on my reference to outside sources?"

"That wasn't up to your usual standard," I said. "But it didn't constitute an admission of anything."

"So we will accept his offer?" Schmidt asked.

"Honestly, you people amaze me," John said in exasperation. "That wasn't an offer, that was a threat. He's got us—Feisal and me, at any rate—over the proverbial barrel. Anybody who knows the details of that extraordinary business, to quote our grandiloquent friend, knows we were in it up to our necks. The only reason we got off scot-free was because we turned our coats and almost got ourselves killed saving the paintings—and because the government didn't want a scandal. If we can't retrieve Tut without the theft becoming public knowledge, he'll make sure we pay for Tetisheri too. So don't start spending your share of the reward. I doubt we'll see so much as a piastre. The best we can hope for is that Feisal will keep his job and I will remain a free man."

"Tsk, tsk," said Schmidt. "I am surprised at you, John. It is not like you to be so pessimistic. The Herr Director General is also over a barrel. He cannot collect that large sum in so short a time unless he informs his superiors in the government of the situation. That is the last thing he wants to do. He would be the scapegoat, be assured of that. He might take others down with him, but he would be the first to fall."

"You have a point," John admitted, looking marginally more cheerful.

The car stopped in front of the hotel and an attendant started unloading our suitcases. Our rooms were ready—*natürlich*. Strutting, Schmidt led the way to his suite.

"I have a point too," I said, dropping into a chair. I'd been brooding about it ever since that interview with Ashraf. I would have brought it up before if anybody had let me get a word in.

"Proceed," said Schmidt, investigating the minibar.

"Didn't it strike you that there was no either/or in that message? Deliver the money, or . . . What? You get another chunk of Tut?"

"Don't say that," Feisal muttered, flinching.

"Why not?" All of a sudden I was hopping mad. "All this fuss and furor over a damned mummy! He's a dead man, Feisal, a very, very dead man."

"A dead king," Feisal said softly.

"Dead man, dead king, what's the difference? If that hand had been lopped off a living person, king or commoner, I'd say we spare no effort to get him out alive and in as few pieces as possible. Hell, I'd do the same for a dog or a cat."

"She is very tender-hearted, our Vicky," said Schmidt, offering me a beer.

I pushed his hand away. "Shut up, Schmidt, I haven't finished. Frankly, I don't give a damn about Tut or any other mummy. I'm not willing to risk my neck or any of your necks, for him—for it."

The other three exchanged glances. I had no difficulty interpreting them: You know how women are, let her get it out of her system.

"Your moral position is unassailable," said Schmidt. "But look at it this way, Vicky. No one has been killed or violently attacked. The case has been remarkably free of bloodshed."

"So far."

"Does this mean you're pulling out?" John asked.

"In your dreams," I said, as I grabbed the beer from Schmidt and took a swig.

I was surprised to see how little time had elapsed; the interview with Khifaya had seemed to last for hours. After we had refreshed ourselves with various beverages, we got to work catching up with our correspondence, verbal and written. It didn't take me long to get through my messages, since Schmidt, my most faithful (read "persistent") communicant, was with me. Feisal fired off a few forceful directions in Arabic, presumably to various subordinates, and turned to John, who was brooding over his mobile.

"Anything of interest?" he asked nervously.

"Not with regard to the present situation. However, if I get out of this I may yet have a business to run. Perlmutter wants a look at the Amarna head."

"Did you give him your number?" I asked.

"No, this call was from Alan. Perlmutter contacted him—the business number, rather. He says he's already forwarded a photo."

"You've done the lad an injustice," I said. "He seems to be doing his job. Why don't you call him back and administer a few pats on the back?"

"He talks too much. I'll text him." John's fingers glided over the keys.

"What Amarna head?" Feisal said.

"That's no concern of yours or Ashraf's. I didn't steal it and I have the papers to prove it."

"I was just asking," Feisal said in a hurt voice.

"Hmph," said John.

"Anything from Jen?" I asked.

"She wants to know where I am and why I haven't been in touch. I'd better ring her, otherwise she might go haring off to London." He met my eye, grimaced, and said, "Later. What have you got, Schmidt?"

"Like your esteemed mother, Suzi asks where I am. I have waited to consult you before replying."

"Tell her you've gone to New York or Buenos Aires," Feisal suggested.

"No, no," John said. "She's bound to find out the truth sooner or later and we don't want your credibility damaged. Let's invent a nice fictitious account of your investigations."

We all joined in. As I might have expected, Schmidt had long since got over his fit of remorse and was enjoying himself hugely. We shot down several of his more outrageous plot ideas, including one in which John and I had dived into the Nile to save him after some unknown villain pushed him in.

"But it will indicate your innocence," Schmidt said, pouting.

"It will indicate that you are a bloody liar," said John. "How about this?"

After a few more suggestions, Schmidt produced something along these lines: "They continue to trust me. So far no suspicious encounters, only normal contacts. Will inform at once of any such, as well as our next destination."

He refused to add "Love."

We decided to let Ashraf dangle awhile longer. "One never knows what may turn up," said Schmidt brightly.

John gave him a hateful look. "If anything turns up, it is likely to be unpleasant. However, I don't want him to think he has only to snap his fingers to make me jump."

"Yes, yes, that is good policy," said Schmidt. "Since we have a few hours to spend, let us visit the museum. I must pay my compliments to my old friend the director."

We went out the back entrance of the hotel and walked across the street to the museum entrance. Feisal had talked Schmidt out of pocketing one of his purchases—a toy AK-47 that looked horribly like the real thing. Security at the museum was tight; we had to go through one line to get into the grounds, and another inside the museum.

The director had left for the day. After exchanging compliments with the guard, Schmidt led the way back into the museum proper. The skylights high overhead were crusted with dirt, the exhibit cases smeared and dusty; mammoth statues and huge stone sarcophagi were crammed into too small a space. Despite its admitted inadequacies, the Cairo Museum—or, to give it its proper name, the Egyptian Museum of Cairo—has a fin de siècle charm that makes modern museums look cold and sterile. We stood in the rotunda discussing what we should see.

"Tutankhamon's treasures?" Schmidt said. "That part of the museum is always very crowded, but perhaps it would stimulate our ambition, *nicht wahr?*"

Feisal made a rude noise.

"I don't care, so long as it isn't a mummy," I said. "My God, that was gruesome. It really is Tut, isn't it? There can't be a mistake?"

"No," Feisal said flatly.

"The little sarcophagus of Prince Thutmose's cat?" Schmidt proposed. "You would like that, Vicky. It is very charming."

John said he couldn't think of anything that interested him less than a cat's coffin. He was in a foul mood, twitching every time someone passed close to us, and I was about to propose that we call the sightseeing off and go back to the hotel when a woman's voice rose high and clear over the medley of languages around us.

"Feisal! Feisal, here I am!"

Feisal spun round. She came trotting toward him, weaving a path through the visitors and waving her arms. Perfect white teeth gleamed in the delicate oval of her face; hair black as the proverbial raven's wing caressed her cheeks. Feisal stood as inanimate as the nearby statue of Ramses II until she caught hold of his shoulders and kissed him resoundingly on both cheeks.

"Why didn't you tell me you were going to be here?" she demanded.

"I thought—uh—you said you wouldn't be at the museum today," Feisal said feebly.

"And you said you were going to Luxor." She patted him on the cheek. "Liar! But I forgive you. Will you present me to your friends?"

"But I know you," Schmidt exclaimed. "We met in New York at the International Congress. You gave an excellent paper on the mummification techniques of the Nineteenth Dynasty."

"And who could forget Herr Doktor Professor Schmidt?" She brushed aside the hand he offered, and kissed him on both cheeks. "*Verzeihen Sie, Herr Doktor*, I did not see you at first."

Schmidt presented us. John was the only peasant who didn't rate the title of doctor. Our newfound friend was Dr. Saida Qandil, author of a seminal work on . . . I'll give you three guesses. She kissed me on both cheeks too. She had to stand on tiptoe. I felt like a big blond ox, the way I always feel around cute little women. I suffered the greeting in a state of numb disbelief. Of all the women in Egypt with whom Feisal could fall in love, it had to be an expert on . . .

"Have you just come? What would you like to see? I will show you around."

"Haven't you got work to do?" Feisal asked.

"No, no, not when friends are here." She gave him a look that could have melted granite. "The Royal Mummies, perhaps? The new room has been finished, you will be impressed at what has been done. Temperature-controlled cases, proper lighting."

The dream image I had had of Tutankhamon laid out on a bed in an air-conditioned hotel suite flashed onto my brain. I drew a dark mental curtain over it.

"I'm not really crazy about . . . mummies," I said. The word stuck in my throat.

"Be a sport," John said. He had been kissed on both cheeks too, and he had obviously enjoyed it. "I would like very much to see the technical advances you've made in dealing with such remarkable objects."

Saida attached herself to Feisal and Schmidt. He kept paying her extravagant compliments which made her emit throaty chuckles. John took me firmly by the arm.

"Get hold of yourself," he hissed.

"But of all the women in the world—"

"Pure coincidence. Mummies, Egypt; Egypt, mummies. The equation is commonplace. If you can't show interest, at least behave like an adult."

Thus chastised, I managed to get a grip. Mummies had never bothered me until now; it was morbid self-consciousness and too damned many dreams about poor battered Tut that had changed my attitude.

It wasn't as bad as I had expected. The room was dimly lit, the cadavers laid out with a certain dignity, with only their faces exposed. One of the effects of the drying process is that the lips pull back, exposing the teeth; a lot of the mummies appeared to be enjoying a hearty laugh—except for the ones who looked as if they were screaming. I was staring down at the noseless face and jolly grin of Thutmose III when Saida edged up to me.

"If it bothers you, don't feel you must stay," she said softly.

"It doesn't bother me at all," I said, with an attempt at insouciance that didn't quite come off. "I just don't understand why people find mummies so fascinating."

"Don't you? Imagine looking upon the actual features of Alexander the Great—of Julius Caesar or King Arthur. Would you be able to resist such an opportunity? These are our kings and great ones, figures from a time so distant they have become legendary." She swept the room with a graceful wave of her arm. "Warriors like Thutmose and Ramses the Great, founders of dynasties. They are all here—except of course for Tutankhamon."

I had been ready for that name, so I didn't react. "You seem somewhat deficient in queens," I remarked.

"Not really. But it is true that there is a gap in the collection which includes many of the most famous royal women—Nefertiti, Hatshepsut, and the wife of Tutankhamon, for example." Her face took on a dreamy look. "I believe they are there in the cliffs of the West Bank, hidden away, awaiting discovery."

"I suppose you'd like to be the discoverer."

"Who would not? But I am not an excavator. I would be called in, perhaps, if human remains were found. But that will not happen soon, there is too much to do to preserve what we already have. We have begun a project to examine all the mummies that are in the museum—there are many, many stored away here. And others in other locations. I would like to see them all brought to the museum."

"All?" I echoed.

Schmidt and John were peering down at a particularly grisly looking specimen—some king who was presumed to have died in battle, with his wounds only too well preserved. His name, I feel no shame in confessing, eludes me.

"Yes, all. Especially Tutankhamon." She extended a dainty forefinger and poked Feisal, who stood nearby. "It is a disgrace that he, the most famous of all our monarchs, the name of all names synonymous with Egypt, is left to rot in that contaminated hole in Luxor. I wish you would speak to Ashraf about it, Feisal."

"I—uh—saw him today," Feisal said.

"You did?" She clapped her hands. "I am so glad. It is time you two made it up. Perhaps you can influence him; he only laughs at me. But now—" She consulted her wristwatch. "We have had enough of mummies, haven't we, Vicky? Let us wash the dust of ages from our throats with an aperitif and decide where we should go for dinner."

I was all in favor of the first part of the agenda. An hour with Saida would have left me limp even if I had not become overly sensitive to the mention of certain words. She fairly crackled with energy.

Tugged along by her arm through mine, I wondered how much Feisal had told her about his past. Did she know about his part in the theft and subsequent retrieval of Tetisheri's tomb? Complete trust between lovers is a beautiful thing, but he was a damned fool if he had confessed all. Would she still love him if she knew he had once planned to help a bunch of crooks steal a great treasure? Would she still adore him if she found out he had lost Tut?

The museum was closing. We dragged Schmidt away from the

bookstore, where a three-foot-high image of the jackal-headed god Anubis had caught his eye, and joined the crowds being shooed out. A row of tourist buses belched exhaust fumes and hawkers of various worthless items closed in on us. As Saida sent them packing with a few well-chosen words, I thought how easy it would be for a would-be assassin to pick off a victim at close range. Any one of the vendors or casual strollers who brushed past us could be carrying a gun. The same had been true in Berlin, though, and in Rome and London. What was the significance of that?

It meant that up until now nobody had wanted to kill one of us. Up until now.

We retired to the comfort of the bar at the hotel, a cozy place with dim lights and soft chairs. Saida flirted indiscriminately with Feisal and Schmidt, but made little progress with John, who seemed even more preoccupied than usual.

"He is your lover, yes?" she inquired, turning to me. "That is nice. Feisal and I have not made love yet. He is very proper. And he is afraid of my father. I tell him there is no reason, Papa is not even in Egypt, he is in Paris. He is a brain surgeon, and my sister is also a medical doctor."

She told her whole life story and expounded her views on marriage, religion, and life in general. "Now you must tell me all about yourself," she said. "I am glad to meet you at last. Feisal has spoken of you often. I was a little jealous!"

"Now you know you needn't have been," I said. "What has he told you about me?"

"That you are a distinguished professor of art history and an official of the National Museum in Munich and a close friend of Herr Doktor Schmidt." She paused invitingly. She had been more than candid with me, and it was hard to resist those big brown eyes and friendly smile, but I remembered one of John's basic rules: Find out how much the other person knows before you let your hair down. Stick to trivia.

So I told her about Clara and Caesar, and my family back in the States, and about my pathetic attempt to crochet a baby cap for my soon-to-be-niece or nephew. She wasn't trying to pump me, I would have bet on that; but she had a way with her, and it was a rare pleasure to gossip with a fellow female with whom I had so much in common. We started swapping funny stories about our work. She told me about the man who had entered her office at the museum carrying a huge wreath of flowers, and asked if he might put it on the coffin of one of the anonymous female mummies. She had been his mother in a former incarnation, he had explained, and she had been haunting him demanding attention. I countered with the story of a visitor whom we found in the torture room trying to get into the Iron Maiden. He kept yelling, "I have sinned, I have sinned," as the horrified guards dragged him away.

"And then there was the time . . ." I said.

"Excuse me, ladies." John, who had seemed to be engrossed in chitchat with Schmidt, turned toward us. "We were discussing where to go for dinner. Feisal said you could recommend a restaurant, Saida."

"Yes, there is one not far from here. I will telephone."

We had to cross Tahrir Square, which was an adventure I hope not to repeat with any frequency. There are a dozen lanes of traffic, none of which obeys any discernible rules. Saida took charge of Schmidt, who had probably had too much beer; I heard his loud chuckles as she guided him across with the skill of a matador sidestepping the horns of the bull. The rest of us followed, less skillfully, but as Feisal pointed out, nobody really wanted to run into us; it would have delayed them.

"Shouldn't you call Ashraf?" Feisal asked.

"Not until we get rid of your girlfriend," John said.

Feisal gave him a hurt look. "Don't you like her?"

"I adore her. Be polite. But get rid of her."

Saida and Schmidt would have made a night of it if John hadn't mentioned that we had to get up early to catch our flight. I almost said, "What flight?"

"What flight?" Schmidt asked.

"Luxor," John said. "Dear me, you are getting forgetful, Schmidt. It's time you were in bed. Come along quietly."

Feisal insisted on taking Saida home. "I won't be long," he promised.

"Ha," said Schmidt. "Were I in your place, I would not come back at all."

We subdued Schmidt. The walk back, and a few hairbreadth escapes crossing the square, sobered him up enough to be sensible, but he could not stop singing Saida's praises.

"A wonderful young woman. Feisal is lucky to have won her heart. We must attend the wedding. Will it be soon, do you think?"

"There may not be a wedding if we can't get Feisal and ourselves out of this mess," I said.

Feisal was true to his word. He got to the hotel only half an hour after we did.

"I had a hard time getting away," he reported.

"Ach so," said Schmidt, leering genteelly.

"She wanted to come to Luxor with us," Feisal went on, ignoring the leer.

"Just what we need," I said. "An expert on mummies with a particular interest in Tutankhamon following us around. Feisal, how much does she know about the Tetisheri affair?"

"You might call it an expurgated version," Feisal said wryly. "A lot of people knew about the retrieval of the paintings, and my part in it. I was appointed to my present job because of my heroism, and over the heads of a lot of people who thought they had a better claim to it."

"I bet you described our mad dash to Cairo, with innumerable villains hot on our trail," I suggested.

Feisal grinned self-consciously. "She led me on. You know how it is."

"You were a hero," I said, patting him on the arm. "So nothing about your initial involvement—or John's?"

"Good God, no. And if she ever finds out . . ."

"She won't," John said impatiently. "If you keep your mouth shut. I trust you talked her out of coming with us?"

"Yes. Have you spoken with Ashraf yet?"

"I guess I've left him dangling long enough. Hang on."

We could hear only John's end of the conversation, but it wasn't hard to fill in the intervening lines.

"We accept your proposition . . .

"I know. I assure you, we won't waste any more time . . .

"Tomorrow. We would appreciate it if you would make arrangements. In view of the fact that our earlier flight was—er—canceled . . ."

He was silent for a while, listening. His expression didn't change much—nothing so obvious as a raised eyebrow—but I knew the outlines of his features well enough to know he'd heard something he didn't like.

"Very well," he said and snapped the cell phone shut.

"What?" Schmidt demanded. "What did he say?"

"He'll see that we catch the ten-thirty flight tomorrow. He'll send his car for us and make reservations at the Winter Palace."

"The Old Winter Palace, I trust," said Schmidt, still feeling no pain. "The New is not acceptable. I had better call and reserve my usual—"

"Shut up, Schmidt," I said. "I mean, please shut up. Something's gone wrong. What's happened, John?"

"The guard, Ali—the only one except Feisal who saw that empty coffin. He's disappeared."

EIGHT

Next morning Ashraf's car delivered us to the terminal and we were whisked through the formalities by an efficient young woman who spoke English with a pronounced public school accent. Once we were on the plane, Feisal said it again.

"He's gone into hiding. Ashraf put the fear of God into him."

I said it again. "That isn't Ashraf's version."

"Oh, I don't doubt he thought he was being affable, but to simple souls like Ali he's the voice of the Almighty, authoritative and unpredictable. Ali may have decided the safest course was to make himself scarce until things settle down."

"Drop it," John said. "We've been over this a dozen times."

And gotten nowhere. Feisal's explanation could be the right one. If I had been in the shoes of the unfortunate guard, I'd have run for cover too.

We were greeted at the Old Winter Palace by the manager, a handsome white-haired gentleman, another of Schmidt's dearest friends, who personally escorted us to the Presidential Suite. It had two bedrooms and two bathrooms, one of which incorporated a tub big enough to do laps in. I could tell by John's expression that he wasn't keen on being separated from Schmidt only by the width of the sitting room, good-sized though it was; but there wasn't anything he could do about it since Schmidt had "forgotten" to reserve another room for us.

After lunch we headed for the West Bank. It's a somewhat tortuous process—taking one of the gaily decorated motorboats across the river, picking up a taxi on the other side, and driving for a considerable distance. I hadn't seen much of Luxor during my last visit, being primarily concerned with avoiding a number of people who bore me ill will. Schmidt had been there many times, but he gaped out the taxi window with that childlike sense of delight that is one of his most charming characteristics, commenting on the changes that had been made and asking questions of Feisal. He didn't get many answers; the closer we got to the Valley of the Kings, the more tense Feisal became. It was with some difficulty that we persuaded him to hop on one of the electric trams that carry visitors to the entrance instead of setting out at a dead run. The sun was high and hot and the air was dusty and I didn't want my chubby little boss to tire himself. Schmidt had decked himself out in one of the white linen suits he had bought in Berlin, and a natty panama hat which I hadn't seen him buy. I wondered what the hell else he had in that overweight suitcase.

The tomb of Tutankhamon is a couple of hundred yards from the entrance to the Valley. I don't know what Feisal had expected, or feared—that the tomb would have vanished along with Ali, or that it had been invaded by importunate tourists—but he let out a long sigh of relief when the rectangular opening came into view. It was closed by a heavy iron gate. A party of tourists was talking with the guards—or rather, to judge by their shrill expletives, trying to argue their way in. One of the men was wearing shorts that bared long hairy legs; the women bulged over the necklines of their skimpy T-shirts. When the harassed guard caught sight of Feisal he let out a cry of relief and ran to meet him.

Feisal disposed of the tourists with a few brusque words. They dispersed, sulking and muttering. Arrogant idiots like that have always been with us and probably always will be. I remembered the story of how Howard Carter had lost his job with the Service des Antiquités by defending his guards against the pushy drunks who had tried to force their way into a pyramid at Sakkara.

After an animated discussion with the guard, Feisal said, "Ali didn't turn up for work yesterday. Mohammed here went to his house to inquire about him; his wife claimed he hadn't come home the night before. I'm going to see her."

"All in good time." Hands in the pockets of his jeans, John gazed thoughtfully at the dark entrance to the tomb. "Can we get in?"

"Why?" Feisal asked.

"The scene of the crime," John reminded him. "I know you're worried about your subordinate, but I should think you'd want to make certain it hasn't been disturbed."

"Yes, that is the correct procedure," said Schmidt. "I have brought a camera to record the clues."

"Good thinking, Schmidt," I said.

"And a notebook and pen." Schmidt thrust them into my hands. I ought to have known I'd be appointed secretary. I thrust them back into Schmidt's hands.

I have been accused by some (John) of learning all my history, except that which pertains to my own limited field, from popular novels. I had read a couple of reports about the discovery of this tomb, including that of Howard Carter himself; it's almost as exciting as fiction. But I will admit that the version I remembered best was in a novel by some woman whose name I couldn't recall. It claimed to be based on actual journals by actual eyewitnesses. I had never bothered to check her facts. Why should I, it wasn't my field.

The last (and first) time I had called on King Tutankhamon, the tomb had been open to tourists. Today, everything looked the way it had before: the massive stone sarcophagus and its heavy glass cover smeared with dust and fingerprints, the golden shape inside. Schmidt stopped me with a warning shout when I was about to proceed into the small tomb chamber. From his pockets he extracted not only a digital camera but a large magnifying glass.

"The lighting is not good," he complained, bending stiffly and squinting through the glass. "Has anyone a torch?"

"No, nor a fingerprint kit," said John.

"Then we must get one." Schmidt increased his angle of inclination, with imminent danger to the seat of his trousers.

"You'll find hundreds of prints," Feisal said. "Mine and Ali's—"

"And those of the miscreants who removed the king." Schmidt straightened and waved the magnifying glass. "Perhaps some of them are in the files of Interpol or another agency."

"To which we have no access," John said patiently. "Go ahead, Feisal. Don't bother looking for footprints, just see if there is anything unusual, anything that is out of place."

"Bloodstains," said Schmidt, his eyes gleaming.

"Shut up, Schmidt," I said. "Please."

The floor wasn't clean. In addition to the dust, there were bits and pieces, scraps of paper and bread crumbs, orange seeds and a pile of mouse droppings. Most of them had been there for weeks, if not months. Schmidt photographed every square inch of the damned place—the dusty floor, the painted walls, the sarcophagus and its contents. After I came across the mouse droppings I abandoned the hunt and joined Feisal, who stood looking down into the sarcophagus.

The golden face, with its beautiful inlaid eyes, stared up at me. It didn't question or demand. It was dead, inanimate. Feisal, fingers clenched over the edge of the glass, said suddenly, "I keep thinking he's still in there."

If you want to hide something, put it in the least likely place, a place that has already been searched, a place so obvious, no one would think of looking there.

I read too many mystery stories. But there was a certain insane logic to that premise; hadn't John said it would be difficult to smuggle Tut out of the Luxor area? What if "they" had come and put him back? Once the ransom was paid, they wouldn't have to risk producing the mummy, they would just have to direct the searchers to the tomb. And what if Ali was the only witness to their second visit? He had disappeared. He couldn't bear witness to anything.

"If he's there, he's missing a hand," I said, trying to convince myself of the absurdity of the idea. "Uh—can you tell whether the coffin lid has been moved since you and Ali put it back?"

Unfortunately Schmidt overheard the question. I say unfortunately because he has an imagination even more lunatic than mine and a greater familiarity with sensational fiction.

"Aha!" he shrieked. "The old Purloined Letter trick! Brilliant, Vicky, brilliant!"

There was no restraining him, and by that time I had half-convinced myself. Even with four of us it was a tricky job manipulating the glass cover and the coffin lid; I couldn't imagine how Feisal and Ali had managed it. Sheer desperation, I supposed. Feisal kept repeating, "Be careful! Don't damage it!"

"Get a grip," John said impatiently. "Pun, deliberate. You can blame any damage on the thieves. Ready? Lift, shift and lower. One, two . . ."

We didn't have to shift the lid far. It was dark down in there; Feisal slid his hand through the gap, which I wouldn't have done, and felt around. His face fell.

"No."

"Are you sure?"

"Yes."

"It was a preposterous idea," John said.

"But it had to be done," Schmidt said.

"Quite so. Leave no stone unturned, no coffin lid unlifted. I see no point in moving it back, do you?"

He addressed Feisal, who shook his head. "If anyone gets this far, we're lost anyhow. Just replace the glass so it doesn't fall and break."

Just, he said. We got the job done, though I pulled something in my shoulder, and Schmidt mashed a finger. Our first casualty, I thought, as I wound a hankie round his hand. Schmidt rather enjoys being wounded in the course of battle; he nobly refused my suggestion that we return to the hotel for more extensive first aid.

"We must go at once to the house of the poor guard and question his wife," he insisted.

"There's no need for you to come with me," Feisal said. "You should get that finger cleaned up, Schmidt, it's only too easy to get an infection here."

"It has bled freely," said Schmidt, admiring the stained hanky. "You will want witnesses, Feisal, and persons skilled in interrogation. Vicky will take notes."

Feisal locked the gate and switched off the lights. We made our way back to the entrance; Feisal hailed a taxi, and I asked, "Don't you rate a car and driver?"

"I rate an ancient Jeep. It's in the shop. It usually is."

From his sour tone I figured he was thinking of Ashraf's upholstered limo and squadron of assistants.

The road led back the way we had come, toward the boat landing. Having failed to force notebook and pen into my hands, Schmidt was trying to make notes. Considering the state of the road and the taxi's springs, I doubted he would be able to decipher his scrawled writing, but it kept him busy and happy. The scenery was monotonous in the extreme, stretches of barren earth reaching back to equally barren cliffs—all shades of tan and brown, with an occasional vivid patch of green. I didn't criticize, since I knew I'd be jumped on by the experts, who would start pointing out fascinating heaps of rubble and telling me what they were.

The taxi stopped in front of a cluster of houses that clung to a rocky hillside. They looked like square boxes, randomly placed, but they were the most interesting things my uneducated eyes had seen since we left the Valley. Some of the flat facades were painted shining white or golden yellow or faded blue, some had scenes of people and camels, ships and airplanes, in nonchalant juxtaposition.

"I thought the authorities were moving these people to a new village," said Mr. Know-It-All Schmidt, without looking up.

"They're about to." Feisal got out of the front seat and wrestled with the back door, which had no inside handle. It gave way finally and I got out. "We'll have to walk from here," Feisal went on. "Ali's house is farther up, near the tomb of Ramose."

"It is a pity," Schmidt said. "They have lived here for centuries."

"And earned a good living robbing the tombs under the houses," Feisal said. "I know, Schmidt, the place is picturesque as hell, and the Gurnawis have fought the move tooth and nail, but it has to be done."

It was picturesque, if you don't mind a lot of dust and stray dogs and barefoot children pestering innocent tourists. Some tried to peddle hideously fake scarabs and small figurines, others just demanded baksheesh. Feisal yelled at them in Arabic. Some of them backed off; the bolder ones circled us and came in from the rear. Schmidt stopped and dug in his bulging pocket. First he produced the magnifying glass, which inspired gasps of longing from the kids. One of them, a skinny boy wearing a ragged T-shirt, reached out. Feisal swatted his hand away.

"Don't give them anything, Schmidt; they have to learn not to beg. That's one of the reasons why we're moving them; tourists complain about being hassled."

"They are poor," Schmidt said. "If you had so little, would you not beg?"

He put the magnifying glass back and came up with a handful of ballpoint pens. They were obviously popular substitutes for cash. The distribution process got a little agitated, with the bigger youngsters snatching from the little ones, and Schmidt in the thick of the melee, scolding and snatching back. A wave of affection swept over me as I watched him. He was a soft-hearted pushover. If there were more like him, the world wouldn't be such a sad place.

Finally Feisal dispersed the young villains with a roar. A few ran on ahead. By the time we reached Ali's house, our arrival had been announced.

The summer temperatures in Egypt hover around one hundred degrees Fahrenheit. The houses have thick walls and small windows to keep out the heat, and the room seemed pitch-black after the blinding brightness outside. As my eyes adjusted I saw that the room was packed with people, mostly women and children, some seated on a low cushioned divan along the side wall, some squatting on the floor. The shadowy forms and bright unblinking eyes were a little uncanny. How long had they been sitting there, unmoving as statues? They couldn't have known we were coming. I got a grip on myself. Obviously our arrival had been announced even earlier than I'd thought, probably the moment Feisal got out of the taxi.

One of the women stood up and greeted Feisal. I recognized the formal *"Salaam aleikhum,"* to which Feisal responded. He knew better than to cut the formalities short; we were offered seats on the divan and glasses of steaming tea and a plate of sweet biscuits. I got a place next to the woman who had welcomed us. Surely she couldn't be Ali's wife. Women wore out fast, but her face was as withered as those of the better-looking mummies in the museum. She was enveloped in black, head, arms, and body—the traditional garb of the previous generation, which most modern women have modified or abandoned—and when she smiled at me and spoke, I saw she was missing most of her teeth. But the eyes, half-hidden by sagging lids, were as bright and piercing as those of a bird of prey.

"This is Umm Ali," Feisal said. "Ali's mother. Drink your tea, Vicky, she asked if you would prefer something else."

I would have risked blistering my fingers rather than offend, but in the nick of time I remembered the technique—thumb under the thick glass of the bottom, fingers steadying the rim. I nodded vigorously at the old lady, bared my teeth in a grin, and sipped. The tea was strong and very sweet. Cavities, here I come, it proclaimed.

I was the last to do my duty. As soon as I had done so, Feisal launched into a series of questions. Umm Ali responded. I couldn't understand a word, so I tried to figure out which of the other women was Ali's wife, nodding and smiling as my gaze met one pair of brown or black eyes after another. One woman, veiled as well as swathed, had eyes of a paler shade; she ducked her head shyly when I looked at her. To judge by her attire, she was too old to be the wife, but what did I know? Mama was obviously the one in charge. The others were probably part of an extended family, which could include sisters and aunts and even more-distant relatives. They didn't say a word. A couple of the men present joined in after a while, adding brief comments, but deferring, as the women had done, to the matriarch. From the back part of the house I heard a donkey bray and a duck quack. A chicken wandered into the room, its head cocked in that deceptive look of intelligence chickens have, and tried to get up on my lap. I pushed it off and smiled apologetically at the woman on my left, hoping I had not been rude. I have nothing against chickens except for the fact that they are not housebroken.

Rejected, the chicken approached John. I hoped it would hop up on him, but something in his frozen glare must have penetrated even its feeble chicken brain. It backed off. I had finished most of my tea and was feeling strangely comfortable; the animal sounds and smells took me back to the days of my childhood on my family's farm in Minnesota, where I learned to love the scent of a well-manured garden.

Feisal broke the mood, addressing me directly. "I don't suppose you understood any of that. Sorry about the chicken," he added.

"No problem. Would I be rude to ask for more tea?"

"Yes," John said firmly.

"No," Feisal said. "But we shouldn't spend more time here. I'll explain after we—"

"I have a question," Schmidt said.

"Later, Schmidt."

"But I—"

"Not now!" Feisal's voice rose. It was his first display of emotion, but I realized he had been holding himself in tight control the whole time.

The concluding formalities took almost as much time as the initial ceremony, but after repeated *"shukrans"* and *"maasalamas"* we edged ourselves out. An escort of children followed us down the hillside to the taxi.

"What was in that tea?" John demanded of me. He brushed a few feathers off his sleeve. "You looked as if you were prepared to squat there indefinitely."

"I was having a nice time," I said dreamily. "They were all so nice. It was a nice chicken."

John gave up on me. "Never mind the bloody chicken; what did they say?"

"They believe he is dead," Schmidt said soberly. "The poor mama asked us to find his body so he can receive a proper burial."

Feisal closed his mouth with an audible snap. "Why don't you go ahead and repeat everything that was said? I wasn't aware your Arabic was that good."

Schmidt realized he had offended, though he didn't know why. "I have been studying," he said humbly. "I understood that much, but not all. I am sorry."

"No, I'm sorry." Feisal shook his head. "I'm a little on edge. If they're right, it's my fault."

According to what Mama had told Feisal, the family had no proof of foul play, but the signs weren't encouraging. Never once had Ali failed to return home after his hours of work. Never once had he stopped at a coffee shop or spent time gossiping with friends. Never once had he taken a trip without telling his mother where he was going and for how long.

"Does he tell the old lady everything?" I asked.

"Wouldn't you?"

"Damn right," I said, remembering those beady black eyes.

"Not everything, I hope," John said.

"Not about the—er—theft," Feisal amended.

"That is what I wanted to ask," Schmidt said.

"I don't think so. I couldn't ask directly. She said something had been worrying him, he had been short-tempered and moody for days, but when she asked, he said nothing was wrong. Then, day before yesterday, he came home looking—I quote—'as if he had seen a vision of Paradise.' Great things were in store for him, for all of them."

"He'd spoken with Ashraf," John said.

"That would be my guess. Why isn't this damned taxi moving?"

"Maybe because you haven't told him where you want to go," I suggested.

The sun was setting behind us as we sailed back across the river. Feisal had allowed as how he ought to check in with his office, which was near the Luxor Museum on the East Bank and go to his flat to change before joining us for dinner. I figured I ought to have a look at Schmidt's wounded finger, which he was exhibiting in an unintentionally (I think) vulgar gesture.

It wasn't broken, just scraped and bruised; with the first-aid kit Schmidt produced from his magic suitcase I cleaned the digit and wound enough bandages around it to satisfy him. We joined John on the balcony, where he was mumbling into his cell phone. I sat as far from him as I could get and enjoyed the view. The river was ablaze with reflected light and the western cliffs had turned a soft shade of purple. Gorgeous as the view was, I couldn't recapture the relaxed mood I had enjoyed for too brief a time. Not without a chicken.

I had allowed nostalgic memories to distract me because I didn't want to think about our reason for being there—about the possibility that the guard's body might be lying in a shallow grave somewhere in the sand of the West Bank. We'd hashed and rehashed theories all the way back. Had Ali, after all, decided to go into hiding? Possible, but not likely, considering his mother's testimony as to his habits and mood. Had he seen or heard something during the robbery without realizing at the time that it was important? Plausible, but that opened up a whole list of other unanswerable questions. When had it dawned on him that he had vital information, and what had he done about it? Would he have approached the thieves and tried to blackmail them? Supposing they were responsible for his disappearance, how else could they have found out he had to be silenced?

John finished his conversation and addressed Schmidt. "Ashraf claims Ali said absolutely nothing to him that would indicate he had new information."

"But how closely did he question Ali?" Schmidt demanded. "Did Ashraf perhaps ask a question or make a statement that triggered a forgotten memory in the mind of the poor fellow?"

"Do you suppose I neglected to ask him that?" John demanded. "If he did, he has no idea what it might have been. You can sit here drinking beer and concocting scenarios all you like, but it won't get us anywhere."

The sunset colors had faded into rose and gray and the voices of the muezzins had died into silence. John's voice had that ugly edge that always rubs me the wrong way. "So what are you doing to get us somewhere?" I inquired. "Not a damn thing that I can see. Time is running out and you—"

John jumped up and headed for the door. "I'm going out. Try not to do anything stupid."

"I thought you told us not to wander around alone," I shouted after him.

The slam of the outer door was my only answer.

"He said *you* were not to go about alone," said Schmidt.

He was the only one left, so of course I picked on him. "Is that what he told you? 'Poor dumb Vicky, she doesn't have the sense of a chicken; do try to prevent her from getting in trouble.'"

Schmidt said, "Tsk, tsk," and sipped his beer.

I took a few deep breaths. "Okay, I apologize. But what I said was true. We aren't getting anywhere. The mastermind isn't doing his job."

"Then perhaps," said Schmidt hopefully, "I should be the mastermind."

"You've got my vote, Schmidt."

"Good. The light is fading; let us go inside and make a plan."

We retired to the sitting room and turned on all the lights. Schmidt opened two more beers and indicated the notebook and pen, which just happened to be strategically placed on the coffee table. I took them. Schmidt began to lecture.

The good ol' boy does have a logical mind. We started with the assumption that Tut was still somewhere in the Luxor area, since the alternative—that he wasn't—meant that he could be anyplace in the world. One of the avenues we hadn't explored was an effort to track the van, but as Schmidt pointed out, that was probably a dead end. Ali had told Feisal the vehicle wasn't the enormous van that had come the first time, but something about the size of a large bus. It probably was a large bus or truck, disguised by panels painted with appropriately mysterious symbols. All the thieves needed was a quiet spot off the road, where the panels could be removed and destroyed. The vehicle, now undistinguished and unnoticeable, would then proceed to . . .

There are a thousand hiding places in the cliffs of the West Bank—caves, abandoned tombs, clefts in the rock. Schmidt insisted the thieves wouldn't put their precious cargo in a place which involved so many risks, from rockfalls to discovery by wandering fellahin. Not to mention the conspicuousness of a large bus heading back into the hills on tracks designed for goats.

"A residence" was the new mastermind's conclusion. "Not a hotel, for obvious reasons, but an environment that can be controlled to some extent, away from extreme heat and dusty air and wandering animals."

"It makes sense," I admitted, impressed by his argument. "Are you sure you didn't do it, Schmidt?"

Schmidt chuckled. "It is all surmise," he said modestly. "But at least it provides us with a starting point."

"Right. Every private house in Luxor and environs."

Darkness hovered at the window. Across the river, lights began to twinkle. I had been dutifully taking notes, but I'd also been listening. When a knock sounded at the door I jumped up and ran to open it.

The well-crafted diatribe I had composed died in my throat. The newcomer wasn't John. It was Feisal.

"Oh," I said.

"Good to see you too," said Feisal. He looked around. "Where's Johnny?"

Schmidt giggled. He is only too well acquainted with American pop culture, past and present. "Never mind," I said, as Feisal gave him a blank stare. "John went out a while ago. He hasn't come back."

"Where did he go?"

"He didn't say."

"You had a fight," said Feisal, enlightened. "I've been expecting it."

"He is, no doubt, exploring new avenues of investigation," said

Schmidt, dividing a look of reproach between me and Feisal. "We have been doing the same. Would you like to hear our deductions?"

Feisal went to the minibar and got out a bottle of some fizzy nonalcoholic lemon drink. I had tried it; it was quite revolting. "Go ahead," he said.

When Schmidt finished, Feisal shook his head. "Fine, as far as it goes. But do you know how many private houses and villas and flats there are in the area? We can't just bang on people's doors and demand entry."

"So we will have to narrow the possibilities by logical deduction," said Schmidt. "Have you any suggestions, Feisal?"

Feisal drained the bottle. "Not offhand."

"What about you?" I asked. "Anything new at the office?"

"Only a dozen messages from various subdirectors, reporting suspicious activities and/or illegal encroachment onto protected sites and/or . . ."

He went on for a while. I had stopped listening, straining my ears for the sound of footsteps or the turn of a key in the lock. Nothing. Surely he'd have got over his fit of the sulks by now.

Schmidt nudged me and I realized he was waiting for an answer to a question I hadn't heard. Observing my vacuous look, he repeated it.

"Are you ready for dinner? Feisal has recommended a restaurant."

"Shouldn't we wait for John?" I asked.

"He'll turn up when he's good and ready," Feisal said. "I'm getting hungry."

At my suggestion, Feisal left a message for John telling him where we'd gone, and I allowed myself to be escorted out of the hotel. Fending off importunate drivers of taxis and carriages, we walked along the corniche past the Luxor Temple. The giant columns glimmered pale gold against the darkness.

"Ah, it is open tonight," Schmidt said. "Shall we go in?"

I was about to say no when I saw someone heading toward the entrance. He was surrounded by other would-be visitors of all sizes, shapes, and modes of dress, but the light glowed off a head of fair hair. The sight of him, engaged in a casual bit of sightseeing after he'd left me to worry, brought my mounting anger to a boil.

"There he is!" I exclaimed. Pulling my arm from Feisal's grasp, I ran after John. Feisal yelled at me to stop, and one of the ticket-takers tried to intercept me. I did a quick end around run past the latter, but by the time I reached the great pylon, John was nowhere in sight. Panting and swearing, I was about to enter the temple proper when Feisal caught up with me.

"What do you think you're doing?" he demanded, taking firm hold of me.

"Didn't you see him?"

"Who?"

Schmidt came puffing up. "Vicky, you must not run off that way."

"It was John," I said. "He went into the temple."

"You must have been mistaken," Feisal said.

"No! I saw . . ."

What had I seen, really? What I wanted to see, what I hoped to see?

"So long as we are here, we will enter and look round," Schmidt said, in the soothing voice he would have used to a whiny toddler.

It was pointless, hopeless, and a waste of time. I knew that even before we passed between the giant statues of some Ramses or other and entered the great open court. The place was vast, with dozens of huge columns and doorways and statues and side chapels, all ideal hiding places for a man who wanted to avoid attention, and with perhaps a hundred people wandering in and out and back and forth. Several of the men had fair hair.

"*Sehr interessant,*" said Schmidt, stroking his mustache. "*Sehr schön.* The most beautiful temple in Egypt, some have—"

"You don't have to be tactful, Schmidt," I snarled. "So I was wrong. Let's go."

The restaurant had a courtyard which looked peaceful and pleasant in the glow of lanterns. A small fountain played in the center, and sitting at one of the tables was John.

Rising and holding a chair for me, he said, "Finally! I've been here some time."

"Where were you?" I inquired very politely.

"Strolling. I stopped at one of the shops round the corner." He handed me a small parcel. I unwrapped it, and found a pair of silver earrings shaped like cats' heads.

It was meant as a peace offering, but I wasn't ready to forgive and forget. "I thought I saw you going into Luxor Temple," I said.

After an infinitesimal pause, John raised an eyebrow. "So that's what took you so long. I presume Schmidt had to inspect every corner of the place."

"I was not inspecting, I was enjoying an aesthetic experience," said Schmidt.

Feisal ordered for us and Schmidt decided to have another Stella. I said, "Schmidt and I have worked out a plan of operation."

"Have you indeed?" This time both eyebrows went up. "May I hear it?"

Schmidt was happy to oblige. "It only remains," he finished, "to narrow down the possibilities."

As I might have expected, John proceeded to demolish our arguments. "What makes you suppose they would worry about a controlled environment? He's been in that tomb for more than three thousand years, and for more than eighty of those years he's been exposed to every form of pollutant imaginable. A few more weeks in a hole in a cliff won't hurt him."

"That would mean he's still on the West Bank," I said, unwilling to abandon our nice, neat theory. "How could they transport him back into the cliffs without being seen?"

"On a cart or wagon," John said. "At night. I doubt they care whether he is banged up a bit. They've already lopped off a hand."

Feisal grimaced. "Don't say things like that."

"Well, what do you think?" John asked. "Is there any point in following Schmidt's suggestion?"

"I think it would be a bloody waste of time," Feisal admitted. "Time we don't have. If we had a lead—any faint, feeble lead . . ."

He looked at John, who shook his head. "What about Ali?" he asked.

"I'm sending some men out to look for him tomorrow. It's common knowledge that he's disappeared, and the theory is that he met with an accident back in the cliffs. Even experienced locals do occasionally."

A waiter began distributing plates and bowls around the table. I recognized rice and a stewed vegetable dish consisting primarily of tomatoes. Feisal gestured to me to serve myself, which I did, discovering eggplant, lamb in several incarnations, and lentils. For a while there was no sound except that of Schmidt masticating.

"It looks as if I'll have to make a quick trip to Denderah tomorrow or next day," Feisal went on. "Someone broke into the storehouse there and made off with a granite sarcophagus basin. They've got a suspect, but haven't tracked him down."

"Where could he have hidden such a thing?" I asked. "It must weigh a ton."

"Thereabouts," Feisal agreed. "Farouk is an old hand at this, though. He and his pals stole a statue of Hathor from the temple a couple of months ago, in broad daylight, with hundreds of witnesses watching. It's never been found."

"Maybe we should ask him where he'd have put Tut," I said.

Nobody found this amusing, not even me.

The Curse of the Omnipresent Cell Phone had reached Egypt; throughout the meal they had been beeping and bopping all around us. When one burst into song nearer at hand I looked at Schmidt. "That has to be yours," I said. "Who else would have Johnny Cash?"

"Don't answer it," John ordered. "Let her leave a message."

"You can't be sure it's Suzi," I said.

"If it is, I'd rather Schmidt didn't talk to her before he gives it due consideration."

"And before I have finished my dinner," Schmidt said, scooping the last of the eggplant onto his plate.

"I'd better check my messages," Feisal said, taking out his cell phone. "I told Ali's brother to let me know at once if they heard from him."

I couldn't blame him for clinging to that hope, increasingly unlikely though it seemed. He had several messages, none of which wrung a comment from him until the last. He let out a strangled squawk of horror.

"Oh, no," I said. "Don't tell me Ali is—"

"Not Ali," Feisal muttered. "But it's bad. Very bad. What am I going to do?"

We waited, holding our collective breaths. Feisal's face was haggard. "Saida. She's coming. Tomorrow. She wants to see . . . him."

NINE

Feisal's first impulse was to cut and run for it. "She can't get in the tomb if I'm not here."

"Wanna bet?" I inquired.

Feisal thought it over. "Bloody hell," he said.

"Perhaps," said Schmidt, "we should enlist her aid. She is very intelligent."

"Tell her the truth, you mean?" said Feisal, horrified.

"Out of the question," John said. "Control your lascivious impulses, Schmidt. It's not her intelligence that interests you. You'll have to ring Ashraf, Feisal. He's the only one who can head her off."

"Yes, right." Feisal pushed his chair back and rose. "Let's find a more private spot."

We let Schmidt pay the check and hurried back to the hotel. A turbaned attendant was turning down the beds and putting little foil-wrapped pieces of chocolate on the pillows.

"The service here is very good," Schmidt said, unwrapping his chocolate.

"Too good," John said, roaming restlessly around the sitting room. "Get rid of him, Feisal. Politely."

"Find anything?" I inquired, after John had looked behind the sofa cushions and under the table.

"No. That's the trouble with all this assiduous service, one can't tell whether the place has been searched. Watch what you say to Ashraf, Feisal. Schmidt, you had better report to Suzi."

"I want to hear what Feisal says first," said Schmidt, settling himself on the sofa.

Feisal got through to Ashraf right away. I found this surprising until it occurred to me that Ashraf must be as edgy as we were, and as anxious to stay in touch.

"Put it on speaker," Schmidt said, all ears.

"Sorry, my equipment is somewhat primitive," Feisal snapped. "Ashraf? Feisal here. We have a slight problem . . . No, nothing like that . . . No, there's been no news of him. But Saida wants to visit a particular site in the Valley tomorrow, and . . . Yes, that site. Can you . . . Good. No, I'm going to Denderah tomorrow, there has been . . . Oh. If you say so. What? Oh. Are you sure you . . . Oh. You're sure. Right."

"Let me guess," I said brightly. "He'll put Saida off. And you are not going to Denderah."

"Very clever," said Feisal, baring his teeth. "Go on."

"Ashraf is coming to Luxor." I was guessing now, but Feisal's expression of deepening gloom confirmed my hunch. "When?"

"Maybe tomorrow. Next day at the latest. He'll let me know."

"Hmph," said John. "He'll expect progress, won't he?"

"Indubitably."

"Then we must make some progress," said Schmidt, taking out his cell. "What shall I say to Suzi?"

"As little as possible," John said.

I must say, the little rascal was good. After the initial fond greetings, his first question was a coy, "Guess where I am?"

Suzi didn't go in for guessing. She knew. Schmidt's mustache twitched; he chewed on his lower lip as he listened to a fairly lengthy speech. "But, *Liebchen*," he began, "I could not find the opportunity . . ." Another longish interruption. Wrong tack, Suzi, I thought, watching Schmidt stiffen and scowl. "You are wrong to reproach me," he said loudly. "They know no more than you. I would swear to it. We are on the trail of the real perpetrators. If you truly care for me . . ." Listening, he put on a smirk I had learned to know well; Suzi had decided to be conciliatory. Too late, had she but known. Then Schmidt let out a bellow. "No! No, you must not do that! You do not trust me! *Ach, Gott!*"

The last fell, it was clear, on deaf ears—the ears of Suzi, at any rate.

"Let me guess," I said. "Suzi is coming to Luxor."

Suzi was stupider than I had believed, or else dangerously confident of her powers of seduction. If I had been in her shoes I'd have begun wondering about Schmidt. She had had sense enough to assure him of her complete trust, and she had promised to stay away from us while she was in Luxor. I didn't believe that promise. It wouldn't be difficult to follow us unobtrusively; Egyptian dress, for men and women both, involves long flapping garments and a variety of concealing headgear. And most men sport beards. Useful things, beards. Suzi was tall enough to pass for a man.

Feisal had declared his intention of heading for the West Bank the next morning to join the search for Ali. After a somewhat acrimonious discussion we decided to join him. Most of the acrimony came from John, who pointed out that we would only be in the way, since we knew nothing about the terrain and weren't in fit condition to climb around the cliffs. Schmidt took this personally and started loping around the sitting room flexing his muscles.

I didn't argue with him. I understood why he wanted to go; action, any kind of action, was better than sitting around stewing and speculating. He even agreed to skip breakfast and head out at sunrise, so we'd have several hours before the heat got too bad.

If Schmidt was going, I was going too. I thought John might try to talk me out of it, but he didn't. Having lost the argument with Schmidt, he retired to our room in high dudgeon (and John's dudgeons are extremely high), leaving me to work out the final details. When I joined him he was already tucked up in bed, reading. He put the book down and held out one elegant, expressive hand. "I'm sorry," he said softly.

It would have been childish to hold a grudge. Besides, the sofa in the sitting room was only five and a half feet long.

Schmidt rousted us out at 6:00 A.M. There was coffee. There was also a heap of square white boxes, the hotel's packed lunch offering. Schmidt delved into one of them as we left the room, and finished a banana before we emerged from the hotel. He had arranged for a car the night before, tactfully refusing Feisal's offer of his Jeep. Schmidt doesn't care for Jeeps, especially the ones that are often in the repair shop. This vehicle was a small van, with plenty of room for us and the lunch boxes. It takes longer to cross the Nile by means of the bridge instead of taking a boat, but Schmidt isn't crazy about gangplanks either, especially the type used by the launches, which are planks about six inches wide. They don't usually wobble, but they look as if they might. Schmidt had been a good sport about the gangplanks the day before, so we tacitly agreed to indulge him this time.

Up front with the driver, Schmidt kept up a running monologue of commentary to which I did not listen. The rest of us didn't talk much. I assumed that John and Feisal, like me, were preoccupied with the ensuing arrivals of a couple of people we didn't want to see. Suzi wasn't answering her phone. Ashraf had ordered Feisal to wait for his call instead of trying to reach him. According to Feisal, Ashraf was not in a good mood early in the morning. It struck me as a very civilized attitude, generally speaking, but I would have given a great deal to be assured that Ashraf had Saida under control. Too damn many people were coming to Luxor. I felt like a nanny in charge of undisciplined children, or a guard single-handedly trying to control a prison break.

The bridge was a grandiose affair, with ornamental statues and posters with enormous portraits of Mubarak. Once on the West Bank, the van headed north, past irrigation canals filled with reeds and garbage. Traffic included carts pulled by morose donkeys, bicycles and motorbikes, people riding morose donkeys, and the occasional tourist bus. Schmidt passed a hard-boiled egg back to me.

"Eat, eat, Vicky. You must keep up your strength for the task ahead."

It turned out to be excellent advice.

Feisal's squad were waiting for us at a predesignated spot, north of the causeway that led from the road to Hatshepsut's temple of Deir el Bahri. The temple is one of the most popular tourist spots on the West Bank, but it was still early, and tourists were not yet in evidence.

Feisal gathered the group round him and began talking and gesturing. It appeared to be a group of volunteers rather than an official squad; clothing ranged from the black uniforms of the security police to jeans and T-shirts, to the standard galabiyas and head cloths; ages ranged from graybeards to kids who could have been as young as ten. He finished with a final wave of his arm, and the men started off in various directions. Two of the youngsters squatted down on the ground, waiting for further orders.

"Might one inquire as to your plan?" John asked. "Supposing you have one."

"I can't think of any good reason why I should explain to you," Feisal said.

John raised one eyebrow. Feisal's emphatic black brows drew together like small thunderclouds. I had a feeling this was going to be a difficult day, in more ways than one. Feisal was drawn tight as a bowstring, hoping not to find what he feared to find, and John had been in a filthy mood for days.

"Now, now, boys, play nicely," I said.

"I am playing nicely," Feisal growled. "All things considered. As it happens, I do have a plan, which would take too long to explain even if you had the vaguest notion of what I was talking about. You three will be with me. Don't wander off."

He inspected us with a critical eye. I'd seen Feisal under pressure, but never in command, so to speak; he was in his element now, on his own turf, and I had to fight an impulse to stand at attention and salute. I passed inspection; I had had sense enough to wear sturdy, low-heeled shoes and loose clothing, and even a hat. John, hatless and lounging, rated a curt "If you end up with sunstroke, don't expect us to carry you."

Feisal snatched a bottle of water from Schmidt, who was trying to insert it into a water-bottle-shaped bag hung on a hook attached to his belt. There were more hooks and tabs all over his vest, one of those khaki-colored garments with approximately a hundred pockets. All the pockets bulged. Most of the tabs were in use—camera, flashlight, Swiss Army knife, compass, and the magnifying glass, among other objects too numerous to mention.

"Don't load yourself down," Feisal ordered. "Yusuf and Ahman will carry the food and water. Hand over that magnifying glass."

Schmidt clutched it protectively. "Will they give it back?"

Feisal replied with another question. "Do you want to set your pants on fire?"

Schmidt gave the magnifying glass to one of the boys, whose grin did not augur well for the return of same, and we set out.

Don't expect specific details; most of the time I had no idea where I was or where I'd been, much less where I was going. Once we had left the temple and its surroundings behind, there were few conspicuous landmarks, only acres of bare brown sandy ground, undulating indiscriminately, backed by ridges of equally bare cliff. Tracks of paler color rambled here and there, up and down. It was the most indeterminate landscape I had ever seen; I couldn't imagine how a search party could operate efficiently. We went up low hills and down them, stopping every now and then to look down into a hole or crevice. The air was still cool, and so clear you could make out the forms of some of the other searchers, who had fanned out from the starting point. The sun had lifted over the hills of Luxor; pale sunlight spread out before us, brightening the western cliffs.

The farther we went, the tougher the going became. The sun rose higher and the slope became steeper. Even with sunglasses the glare was hard on the eyes. Heaps of loose scree, ranging in size from pebbles to good-sized rocks, had been rolled down by wind and water, piling up at the base of the cliffs and sliding down the hillside. The other searchers were no longer in sight, but every now and then we encountered a local villager on business of his own; more and more frequently we were forced to circumnavigate piles of rock or declivities of varying depths. When we stopped and passed round the water bottles, Schmidt lowered himself carefully onto a boulder. Glancing at his flushed face, Feisal said, "Rest for a few minutes. It's all uphill from here on."

In my opinion it had been pretty much uphill all the way. I accepted a bottle of water from Yusuf, or maybe it was Ahman. The liquid was warm as blood. I shaded my eyes and looked up—straight up. We were getting close to the base of the cliffs, which were for all intents and purposes perpendicular.

"I hope you don't intend to climb those," I said, gesturing. "If you don't mind my asking."

Feisal's tight lips relaxed. "Sorry I was a little brusque back there. I don't mind your asking, but I'm afraid any explanation would be meaningless without a map."

Schmidt coughed. "We are not far from DB 320, is it not so?"

Feisal stared at him, and then let out an actual, genuine laugh. "Touché, Schmidt. Have a sandwich."

"I am already doing so," said Schmidt, who was already doing so. He had extracted one of the lunch boxes from the jealous hands of Ahman, or maybe it was Yusuf.

"Is DB 320 a tomb?" I asked.

"Right. They're numbered, with each area having its own grouping. KV refers to the Valley of the Kings, DB to the Deir el Bahri region."

Even Feisal seemed willing to rest for a while longer. Or maybe he was just reluctant to go on. The cliffs were full of tombs on various levels, not to mention crevices and natural holes. If Ali hadn't disappeared of his own free will, there were only two possibilities:

an accident, in which case he shouldn't be too hard to locate; or foul play and subsequent concealment, in which case his body might be undiscovered for years.

Schmidt directed the boys to pass the lunch boxes around, and to help themselves. Nibbling on a very warm cheese sandwich, I looked out across the landscape. In the distance I could see the green strip of cultivation and a sunlit sparkle on the river beyond the green. Deir el Bahri was out of sight, concealed behind the curve of the cliffs.

"What's that building?" I asked, indicating a structure some distance below. It was constructed of mud brick, the same color as the earth around it; only its rectangular outlines allowed me to make it out.

"Metropolitan House," Feisal answered. "It was once the headquarters of the Metropolitan Museum team; they worked in this area for years. If you're thinking what I think you're thinking, Vicky, forget it. The place isn't abandoned. It's now being used by a Polish expedition.

"And that one?" I asked, indicating another low-slung building.

"It belongs to a British archaeological group, FEPEA. They usually come out in October for six months or so."

"An admirable organization," Schmidt declared. "I have been privileged to visit with them on several occasions. Their archives contain some remarkable material. It should be of particular interest to you, John."

John had been uncharacteristically silent that morning. He remained so, staring at the distant outline of FEPEA headquarters with a remarkably vapid expression. I nudged him.

"Are you all right?"

"What?" He started. "Yes, certainly. Shouldn't we get on with this?"

On we trudged, stopping more and more often to let Schmidt catch his breath. There wasn't an inch of shade even at the base of the bigger boulders; the sun was high overhead. To be honest, I was losing interest in the whole business. How on earth could anyone hope to find one human body in this wilderness? Even the living were diminished by the towering cliffs.

Only once did something happen to shake me out of my fatalistic mood. Rounding a finger of cliff, we saw, projecting from the rubble ahead, an irregular dark shape. It moved slightly, like a feebly gesturing arm.

Feisal dived for the heap of debris and began digging with his bare hands. The rest of us stood frozen until he straightened up and held out a torn scrap of fabric.

"It's from a woman's robe," he said, breathing hard. "Black. Faded."

He and the two boys leveled the heap of rock, though a second glance had indicated it wasn't high enough to have concealed a body. Some careless female had snagged her hem, and not recently. The fabric was so rotted, it tore at a touch.

"That's it," Feisal muttered, wiping his damp forehead with a damp handkerchief. "You three start back. I'll catch you up."

"We cannot abandon Feisal," said Schmidt the indomitable. His face was red and his mustache hung limp with sweat. Even his giant hat hadn't protected him entirely from sunlight reflected up from the surface. Guilt swamped me. I ought to have kept a closer eye on him.

"He'll get along better without us," John said. "I don't think I can go any farther, Schmidt."

He tried to look wan and wilted, which isn't difficult for him. That air of aristocratic ennui serves him well.

Schmidt made clucking noises. "Ach, poor John. We will start back at once."

He detached his compass and Feisal said, "You won't need that, Schmidt, just head straight for FEPEA house and tell your driver to meet you there. He'll know where it is."

Schmidt started collecting his gear. Both boys denied any knowledge of the magnifying glass; while Schmidt was arguing with them I said softly to John, "Well done. You put on a good show of exhaustion."

"It wasn't a show."

Feisal extracted Schmidt's magnifying glass from one of the boys and went on with the boy—Yusuf—in the direction we had taken originally. He was out of sight almost immediately, behind an outthrust spur of rock. We started toward the river, accompanied by Ahman, the other boy, who carried a few remaining bottles of water and the last of the lunch boxes. It was downhill most of the way, but the sun was high overhead and by the time we reached our destination we were all drenched in sweat, except for Ahman, who was as brisk as a goat.

The compound, for such it proved to be, was on the edge of the cultivation. Palm trees and patches of greenery surrounded various structures which were presumably designed for storage and laboratory functions. The main house was a good-sized building, constructed of local mud brick that had been repeatedly patched and repaired, but the design was unusual for that part of the world. A veranda enclosed by screened arches stretched across the front of the house. John tried the door, which was also screened.

"It's unlocked," he said. "Let's get out of the sun. Have a seat."

The shade felt heavenly. The only pieces of furniture on the veranda were a wicker armchair with faded cushions and a rickety table. Empty pots of various sizes stood on the window ledge. Schmidt collapsed onto the chair and whipped out his cell phone. He hadn't been able to reach his driver earlier. This time he succeeded.

"He was in the restroom," he explained, supplying a tidbit of information I didn't need to know. "He will come at once. Let us finish the lunch while we wait, eh?"

John perched on the wide window ledge. I joined him and looked around. "The caretaker hasn't been doing his job," I remarked, indicating the withered vines that had been trained to climb around the arches.

"He comes every week," said Ahman.

It was the first time he had spoken English or given any indication that he understood the language. There's a child among you taking notes, I thought, and scolded myself for falling victim to the unconscious superiority we feel for people of other cultures. I hoped I hadn't said anything rude about him or his country or his relatives.

"Is he by chance your father?" John asked.

"The brother of my father. He is a good man."

I was about to apologize for implying otherwise when I heard a sound at one of the closed windows of the house proper. An apparition met my startled gaze. Standing on its hind legs, scratching vigorously at the pane, was a large fluffy cat, striped in black and gray. Its mouth opened. A faint but peremptory mew penetrated the glass.

John went to the door. The handle turned and the door opened; the cat disappeared from the window and shortly thereafter marched out, bristling with indignation. Spotting the sandwich Schmidt was holding, it headed straight for him.

"A beautiful animal," cooed Schmidt, dispensing scraps of chicken.

"Hmmm," said John. "Was it supposed to be shut in the house?"

Ahman replied, from outside the veranda. I hadn't even seen him move. "No."

"What's the matter?" I asked.

"Nothing." He was staring at the cat, the whites of his eyes very much in evidence.

"You aren't afraid of the cat, are you? Who does it belong to?"

Ahman opened the door just wide enough to slip in. "It lives here."

"All the time? Who feeds it when the staff is away?"

"Everyone. It goes where it likes and does as it likes, and when it comes to a house it is given what it likes. People bring food to it."

"Oho," said Schmidt interestedly. "It is a locus genii, then."

Ahman looked bewildered. "A supernatural guardian spirit," I translated.

Tiring of this meaningless commentary, Ahman said, "It is not an ordinary cat. It goes where it likes and—"

"I understand," John said, smiling. "I expect the creature has a den in one of the outbuildings and lives on mice and rabbits."

"And dogs," Ahman said seriously. "The dogs run from it."

I could almost believe it. The animal was huge, a good three feet from the tip of its nose to the end of its enormous tail, which was now raised in feline approval as it finished Schmidt's chicken.

"Someone seems to have fed it recently," John said. He indicated the bowls on the ledge. "They're all empty. Give it some water, Schmidt."

The water was received with the usual feline appreciation; that is to say, the cat condescended to drink.

"It appears it hasn't eaten or drunk since yesterday," John said. "So it must have been shut in the house last night."

He got up and went to the door, which he had left open.

"We shouldn't go in," I said. "Isn't that breaking and entering, or something equally illegal?"

"Just entering," John said. He added, "The cat couldn't have let itself in, which means someone has been here. As good citizens, we are obliged to make certain the place hasn't been robbed."

The central block of the house was devoted to offices and a handsomely appointed library. Bookshelves stretched from floor to ceiling and several tables, equipped with reading lamps, occupied the center of the library. Schmidt went at once to the bookshelves and began reading titles. "It is one of the best Egyptological libraries in the country," he said admiringly. "Here are all the volumes of the Amarna Tombs series, and the *Denkmäler* of Lepsius, and . . ."

I let him ramble on while I inspected the contents of a pair of glass cases flanking the door. Expecting to find precious manuscripts and/or choice artifacts, I was somewhat taken aback to see a smallish, old-fashioned gun, a large knife, and a piece of folded fabric, roughly triangular in shape. The light was poor. I was trying to figure out what on earth it was when John forcibly removed Schmidt from the bookshelves and ordered us into the next room.

It had to be the director's study. The desk was a massive piece of solid mahogany, hand-carved with Egyptian motifs, with crocodile heads forming the drawer handles. Oriental rugs in a glorious medley of colors covered the floor; a table was surrounded by high-backed leather chairs. The chairs showed evidence of being used as scratching posts. The long sofa against one wall was piled with cushions. There was a stone-faced fireplace along the inner wall, for those chilly desert nights, with a pair of crossed swords on the wall above it. It was a wonderful room, dignified and cozy at the same time. Even the filing cabinets were handsome articles of furniture, massive structures of polished wood. I was admiring the effect and wondering where I could get hold of a pair of crossed swords (and a comfy sofa) for my office when I heard a faint sound, no louder than a mouse's scamper. I knew it probably was a mouse but it reminded me that we had no business being in the house.

"Let's go," I said uneasily.

"Yes, the driver is probably waiting," Schmidt agreed. "Come, puss, puss, good puss, you do not want to be locked in again."

The car and driver were there. So was Feisal. One look at him told me we were not about to hop in the car and go home.

"Let me have your camera, Schmidt," he said.

Wide-eyed, Schmidt started fumbling in his pockets. For a few seconds no one spoke. Then John said evenly, "Is he dead?"

"Yes."

"Then he can wait a little longer," John said. "Where, how, and when?"

The flat, almost callous tone was, contrary to expectations, the right one. Feisal replied as flatly.

"We won't know when or how until we get him out. I want to get photographs before we move him. He was at the bottom of a narrow ravine a few hundred yards back from the top of the cliff."

"Can we do anything?" I asked. It was a feeble attempt to convey the sympathy and distress I felt, but something told me not to go any further.

"No. I've rung the police. I tried to reach Ashraf, but he's on his way to Luxor even as we speak. I left a message. You may have to deal with him. Go back to the hotel and wait for me."

Mutely Schmidt offered him the magnifying glass. As a gesture it was perfect: heartfelt and absurd at the same time. Feisal's frozen face cracked into normalcy. "Thanks, Schmidt."

After he had left, covering the ground with long, quick strides, Schmidt and I stood staring helplessly at each other. Neither of us could think of anything to say that wasn't banal or useless.

"What are you waiting for?" John demanded. "Get in the car."

"Shouldn't we lock up?" I asked.

"What with? We haven't a key. Yusuf—"

"Ahman," said the individual addressed.

"Sorry. What time of day does your uncle usually come here?"

Ahman shrugged. The gesture might have indicated lack of comprehension, indifference, or ignorance of the answer.

"Bloody hell," said John. "We can't wait indefinitely. Where does he live and what is his name?"

Ahman gave him a blank look and shrugged again.

"Feisal will know," I said. "The kid isn't going to tell you anything, John, he's afraid his uncle may be in trouble. Give him some baksheesh and let's go."

A long unpaved version of a road led down to the main highway bordering the river. Rejoicing in the blast of cold from the car's air conditioner, I took off my hat and shook out my damp hair.

"Someone searched that house," I said.

"A somewhat sweeping statement," said John.

"The director's study, anyhow. Two of the chairs had been pulled away from the table and—"

"Several desk drawers were open an inch or so."

"Oh," I said, deflated. "You noticed."

"There were a few other indications, subtle but suggestive, that someone had been in that room recently."

"How did he get in? A hefty bribe to the uncle of Ahman?"

"I don't think so. The lock had been forced. An easy job, with a clumsy, old-fashioned lock like that one."

"What was he looking for?" I asked. "A place to hide . . ." Ali's name had been mentioned; there was no avoiding the subject any longer. "To hide a body? And then the killer decided it wasn't a good place after all?"

"Not likely." John's mouth shut tightly. But I was on track now, I didn't need any help from him.

"Not likely," I agreed, thinking aloud. "There would be no

hope of making Ali's death look accidental if his body were found there."

"Perhaps it was Ali who went there, looking for the mummy," Schmidt offered. "And the thieves caught him."

I shook my head. "The place had been searched. They, or he, or she, or whomever, wasn't looking for Tut, they were looking for something relatively small."

John leaned back, arms folded, and stared out the window. The car swerved around a camel loaded with bundles of some variety of herbage.

"What are you thinking about?" I asked, poking him.

"A long cold shower."

I had to admit it was the best idea I'd heard for a while.

John didn't join me in the shower. Perhaps, I mused, as the lovely element caressed my sticky self, the idea had struck him as somewhat inappropriate. I wasn't in the mood either. I had never known Ali, but Feisal's description and the collective memories of his family had painted the picture of the man: hardworking and honest, struggling to make ends meet against considerable odds. One of the common people. And worth more than any dead king.

We had found several messages tucked under the door of the sitting room. When I came out of the bedroom, toweling my hair, John was reading them.

"Let me see," I said.

"Be my guest." John went into the bathroom and closed the door.

Schmidt, pink and scrubbed and wrapped in one of the terry-cloth robes supplied by the hotel, joined me before long.

"We are popular," I said, handing him one of the slips of paper. "Ashraf has already been round to see us."

"Aha," said Schmidt, perusing it. "He is on his way to the West Bank. That implies that he has received Feisal's news about Ali. Who is that one from?"

"Somebody I've never heard of."

"It is addressed to me," Schmidt said indignantly. "You opened the envelope?"

"John did. I did not read it," I said virtuously. "Who is Jean-Luc LeBlanc?"

"A distinguished French archaeologist. His team works at Karnak. He has heard I am in Luxor and invites me to visit him."

"French, eh? We've had suspicious encounters in Germany, Italy, and England. Maybe we shouldn't have skipped Paris."

"Jean-Luc cannot be an object of suspicion. He is a distinguished—"

"Right. This next one sounds like an American. Only a few more Western countries to be heard from. Is she another distinguished archaeologist?"

Schmidt looked at it and shook his head. "She writes to John, not to me. 'I am staying at the Mercure, please call me as soon as possible.'"

John emerged. He had exchanged his sweat-stained shirt and jeans for a suit and tie. (Regimental or public school, I presumed.) I handed him the message.

"One of your floozies?"

"I do not have floozies. Not even one."

He gave me a fond smile and bent over to kiss me on the top of the head.

"Who is she?" I asked, resisting distraction.

"An admirer, I expect. I have quite a number of them."

"You don't recognize—"

The unmistakable voice of Johnny Cash made itself heard. Schmidt fumbled in the pocket of his robe. "Where is my cell phone?"

"Probably in your bedroom," John said. "You had better answer, it might be Feisal. I'll help you look."

Schmidt's phone was on the table next to his bed, which was strewn with articles of clothing. I've tidied up after Schmidt so often it has become a habit; ears pricked, I began collecting cast-off garments. Among them was a rather large pair of boxers printed with hearts and bluebirds. Schmidt shares my fondness for fancy lingerie.

After an initial exclamation of distress, Schmidt didn't say much. He rang off, and John said impatiently, "Well?"

"Feisal is on his way here," Schmidt said. "With Ashraf."

"Fast work," John muttered. "Was it murder?"

"They will have to wait for the results of the autopsy. He had a fatal wound of the head and several broken bones, but they could have resulted from a fall."

"Has his family been notified?" I asked.

"I forgot to ask." Schmidt ducked his head. "I am ashamed."

"You've no reason to be ashamed, Schmidt," John said gently. "You're a good man."

It was a rare tribute, and Schmidt reacted by leaking tears. By way of distraction I suggested we fill out a laundry form. He must be getting low on white linen suits by now. Such proved to be the case. Schmidt fished out clothes from the floor of the wardrobe. It took a while to sort and list them and put them into the bag provided.

"I'll call to have them picked up," I said briskly. "You get dressed, Schmidt."

"Yes, yes, we will soon be having guests. I will call the room service and—"

"I'll do it. Beer?"

Schmidt nodded. Activity had got him out of his mournful mood, but he looked sober. "Time is running out, Vicky. How many days have we left?"

I tried to think. Ten days, Ashraf had said. That had been two days ago, and the message had been delivered to him . . . when? A day or two before we saw him.

"I don't know, Schmidt. Fewer than I'd like."

"You were right, you know, in what you said. A dead king is less important than a living creature. But we must persevere, to help our friends."

"Of course." I patted him on his bald head.

I towed the bulging bag of laundry out into the sitting room and called housekeeping and then room service. Then I sat down on the sofa and picked up the notebook and pen. The problem was one of simple arithmetic, but so much had happened I was beginning to lose track of the time. Our unscheduled meeting with Ashraf had taken place Tuesday morning. At the latest he would have received the "ransom" note the day before. So when we saw him there were nine days left, not ten. We had arrived in Luxor the following day, inspected Tut's tomb and visited Ali's family.

Eight days.

Today on the West Bank.

Seven days.

Or had I miscounted? At best we had a week. Maybe less.

I was doodling aimlessly on the page, drawing vultures and jackals, when the laundry maid—a gray-haired, timid little woman—arrived. We got excellent service, thanks to Schmidt's habit of tipping everybody for every move they made. I was fishing in my pocket looking for a few stray pounds when Schmidt came out and provided them.

"You look very natty," I said. "How about a rose for your buttonhole?"

"It does not seem fitting. A black armband, do you think?"

"That would be overdoing it," I said, wondering whether a black armband formed part of his usual travel wardrobe.

"Perhaps you are right. Where is John?"

Yes, indeed, where was he? The bedroom door was closed. I opened it and looked in. Not a sign of him there or in the bathroom.

"Goddamn him," I said. "He's done it again." I ran to the balcony and leaned over the balustrade. Three stories below, the corniche provided its picturesque view of camels and carts and cars and carriages, with a bustle of pedestrians strolling along the sidewalk or weaving their way through the traffic on the street. None of the foreshortened forms was familiar.

Uttering incoherent curses, I started for the door. Schmidt inserted his solid form between me and the egress.

"You waste your time, Vicky, you cannot find John when he does not want to be found. Why are you angry? He will turn up, as he did the other night."

"He's up to no good, Schmidt. He knows something he hasn't told us."

"If he is," said Schmidt, ponderously shifting position as I tried to slide past him, "it is because he is following a lead he can best pursue alone. You have no proof that he is concealing important information."

Unbidden and unwelcome, the memory of John's meeting with Helga, the dealer in Berlin, came back to me.

"Schmidt," I said, "what does Helga look like?"

"Who?"

"The antiquities dealer in Berlin. What does she look like?"

"Oh, Helga von Sturm. Why do you—"

"Just tell me, okay?"

"She is a handsome woman. Not young, you understand, but soigné and elegant, always expensively dressed. She is very success-ful, and can afford—"

"So it wasn't she John met in Berlin." I slammed my fist onto the table. "Ouch. He lied about that, he's lying about the woman who left that note. When he comes back, I'm going to tie him to a chair and torture him till he comes clean. I'm going to—"

"I am sure he has only gone to the bank or to purchase a news-paper," Schmidt said. Someone knocked at the door. "Ah—there, you see."

Primed and ready, I opened the door. A waiter with a cart shied away when he saw my expression. I forced my face into nonthreat-ening lines and stood back.

"What is all this?" I demanded. "I only asked for beer."

"I spoke to the room service too," said Schmidt. "I feared you would forget that we must offer hospitality to our friends, who have been hard at work in the hot sun. No doubt they will want . . . Ah. Just in time, they are here."

We got Feisal and Ashraf in and the waiter, properly baksheeshed, out. It was obvious they had come straight from the West Bank; Feisal's once-crisp shirt hung limp and the dust on his face was streaked with runnels of sweat. Ashraf was carrying his jacket and his two-hundred-dollar shoes were covered with dust. He hadn't forgotten his manners, though; he waited until I had sat down be-fore sinking into a chair. Schmidt bustled about, offering fizzy drinks and platters of hors d'oeuvres.

"Just water," Feisal said hoarsely. He twisted the cap off a frosty bottle and drank deeply. *"Alhamdullilah,* that's good. Where's Johnny?"

"Out," I said, snapping the word off.

"When do you expect him back?" Ashraf asked.

"I don't know."

"Ah." Ashraf leaned back and loosened his tie. He'd hurried off to the West Bank without stopping to change. "Then perhaps you, his associates, can tell me how your investigation is proceeding."

He looked inquiringly from me to Schmidt. I kept my mouth shut. Feisal shut his. Sensing a certain level of discomfort all round, Schmidt burst into speech.

"Today's tragic development has altered the picture, *Sie verstehen.* We must analyze the ramifications before we can fully comprehend how they fit into the overall pattern."

"So there is a pattern?" Ashraf inquired.

Feisal stood up. "If I may make use of your bathroom, Schmidt, I'd like to wash up."

Without waiting for an answer, he disappeared into Schmidt's room.

"Feisal has not been forthcoming," Ashraf said smoothly. "He referred me to Mr. Tregarth. I did not press him, since he is clearly distraught about the death of his subordinate."

Schmidt, for once at a loss for words, shoved a plate of cheese and sliced smoked turkey at him. Ashraf looked ruefully at his dirty hands.

"With your permission, I will emulate Feisal."

I waved him toward the other bathroom. As soon as the door had closed behind him, Feisal popped out of Schmidt's room, toweling his hands.

"Talk fast," he ordered. "Has anything happened? Anything encouraging?"

"No," I said, glancing at the outer door. It remained uncompromisingly closed.

"Damn. I can't keep putting Ashraf off, he wants some indication of progress."

"Make something up," I said.

Feisal directed a desperate stare in my direction, and Schmidt said brightly, "I can do that."

Ashraf reappeared, wearing his jacket. He had given his shoes a quick rub, probably with one of my towels, but what did I care?

"So," he began.

"So it appears," said Schmidt, hands raised and fingertips together, "that our preliminary theory was correct. The missing object is hidden somewhere in the Theban hills. Ali came to the same conclusion and went to look for it. He surprised the men guarding the cache and they were forced to silence him. What did you say to him, Dr. Khifaya, that might have given him the idea?"

That was taking the fight into the enemy camp, all right. Ashraf looked startled, and then thoughtful. "Nothing that I can think of. He was speaking from the taftish, to which I had summoned him; I cautioned him to watch what he said, since there were others present. I did most of the talking . . . Let me see. I told him that the theft had been discovered, and cut him off when he began babbling; assured him that I did not hold him responsible . . ."

"That I was the one responsible," Feisal said, scowling.

"What is the American saying? 'The buck stops here'?"

"That means you," Feisal said. The two glowered at each other. I could see the family resemblance now, they glowered similarly.

"Do not quarrel," Schmidt said. "You are getting off the track. What else did you say to Ali?"

Ashraf rubbed his forehead. "Not much. To notify me at once if anything out of the ordinary occurred."

"Vague," I said critically.

"I couldn't be more specific," Ashraf insisted. He was on the defensive now, which was just where I wanted him. "Not over the telephone."

"No suggestions as to where the—er—missing article might be? No orders to search for it?" Schmidt demanded.

"No, I tell you. How could I propose an idea that hadn't occurred to me? May I ask why it occurred to you lot?"

"I will explain," said Schmidt, peering owlishly at Ashraf.

The explanation took a good ten minutes. Feisal couldn't sit still; he paced and sat down, jumped up and went onto the balcony, came back, sat down, jumped up, paced. When Schmidt couldn't drag it out any longer, he stopped talking and gave Ashraf a smug smile.

"It does open up a possible line of action," the latter admitted. "But there are difficulties. If Ali's death was not an accident—and we still have no actual proof that it was not—we must assume the murder did not occur near the place where his body was found. That leaves a large territory to be searched. Furthermore, how can I send search parties into the hills without telling them what they are searching for?"

"And without warning them that if they find it they could be murdered," I said.

"That too," said Ashraf.

Not a sound at the door.

"You disgust me," I burst out. "All of you. A man is dead, a good, harmless man, and all you can think of is how to keep this business a secret. You're willing to risk more lives to retrieve a dried-up corpse."

Ashraf's expression was so tender and kind I wanted to paste him one. That was the attitude he expected from a woman. If he had praised me for it I would have hit him. It might have been Feisal shaking his head or Schmidt's fit of frantic coughing that warned him. All he said was, "If I decide to send out search parties, they will be armed and expecting trouble. We can easily find an excuse that does not involve—er—*him*. A missing tourist, perhaps. When did you say you expected Mr. Tregarth to return?"

Back at you, Vicky.

"When he's good and ready," I said. "Have some cheese."

TEN

The sun sank slowly in the west, as it is wont to do, the muezzins sang the praises of God, and still John had not returned. Feisal kept running out onto the balcony. I kept trying not to look at the door. Schmidt tried his best to distract Ashraf, but eventually he was reduced to mentioning dinner. Ashraf declined his invitation to join us.

"I have an appointment this evening. I will meet you at your office tomorrow at eight, Feisal."

It was an order. Feisal acknowledged it with a surly nod, and Ashraf strode out. I collected the messages we had received and for want of anything better to do, began rereading them in the forlorn hope that we had missed something. The note from the unknown American female provided nothing new. I picked up the one from the French archaeologist and wrinkled my brow over it. My French isn't as good as Schmidt's. It took me a while to decipher the crabbed handwriting.

"Wait a minute," I said. "What's this about Karnak? 'I have received permission to enter the temple tonight after the Son et Lumière and hope that you will be able to join me.'"

"Ah, that is most *interessant*," said Schmidt, perking up. "It is a rare privilege, seldom granted, to see the temple by moonlight."

Feisal looked up from his frowning contemplation of the floor. "Rare is right. How did LeBlanc manage that?"

"He apologizes for not notifying you earlier," I went on. "He only learned of the plan this morning. Feisal, who is in a position to arrange this?"

"Not me. Not without permission from a higher authority."

"Ashraf?"

"I suppose so. What are you getting at?"

"I'm not sure." I grabbed hold of my head with both hands, as if that would keep the wild ideas flooding into my brain from leaking out. "Let me think. Ashraf must have been the one who set this up. He invited LeBlanc, and maybe a few others. He didn't invite us, though."

"That was not kind of him," Schmidt said, pouting. "It is a rare opportunity, a once-in-a-lifetime—"

"Exactly! So why didn't he?"

Feisal opened his mouth. "Shut up," I said distractedly. "Remember what I said before—that there had been no either/or in that message from the thieves? Something else was missing—a means of contact. They said they'd be in touch. Suppose they have been. Suppose that's why Ashraf came to Luxor. To meet with one of them. At the temple of Karnak, late at night, when only a few people are around. But not us. He didn't count on Schmidt's wide circle of dear old friends. He doesn't want us to be there."

Feisal's eyebrows wriggled. "Is paranoia rearing its ugly head?"

"Not raising its head, upstanding, yelling, and waving its arms.

They have to make contact with him sooner or later. How else can they collect the ransom?"

Feisal said something under his breath. I turned on him. "What was that?"

"I said, wire transfer. You need to move up into the twenty-first century, Vicky."

"Oh," I said, momentarily deflated.

"No, she is right," Schmidt declared. "He must confirm that he has received their message and will agree to their terms, *nicht wahr*? They would not give him a telephone number or a post restante, or any other address that could be traced. A personal meeting may be old-fashioned, but it is the safest way. When the actual exchange takes place, it will be carried out in the same manner."

"Yes! And the ambience is perfect for the first meeting—dark and deserted, isolated—those vast spaces, huge statues and towering columns, people wandering romantically through the shadows—just enough people to make it look legitimate . . ." Feisal's eyebrows continued to convey skepticism, but I had convinced myself. "If Ashraf were fool enough to bring along a squad of cops they would be spotted right away. He wouldn't dare risk it, it would queer the deal and the next thing you know he'd get Tut's head delivered to his door, and the price would go up."

"Hmmm." Feisal scratched his bristly chin. "Why didn't he let us in on the program?"

I was pacing, waving my arms like Mr. Paranoia. It was all coming together. "Ego. The man's an egomaniac. He thinks he can pull this off without us, take all the credit, maybe even persuade his contact to turn on his bosses and reach a private agreement. He doesn't trust us. After all, what have we accomplished so far? Damn little. He gave us a chance, today, to prove we were making progress. We couldn't because we still haven't a clue."

"Almost," said Feisal slowly, "you convince me."

"It can do no harm to proceed on that assumption," Schmidt said, nodding at me. "We should certainly be present, if only for the experience."

"And I'll tell you who else will be present." I was at full throttle, roaring along the track. "John. He read that note. He reached the same conclusion I—we—have. He skun out of here before Feisal and Ashraf arrived because he knew it would be more difficult to get away from four of us."

"How can he gain entrance, though?" Schmidt asked. "LeBlanc said he will have told the guards to admit me and my party, so one must assume that only those on a select list will be allowed in."

"There are ways," Feisal said. "He could attend the Son et Lumière and not leave with the other viewers. There are plenty of places to hide. Or climb over the enclosure wall, or—"

"If anyone can find a way, John can," I said. "So . . . we go?"

Feisal raised his shoulders in a shrug. "What have we to lose?"

I could think of several things. I refrained from enumerating them.

It was obvious to me by then that wherever he might be, John had no intention of returning anytime soon, but Schmidt insisted on leaving a message at the desk telling him that we were having dinner at the hotel. Feisal appropriated John's razor and certain items from his wardrobe, including a tie (regimental?), which was de rigueur in the restaurant. John hadn't taken anything with him except his precious self, which might have suggested to a trusting soul that he had not left us in the lurch. It didn't convince me. For all I knew, he might have a pied-à-terre and another wardrobe elsewhere in Luxor. Or he could be on a plane to Cairo, or Berlin, or Kathmandu.

We had time to kill (and Schmidt was paying), so we dallied over a five-course meal and drank a lot of wine. My initial enthusiasm had faded a bit and I began to wonder if I was on the wrong track. My scenario made perfectly good sense, but so do the plots of a lot of novels.

Schmidt, full of wine and sipping a brandy, had become a convert. He has a head like a rock, though, and it was he who brought up the unpleasant subject of possible pitfalls.

"We must make a plan," he declared. "In case something goes amiss."

"Something is sure to," Feisal said morosely. He hadn't had any wine.

"First," said Schmidt, ignoring this, "we stick together, yes? We do not separate for any reason."

"Fine so far," I agreed. "Second?"

"We find Ashraf and follow him, but at a discreet distance, being sure he does not see us."

Seemed to me we had already hit the first snag in the plan. Three people don't lurk well, especially when Schmidt is one of the three.

"When he meets his contact," Schmidt continued, "we stay at a distance, we do not interfere unless it appears that Ashraf may be in trouble. Then we follow the man he meets."

"All of us?" I said dubiously.

"We must not be separated," Schmidt insisted. "If by chance one of us is, she must return immediately to the entrance and wait."

"What do you mean, she?"

"She or he," Feisal said. "That goes for you too, Schmidt. All right, I think that covers the main points. The rest is in the hands of God."

After dinner we went back upstairs to collect our gear. Schmidt left his bedroom door open, so when I heard him talking I felt no compunction about eavesdropping. I had no difficulty in deducing that it was Suzi on the other end. He kept saying "no" and "but" and sputtering.

"Where is she?" I asked, once he had broken the connection.

"In Luxor. She would not tell me where she is staying. She is not pleased with me. She asked why I did not inform her about Ali."

"She's really on top of things, isn't she? What else?"

"She tells me nothing," Schmidt said angrily. "It is all reproaches and demands and complaints. I am through with her. *Gott sei Dank* that I found out what sort of woman she was before I—er—"

"Oh, Schmidt," I said. "Were you about to propose? I'm so sorry. I didn't realize matters had gone that far."

Schmidt squared his shoulders, insofar as they were capable of that shape. "There are other women in the world. I will forget her. Go, Vicky, and get ready to leave."

"I am ready. Don't I look respectable enough?"

Head on one side, Schmidt studied my ensemble, which was neat if not gaudy—navy pants and a long-sleeved blue shirt, sneakers (blue) and a (blue-and-green) striped scarf. "I like it better when you wear a pretty dress. But for tonight's adventure, perhaps trousers are more suitable. A shawl, perhaps? The nights grow quickly cold."

Picturing myself in a fringed shawl, I was moved to mirth. "Shawls are nuisances, Schmidt, they catch on things and slide off."

"A jacket, then. Something," said Schmidt pointedly, "with pockets."

His jacket had plenty of them—another of those archaeologist-type garments. Many of the pockets bulged.

"What have you got in there?" I demanded, indicating the bulgiest pocket.

"A flashlight. Here is one for you."

"Not a bad idea, Schmidt. Thanks."

Before I could pursue my inquiries, Schmidt made shooing gestures. "Put it away and let us be off. We should arrive early in order not to miss Ashraf."

The moon was gibbous. Now there's a word that resonates: gibbet, giblet, gibbering . . .

It means not quite full. Perfectly harmless word. And support for my hypothesis, that Ashraf had ordered the temple opened for purposes of his own. Full moon was the traditional time, when the brilliant Egyptian moonlight is at its brightest. There would be a lot of dark in there tonight.

Feisal had been rude enough to suggest that maybe Ashraf's motive for violating tradition was personal or, as Schmidt would have said, romantic. He was a busy man, and if the lady he wanted to captivate had an equally full schedule (with, let us say, a husband), Ashraf would have to improvise.

"That's disgusting," I scolded. "Shame on you for implying Ashraf is a philanderer."

"What a ladylike vocabulary you have," Feisal scoffed. "And what a naive mind. Ashraf has women hanging off him."

"Tsk, tsk," said Schmidt. "He is a married man, is he not?"

"What does that have to do with it?"

Schmidt said, "Tsk, tsk."

The last Son et Lumière attendees were leaving the temple when we got out of the taxi and headed for the entrance. Schmidt pulled me aside into the shadow of a sphinx—there was a row of them on either side of the path—and indicated two people going in the other direction.

"Suzi!" he hissed.

"Which one?" They were about the same height, wearing the unisex uniform of jeans and shirts, baseball caps and sneakers. I heard a fragment of what sounded like Swedish from one. The other laughed and put his or her arm around her or him. "Now you're getting paranoid, Schmidt. Come on."

The last of the lights inside the enclosure went out, leaving only a single source of illumination at the entrance. A uniformed guard was dragging a barricade across the opening. "The temple is closed," he intoned.

I expected Schmidt to greet him by name, but apparently Schmidt didn't know absolutely everybody in the world. The guard recognized Feisal, though, and when Schmidt announced himself, the guard nodded. "Yes, Dr. LeBlanc has given your name. This lady is with you? Enter."

We passed through a pyloned gateway into an open court. It was a clutter of shapes. Column bases, more sphinxes, slabs of carved stone, and broken statues were outlined in black by the gibbous moon. A few dark forms moved slowly in and out of the shadows. There wasn't a sound except for the faint crunch of gravel under our feet. When Schmidt let out a shout, I jumped clear off the ground.

One of the featureless forms trotted toward us and turned into a neat little man with a neat little goatee and neat gold-rimmed glasses. He and Schmidt embraced and exchanged enthusiastic exclamations in French. Schmidt introduced me and LeBlanc kissed my hand. His goatee tickled, but I didn't mind. I like having my hand kissed.

"And you know Feisal, of course," Schmidt went on.

Feisal got kissed on both cheeks. Very French and also very Egyptian.

"Feel free to go where you like," LeBlanc said, speaking English for my benefit. "I would offer to show you around, but you know the temple as well as I, if not better."

"You will want to greet your other guests," Schmidt said. "Who else will be here?"

LeBlanc mentioned several names, none of which was familiar to me. "And the secretary general, of course. Without him I could not have arranged this favor."

"Aha!" The word just popped out of me.

"Pardon?"

"Sorry. I was thinking of—of something else."

"And why not?" LeBlanc smiled. Gold teeth matched his gold spectacle frames. "It is a spot for mystery and magic, for romance, for dreams. Enjoy!"

"See what I mean?" Feisal hissed into my ear. "In a setting like this Ashraf could have his wicked way with any female."

"Not me." I shivered involuntarily. "I can feel eyes, all those empty stone eyes, staring. Who's that?"

Feisal followed my gesture. "Ramses the Second."

"A dead king," I muttered. "Dead kings, staring."

"They couldn't care less," Feisal said. "Pull yourself together, Vicky. We've got to locate Ashraf."

I pulled myself together and poked Schmidt, who was staring dreamily at Ramses the Second, who stared stonily back. "This is hopeless, Schmidt. I remember the plan of Karnak; it's vast, enormous, unending. How are we going to find one man in all this?"

"*Man tut was man kann,*" said Schmidt. Then, believe it or not, he giggled. *"Tut! Tut!"*

Feisal growled and I said, "I hope you didn't do that on purpose."

"No, no, it was a fortuitous joke, you understand. The quotation means, 'One does what one can,' and the German verb form *'tut'* is the third-person—"

"We get it, Schmidt. Lead on."

Schmidt led the way past Ramses (a much smaller figure next to him was female, presumably his queen) and through another gateway into a forest of stone. I had been in the Hypostyle Hall once before, but that had been in the daytime. At night, with only the moon to light them, the towering columns were even more overpowering. We were midgets, insects, next to those mammoth shapes. They surrounded us and diminished us. A few other insects crawled in and out of sight among them.

My idea of romance is a cozy little room with a fire on the hearth and a lot of soft cushions and a bottle of something on ice. Or maybe a secluded pool, surrounded by palms and hibiscus and vines waving gently in a tropical breeze. Or maybe . . . Whatever it was, it wasn't a big dark stony place where the shadows whispered words I couldn't quite hear.

"Romantic?" I said aloud.

"Shh." Schmidt came to a halt and pointed. "There. Is that not—"

Pale light sifted down between the giant columns and glimmered off a head of fair hair.

"Not John," I said.

"How can you be sure?"

"If it were John you wouldn't see him at all. Probably some visiting archaeologist."

We went on along the main axis, stopping to look down the intersecting aisles as we crossed them. The futility of our search became increasingly apparent to me; the few people we spotted were so diminished by distance and darkness, I couldn't even tell whether they were men or women.

I caught hold of Schmidt's sleeve. "This is only one part of the temple, isn't it?"

"Yes, yes, there are long sections beyond. Several more pylons, a temple of the Eighteenth—"

"Why wouldn't Ashraf be meeting his contact there? This is an impossible place to search."

"But it is perfect for a private rendezvous. One cannot be cornered," said Schmidt triumphantly, "because there are no corners! And concealment can be attained in a split second."

And one could go on playing hide-and-seek indefinitely. Every column looked like every other column and each was big enough to hide several people.

I didn't have the heart to call a halt, though. Schmidt was having a wonderful time, tiptoeing and squinting at nothing in particular, and I was getting over my fit of nerves.

Then Schmidt let out a stifled shriek and disappeared.

I wasn't looking at him when it happened. He had fallen behind Feisal and me—not far behind, only a few yards. Having concluded that nothing nasty was going to happen, I had relaxed my guard and was going through the motions, peering dutifully from one side to the other. I spun around. No Schmidt. Gone, just like that.

I ran back, yelling his name, and made a quick right turn into the next intersecting aisle. There was enough light for me to see some distance along the line of huge columns. At the far end, a long way off, was a human figure. It couldn't be Schmidt, he couldn't have got that far. Oh, God, I thought, please, no—not Schmidt . . .

A hand covered my mouth and a muscular arm pinned my arms to my sides. I kicked back, heard a grunt, and then a swear word. "Stop that," Feisal muttered. "He's okay, I found him."

I went limp with relief. Feisal let me go. "Keep quiet," he said softly. "This way."

I hadn't gone quite far enough. Schmidt was in the next aisle down. He was talking to someone. They were both hidden from view by one of the damned columns, and their voices were so low I couldn't make out what they were saying until we stood on the other side of the column.

The other person was speaking. It's hard to identify voices when they whisper; the speaker might have been male or female. The first words I heard were ". . . want to help. I'm on your side, you know."

"Do you really mean it?" came next, in Schmidt's version of a whisper.

For several long seconds there was no sound except for some heavy breathing. Feisal squeezed my arm. I looked up at him. He grinned and raised his finger to his lips.

I was sorely tempted to burst upon the pair with rude comments, but discretion dictated otherwise. No, I would wait to hear what Schmidt had to say. If he fell under the spell of Suzi again, we would have to deprogram him. The other person had to be Suzi; Schmidt hadn't had time to make another conquest. She must have followed us from the hotel . . . Unless Schmidt had told her where we were going. Honestly, I thought, you can't trust anybody.

Feisal put his mouth against my ear. "I'm going to follow her. Get hold of Schmidt and go back to the entrance."

"He told us not to—"

He faded into the shadow and became invisible.

I had had enough. Reaching into my pocket, I took out Schmidt's flashlight and switched it on. A faint sound behind me made me whirl in that direction; in the beam of light I thought I saw something duck back behind a column. Another sound from the opposite direction. Shadows raced from the light as I turned back to see Schmidt step into view. He raised his hand to shield his eyes.

"What—" he began.

I grabbed him by the collar with my free hand and shook him. "What do you mean, what? I'm the one who should say 'What?' How dare you scare me that way?"

"It was Suzi," Schmidt said calmly. "She caught hold of me and pulled me behind that column. She is very strong for a woman. I was too surprised at first to resist, and then she persuaded me that I must listen to what she had to say. Where is Feisal? I told him not to leave you alone."

"You left me alone."

"It was not my fault, but I don't blame you if you are angry." Schmidt tried to appear penitent. He didn't really succeed; the very curve of his mustache was smug. "I found out much of interest, and got back into her good graces. She begged my pardon and said she believed me; that she is on our side now."

"Did you believe her?"

"Of course I did not. But it seemed to me wise to act as if I did. Vicky, she says John is here at Karnak. She saw him not five minutes ago. Turn off the flashlight and I will take you—"

"Damned if I will. I've had enough dark."

"He will see us approaching."

"No, he won't because we aren't going . . . Hmmm. Where was he when she saw him?"

Schmidt pointed down one of the endless aisles. "Going in that direction. What will you bet me that he is following Ashraf?"

"Ashraf is being followed by John who is being followed by Suzi who is being followed by Feisal and us? This is ludicrous, Schmidt. I'm going back to the entrance and you are coming with me."

"Feisal is following Suzi?"

"Just come quietly, okay?"

There was only one way of making certain he did, and that was to start back myself. I knew my Schmidt wouldn't leave me alone.

We had only gone a little way when a long, high-pitched cry echoed down the aisles. The sound was as shocking as an explosion in the pervasive silence, and it went on and on, broken by brief pauses which wrenched at the hearing almost as painfully as the cries themselves.

The flashlight beam wobbled violently as I pivoted, trying to locate the source. Schmidt tugged at my arm. "This way!"

"Schmidt, we can't—"

But I knew we had to. Feisal was out there somewhere.

As we swerved around columns we ran into a man coming the other way—another way, anyhow, there weren't any discernible directions in that maze. I directed my light at him in time to keep Schmidt from knocking him flat. He was even chubbier than Schmidt; they bounced off each other and rocked to a stop.

"Wolfgang!" Schmidt exclaimed.

"Schmidt! Is it you? *Was ist gefallen? Wer hat geschriehen?*"

"*Ich weiss nicht. Kommen Sie mit.*"

"Your flashlight, Schmidt," I said breathlessly.

"*Ach, ja, ich habe vergessen.*"

He had, understandably, neglected to introduce Wolfgang; I deduced that he was a member of one of the archaeological groups working in the Luxor area. The screams had stopped, but after we'd gone a little way I began to hear voices. We weren't the only ones who had responded. Some must have been closer to the scene than we, since already a small group of people had gathered around a figure seated on the ground, hands clutching his head. Everybody was talking at once, offering advice in a variety of languages.

"Don't try to get up."

"Lie down, you are bleeding."

"Send for an ambulance!"

"Stand back, give him air."

Among the spectators was Feisal. We trotted up to him and he spared us a quick glance. "It's Ashraf. He's not badly hurt. All right, friends, your assistance is appreciated but unnecessary. He slipped and hit his head, that's all."

"I was afraid it was you," I mumbled.

"No, that was me screaming. I heard a muffled cry and the sound of a fall, and found him flat on the ground. I didn't want to leave him alone while I went for help."

"He didn't slip, did he?"

"Later. Come on, Ashraf, let me give you a hand."

"He may have concussion," Schmidt said. "Should we not wait for a medical person?"

"He could die of old age before we got a stretcher in here," Feisal said. "Are you offering to carry him?"

Ashraf lowered his hands and looked up at us. Blood trickled down his neck. "I don't require to be carried. A slight accident, as Feisal said. I hope I have not spoiled this experience for you."

He got slowly to his feet, waving Feisal away. The spectators made polite disclaimers, but they began to drift away singly and in pairs, returning to the entrance. The show was over, in any case. The light had faded. The gibbous moon was setting.

"Take my arm," Feisal said. "Nobody's looking, you needn't show off any longer."

"Go away," Ashraf said through his teeth. "Leave me alone."

Wolfgang, the only one of the outsiders left, took this personally. He chugged away, muttering and shaking his head.

"You too," said Ashraf, squaring his manly shoulders and distributing an indiscriminate glare at the rest of us.

"Fat chance," I said. "You owe us an explanation, Ashraf. Whom did you meet? Where did he go?"

"She," Feisal said.

"What?" I stared at him.

"I saw her running away," Feisal said. "She had a scarf pinned round her head and she was wearing a skirt. And don't try to tell me it was a man in a head cloth and galabiya, I know the difference."

"I suppose," said Ashraf, "that if I told you I had an appointment with a lady friend—"

"We wouldn't believe it," I assured him. "So your contact was female." I succumbed, I admit, to sexist prejudice.

For all his bravado, Ashraf wasn't at his best. He sagged a little, and when Feisal put an arm round him he didn't shrug it off. "It was clever," Ashraf admitted. "I had come prepared to defend myself should it be necessary. Finding a woman lowered my guard."

"Why did she hit you?" I asked.

"She didn't. We were getting along nicely when someone came up behind me." Ashraf showed his teeth in what was certainly not a friendly smile. "It was your friend Mr. Tregarth."

ELEVEN

Ashraf refused to see a doctor. He was steady on his feet, and it was two o'clock in the morning, so we decided to take him back to the Winter Palace. The yawning guard assured us we were the last to leave the temple. I doubted, not his veracity—he probably thought he was telling the truth—but his accuracy. But by that time I didn't give a damn who was still chasing whom around the columns or climbing over which walls.

After protesting our intent, to no avail, Ashraf lapsed into silence and refused to answer questions. The streets of Luxor were dim and deserted, with not even a taxi in sight, but of course the director's car awaited. Nothing so prosaic as an ordinary EgyptAir flight for Ashraf; he had had his chauffeur drive him to Luxor.

When we arrived at the hotel, I stopped at the desk to ask for messages and was informed, with appropriate hauteur, that they would have been delivered to our room. Mr. Tregarth had not picked up the one we had left earlier. The news came as no surprise.

Schmidt dug out his first-aid kit and Ashraf submitted fairly graciously to my ministrations, such as they were. The blow had landed just behind his right ear, resulting in a bump and a small cut. He refused my offer to shave off the hair around the cut, so I had to settle for dabbing on an antiseptic cream. I smeared on quite a lot of it, messing up his nice haircut, since by that time I had had it up to here with Ashraf.

He had resigned himself to the inevitable by then—the inevitable being three annoyed people who were prepared to use force to prevent his leaving—and he'd also had time to think things over.

"How did you know?" he inquired, taking a sip of the fizzy lemon drink with which Schmidt had supplied him.

"We're asking the questions," I said, folding my arms. "Why didn't you tell us you had heard again from the thieves?"

"The second message warned me of what would happen if I confided in anyone else."

"Another piece of Tut?" I asked.

Ashraf shuddered. "Please, don't say such things."

"But we aren't the police," Feisal said. "That was an idle threat; they couldn't know whether you had told *us*."

"They would know if you turned up at the right place at the right time," Ashraf said with sudden fury. "Which you did. You were seen. She was extremely angry. I swore by every saint in several pantheons that I hadn't said a word to any of you. Fortunately she believed me."

"What a nice, trusting lady she must be," I said. "Some conspirator!"

Ashraf leaned back, legs extended, ankles crossed, lips curving in a smile. "She was amenable to persuasion. But perhaps I should start at the beginning."

He had found the second message waiting for him when he arrived at his house in Luxor. (He had others, Feisal told us later, at Sharm el Sheikh and Alexandria.) It instructed him to meet his contact in the Hypostyle Hall at Karnak between twelve midnight and 1:00 A.M. They were thoughtful enough to give him twenty-four hours to arrange the matter. If he failed to show up, he would have cause to regret it.

"I came to you to ask whether you had made any progress. You presented me with a variety of unfounded theories, but no facts. It became evident to me that you were incapable of carrying out your assignment, or unwilling to do so. So . . ." He took out a fancy silver case, extracted a cigarette, and lit it with a fancy silver lighter. "I decided to proceed on my own. I invited a number of dignitaries and archaeologists to justify my reason for opening the temple. I staked myself out near the entrance in the hope of identifying my contact when he entered; when I saw you three, I realized I ought to have anticipated that Dr. Schmidt would learn of the occasion from one of his several thousand dear friends, and that you would be unable to resist enjoying the experience."

"Enjoy, hell," I said. "We went because we had figured out what you were up to. The fact that you hadn't invited us was suspicious."

"It was ratiocination of the most brilliant kind," Schmidt added.

"If you say so," Ashraf said, not believing a word of it. "In any event, I decided your presence would not interfere with my plan. I had been given a specific cross-reference, and the area is extensive." He blew a perfect smoke ring and leaned back to admire it.

"Go on," I said. We should have banged him on the head again in order to keep him off balance. He was enjoying his place in the spotlight.

"As I said, when I encountered a woman I was taken by surprise. However, she gave me the word I had been told to expect—"

"Mummy?" I couldn't resist.

"How did you know?" Ashraf demanded in surprise.

I had meant it as a feeble joke, but I wasn't about to admit it. Smug is a game two can play. I gestured for him to continue.

She had been angry and visibly nervous at first, "but I soon put her at her ease. We—er—negotiated. I promised her immunity and a safe haven if she accepted my offer."

"How much?" Feisal asked bluntly.

Ashraf hesitated. "Two hundred and fifty thousand, for herself."

"In exchange for Tut's current address?" I asked.

Feisal and Ashraf both flinched. "I wish you wouldn't be so frivolous about this," the latter said. "In essence, yes, that is what we agreed. We were about to set up our next and final meeting when your friend interfered. When I recovered from that cowardly blow, he and she were both gone."

He lit another cigarette, looking pleased with himself.

He'd told a plausible story, one that made him look like both hero and victim. I wondered how much spin he'd put on it. I was prepared to believe that one of the gang was ready to make a deal. Criminals are not noted for loyalty to one another. Ashraf had private means. He could probably raise that much if he had to.

"Ashraf, you damned fool," I said. "Didn't it occur to you that someone would be keeping an eye on your lady friend? I hope for her sake the other guy didn't overhear too much. Crooks have ways of dealing with traitors."

"He must have overheard a good deal," Ashraf admitted. "He struck me down just as we were about to come to an agreement."

We had to come to it, sooner or later. "He was behind you," I said, in a last-ditch effort. "How do you know it was John—Mr. Tregarth?"

"I caught only a glimpse. I heard a sound, and started to turn. But I saw enough. How many fair-haired individuals were present tonight?"

"Several, I should think."

"But only one who is involved in this affair," Ashraf said triumphantly. "Up to his neck, I should add. Why would he have gone to the temple unless he knew a meeting was planned? You claim you were able to anticipate my intentions through—ratiocination, was it not?—and I am willing to consider the possibility that Tregarth has deceived you as he tried to deceive me; but the evidence against him is strong. If he was not there, where was he? Where is he now?"

"He'll turn up," I said. "With a perfectly good explanation."

"Let me know when he does." Ashraf put out his cigarette and stood up. "It is late and I am feeling a trifle fatigued. Can I give you a lift, Feisal?"

Feisal looked as if he would like to refuse, but exhaustion overcame pride. None of us was in the mood to go on rehashing the affair. The two men left; Schmidt trudged off to his room; I hung a Do Not Disturb sign on the door into the hall, peeled off the outer layers of clothing, and collapsed into bed.

I was so tired, every muscle in my body ached, but my brain wouldn't shut down. Ashraf had presented a circumstantial but damning case. He wasn't the only one who claimed to have seen John. Suzi had too, if we could believe her. And what had become of Suzi? Feisal had been following her when he heard Ashraf being attacked. Could it have been Suzi who hit him? She had blond hair, cut short like a man's. That was all Ashraf had seen, the glimmer of light on a head of fair hair. Feisal had only seen a woman who was wearing a head scarf.

The windows were rectangles of pale gray. Dawn wasn't far off. I was too exhausted to get up and close the drapes. I pulled the sheet over my head and fell asleep.

B right sunlight hit me in the eyes and woke me. My watch informed me it was almost ten. I rolled over onto the cold, empty space next to me. The rustle of bedclothes produced a knock at the door.

"Are you awake?" Schmidt, who else. He must have been standing right outside, with his ear pressed to the panel.

"No."

"I will order breakfast." Footsteps retreated.

Having been left with no choice in the matter, I dragged myself into the shower. In fact, I felt better than I had any reason to expect. My subconscious hadn't come up with any answers to the questions that had kept me awake the night before, though.

I got dressed, realizing I had better send some laundry out too. I was buttoning my last clean shirt when the door opened, after what I can only call a perfunctory knock.

"You are dressed," said Schmidt.

"Sorry about that."

"There is coffee," said Schmidt, resigned. "And Feisal is here."

I didn't ask whether John had returned. Schmidt would have said so.

The waiter had been and gone and Schmidt was tucking into a plate of eggs and turkey sausages. I accepted a cup of coffee from Feisal.

"Did you get anything useful out of Ashraf?" I asked.

Feisal made a wry face. "All he did was gloat about his cleverness and scold me for queering the deal."

"How much of his story do you think is true?"

"The basic facts, I believe," said Schmidt thoughtfully. "But there are many unanswered questions. I have now heard Suzi's version of what transpired."

"You've been a busy little bee this morning. Sorry I overslept."

"A man in my physical condition does not require much sleep." Schmidt smeared jam on a roll. "In accordance with my new policy I expressed concern over her safety and offered to tell her what had happened to Ashraf, since I assumed she would already have heard of it."

"Well done." The jam was all gone. I opened a little pot of honey. "Well? What did she say?"

"She did not see the attack itself, only Ashraf's fallen body. Hearing Feisal approach, she hid herself and watched."

"Those useful columns," I murmured. "How did she get out of the temple?"

"Walked out, I expect," Feisal said. "The guard wasn't told to keep track of people leaving. Isn't anybody going to ask how I spent the morning?"

I made encouraging noises, through a mouthful of bread and honey.

"Not happily," Feisal said. "Ali's family wants his body back. They sent a delegation—all the men in the family—to my office. I had to tell them the autopsy wasn't finished. They didn't like it."

"According to Muslim law, the body must be buried before sunset of the day of death, or at latest the following day," Schmidt informed me.

"It was too late for that when the body was found, wasn't it?" I asked.

"You don't reason with people who are in emotional distress," Feisal said. "I'm going to the village to see the rest of the family, try to explain. Do you want to come with me?"

I didn't want to. It was bound to be an upsetting experience. But maybe our presence would make it easier for Feisal.

He waited while I got my laundry together and Schmidt loaded his pockets with a variety of useful and useless objects, including the beloved magnifying glass, which Feisal had returned to him. One never knows when one will stumble across a Clue.

Since we did not have the limo at our disposal, we crossed the river on one of the boats. I like the boats; they have bright awnings and soft, if faded, cushions on the seats, and they have names like *Rosebud* and *Cleopatra* and *Nefertiti*. Watching Schmidt wobble across the gangplank added a certain element of suspense to the entertainment. Feisal's Jeep was waiting on the other side.

"I have to stop by the Valley later," he explained. "But I want to get this over with first."

This encounter was a repeat of the first—the same swarm of importunate kids, the same darkened room and watching eyes, the same offer of tea and biscuits, the same chicken, or a close relative of same. I ended up sitting next to Umm Ali, who ducked her head in greeting and returned my mispronounced *"Salaam aleikhum"* with a few words in Arabic that weren't in my current vocabulary. Schmidt sat in a chair across from me, his face somber. Everybody stared at Feisal.

They listened in silence to his brief speech. The silence lengthened. The chicken flapped up onto Schmidt's knee. He patted it absently.

"Please, Feisal, express our sympathy to the family."

"I did. We may as well go. My explanation wasn't well received," he added morosely.

I put my glass of tea on the little table and stood up. I felt a need to do or say something, not just walk out. Feeling miserable and ineffectual, I said, "I'm sorry. So very sorry. If there is anything we can do . . ."

The old lady got to her feet. One bony hand shot out and caught hold of mine. Standing on tiptoe, she looked up at me. The sharp black eyes were blurred with tears. She spoke softly and urgently, squeezing my hand. Her fingers felt like birds' claws, thin and strong.

Feisal translated, his voice hoarse. "'My son was murdered. Find his murderer, sitt, so that he can rest in peace.'"

"I will," I said. "*Aywa.* Yes. I promise. *Inshallah.*"

Feisal didn't have to translate. The old lady nodded and sat down. "*Inshallah,*" she echoed.

God willing. Nobody makes a promise without adding that. In the end it is in the hands of God. But by her God and mine, I meant to do my damnedest.

Schmidt was openly wiping his eyes when we emerged from the house. "That was very beautiful, Vicky."

"It was the right thing to say," Feisal admitted. He gave me an odd look. "I can't imagine why she should appeal to you. In this culture—"

"Yeah, yeah, I know, men rule the roost. Maybe some of the women know better."

Feisal's Jeep needed new springs (among other things). Schmidt kept bouncing off me as we hit potholes and swerved to avoid various fauna and other vehicles. A cloud of dust traveled with us, most of it inside the vehicle.

"Tell him to slow down," I yelled at Feisal, who was up front with the driver.

"We're late," Feisal yelled back.

Late for what? I wondered. I didn't ask. The Jeep hit another pothole; Schmidt ricocheted off the window frame and onto my lap.

Feisal deigned to explain after the driver had dropped us off at the entrance to the Valley of the Kings. "I'm meeting Ahmed

Saleh, the subinspector in charge of western Thebes. He's miffed because I haven't been answering his calls. He's a born complainer, but I figured I had better shut him up before he goes over my head. Or," Feisal added, "behind my back, with a knife in his hand."

"Is he after your job?" I asked.

"They're all after my job. For ten piastres I'd let them have it."

The subinspector was not at the guards' kiosk. Feisal's irritated question got an expansive gesture and an explanation Feisal cut short.

"He's gone on along the main path. Confound him, I told him to wait for me here."

He lengthened his stride. There's no denying we were all a little sensitive about that particular tomb; like a murderer who is guiltily conscious of where the body is hidden, we got nervous whenever anyone went near it.

The sun was past the zenith. Many of the tourists had gone off to lunch, but there were enough of them left to slow our progress; we had to veer around groups clustered around a lecturing guide, and a few of those maddening trios and foursomes who spread themselves out across the path, yielding the way to no one. When we came in sight of the tomb—The Tomb—Feisal screeched to a stop. Dust spurted up from under his heels.

Perched on the enclosure wall above the entrance was a pretty little woman wearing a becomingly arranged head scarf and a full skirt which spread out around her in an amber pool. She was looking down, and seemed to be chatting with someone who was out of sight on the steps below.

Feisal let out a bellow. The woman looked up, displayed a set of gleaming white teeth, and sprang to her feet.

"Here you are at last," she cried, hurrying toward him. "Saleh, here he is."

Feisal put out a hand to fend her off. Unperturbed and still beaming, Saida threw her arms around me. Over her head I saw a man emerge from the depths of the stairs and come toward us. He didn't seem to be in a hurry.

"What the hell are you doing?" Feisal shouted. "I told you no one was to be allowed in that tomb."

Mr. Saleh's most conspicuous feature was a magnificent black beard, which he kept stroking nervously. He greeted his superior with an ingratiating smile and looked imploringly at Saida.

Like the lady she was, she came to his rescue. "He was only inspecting the steps, Feisal. I asked him—"

"What's to inspect? They're steps!" Feisal lowered his voice a few decibels. "You asked him, did you? And smiled and fluttered your lashes and—"

Her melting brown eyes congealed like hardening fudge. "Don't you dare talk to me that way!"

I detached myself from Saida's fond embrace and took Feisal's arm. "Watch it," I muttered.

"What?" He stared at me and, with a visible effort, got himself under control. "Oh. Right. I'm sorry, Saida."

Saida, now in Schmidt's fond embrace, said cheerfully, "I forgive you."

"As for you, Saleh," Feisal began.

"I was only—"

"Never mind. What did you want to see me about?"

"It can wait. There is no problem. Whenever you can spare the time, Chief Inspector."

He was backing away, step by step, as he spoke. Feisal nodded curtly. "Later, then."

"Yes, sir. As you say." He beat a hasty retreat, but I caught a glimpse of his face before he turned, and I understood why Feisal had mentioned knives in the back.

"Oooh," Saida cooed. "I do love you when you are being masterful."

"Knock it off, Saida," Feisal growled. "What are you doing here?"

"Here in Luxor or here in the Valley?" She studied his flushed face and sobered. "I suppose I can travel where I please? I tried to reach you this morning but you did not answer your phone. Then I called your office, and they told me you would be in the Valley this afternoon. When I arrived, Saleh was at the guard post. He graciously accompanied me."

She stopped talking and looked inquiringly at him, as if inviting him to reply. The eyes were melting and the lashes were fluttering. Poor bemused Feisal was trying desperately to think of a way of dropping the subject, but I, immune to melting eyes and so on, realized we were in for it. She was not the lady to let him off the hook or quit excavating when she suspected something important lay just beneath the surface.

"All right, Saida," I said. "Let's stop playing games. What are you after?"

She burst into speech, eyes blazing and hands weaving patterns. "Honesty! Candor! The trust of the man who says he loves me! You insult my intelligence, Feisal. Do you think I am too stupid to put two and two and two and two together? For days you have been worried and afraid—"

Stung, Feisal interrupted at the top of his lungs. "What do you mean, afraid?"

Saida brushed the interruption aside with a sweeping gesture. "Your friends, your famous friends, who helped you to save Tetisheri, suddenly appear. They are interviewed by Ashraf, who does not waste time on social courtesies. They visit the museum and one of them, a lady who is not known to suffer from squeamishness, expresses a dislike of mummies. I begin to wonder. And then Ali, poor Ali, who had not an enemy in the world, disappears and is found dead. I begin to ask questions. It is not difficult to get answers if you know what questions to ask. Ali was not the only one to see that interesting van stop at the tomb. The others thought nothing of it, because no one told them they should! They believed it was an official visit. But it was not, was it, Feisal, because if it had been you would have told me about it. Me, of all people. Me, who has been nagging Ashraf for years to take better care of—"

Feisal covered her mouth with his hand. Over his fingers her eyes widened until the whites showed all around the dark pupils. She pushed his hand away.

"Oh, no," she whispered. "Tell me. Do not spare my feelings. Is he—did they—"

Schmidt's resigned expression mirrored my own thought. Denial would have been futile. She'd insist on seeing for herself, and a flat refusal would only strengthen her suspicions.

Feisal's silence had the same effect. He was the picture of guilt, shoulders bowed, head hanging. He was seeing not only exposure, but the loss of his beloved.

"They took him," I said. "They're holding him for ransom."

Men think they rule the roost, but some women know better. Saida blew out a breath of relief. She had feared the worst—the destruction or mutilation of the mummy. "Well, then," she said briskly, "we must get him back. And when we do, Feisal will be the hero, and Ashraf will look like a blithering idiot!"

It was a pretty ambitious agenda, and I could see trouble brewing if Saida stuck to it. I started to point this out, but nobody heard me, since the lovers were wrapped in a passionate embrace and

Schmidt was watching with romantic relish. Once the two had untangled themselves, Schmidt said, "Let us go somewhere for a nice lunch, eh?"

"We need to talk, Schmidt," I said.

"Talking and eating are not mutually exclusive. In fact," said Schmidt, "I think more clearly when I am eating."

We found a restaurant across the street from one of the big temples—Medinet Habu, I think it was—where the proprietor greeted Feisal by name and promised to produce anything we wanted, so long as it was chicken or rice. We settled ourselves with various beverages at one of the long tables while he went off to cook it. Wary cats brushed against our ankles. The place was cool and shady and a little shabby, and the view was about as good as it could get: the great pylons of the temple, pale gold against an azure sky.

"Now," said Saida, "tell me everything."

Schmidt was more than happy to oblige, interrupting himself from time to time to tell the cats to be patient, there would be chicken. Saida listened attentively, her head cocked and her elbows on the table. When Schmidt wound down, she said, "So you have not the slightest idea where he might be?"

I thought she was referring to Tutankhamon until she turned those big brown eyes to me. "You feel that he has betrayed you?"

My first reaction was anger. Nobody else had been rude enough to suggest that John had made a fool of me, that his protestations of innocence had been false, that he was the one behind the whole scam. I hadn't wanted to talk about it either. Meeting her sympathetic but steady gaze, I realized it was time I did.

"He's certainly told me a pack of lies," I said. "From the very beginning."

"Are you sure?" Schmidt asked anxiously.

"Oh, yes." The dealer in Berlin who wasn't a dealer, the so-called monsignor who probably had nothing to do with the Vatican . . .

"But that does not prove he is guilty of stealing—" Schmidt began.

"Shh," we all three hissed.

He continued, ". . . him. He—John—may be pursuing a Clue."

"Without telling us?" Feisal demanded. He looked as if he too was relieved to be able to discuss what had been weighing on his mind.

"Candor is not one of his most conspicuous characteristics," I said.

"He would not want to endanger us," Schmidt insisted. "Especially Vicky."

"You are such a bloody romantic, Schmidt," Feisal growled. "Face it. He was always the most obvious suspect. He has the connections and the insane imagination. If I hadn't provided him with an excuse to come to Luxor he'd have invented one, so he could be on the scene for the final negotiations."

There was pain as well as anger in his voice. It hurts to think you have been betrayed by someone you trusted.

Only Schmidt, the bloody romantic, spoke up in John's defense. "I will not believe it until he admits it." He considered the statement and then added, "Perhaps not even then."

"All right, let's go over it again," Feisal said wearily. "He was in the temple last night—"

"Along with a number of other dubious characters," I interrupted. "Let's not go over it again. We've got to stop speculating and guessing and concentrate on locating it . . . him. And I don't mean John. Anybody got a bright idea?"

The food (chicken and rice) arrived, along with bowls of stewed tomatoes and bread and hummus. The genial host left, the cats came out from under the table, and we stared stupidly at one another until Saida banged her fist on the table.

"Vicky is right! To begin with, let us assume that he is still somewhere in the Luxor area."

"That's an unverified assumption," Feisal said.

Saida gave him a scornful look. "We have to start somewhere, and it is a logical assumption, given the difficulties involved in transporting him elsewhere. The second assumption—"

Feisal opened his mouth. Saida raised her voice a notch and went on. "Which is also logical, is that he is still on the West Bank. Shall I explain to you why?"

"A conspicuous vehicle like that would have run a greater risk of being noticed on the streets of Luxor," Feisal said in a bored voice.

"Very good," Saida said condescendingly. "Whereas, on this side of the river, there are sparsely inhabited areas where, with caution, the vehicle could pull off the road, transfer its passenger, and remove the distinctive camouflage. Disappear, in other words."

We'd considered some of those points before, but hearing them laid out in that incisive contralto carried greater conviction. Feisal wasn't ready to admit it, though. "So you've narrowed it down to a few hundred square miles. That shouldn't be a problem."

"Go to hell," Saida said pleasantly. "To proceed. There are two general types of hiding places for such an object—a cave or abandoned tomb in the cliffs, or a room in a structure of some sort."

I remembered my dream, of Tutankhamon laid out on a bed in a fancy hotel, with the air-conditioning going full blast. Crazy, of course, but . . .

"They would want to protect him as much as possible, wouldn't they?" I asked. "Away from dust and insects and predatory animals and rockfalls and so on. And there would be less chance of someone stumbling on the hiding place by accident if it had walls around it and doors that could be closed and locked."

"But Ali's body was found in the cliffs." Feisal was still fighting a rearguard action.

"Pah," said Saida. "The villains would take him far away from the place where he met his death." She looked around. Schmidt and the cats had eaten all the chicken. "Let us go. Vicky, would you like to visit the loo before we start back?"

She led the way to a room at the back which, to put it as nicely as possible, would not have rated even one star in a guide to elegant restrooms. I will spare you the details, except to mention that I understood why she was wearing skirts instead of trousers. While we washed our hands at a stained basin with a well-used scrap of soap, she gave me a sidelong glance and sighed.

"Men are very pleasant to have around, but they are deficient in common sense, poor things. You saw at once the logic of what I was saying."

"They don't think the way we do, that's for sure."

"Except for your lover?"

She had got me away for a little girl talk. I liked her a lot but I wasn't in the mood for confidences. Not yet.

"John doesn't think the way anybody else does," I said with perfect accuracy.

"You are worried for him, aren't you?"

I accepted a handful of tissues which she produced from the billowing folds of her skirt. There was a towel, hanging on a hook by the sink, but I'd rather have wiped my hands on the floor.

"I haven't made up my mind," I said.

Schmidt had fallen in love with Saida early on, and when she asked for the loan of his notebook and pen he was ready to kneel at her feet. Their heads together, the two of them made lists while we drove to the boat landing. Once we were on the East Bank, Feisal and Saida went off arm in arm, destination undeclared, and Schmidt and I headed for the hotel.

The telephone was ringing when we entered his suite. I pounced on it; why kid myself, I was still hoping a familiar voice would announce a triumphant return, with Tut under one arm and the principal perp under the other. The caller was from housekeeping, asking if she could bring my laundry.

She'd come and gone and Schmidt was in the shower and I was about to head for mine when there was a knock at the door. Hotel employees popped in and out all the time, offering small services in return for badly needed small tips, so I assumed it was someone with a vase of flowers or a bowl of fruit. Instead I beheld a woman who was a total stranger. Her wash-and-wear gray pantsuit and low-heeled shoes reminded me of my Aunt Sue's going-out-for-lunch-with-the-girls outfits. Horn-rimmed glasses framed faded brown eyes, and brownish hair streaked with gray had been pulled back into a bun set off by a coquettish red bow. She was clutching an enormous purse, held in front of her. I half-expected her to ask me to contribute to the local animal shelter or subscribe to *Ladies' Home Journal.*

Her eyes tried to see past me. Since I pretty well filled the doorway and she was considerably shorter than I, they did not succeed.

"Yes?" I said, meaning no, what do you want?

She cleared her throat and said in a soft, precise voice. "I would like to speak to Mr. John Tregarth."

"Sorry," I said, "he isn't here."

"May I ask when you expect him back?"

"I don't know. That is," I amended, "you may ask, but I can't give you an answer."

"Oh."

I figured I had been polite enough for one day. This had to be another of John's ambiguous acquaintances. She didn't look like a crook, but then the best of them don't.

"Won't you come in?" I asked, stepping back and stretching my lips into a smile.

The smile may have been a mistake; it probably showed altogether too many teeth. She shook her head. The red bow bounced. "No, thank you. I—I will come another time."

"Who the—who are you?" My tone of voice and the hostile stare that accompanied it alarmed her. She jumped back, lifting the purse like a shield. Her eyes, magnified by thick lenses, were wide with alarm. I was afraid she'd start to scream and I'd be arrested for threatening a harmless lady who was twice my age, so I produced a modified version of the smile and said, "I mean—can I help you?"

"No. No, thank you. It is a private matter. But very important. I left a message earlier."

"Oh, are you . . ." I couldn't remember the name.

"If you will be good enough to ask him to telephone me at the Mercure? Thank you. I am sorry to have bothered you. But it is very important."

I had lied when I had pretended to Saida that I wasn't worried about John. I was worried and angry and frustrated, and here was a possible lead to his motives if not his current whereabouts. I was almost ready to grab her and drag her into the room and take my chances with the screaming when the portly form of Mahmud, the room steward, came into sight. He was carrying a vase with a pink rose in it.

"Goddamn it," I said vehemently.

Ms. Whatever let out a ladylike shriek and ran. Mahmud beamed and bowed and offered me the vase. I waved him in. "Put it on the table."

Schmidt's suite was at the far end of a long corridor. The unknown personage was still in sight, trotting as fast as she could toward the elevators. Just as well Mahmud had heaved into view, I thought. He had given me time to reconsider my initial impulse.

Across the hall from where I stood, two long flights of stairs led down to the mezzanine of the New Winter Palace lobby, where it was connected to its older neighbor. I made a dash for them, leaving the door open. If I moved fast enough and if the elevator was slow, as it usually was, I might reach the Old Winter Palace lobby before she left.

I went down the stairs at a breakneck pace, hanging on to the rail to keep from falling, and pelted along the corridor that led into the older building, and down the stairs to the lobby.

My first quick glance around the lobby failed to find her. A second, more deliberate glance, also came up empty. I didn't run, but I walked really fast to the front entrance. From the terrace I had a good view of the street one story below. Conspicuous by its absence was a small figure in a gray pantsuit.

"Goddamn it," I said.

Continuing the pursuit would probably be a waste of time. Now that I had calmed down, I realized I shouldn't have pursued at all. After all, I had her name and current address—assuming I could find her original message. I had no idea what had become of it. I ought to have made nice instead of frightening her into flight.

When I got out of the elevator I saw Schmidt standing in the open doorway of the suite, swinging from side to side like a pendulum. He saw me and let out a shout.

"Where have you been? How could you alarm me so? Never do that again. *Herr Gott,* do you not know better than to open a door when I am not present to defend you?"

I apologized and explained. Schmidt's eyes narrowed.

"You are starting at shadows, Vicky. This woman, whoever she may be, cannot have anything to do with the Tutankhamon affair or she would not have given you a name and an address. Now come and change. Feisal has just telephoned; he and Saida are joining us for dinner."

When I emerged from the bedroom, clean and freshly clothed and more or less in my right mind, Saida and Feisal were sitting on the balcony with Schmidt, watching the sunset. Saida was telling us what we were going to do next.

"We begin tomorrow at daybreak," she declared, waving a piece of paper. "I have made a list of places to be searched."

I took the list from her. It filled the entire page. "Us and what army?" I inquired. "We can't go bursting into the headquarters of respectable organizations like the German Institute or—"

"Who said we would burst? We will visit, as colleagues."

I glanced at Feisal, who avoided my eyes. I couldn't count on help from him, or from Schmidt, who was bouncing up and down in his chair, delighted at the prospect of active detecting. I was trying to decide whether to throw the cold water of common sense on the scheme or let them amuse themselves when there was a knock at the door.

"Saved by the knock," I said, and went to answer it.

It was a hotel employee carrying a plastic bag with the logo of one of the expensive shops in the arcade. "For you, lady," he said, offering me the bag.

Schmidt had rushed to my side, his right hand in his pocket. Visibly disappointed at seeing a harmless messenger instead of a knife-wielding assassin, he withdrew the hand. Instead of a weapon, it held a wad of banknotes.

"Wait a minute," I said. "That can't be mine. I haven't bought anything at Benetton."

"You ordered it," the man insisted. "It came to the desk just now."

Schmidt took the bag and handed over baksheesh.

"It is a present for you, perhaps," he said, closing the door. "Let us see if there is a note."

What there was, under a layer of tissue, was a wooden box inlaid with mother-of-pearl. The sort of box you can find at any shop in the suk.

"Oh my God," I said.

My exclamation brought Saida and Feisal in from the balcony. We stood around the table staring down at the box. I couldn't bring myself to touch it.

"It is very pretty," Saida said politely. She reached for the box. Feisal knocked her hand away. His face was an ugly shade of gray. "Let me," he said hoarsely.

She hadn't seen the other box, but his reaction and the fixed glares of Schmidt and me were enough to jog her memory. She shied back and raised her hands to her mouth. "Oh, no," she whispered. "Not another . . ."

The catch was stiff. Feisal pried it up and removed a layer of cotton wool.

It was a hand, but not the hand of a mummy. By the look of it, the body to which it had been attached had lost it within the past twenty-four hours.

TWELVE

Saida made it to the bathroom in time. Swallowing strenuously I followed her and sat on the edge of the tub until she was through.

"I'm sorry," she gasped, raising a pale face.

"It's okay." I offered a glass of water and a handful of tissues. "You're blasé about mummies; I'm not. But I expect I'm more accustomed to fresh corpses than you are."

She got unsteadily to her feet and took the glass. "Vicky. Was it . . . It wasn't his?"

"No." I hadn't thought it was, not even for an instant; I knew those long, elegantly shaped hands too well. The very idea that it might have been made my stomach churn. I went on, deliberately matter-of-fact, "It was a woman's hand. Small, brown, traces of henna on the nails and skin."

"I'm all right now." She squared her slim shoulders. "We must look again. Try to determine who it was."

I had a pretty good idea of who it was.

Feisal had turned away from the exhibit and lit a cigarette. Schmidt was still peering down into the box.

"It is the hand of a woman," he said.

"An Egyptian woman." I joined him and forced myself to have another look. "She was already dead when they cut it off. There's very little blood."

Saida let out a long shuddering sigh. Feisal put an arm around her shoulders. "The woman Ashraf met last night," he said, and blew out smoke in a long exhalation.

"It's a reasonable guess." I was sorry I'd quit smoking. Then I remembered I had another bad habit. I went to the minibar and selected two small bottles more or less at random. At that point I didn't care what I drank so long as it was alcoholic.

Schmidt took the glass I handed him. "*Vielen Dank,* Vicky. Are you all right?"

"As right as one can be under the circumstances." Scotch jolted down into my queasy interior, which welcomed it heartily. "What are we going to do with—with it?"

"Notify the police, of course," Feisal said.

Schmidt carefully lowered the lid of the box. "Not of course, my friend. Not until we have had time to consider this. There was a message."

The slip of paper in his hand must have been under the horrible thing. It certainly hadn't been on top of it. Bless the old dear, he had more guts than any of us. Bushy brows raised, he held it out. When no one offered to take it, he read it aloud.

" 'You are responsible for her death. The price is now four million. You have three days.' Well, Feisal? Do you want to show this to the police? Even if we do not hand over the note they will want to know why the box was sent to us."

Feisal ran a hand through his hair. "What do you suggest?"

"Ashraf," I said.

At first Feisal resisted the idea of calling his boss. "He'll only make matters worse. This would never have happened if he hadn't tried to be clever."

"Exactly," I said. "It's his mess, and I vote we shove it in his face."

"So do I," Saida said. "Schmidt? Yes. You are outvoted, Feisal."

Ashraf answered on the first ring. Feisal was uninformative but peremptory. "No, I can't tell you what the problem is, but it's bad. Just get over here, right now."

Then we waited. He was there sooner than I had expected. He had to be pretty worried to respond so quickly, but, being Ashraf, he wasn't about to admit it.

"I was on my way to an appointment," he said stiffly. He was dressed to the nines, a monogrammed hankie tucked in his breast pocket, which bore the insignia of a Cairo sporting club. "What is so—"

The sentence ended in a hiss of breath. I had cleared everything off the table except for the box, and was standing in front of it. I stepped to one side with a graceful wave of my hand; there it was, conspicuous as a signboard even to one who had not seen the first delivery. I felt a little guilty when I saw the blood drain from Ashraf's face. But only a little. He was afraid it was another piece of his precious mummy.

I felt even less guilty when his reaction to the reality was visible relief. "I thought," he began, and then turned on Feisal. "Did you arrange this charade? I know you dislike me, Feisal, but to torture me in this way—"

"It's not a charade," I said furiously. "And it's not a damned dried-up mummy that's been dead for three thousand years. Sit down and shut up, Ashraf. Give him the note, Schmidt."

I gave him two seconds to read it and then said, "This was meant for you, Ashraf. It was safer for them to deliver it here rather than approach you directly, after the dumb stunt you pulled last night. What are you going to do about it?"

"Four million," Ashraf mumbled, staring at the paper.

"Can you raise that much?"

"Not in three days. Not without stripping myself of every asset I own."

"Then it seems to me your only recourse is to inform the Ministry."

Ashraf let out a bleat of protest. "What other option have you?" I went on remorselessly. "Leave it to them to decide whether to raise the money or risk the negative publicity. If I were in their shoes I'd choose the latter alternative. The gang may take the money and not return your precious Tut. For all you know, he's already been destroyed."

Ashraf drew a long breath. He tossed the note onto the table. "There is another option," he said. "We must locate these villains before the deadline."

"Any ideas?" I inquired sarcastically.

"Keep looking. We have three days. I have the authority to request police assistance. I will tell them we are searching for a missing tourist who may have been kidnapped."

"It's worth trying," Feisal said. "Schmidt, you questioned the concierge. Did he give you a description of the man who delivered the parcel?"

"Only that he was a neatly dressed man who said he was a clerk at the store in question. The lady had wanted an object which was not in stock, and they promised to procure it for her and deliver it to the hotel. They had a card with her name on it."

"My name," I added helpfully.

Eyeing Ashraf closely, Schmidt added, "We discussed whether or not to notify the police, and concluded it was only fair to consult you first, since you were the last known person to see her alive."

Ashraf's jaw dropped. "What are you implying?"

"I state a fact," Schmidt said. "Which in duty bound I will feel obliged to mention to the police. You are the only one of us who can give them a description of the woman."

You had to admire Ashraf's nerve. Schmidt's one-two punch had shaken him badly, but he wasn't stupid enough to start spouting denials. We gave him time to think it over. After a long interval he straightened and looked up at Schmidt.

"Very well, Herr Doktor, the police must be kept out of this for the time being."

"That," said Schmidt, "is your opinion. We have invited it but the final decision is mine—ours, I should say."

He could have the first person singular, as far as I was concerned. So far he had played it brilliantly. John couldn't have done better.

"You do not deny," Schmidt went on, "that the severed member most probably belonged to the woman you met at Karnak?"

"Don't interrogate me as if I were a suspect," Ashraf said with a flash of temper. "I don't deny it is possible—likely, even. However, I bear no responsibility for her death. I don't know who she was or where she went. I was struck unconscious, remember? You had better question the man who hit me."

"It wasn't John," I snapped.

"You would say that, of course," Ashraf said, giving me a sympathetic look.

I saw the same look on a couple of other faces, and lost the remains of my temper.

"Oh, for God's sake, haven't any of you heard of wigs and hair coloring, and hats and turbans? John of all people knows how light, even dim light, shines on fair hair. If he was there, and I suspect he was, he'd be wearing some sort of disguise."

"Ah," said Schmidt, stroking his mustache and nodding.

"He was there, however, you believe?" Ashraf pounced. "Then he could have overheard her betrayal. Or learned of it later from one of his confederates."

"Or got the information from a Ouija board," I said. Schmidt and I exchanged meaningful glances. We were on the same wavelength, good ol' Schmidt and I, perhaps because we were the only ones who weren't obsessed with the well-being of Tutankhamon.

"Okay," I said. "We'll try it your way, Ashraf. It's your decision whether or not to come clean to the Ministry. But from this moment on, you let us in on every move you make and every thought you think. You mucked up good and proper when you tried to go it alone."

"They will be in touch again," Schmidt added. "To designate when and where you are to hand over the ransom. You will notify us immediately of this."

Ashraf's sour expression showed how little he liked being ordered around. He had no choice but to agree, however. His last faint hope rested with us. I couldn't blame him for finding that idea depressing.

When he got up to leave I offered him the box. He backed away, hands raised in rejection. "It's yours," I said firmly. "Anyhow, you are better able than we to find a secure hiding place. The hotel personnel are in and out of this room all the time."

He agreed, after I had replaced the box in its original bag, and went out carrying it at arm's length the way I remove the remains of the unlucky small animals Caesar occasionally manages to catch. Fortunately he's not very good at it.

It was amazing what a relief it was to have that box out of the room; it had permeated the air like poison gas. Schmidt mentioned the room service, and we agreed we might be able to force down a morsel or two. Saida got out her list again. Before she and Schmidt could start on it, I said, "Hey, Schmidt, can I borrow your cell phone?"

"What is wrong with yours?"

"It's dead. I guess I forgot to plug in the battery." I'm usually a comfortable liar, but Schmidt's innocent blue eyes made me plunge into unnecessary explanations. "I just want to call Karl and find out how Caesar is doing. I'll pay you back."

"*Ach, nein,* there is no need." He handed it over and I retreated into the bedroom. As I had expected, the number was on Schmidt's frequent-call list.

The next problem was how to get away without Schmidt. I considered a number of ideas, none of them very nice and a few downright dangerous. Getting Schmidt drunk was not nice, and it had drawbacks. He was inclined to challenge people to duels, and once he passed out it was impossible to rouse him for hours. I pondered the problem as I picked at my food—turned out I wasn't very hungry after all—and was still pondering when he said casually, "I am going out for a while. Stay here and lock the door."

"Going where?" I demanded.

Schmidt chuckled. No cherub in a Boucher painting could have looked more innocent. "I wish to shop."

"What for?"

"A galabiya and a scarf. In case I need to disguise myself."

The explanation made perfect sense, if you knew Schmidt as I knew Schmidt, and it suited my plans perfectly. "And," Schmidt went on, "I will get one of each for you too. The shops in the arcade are open late. I will not be long. Feisal and Saida will come with me."

If I hadn't been so anxious to carry out my own scheme, I might have realized he was babbling unnecessarily, just as I had. Saida indicated her willingness to participate, and off they went.

I had told her I would call her back. She was waiting for the call.

Unlike some heroines, I am not the girl to trot out onto the dark streets of a strange city in order to meet with an individual whose motives are open to question. The lobby of the Old Winter Palace is quite large, with groupings of chairs and sofas scattered here and there. I selected the grouping farthest from the door and the elevators and sat down, holding a book up in front of my face and peering over the top of it. She wasn't long. I recognized her as soon as she came through the door, although her hair was a cascade of auburn tresses and she was made up like a Hollywood celebrity. Lipstick enlarged her narrow lips and she had on so much mascara and eyeliner, she looked as if she'd been punched in both eyes.

The guard at the security desk gave her elegant handbag only a cursory search and waved her on through. She'd spotted me by then and came straight toward me.

"It's a delightful old hotel, isn't it?" she said.

"We don't have time for small talk, Suzi. Schmidt is on the loose and due back before long."

Her lips stretched into a half-smile. "Fair enough. What do you want?"

"I want to know everything you know. Candor goes against the grain with you people, but you ought to realize we have the same end in mind."

"I'm not so sure about that."

"Okay, I'll tell you what I want. The damned mummy retrieved, and the perps caught before they can do any more damage."

"Seems reasonable," Suzi murmured.

"Your turn."

She took a small hand mirror from her purse and pretended to inspect her makeup. "I don't want you or Anton harmed. I'm very fond of him, you know."

I thought of several caustic comments, but stuck doggedly to the subject. "What do you want most? Don't tell me your priorities are identical to mine."

"Frankly," said Suzi, manipulating the mirror, "I don't give a damn about the mummy. They can smash it to pieces for all I care. The people who pulled off the heist are small-fry, hired thugs. I don't give a damn about them either. I want the man in charge."

"John? Why? Forgive my rudeness, but you seem a trifle obsessive about him."

She put down the mirror and looked me straight in the eye. "I spotted him on the cruise, but I couldn't be absolutely certain I was right until I went over his dossier and put a number of hints together. Laws vary, and so do the statutes of limitations. I realized it would be very hard to pin any of his past escapades on him. But I didn't believe the leopard had changed his spots. I knew he'd revert to his old ways sooner or later, and then I'd catch him in the act."

Never trust people who look you straight in the eye. I said again, "Why? Why him? You must have other cases on the docket."

"I'll tell you the truth, Vicky." A small self-deprecating smile joined the candid gaze. "He's become something of a legend in the business, not only because he has gotten away with so many shady deals but because of their bizarre nature. Nailing him would be like—like identifying Jack the Ripper. Come on, Vicky, you know he's been lying to you and Anton all along. Using you, betraying your trust."

"He certainly has told me a lot of lies."

"You don't resent that?"

"Oh, I resent it a lot," I said with perfect truth.

"Then collaborate with me. If he's innocent, fine; I'm wrong and will admit it. If he's not, you ought to be as anxious as I to catch him. It isn't as if you'd be handing him over to the hangman, he'd only spend a few well-deserved years in jail."

"Well . . ."

"I know where he is."

I leaned back and crossed my legs. "I thought you might. You followed him the other night, didn't you?"

"Yes. The place was crawling with people following other people. Most of them converged on your friend Feisal, who was yelling his head off, but I stuck to Smythe—or Tregarth, if you prefer—who had taken off after the woman, the one Khifaya met. I had to climb a damned wall; it took me a while. I was afraid I'd lost him but I finally glimpsed him just as he caught up with her, outside a house behind the temple. They talked for a minute, maybe less. Then she twisted away from him and ran. That distracted me. It shouldn't have, but it did, for a vital second or two. When I looked back he was gone. He had to have entered the house. He hasn't come out since."

That wasn't the story she had told Schmidt. She must have concluded she couldn't entirely trust him, but she was still hanging on to him in case he might prove useful.

"Why haven't you gone in after him?" I asked.

Her lips twisted. "Regrettably, we are constrained by the laws of the country in which we are operating. The place is owned by a well-to-do Egyptian of impeccable character, who sometimes rents it out on short leases. In order to get a search warrant I'd have to go to the police. For obvious reasons I don't want—"

"Oops," I said. "Duck. There's Schmidt."

Suzi slid down until only the top of her head showed over the back of the chair. I peeked out from behind my book. Schmidt didn't look in our direction. In addition to several parcels he'd acquired a gaudily ornamented stick with dependent strings of beads, which he swung jauntily as he passed the elevator and went on along the corridor.

"It's okay," I said. "He's gone toward the bar. But you had better make it quick. What do you want me to do?"

"Get him to leave the house. I've had the place staked out. He may have spotted some of my people. I'll call them off. That should be evidence of my good faith."

That and a crucifix on which you would swear, I thought.

"Tell me where the place is."

The description she gave was sufficiently detailed. I nodded. "I think I can find it. I'll have to reconnoiter first."

"When?"

"Tomorrow. In daylight."

"And then?"

The questions were coming hard and fast, like the cracks of a whip. She was so eager, she had forgotten to be persuasive.

"Then, if all goes well, I'll try for it tomorrow evening. Before dark. I'll call you. Now get going."

"You won't be in danger, Vicky. I promise."

Seemed to me I'd heard that song before.

We had cut it close. I was waiting for an elevator when Schmidt emerged from the bar, patting daintily at his mustache with a hanky.

Seeing me, he broke into a trot and a litany of complaints. What was I doing in the lobby? Why had I not followed his orders?

"I was worried about you," I explained. "You were gone so long. Where are Feisal and Saida? You promised to stay with them. Have you been in the bar all this time? Boozing it up while I fretted?"

"Feisal and Saida escorted me back to the hotel—as if I were a little boy," Schmidt added indignantly. "They then went on their way. I was in the bar only for a single glass of beer. It is a historical room, where Howard Carter often went when he was working on the tomb of Tutankhamon. Would you like—"

"No, thanks. I'm beginning to resent Howard Carter. If he hadn't dug Tut up we wouldn't be in this mess."

"And how is Caesar?" He followed me into the elevator.

"Who? Oh." I had forgotten I was supposed to have been inquiring after my dog. "Fine. Where'd you get the fly whisk?"

"It is not a fly whisk, it is one of the royal scepters," Schmidt explained. "The flail, as it is sometimes called." He swished the strings of beads.

"Very nice. What else did you get?"

Showing off his purchases took a while. Schmidt has a weakness for bling. Instead of simple inconspicuous galabiyas, he had purchased gaudy garments made for the tourist trade, trimmed with colored or metallic braid. I was moved to mild protest. "I thought you wanted something you could wear as a disguise."

"Like this?" He dug into another of the bags.

Galabiyas are made to the same basic design: straight, ankle-length garments with long sleeves. They go on over one's head; the neck opening is just a hole with a slit down the front. The first one Schmidt produced was pale blue, the second had narrow stripes of brown and white, the third was tan. At my suggestion Schmidt tried them on, one after the other. Even the shortest dragged on the ground. Hoisting his striped skirts, Schmidt trotted into his bed-room and came back with a pair of scissors. I crawled around him, hacking off a foot or so of fabric all around, and sat back to study the result.

"It won't do, Schmidt. A ragged hem might pass, but not when the rest of the garment is in pristine condition. And don't expect me to fix it, I can't even sew on a button."

"The nice lady from housekeeping will do it for me. Now let us make for me a turban."

We tried, using the white scarves Schmidt had bought. The ends kept coming loose and falling down around Schmidt's ears. Unper-turbed, Schmidt produced a large white-and-red-checked cloth which he draped over his head and tied in place. He looked like a musta-chioed member of Hamas or Hezbollah. I refrained from criticism, since I had no intention of letting him go out on the street in the outfit.

Well, it passed the time. Schmidt handed over the stripy robe to a beaming "nice lady," who knew she would earn a week's wages for an hour's work, opened a Stella, and whipped out his cell phone.

"I must report to Suzi so that she will remain unwitting of my defection."

Somehow I wasn't surprised when Suzi failed to answer. Schmidt then went through the messages waiting. "Here is one from Hein-rich asking how he should respond to a request for you to speak at a meeting in Zurich."

"That fink! Why did he go to you behind my back?"

"He says you do not communicate with him."

"He doesn't communicate with me either. He's after my job, try-ing to make me look bad."

Schmidt chuckled. "That is what you call an uphill struggle. Here is another from him, asking why you do not communicate.

Foolish young man. And this . . . Hmm, hmmm, only unimportant reports. Ah! Wolfgang has called."

I waited until he had listened to the message, and then said, "The guy we—er—ran into at Karnak?"

"Yes. He regretted that our encounter should have ended so abruptly and asks me for lunch tomorrow."

"He wants to pump you about the so-called accident."

"*Aber natürlich*. I would do the same. Shall we go?"

"I thought you and Saida had tomorrow's schedule all worked out."

Schmidt tugged at his mustache. "Yes, but I am not so sure she is on the right track. How could an object of such size be concealed in a place where there are always people?"

"True, Schmidt. Why don't you put Wolfgang off? Rain check, and so on. We don't have time for social activities. I take it Saida and Feisal are planning to come for breakfast? We'll reconsider our plans then."

Schmidt went off with his parcels and his beer. He forgot the flail, which was lying on a chair. I picked it up and gave it a tentative swish. The beads made a sound like a baby's rattle. As a potential weapon it lacked gravitas.

After I had washed and brushed and so on, I sat down on the side of my bed and called a number I had rung every night for the past four days. As before, there was no answer.

The bed had been turned down and not one but three foil-wrapped chocolates rested on the pillow. I unwrapped one. Maybe a sugar surge would stimulate my thought processes. I hadn't had time to consider my conversation with Suzi and what I meant to do about it.

The pale blue galabiya Schmidt had pressed upon me lay across a chair. It would be about as useful as a belly dancer's costume.

(Schmidt would probably get one of those for me next.) I couldn't pass as a man without, at the bare minimum, a properly wound turban and something to darken my hands and face. What I needed was a black woman's robe and face veil. They sure didn't sell them in the suk. I considered possibilities as I unwrapped the second chocolate. The "nice lady" from housekeeping might be able to get one for me—but negotiating with her while Schmidt was around wouldn't be easy. Saida would know how to get one—but I didn't want her in on this.

There was only one other option. I ate the last chocolate and got into bed.

That must be the house I was told about," I said, pointing. "It's the only one around that fits the description. Do you know it, Feisal?"

Feisal leaned past me to peer out the window of the taxi. We had hired one of the nondescript vehicles that wait for fares outside the hotel.

"Yes, I know it. When are you going to tell us how you learned of this place and why it's important?"

Saida whipped out her notebook. "Is it on my list?"

"How the hell should I know?" Feisal demanded. "Vicky—"

"Later. Just keep a lookout."

Someone might reasonably have asked "What for?" The house was surrounded by a high wall made of whitewashed mud brick. Only the tops of trees and the roofline of the building inside were visible. A wooden double-leafed gate, wide enough to admit a delivery truck, was closed. Sitting next to it on a straight chair was a man wearing a raggedy galabiya and head cloth. He glanced incuriously at the taxi. There were a few other people around—two women robed in black towing a protesting child between them, a huddled figure apparently asleep under a dusty palm tree, a man driving a donkey cart piled with greenery.

The taxi driver addressed Schmidt, who was sitting beside him. "Is this where you wish to go? Shall I stop?"

"No!" I said emphatically. "Keep going. Slowly."

I pushed Feisal away from the window and craned my neck as we cruised past. It was the back of the house in which I was interested. I couldn't see much. The right angle of the wall went on for some distance. It was as blank and uninformative as the front wall.

"The effendi is not there," the driver offered. "He lives in Cairo most of the year."

"Who is living there now?" I asked.

The string of blue beads hanging from the rearview mirror tinkled musically as the taxi turned onto a road that led away from the house. "Strangers. Also from Cairo, perhaps. They have their own vehicles. They came a month ago. They are not friendly people. They do not buy at the local market."

"What about servants?" I asked. "Have they hired local people?"

An expressive shrug. "No."

I was sorry to hear that, though it didn't surprise me.

"Where now, sitt?" the driver asked. He had apparently accepted the fact that I was the one in charge.

"A café," said Schmidt promptly. "The nearest."

An extremely chilly silence ensued, enlivened only by hostile glares from Feisal. My colleagues had realized they weren't going to get the information they wanted while the helpful, English-speaking driver was present. He selected a place (probably owned by a friend or cousin) on one of the streets of town, away from the corniche. We accepted his offer to wait.

"Very nice," said Schmidt, as we settled at a table.

Very nice and very empty. We were the only patrons. Feisal fizzed quietly like a lit fuse while Schmidt discussed food with the waiter. When the latter had gone into the kitchen, Feisal leaned forward, pushed aside a vase with two rosebuds in it, and planted his arms on the table.

"All right, Vicky, we went along with you on this expedition and refrained, as you requested, from questions. Now let's have it."

"I will tell you everything," I said.

"Hah," said Schmidt.

I did tell them everything. Almost everything. Schmidt's eyes narrowed and widened, narrowed and widened, as I described my conversation with Suzi. Feisal's eyebrows wriggled. Grinning, Saida took out her notebook and pen.

I stopped talking when the waiter came with our coffee. The usual alternative to Turkish coffee is Nescafé and a pot of hot water. I was happy to settle for that. There were no grounds involved.

Nobody had interrupted me. They were too busy trying to take in the flood of information I had supplied. Saida was the first to recover.

"As I expected! A woman is the first to make a vital discovery!"

"It's a possible lead," I said modestly. "She could have been feeding me a line. I didn't see anything suspicious."

"Precisely what you would expect to see if it were the headquarters of the gang," Saida cried.

"Hmm," said Feisal.

"What do you think, Schmidt?" I asked. I was beginning to worry about him. He had barely spoken, and I had hit him with the equivalent of a sockful of sand.

"I think," said Schmidt, "that you are deceitful and dangerous. And even more clever than I had realized. At least you had the sense to let us in on this instead of going alone to reconnoiter."

"I am all those things," I admitted. "And so are you, Schmidt, so don't give me a hard time."

"I do not because I know what drives you," Schmidt said. "But we will not speak of that. We agree, do we not, that the house is suspicious? Strangers who have been in residence for a month, who do not mix with the local population, who live behind high walls with a guarded gate. Suzi would have no reason to lie to you. She wants your help."

"And she's perfectly willing to use you as a decoy," Feisal added. "Forget it, Vicky. Not even to retrieve Tutankhamon would I permit you to take such a chance."

"Aw, gee," I said, patting his hand. "That's so sweet."

"You are a dreadful woman," Feisal said, without rancor. "Can't you accept a statement of affection without making a joke of it?"

"No, she is afraid of serious emotions," Schmidt explained. "We who love her accept this."

"Shut up, Schmidt," I said. "Please."

Schmidt patted my hand. "It is a subject for another time, perhaps. Assuming that Suzi is speaking the truth, that house may be the present headquarters of the gang. In which case, Tut—er—he may be there."

Lips pursed and eyes shining, Saida chortled, "Yes, he must be. And it is Vicky who has found the vital clue! A woman!"

Nerves were a trifle strained. Feisal turned on his beloved with a sneer. "As it turns out, you weren't so clever, were you? He's not on the West Bank. You were wrong."

"Not at all," Saida said serenely. "Mine was only one theory among others."

"The first part of the scenario was right," Schmidt said, before a jolly little lovers' quarrel could develop. "They changed the look of the van while they were still on the West Bank, or transferred him to another, more inconspicuous, vehicle. No one would have paid particular attention to a small van or truck on the bridge or on the streets of Luxor. The house is isolated; they could drive straight into the courtyard. It is the right place. It must be. So. We go in tonight, *nicht wahr?*"

His mustache bristled. I said, "If you mean go in, as 'in with guns blazing,' the answer is forget it. This is going to require some planning."

"Exactly," Feisal said, giving Schmidt a stern look.

We discussed it for a while. As Feisal kept telling Schmidt, we couldn't involve the police without getting a warrant, for which we had no cause. Ashraf would go ballistic at that idea. The most interesting suggestion came from Saida.

"Vicky and I will approach the guard at the back gate. Yes, yes, Feisal, there is certainly a back gate. He will be disarmed by the appearance of two helpless, harmless females. We will persuade him to let us in. Then we will begin screaming for help. That will provide an excuse for you and the others to break in."

Schmidt said, "No, we cannot allow you to take the chance. I will approach the guard, wearing a veil and habara."

I said, "Not to disparage your powers of seduction, Schmidt, but—"

Feisal said, "What others?" Then he said, "That is the most absurd scheme I have ever heard, and if you suppose for one second that I will allow—"

The appearance of the waiter, wondering what the yelling was all about, put an end to the argument. Schmidt asked for more coffee and I took advantage of the relative quiet.

"Okay, this is the plan. I call Suzi and report. Feisal, you arrange a meeting with Ashraf. One of them may have an idea."

"That is not a plan, that is procrastination," Schmidt exclaimed. "If we are to go in tonight—"

"We are not going in tonight. We need time to think and make arrangements."

"Time," Schmidt intoned, "is running out."

"Shut up, Schmidt."

To show my good faith, I called Suzi and let the others listen in. She had already been informed of our appearance that morning and scolded me for bringing the others with me. I responded with whining excuses which, if she'd had the sense God gave a goat, would have warned her to back off. An exasperated sigh followed my explanation that I wasn't ready to take action that night. "Meet me in the lobby, same time, same place, tonight," she said crisply. "I'll have a plan worked out."

"She's a charmer, all right," I said, ringing off. "Your turn, Feisal. Tell Ashraf we'll meet him later at—someplace on the West Bank. Deir el Bahri, maybe."

Nobody asked why the West Bank. That was a relief, since I couldn't explain my reasons.

The taxi driver was reluctant to part with us, but we couldn't have conversed freely in the presence of someone whose English was so good. After he had dropped us at the hotel, Schmidt proposed lunch. Over his protests and those of Feisal—"we aren't meeting Ashraf until three"—I managed to hustle them all onto a boat by telling them the simple truth.

"I want to visit Umm Ali. I wouldn't want her to think we had forgotten her or her son."

We picked up a taxi on the other side and went to the village.

I wondered if the kids posted lookouts. They converged on us with the speed of paparazzi tracking the latest pop culture celebrity. Among them I saw a familiar face. I stopped.

"Hey, Ahman. I'm sorry about your uncle."

The cheeky grin faded, the outstretched hand dropped to his side. "It's okay," I said quickly. "I just wanted to know—"

He slid away. I didn't go after him. It had been a random shot, but his hasty retreat strengthened my hunch. Young as he was, he had been taught the lessons his elders had learned from years of exploitation and adversity: don't answer questions, or show emotion to *strangers*, however well-intentioned. They are not one of us. They don't understand.

The men were in the courtyard, smoking and sitting. That was a relief; I wouldn't have to face the entire family. I dealt with the next hurdle by the same method that had worked up till now. The truth.

"Stay here," I told the others. "I want to talk to her alone."

"You don't speak Arabic," Feisal protested.

"Don't worry, I'll make myself understood."

She'd had enough advance notice to arrange herself on the sofa, erect and formidable as a graven image. There were several other women present, including the veiled gray-eyed female I had noticed before. After gabbling my way through the formal greetings, I addressed gray-eyes.

"Do you speak English?"

"A little only, sitt."

I had concocted a couple of wild theories about her. I'd been wrong on all counts. The face she bared when she put her veil aside was that of a young Egyptian woman, smooth-cheeked and unfamiliar.

"Tell Umm Ali I think I know who murdered her son. Tell her I need her help."

Another example of unconscious prejudice made me cringe when a murmur of comprehension ran around the room. The younger women had remained modestly silent in the presence of the matriarch, but I ought to have known some of them understood and spoke English.

I told them what I wanted.

When I emerged, blinking, into the sunlight, my backpack bulged, but not enough to provoke comment. So far so good. One step at a time. The next step was going to be a giant step, though.

Nobody was hungry except Schmidt, who is always hungry. Since we had time to kill, we found him a restaurant.

"Now we must discuss what to tell Ashraf," Saida said, digging into a bowl of hummus with a chunk of bread.

"The truth," I said absently. "It seems to be working."

Feisal ignored the last statement. He and Saida got into one of their standard arguments about who was to say what to whom and why. Schmidt drank beer and ate and watched me. He knows me too well, does Schmidt. The truth, the whole truth and nothing but the truth . . . It had to work. It was my only option.

I didn't get my chance until we were almost finished eating and Schmidt announced he was going to the bathroom.

"Me too," I said, and followed him.

The room in question—one room—was around the side and toward the back. Schmidt paused, politely inviting me to precede him.

"Schmidt," I said softly, "I am depending on you as I have never depended before, and that's saying a lot. Will you promise to do exactly what I tell you, no arguments, no questions?"

Schmidt said, "Yes."

I wanted to hug him. So I did. When I had finished explaining my plan, such as it was, he said only, "How will you get away from Feisal and Saida?"

"I haven't figured that out yet."

"I will make a distraction."

"God bless you, Schmidt."

"Now you promise that you will do exactly as you said. If I do not hear from you by five, I will come in after you."

"Fair enough. It could be a wild-goose chase, Schmidt."

Schmidt nodded. "For your sake, I hope it is. Be careful." With great dignity he entered the loo and closed the door.

THIRTEEN

Schmidt scampered out onto the road right in front of a camel. The camel howled, or whatever they do—it's a horrible sound—its rider screamed, and Schmidt, writhing on the ground, added a few howls of his own. I stood frozen for a second or two; then a fat, white-clad arm waved imperiously, and I realized that this was Schmidt's idea of a distraction and that he had fallen, not been knocked down.

When I emerged from the loo, swathed in black, Schmidt was still carrying on at the top of his lungs. I could hear him but I couldn't see him because his prostrate form was surrounded by a crowd—Feisal, Saida, the camel driver, the camel, the cook, the waiter, and a motley collection of passersby. One, I was happy to see, was a woman, unveiled but robed in black, carrying a baby. I sidled up to her and stood watching with the other spectators. Nobody was leaving the scene, it was just too darned interesting.

Finally Schmidt allowed himself to be raised to his feet and led back into the restaurant. He was doing his best to cover my retreat, insisting that it was his fault, that the hysterical camel rider was not to blame, that he wanted water, beer, and the arm of Saida to support him. My newfound friend shifted the baby to her other arm and spoke to me. I shrugged apologetically and pointed at the spot where my ear lurked under the head covering. She smiled and offered me the baby.

I took it as it was meant, as a gesture of goodwill and sympathy. I also took the baby. The baby did not approve. As Mama and I started off down the road, side by side, it began to cry. The veil covering my face might have put it off, or maybe it was just me. I don't have much experience with babies. It was too good a disguise to give up, though. Feisal and Saida had realized I was missing. They had hurried out of the restaurant and were making little dashes along the road, first in one direction, then in another, shouting questions at everyone in sight. The two ladies in black, one of them toting a screaming infant, didn't register on their radar.

I parted company with the baby, to the relief of baby and Mama, as soon as we were out of sight of the restaurant. Hiccuping sobs succeeded the screams when Mama took it. I thanked her for the treat by ducking my head, and then struck off to the right.

I was still some distance from my destination, but I was in no hurry. Trudging along the path, I went over my program. It was simple: Get into the house unobserved, find a place to hide, stay there until something happened . . . or it didn't.

I have a lot of faith in hunches, which are often based on evidence observed but unprocessed by the conscious mind. In this case, the processed evidence was thin. A house that fit all the specifications we had come up with, a house purportedly unoccupied, but which had been entered within the last few days, a house where I had thought I might have heard a suspicious noise, a house whose custodian hadn't been carrying out his duties. A house shunned by the locals because it was haunted by a demon cat. I could be way off base on all those counts. The only way of finding out for sure was to do what I was doing now.

Dust sifted into my shoes and whitened the hem of my robe as I plodded along. What did I have to lose, after all? If my hunch was wrong, a few hours of my time. If I was right . . . A few years of my life?

Don't be such a pessimist, Vicky, I told myself. If you're right you stand to gain a lot.

I began to understand why some Muslim women regarded the veil as protection rather than a sign of subjugation. The people I met along the way paid no attention to me. The men didn't even look in my direction. The closer I got to the house, the fewer people I encountered. That was either a good sign or a bad one—good because it showed the locals did avoid the place, bad because anyone approaching was conspicuous. I slowed to a slower shuffle.

The first item on my program was the hardest—getting inside without being observed. I didn't see any signs of life, but it wouldn't have been sensible to march up to the front door and knock.

Someone had gone to considerable lengths to establish and maintain a garden. There must be water somewhere, an irrigation ditch or pool, although most of the plants might be varieties that can survive in hot, dry conditions. I'm no gardener; the only ones I recognized were cacti and palms, and stands of the dusty green tamarisk that is common in the area. I hadn't cased the place in detail on our first visit, having no reason to do so, but I remembered a view of some kind of green stuff outside the window of the director's study. I wandered off to the right, following a narrow track that appeared to go in the direction I wanted—around the house, toward the side. The grounds were more extensive than I had realized. Wings stretched out at odd angles, and I could see other buildings and sections of wall through the trees. More to the point, a grove of low, shrubby trees, vine-entangled, ran along the side of the house, from the veranda toward the back.

It was mid-afternoon, when people in hot climates stay indoors, napping or resting. I couldn't be seen from the house, thanks to those convenient trees; a quick look around assured me that there wasn't another soul in sight. It wasn't going to get any better than this. I divested myself of my black shroud; it left me feeling naked and exposed, but the folds of fabric encumbered easy movement and no disguise was going to do me any good if I was found inside. And now I could get at the objects I had stowed away in my pockets. I had abandoned the backpack, with the pious hope that an honest soul would turn it in to the proprietor of the restaurant, or that Saida would retrieve it. I took out my wristwatch. Quarter to three. It had taken me too damn long to get here. Siesta time would end soon.

I moved carefully, pushing branches aside instead of plowing through. The trees, whatever they were, prickled. The vine was a pretty thing, covered with sprays of little pink flowers. It had climbed and intertwined, reaching for light, and it provided a screen so thick I didn't see the window until I was almost upon it.

The window was open.

Seeing the first actual confirmation of my wild theory shocked me into a brief mental blackout. I guess I had never really expected to get this far. It took several seconds for me to get my wits, or what passes for them, back.

The couch is under the window, I reminded myself. The sill is about four feet above the ground. Now, before you rush in where angels fear to tread, make sure nobody is there. That's not too hard. Look and listen and take it slow.

The room was shadowy and still, except for a buzzing, which, after a heart-stopping second, I identified as a gathering of flies. The doors, one to the library and one into the central hall, were closed. The couch was unoccupied. One of the high-backed chairs had been pushed away from the table. Otherwise the room looked pretty much as it had before.

John would have been over the sill in a single movement. John. I didn't let myself think about him. It took me three movements: one foot in a crack, a knee on the sill, the other knee onto the couch.

The sound wasn't loud, just a faint squeak of rusty springs. It was echoed by another sound, a cross between a snore and a snort.

I was under the couch before the snort stopped. There's nothing like sheer terror to inspire agility. Someone was sitting in that big chair. I hadn't seen him—or her?—because of the high back. Luckily for me, the occupant had been napping.

The couch was long enough to conceal me, but there wasn't a lot of room underneath, thanks to those sagging springs. One of them poked into my derriere and another into my left shoulder. I didn't dare wriggle around to find a more comfortable position. The snoring had resumed—not in a steady rhythm, but the intermittent noises of a sleeper who has been disturbed and has not sunk back into deep slumber.

I lay there for what seemed like hours. Nobody had dusted under the couch in recent memory; I kept swallowing sneezes. My nose itched. Splinters dug into my cheek. By turning my head sideways, a millimeter at a time, I found I could see out from under the spread. The view was limited; however, it included the suspect chair and one of the doors, the one leading to the central hall. Something new had been added, after all; a pile of buff storage boxes next to the library door.

None of them was long enough to hold Tutankhamon.

The sleeper's breathing had evened out and so—finally—had mine. Now for the next maneuver.

My left arm was straight at my side, my right slightly bent at the elbow. My mobile was in the right-hand pocket of my pants. I could only move horizontally unless I wanted to risk another screech from the rusty springs. If I hadn't let that snore panic me I would have got the cursed phone out before I squashed myself under the couch. With the same slow deliberation, flinching at every rustle of fabric, I got my hand down and in the pocket. I was breathing fast, from sheer nerves, when my fingers closed over the cell, and I was sorely tempted to proceed by feel alone. I knew I couldn't risk it, though. This call had to be dead right, and fast. By the time I got my hand up to my face I was sweating bullets, and not from the heat, though it was pretty warm under there.

Discomfort was succeeded by numbness and, believe it or not, drowsiness. (I am told by those who know that this is not an uncommon reaction to stress.) The room was dim and quiet, except for the soothing buzz of insects. I was on the verge of dozing off when there was a knock at the door. It woke me as effectively as a shout in my ear.

It also woke the occupant of the chair. I heard the rustle of cloth as he shifted position, and then a brusque order. The door opened and the chandelier over the desk blazed. John came in.

He looked as sleek as a well-fed cat—not a hair on his head out of place, not a mark on him. His hands were in the pockets of his khakis, his shirt, open at the throat, was one I'd never seen before—a rather girlish baby-blue-and-white-striped. He stopped a few feet inside the room and tilted his head inquiringly. The man sitting in the chair barked out another baritone order. The door closed.

They played the old "Let the other guy speak first" routine for a short time. John had been playing it longer. The other guy said, "I trust you have been given everything you require?"

It was the first time he had spoken more than a single word. The language was English, the accent well-educated British. I knew I'd heard that voice before, but I couldn't place it. My head was buzzing as loudly as the flies. He hadn't been injured. He was shaved and brushed, neat as a pin. But someone had opened the door for him. Someone was outside, in the hall, guarding the door. Not yet, I told myself. Wait.

"Come off it," John said pleasantly. "There's no one listening. Shall we proceed to the next stage of negotiations?"

"You've nothing to negotiate with."

From beneath the couch, I could see as John raised an eyebrow. "Then let me put it another way. What are you planning to do next?"

"To you?" The other man laughed. Damn, that laugh was familiar! He went on, "Nothing at all. Don't tell me you haven't figured out my plans for you?"

"Oh, that. It was the obvious course."

"Obvious?" His voice rose. "Most people in my position would have—"

"Now, now," John said, in the tone he would have used to a peevish child, "don't get excited. You've done very well for an amateur."

He was trying to bait the other man, for no good reason that I could see, except that he couldn't resist being cute. Then it dawned on me. I was a little upset, or I would have seen it immediately.

The chair legs let out a screech as the other man pushed back from the table and sprang to his feet. The two of them confronted each other like mirror images—lean and tall, fair-haired, dressed almost identically. I ought to have recognized the voice and the laugh, but the very idea of his being here was too preposterous to accept. Even now I had a hard time believing it.

John's little game didn't work. Alan was unarmed, and he knew better than to tackle John with his bare hands. If I had been in his position I'd have been armed to the teeth, but that was Alan's problem—he had to outdo John on John's terms, beat him at his own game. Besides, he wasn't risking bodily harm; he had help right outside the door.

Alan managed to get his breathing and his temper under control. "How kind," he said, in a fair imitation of John's drawl. "You can't admit, can you, that I've succeeded where you would have failed? This operation exceeds any and all of your childish games. It will go down in the annals of crime."

"Is that the only reason you had me brought here?" John asked. His eyes moved fractionally, from Alan's face to his hands and back. He was calculating the odds. They were against him, and he knew it. "To boast? Should that be the case, I hope you will excuse me."

I had preprogrammed the call. I only had to press one button. I kept hoping Alan would really lose his temper and start yelling, but I didn't dare wait any longer. I pushed the button.

"Sit down," Alan said tightly.

"What would be the point? Unless you want my advice."

"I don't need your damned advice! I know precisely what I'm doing. In a few days I'll walk away with four million pounds in hard cash, and you will be found unharmed and unconfined in company with the stolen mummy of Tutankhamon. Even your trusting friends can't get you out of this. You haven't been exactly forthright with them, have you?"

"I daresay several incidents will lend credence to the assumption of my guilt," John admitted.

Schmidt, Schmidt, where are you? I thought wildly. Now's the time. He's here, where he has no business being, and no excuse for being here. I've heard his confession. Come on, Schmidt, call in the troops.

I hoped to hear alarms and excursions, gunfire, shouts, explosions. What I got instead was a door bursting open, banging back against the wall. It wasn't the door to the hall. I stuck my head out from under the couch and saw what I had hoped not to see. Schmidt had come in through the library. Schmidt. Just Schmidt, all alone. He was brandishing what appeared to be, and almost certainly was not, an automatic pistol.

Alan spun round to face Schmidt, John nodded a gracious greeting, and—driven beyond endurance—I yelled, "Bloody hell, Schmidt, what do you think you're doing? You can't kill anybody with a toy gun!"

"It is not a toy," Schmidt yelled back. He proceeded to prove it.

We were yelling because the long-awaited cacophony had finally burst out—gunfire, crashes, yells, and in the case of Schmidt, a fusillade fired back into the library toward several persons who were about to follow him into the study. They ceased to follow and Schmidt slammed the door shut.

"*Also,*" he panted. "Put up your hands, Mr. Whoever-You-May-Be. It is a fair cop. *Guten Abend,* John. Where is Vicky?"

"Here," I said faintly.

John sauntered to me, bent over, and offered me his hand. "Well, well," he said. "Fancy meeting you here."

My appearance distracted and alarmed Schmidt. "Is she hurt? Is she safe?"

For a few vital seconds nobody was looking at Alan. A musical clatter drew our attention back to him. If I had had false teeth I would have swallowed them when I saw that he was now brandishing one of the swords that had hung over the mantel. The other one lay on the floor near the fireplace.

"Oh, for God's sake," John said, hauling me to my feet. "Put that down, you damned fool."

"Yes, drop it," Schmidt ordered. "Or I will fire."

"No, you won't," Alan said breathlessly. "In the first place you are too much of a gentleman to shoot a man armed only with a sword. In the second place, you emptied the clip just now."

Schmidt let out a string of *Mittelhochdeutsch* swear words and began searching through his plethora of pockets. John edged toward Alan and came to a sudden stop as the blade whistled past his face.

"Pick up the other one," Alan said, baring his teeth. "We'll see who is the better man."

"You," John said hastily. "No question. I give up. I can't fence."

"I happen to know that you can. Not as well as I, however. Those reenactments at which you chose to sneer honed my skills. Pick it up or I'll carve my initials in Vicky."

I would never have supposed that one blade could hold three people at bay. It can, if the other three haven't so much as a knife, and if it moves as fast as it did when Alan wielded it.

"Pick it up," he said again.

"Not much choice, really," John said, his casual tone at odds with his tight mouth and narrowed eyes. "He's gone over the edge. All those fantasy games . . . Oops."

He ducked just in time, and scooped up the fallen sword. I jumped back as Alan swung in my direction. Schmidt wobbled indecisively, still searching his damned pockets.

"Call for help, Schmidt," I shouted. "Where is everybody?"

From the continuing sounds of battle, it was evident that "everybody" was fully occupied. Alan's gang was firing back, from all four sides of the house.

"Just hold him off," I said to John.

His lips moved soundlessly but eloquently. I didn't blame him for wanting to call me bad names; it had not been one of my more brilliant suggestions. I knew he could fence a little. I'd seen him do it—with an opponent who was fat, drunk, and essentially incompetent. Alan was none of the above and he was in a state of manic exhilaration. I don't think he cared any longer about the money or the game. All he cared about was inflicting as much damage as possible, with his own hands, on the man he admired and hated and envied most.

John managed to parry the first pass. The next three opened up cuts on his cheek, forearm, and side. He avoided some of Alan's thrusts by various moves that looked unorthodox even to my uneducated eyes, ducking and twisting and weaving, but he was breathing hard and he kept retreating. Schmidt had finally located another clip and was trying to slide it into the gun. He was swearing. Alan was laughing. That laugh was one of the ugliest sounds I had ever heard. I picked up a poker and tried to get behind Alan. He whipped round and knocked the poker out of my hand before turning back to John and parrying his clumsy thrust with insulting ease.

"Touché," he yelled and ran John through the right arm.

The blade fell from John's hand. His back against the wall, he slid slowly down to a sitting position. He was bleeding from half a dozen cuts, none of them except the last serious, and he was too out of breath to speak. I ran to him and knelt beside him, supporting his sagging body.

"Shoot, Schmidt," I yelled.

"*Allmächtigen Gott im Himmel*, curse the *verdammt* gun," said Schmidt, at the top of his lungs. He tossed the gun aside; I let out a shriek, which rose to siren pitch as Schmidt picked up the sword John had dropped.

There was still noise somewhere in the background, but none of it penetrated my horrified brain. All I could think was that Schmidt, the self-proclaimed greatest swordsman in Europe, had finally lost his mind. And he wasn't even drunk.

Struggling to sit up, John gasped, "No, Schmidt, don't, for God's sake, don't—" Schmidt assumed the position—I guess it was the position—and bellowed challenges in various languages, ending with *"En garde!"* Alan was laughing so hard I thought he would fall over. That annoyed Schmidt. He took a step forward and . . .

I can't describe what happened. All I saw was a whirlwind of flashing steel, all I heard was the ring of metal on metal. When it stopped, Alan had fallen back, out of range of Schmidt's weapon. He wasn't laughing anymore. His eyes were big as saucers and his mouth hung open. Schmidt stood planted in the exact same spot, teeth bared and mustache bristling. "Ha!" he shouted. "Have at you!"

It went slower this time. Alan poked his sword at Schmidt and Schmidt knocked it away with contemptuous ease, before poking back at Alan. John started squirming, trying to pull away from my tenderly supportive arms. "Damn it, Vicky, get out of the way! I can't see." His voice rose in a howl of delight. "Get him, Schmidt! Let him have it!"

When the two broke apart this time, blood was streaming down Alan's left arm. With slow dignity Schmidt took a single step forward and went at it again, forcing Alan back. I was vaguely aware of a voice babbling close to my ear. Every sentence ended in an exclamation point.

"The greatest swordsman in Europe! He was, by God, he was! A-to-Z Schmidt, Alphabet Schmidt—Olympic gold medalist, world champion! We were made to watch the films! I ought to have known! But it was almost twenty years ago, and he's always been good old Schmidt . . ."

Schmidt's fat old arm moved with the quick precision of a metronome. Alan was streaming blood from multiple cuts. Schmidt's revenge, I thought wildly. He's doing the same thing to Alan that Alan did to John.

This time it was Schmidt who stepped back. His breathing was ragged, but Alan was also gasping for breath, more from disbelief than exertion, I thought.

Schmidt intoned, "Do you yield?"

Melodramatic to the end, Alan cried, "Never!" and attacked.

Two quick passes; then Schmidt dropped to one knee and lunged, arm and sword in a single straight line. The point entered Alan's chest.

For several long seconds there wasn't a sound, not even that of exhaled breath. I will never forget the look on Alan's face. Not pain, not anger—utter disbelief. He fell slowly, first to his knees, then onto his side, pulling the weapon from Schmidt's hand.

John removed himself from my limp embrace and staggered to his feet. "Schmidt," he said softly. "Schmidt, I . . . You . . ." and then, almost prayerfully, "Christ."

He knelt by Alan and turned him onto his back. The hilt of the sword swayed gently, like a flower on a stem. Schmidt hadn't moved. Still on one knee, he said, between gasps, "Vicky, will you please give me a hand?"

"Schmidt, are you hurt?" I hurried to him.

"No. It is . . . Well, you understand, it is my knee. Just help me up, please."

I took his hand and pulled. Accompanied by a series of popping noises, Schmidt rose like a wounded whale. *"Ach, Gott,"* he wheezed, leaning heavily against me. "I have killed him. I did not mean to. God forgive me."

"He's not dead," John said. "But he's in bad shape. Call for an ambulance."

"It's on the way," said a voice I hadn't heard for some time.

Sans auburn wig and avec gun, Suzi stood in the door of the library. Behind her I saw several other familiar faces. I don't know how long they had been there. I wouldn't have noticed a stampede of buffalo.

"Typical," I said bitterly. "Where were you when I needed you?"

"I came as soon as I received your message," Suzi said.

"Swell," I said. "There's your thief, Suzi. And there, wounded but undaunted, is the man whom you wrongly suspected." I flung my arm out. Never one to miss a cue, John got slowly to his feet. I went on with mounting passion, "If you ever bother us again, I'll make sure your bosses hear how you screwed this one up. You weren't looking for the perpetrator, you were blinded by your desire to nail John. He might have been killed if it hadn't been for—"

"Schmidt," John said, swaying theatrically. "Anton Z. Schmidt, the greatest swordsman in Europe."

The lunge, you see, becomes difficult with middle age," Schmidt explained. "The knee joints do not cooperate so well. Hence a fencer must rely on the strength of his arm and his expertise. He knew that, and did not think I would attempt it."

The words "middle age" didn't raise a single eyebrow. Schmidt could have described himself as "a mere youth" and none of his adoring fans would have contradicted him. Especially me.

"Oh, Schmidt," I said. "I do love you."

"You have said that before." Schmidt's eyes twinkled. "But you can say it as often as you like." He examined his empty glass. "I believe I will have more beer."

John beat me to the minibar. I was ahead on points, though, since I had phoned the hotel to order the beer before we left the battlefield.

The word was not inapropos. Alan's allies had put up a pretty good fight, barricading most of the windows and defending the doors. Loyalty probably had little to do with it; anyone trying to leave the house, with or without a white flag, might have been mowed down. People with guns like to shoot them. They don't always shoot straight when they are excited, though, and miraculously, no one had been killed.

Our allies, summoned by Schmidt, had waited for my signal before moving in. (Schmidt was in command because he was the only one who knew where I had gone.) They were a motley lot and it's a wonder they didn't start fighting among themselves—Suzi and Ashraf and their "assistants," Feisal and a band of men from the village, and, of course, Saida. Schmidt was the glue that had held them all together. Feisal said he sounded like a French revolutionary stirring up the mob. "Avenge the murder of Ali! Retrieve the stolen treasures of Egypt! Rescue the beautiful American girl and save her lover!" I don't know where they got all the guns and I had sense enough not to ask. Feisal wouldn't let Saida have one, so she threw rocks. She claimed to have brained at least two of the enemy.

She and Feisal had come back with us to our now dear and familiar home away from home at the Winter Palace, leaving Ashraf and Suzi to direct the cleanup operations. John flatly refused the assistance of the ambulance personnel. "It's a nice neat stab," he said approvingly. "And I need a clean shirt. Alan has frightful taste."

"That's one of Alan's?" I asked.

"Did you suppose I had another wardrobe hidden away in Luxor?"

His voice wasn't exactly accusing, but I couldn't meet his eyes. "What was I supposed to suppose?" I demanded.

"Never mind, darling, I forgive you. I will tell all in due course. In the meantime I could do with a little first aid."

"And beer," said Schmidt.

He had his beer, and John and I had something a little stronger. After I had patched John up—a job at which I had become only too adept—and he had selected a shirt in a much more becoming shade of blue, we took turns telling our tales. I have to admit John's was the most interesting.

"I shall begin at the beginning," he announced, fondling his glass of Scotch, "and continue until I reach the end. Kindly do not interrupt with questions. An occasional inquiring look will indicate you require elaboration of a particular point."

Saida chuckled. John raised an eyebrow at her, cleared his throat, and began at the beginning.

"As soon as I read that message from LeBlanc I felt certain Ashraf had arranged the moonlight visit in order to facilitate his meeting with his contact. It was well thought out, really; the place is so huge he could select a safe spot, yet there were enough people wandering around to confuse potential followers. He certainly succeeded in confusing me. After a while I couldn't tell who was following whom, though I began to realize that far too many of them were following me. When the meeting actually took place I was some distance away. I saw that Ashraf's contact was a woman, but I couldn't hear what they were saying. When she bolted I went after her. My motives were not entirely altruistic, I admit . . . Vicky, will you stop giving me what you presumably believe to be inquiring looks?"

"I want you to skip the elegant syntax and get on with it. You followed her because you thought she would lead you to the headquarters of the gang."

"I didn't mean her to get that far. I was reasonably certain we could shake a confession out of the poor creature and I certainly didn't intend to get within arm's reach of the bad boys. She was too quick for me," John admitted with obvious chagrin. "She knew where she was going and I didn't. I didn't catch her up until she had actually reached the house, and when I intercepted her she shrieked like a banshee. They were obviously on the lookout for her. The door burst open and several large unkind men dragged both of us inside. No, Vicky, I did not put up a fight. I do not fight large men armed with knives when I'm outnumbered six to one. They had me trussed up like a turkey, blindfolded and gagged, before I could reason with them, and then they bundled me into a cart, with a sack of some heavy granular substance on top of me, and drove away. The whole business didn't take more than two minutes."

He paused for a refreshing sip and I said, "So by the time clever Suzi arrived, you were long gone. Probably by way of the back gate. She's dead, you know."

He knew I wasn't referring to Suzi. "I do know. Alan told me, in lurid detail. She had tried to make a separate deal. I'm sorry. She was a relatively new recruit whose only crime was attempted extortion.

"What with being banged around in the cart and mashed by heavy objects, I wasn't in top-notch condition when we arrived at our destination. Expecting the worst, as is my habit, I was pleasantly surprised when they unwrapped me quite gently and supplied me with a nice soft chair and a glass of brandy. I recognized the surroundings at once and it dawned on me that the thieves had been using the FEPEA house as a secondary headquarters. The house on the East Bank served them well at the start, but if anything went wrong—which it did—they needed a fall-back location. I was gazing about, trying to find an exit, when Alan made his appearance. I was not surprised to see him. I had already realized he must be involved. Ah. I see from a number of doubtful glances that I must justify that statement.

"You had mentioned seeing me at Luxor Temple. I knew I hadn't been there, and it occurred to me that perhaps your sense of recognition was based on the resemblance between me and Alan. That got me started thinking. I had hired him in part because of his computer skills. It had become obvious that someone had got into my closed files, the ones that listed my former rivals and associates—"

"Damn it," I burst out. "You said some time ago that you had severed relations with that lot."

"I did. In the sense that I had not communicated with any of them until—"

"Berlin. Rome. You didn't ask the monsignor about missing relics, you bribed him to give you information about current criminal gangs. And every word of that conversation you reported having with Helga was a flat-out fabrication."

"I thought I made it sound quite convincing," John said with a complacent smile.

But then he looked directly at me, and now it was his eyes that fell. "I had promised you I would cut off all contacts with my former associates. I lied. I had to. You'd have argued and protested, and those files were too valuable to destroy. I always expect the worst. The worst happened."

"How true," Schmidt exclaimed. "The present situation has justified your decision."

They nodded gravely at each other. "So," John resumed, "when I spotted Alan at Karnak, flitting about in the moonlight, I wasn't surprised. He didn't bother with a disguise, because he wanted to be taken for me. Such proved to be the case. The light was poor and people see what they expect to see."

"Never mind the lectures on crime," Feisal said impatiently.

"Oh, I find them fascinating," Saida exclaimed. "Do go on."

"Well, the lad was quite full of himself," John said. "Another sign of an amateur is that he talks too much, which Alan proceeded to do. Psychologically he's an interesting case. He hates my guts but he wants to be me, only better—or, from another point of view, worse. His role-playing was a way of compensating for his dull existence. Then I entered his life and he realized he didn't have to play hero. The dashing Cavalier became the Dark Lord, the master of crime. Evil, as someone has said, is more interesting than good."

"Yes, yes," said Schmidt eagerly. "Many more visitors to the fantasy conventions come attired as Darth Vader or Saruman or storm troopers than as—"

"Who?" Feisal said in bewilderment.

"The bad guys," Saida translated. "I'll explain another time, dear boy."

"As I was saying," John remarked loudly, "he told me everything. He started making deals on the side, cooking the books with a skill I couldn't hope to match. He made copies of my keys, got into locked desk drawers and the safe."

"So he was the one who searched your flat?"

John's brow wrinkled. "Must have been. Though I don't understand why he—"

The phone rang. I picked it up, since no one else seemed inclined to move. The concierge's voice informed me that someone was at the desk asking for us. "Send him up," I said and hung up.

"It must be Ashraf," I informed the others. "That was quick."

"He has found him," Feisal exclaimed. *"Alhamdullilah!"*

"Unless it is Suzi." Schmidt looked severe. "I will not see her."

I was curious to hear Suzi's accusations, excuses, or whatever, but Schmidt's word was law that evening, and Suzi could wait. I meant to have a long talk with her at some point. In private.

"I'll get rid of her," I said, going to the door. The knock had been somewhat tentative. Maybe Suzi was feeling apologetic. When I saw who the caller was, I went on offense. "Suzi sent you, didn't she? She didn't have the nerve to come herself."

The little woman with the big hat said, "Who is Suzi?"

"Oh, come on, you're one of hers, you have to be. I fingered you some time ago."

The woman drew herself up to her full five-feet-two-inches. "I have come to see Mr. Tregarth. Don't tell me he isn't here, I bribed the concierge to inform me when he returned. This time I will not be put off."

John had overheard. He came up behind me. "I'm Tregarth. How may I—"

"I know you are. I have been trying for days to see you. If you don't let me in, I will sit outside the door and—and do something disruptive."

She was trying to look fierce, but I have never seen a countenance or a form so unintimidating, or heard a threat so absurd. John passed his hand over his mouth to hide a smile, and waved me back. "Do come in, Miss—Ms.—Mrs.—"

"My card." She handed it to him and swept into the room. Schmidt rose gallantly to his feet; Saida poked Feisal, who was sunk in happy dreams of Tutankhamon, and he followed suit.

"Oh, yes," John said. "I remember now. I don't believe we ever met, though. You dealt solely with my mother . . ."

His voice trailed off. A series of rapid, strong emotions passed over his face, and then he burst out, "You were the one who broke into the house and searched the attic!"

"Please." She looked up at him from under the hat. "Please don't shout at me, it makes me very nervous, and when I am nervous I start shouting back. Just let me explain. I have done wrong and I am here to confess and to make restitution. I don't know what came over me!"

"Tsk, tsk," said Schmidt, at John. "Madam, do not be alarmed. No one will shout at you while I am here."

"How kind you are." She smiled at him. Up at him. She had a dimple. From a chain round her neck, barely visible in the vee of her prim blouse, hung a fat gold ring. The Ring. An exact duplicate of the one Schmidt owned. A hideous foreboding came over me.

"Please have a seat," said Schmidt the chivalrous. "May I offer you a beer, Miss—Ms.—"

He snatched the card from John's hand and looked at it. "Ah! It comes back to me now. I know your name. I know all of them!"

"How many does she have?" I asked, unwillingly distracted.

"Three, is it not?" Schmidt got a modest smile of acknowledgment. "Two are noms de plume, you understand."

"Then the name on the note you left—"

"Is my real name." She smiled apologetically. "I have to use it when I travel, because of credit cards and passports and that sort of thing. I know it is confusing. I get mixed up myself."

"But the pseudonyms are necessary," Schmidt exclaimed. "Because of your many admiring readers. I wrote to you once a fan letter, and you sent me an autograph."

"I remember. You asked for a photograph, and I was sorry to refuse, but I make it a rule never to—"

"Send photos as if you were some sort of media celebrity," Schmidt cried. "An admirable attitude. I fully understood."

"Would you like the rest of us to leave?" John inquired in a devastatingly polite voice.

Schmidt said "Hmph" and the woman—whose name I still didn't know—turned pink. "Let me make my confession, please. It was I who broke into your family home, I who searched your flat, I who have followed you across Europe in various disguises. I was temporarily deranged."

John leaned over and delicately removed the hat. They looked each other in the eye. The corners of his lips turned up and he said, "Yet I suspect you rather enjoyed it, didn't you? Especially the disguises."

A fleeting smile echoed his. Then she said primly, "That is not the point. You see, the journals your mother sold me some time ago formed the basis for a very successful series of novels. Then— then I ran out of journals! I knew there must be more, since there were gaps in the chronology, but your mother denied having them, and she refused to let me search for myself. I was desperate."

"Why didn't you just make something up?" Saida asked interestedly. "Isn't that what novelists do?"

"No, she could not do that," Schmidt exclaimed. "Not a writer of integrity like this one, whose work has always been based on true history."

"Thank you for understanding," said the writer of integrity, who had just admitted to having broken into two different dwellings. "However, that does not excuse what I did. I found three of the missing journals in the attic of your home, Mr. Tregarth (you really ought to get someone in to clean the place properly). I took them. I will return them if you insist, but I beg you will accept my check and my heartfelt apologies instead."

Leaning against the back of the sofa, John said solemnly, "How much?"

"Stop teasing her," I exclaimed. She was genuinely repentant, and very short. I have a soft spot for women like that.

"I think she's rather enjoying that too," said John. He got a fleeting but unregenerate grin in reply. "All right. Same price as the others. Agreed?"

"Oh, yes! Thank you so much." She only hesitated for a second. "And if you should know of any more . . ."

"Have you searched the library of the FEPEA headquarters?" Saida asked. She had recognized a kindred spirit, even if this one was pretending to be a sheep.

"I tried, but I did not succeed. And that is one of the reasons why I have been trying to talk to you, Mr. Tregarth. That house, which is sacred to the memories of your distinguished ancestors, is now occupied by a group of suspicious individuals. When I approached the house five days ago—"

"With the intent of committing another burglary?" John broke in.

"Who cares?" I exclaimed. "Tell us about these individuals."

"I meant to proceed with complete decorum this time" was the indignant reply. "I had observed evidence of someone being in residence, so I knocked at the door. Eventually it was opened by a person who spoke emphatically to me in Arabic. I do not understand the language well, but his gestures made his meaning clear. When I offered my card, he shut the door in my face."

"Good God," Feisal exclaimed. "You must have a guardian angel looking after you. You might have been killed or kidnapped."

"They wouldn't risk violence," I said. "They wanted to avoid anything that would draw attention to them. Five days ago, you said?"

"Yes. That was why I was emboldened to approach Mr. Tregarth, since I felt he ought to be warned of their presence. I hope—I do most sincerely hope—that my failure to speak out has not caused trouble. I can't help but notice you appear to have been injured."

She certainly couldn't, since John had insisted on a sling and a copious application of bandages to the cuts on his hand and cheek. He murmured something vague and deprecatory, and I said, "It wasn't your fault, you tried your best."

"You are most kind. I also felt obliged to inform him that his assistant is a venal young man who does not deserve his trust. He charged me a hundred pounds for the use of the key to your flat."

"Ah," I said.

John cleared his throat. "I appreciate your telling me."

"It was my duty." She picked up her hat and rose. "Thank you for overlooking my malefactions. I will send a check tomorrow."

Schmidt bounded up. "I will escort you back to your hotel."

"No, no, I have taken enough of your time. It has been a pleasure meeting you, Herr Doktor."

"The pleasure is mine! At least allow me to see you into a taxi."

They went out together. Rebound, I thought. One-hundred-and-eighty-degree rebound. The marriage of true minds, not the lure of the flesh. Shared interests, mutual respect . . .

The silence that followed their departure could only be described as critical. If John had replied to her first message, we would have learned several facts of interest. Maybe they would have made a difference. Maybe not. But as my mom always says, it never hurts to be polite.

Schmidt's return gave John an excuse to change the subject that was in everyone's mind. "Back so soon?" he inquired.

"I wanted to entertain her in the bar, but she would not stay," Schmidt said. "A delightful woman, is she not? An admirer of J.R.R. Tolkien too! She is leaving Egypt tomorrow, but she was good enough to give me her telephone number. John, had you but had the common courtesy to respond to her first—"

"Water over the dam," John said hastily. "As I was saying earlier . . . Confound it, now what?"

"Ashraf, I hope," I said, going to answer the knock at the door.

"If it is Suzi . . ." Schmidt began.

"I know, I know."

It was Ashraf, though I almost didn't recognize him at first. His hair stood on end, his face was streaked with dust, and his eyes were wild, and when he spoke his voice cracked.

"He wasn't there! He's still missing!"

FOURTEEN

We restored Ashraf with brandy—permissible for medicinal purposes—and barraged him with questions.

"What do you mean, he wasn't there?" Feisal cried. "Where else could he be? You didn't search thoroughly!"

"We tore the place apart." Ashraf spread his dust-smeared, splinter-riddled hands. "Not only the main house, but every outbuilding. That woman—that dreadful woman—has gone to investigate the villa at Karnak, but I cannot believe they would have left him there unattended."

"No," John said.

"Where can he be?" Ashraf's voice rose in a poignant plea.

"Well, now, that's the question, isn't it?" John said coolly. "Let us control our emotions and examine the matter logically."

"Please," I said. "Not another lecture on crime and the criminal mind."

"Just crime, darling. I was about to go into that aspect of the matter when we were interrupted. If anyone has a better suggestion . . ." Eyebrow lifted, he swept his audience with an inquiring eye. No one responded. Ashraf had relapsed into gloomy despair, Feisal was pacing, Schmidt watched John with amiable expectation, and even Saida was fresh out of ideas. The blow had been devastating; it had never occurred to any of us that the damned mummy wasn't there.

I refrained from additional criticism. John had been through a lot lately; as he had frequently remarked he hates being hurt, and his amour propre had also taken a beating. He had, to put it rudely, screwed up not once but several times. So I folded my hands and gave him an encouraging nod. He would have gone ahead anyhow.

"This," said John, "was an expensive operation. It required a number of people to carry it out, people with special skills. There aren't as many of them as you might suppose, particularly in this part of the world—not terrorists, not politically motivated, a criminal organization pure and simple, interested only in the money. After checking my sources I had determined before we arrived in Egypt that one group was the most likely. They had pulled off several rather neat thefts of antiquities, from storehouses and in one case from a well-guarded temple."

"Denderah," Feisal exclaimed.

"Right. The modus operandi in that case was similar to the one employed here. Now you may well ask why, if I had identified the group in question, I didn't tell you. The answer is that the gang itself was unimportant. They are for hire, they carry out orders. I wanted the man who had hired them, and at that point I didn't have a clue as to his identity. There were too many possible motives, too many possible suspects.

"Gangs have their uses, but they also have inherent disadvantages. They're in it for the money. So if somebody offers them more money, they may decide to take it and run. Or if something goes wrong they may decide to save their own skins—and run. That's why I don't use them. You simply can't count on the buggers. Vicky, you're twitching. Am I boring you?"

"Yes."

"Me too," Feisal snarled. "Where is all this leading?"

"I am trying to explain," said John loftily, "why I didn't let you in on my deductions. You were all suspects. Yes, Feisal, even you. You would have been happy to see Ashraf disgraced and you the hero who had saved Tut. The only people I didn't suspect were Vicky and Schmidt, and both of them have a deplorable tendency to take matters, and in Schmidt's case, weapons, into their own hands."

Taking this as a compliment, Schmidt chuckled and opened another bottle of beer. "I didn't have any damned weapons," I said grumpily. "Schmidt, how the hell did you get hold of that gun?"

"I got it the night I went shopping with Saida and Feisal," Schmidt explained. "From a taxi driver, after they had left. There are ways to find things, Vicky, if one knows the ropes."

Feisal rolled his eyes heavenward. "I don't want to hear about it, Schmidt, and I don't want to hear any more theories. I want to know what the hell has happened to Tutankhamon!"

"So do I," Ashraf said. "If you're so bloody clever, Tregarth, answer that."

John went to the minibar. "I never drink to excess, but I think this evening I'm entitled to approach that level." He winced theatrically and rubbed his arm. "Tut? He's at the FEPEA house, of course."

Ashraf was too infuriated for coherent speech; he sputtered and waved his arms. Feisal swore eloquently. "Impossible. We searched the place from top to bottom."

"You didn't look in the right places," John said.

John refused to say more, claiming he was feeling faint and needed his rest.

"Tomorrow," he said wanly. "I—I may be up to the job tomorrow."

"Tomorrow be damned," Feisal yelled. "I'm heading there right now."

"I strongly advise against that," John said. "You've left some of your people guarding the place, I presume? He'll be perfectly all right." He had to raise his voice to be heard above the threats and curses. "Do you want the man who is behind this? Then be patient. It will be worth the wait. Trust me on this."

We got Feisal and Ashraf out before they could commit bodily assault on John. I was tempted to join them, but I was beginning to get an inkling of an idea. I think Saida was too. She hadn't joined in the general outcry.

The cat was the first to greet us. It came round the corner of the house, tail erect, and made a beeline for Schmidt.

"She remembers," Schmidt said happily, stooping to stroke the animal's head.

"It's a he, Schmidt," I said, from the other end of the cat. "Definitely a he."

"I was worried about you," Schmidt informed the cat. "I ought to have known that you would be sensible enough to stay away from a place where there were loud noises and projectiles."

Schmidt held the door for me and the cat. The others were in the director's office. Schmidt stopped and looked down at the dark stain on the Bokhara rug.

"It's okay, Schmidt," I said, patting his shoulder. "He's still alive."

Schmidt sighed. "Barely. But it was necessary. He might have killed you or John."

The dark stain wasn't the only evidence of violence. The study looked the way my living room looks most of the time—chairs pulled out or knocked over, various objects strewn around the floor. Among the latter were the two swords. The tips were darkly stained.

"Tsk, tsk," said Schmidt. "Such beautiful weapons, to be treated so cavalierly. They should be cleaned and replaced."

"Not by you, Schmidt," I said. "Ashraf, you had better get some of your henchmen in here to repair the damage before the expedition arrives, or you'll have some explaining to do to."

"I suppose that is true," Ashraf admitted. Something crunched; he lifted his foot and examined the sole of his brogue. "Broken glass. Where did that come from?"

"In the mad rush to the rescue last night, someone knocked over one of the display cases," John said, looking into the library. He bent over and delicately extracted a knife from amid the shards of glass. "Nice weapon."

"The founders must have been a bloodthirsty lot," I said.

"Life was hazardous in those days," John said, admiring the knife. It was a good eight inches long, and showed signs of use.

"Never mind the nostalgia," Feisal growled. "Where's Tutankhamon?"

John came back into the study. He put the knife down on the table. "Here."

"I tell you, we looked everywhere," Feisal insisted.

"You were looking for a coffin-shaped box approximately six feet long," John said.

The words fell like lumps of lead thudding onto a defenseless head. Feisal's jaw dropped. Ashraf choked. Saida said calmly, "I thought so."

John went to the file boxes piled in the corner. They were of heavy cardboard, squarish in shape, none longer than three feet. The one on top was about a foot square. With the slow deliberation of a magician preparing to produce a rabbit from a hat, John removed the lid and lifted a few loose papers. The head of Tutankhamon smiled shyly up at us.

"Ham," I said. "Show off. Charlatan."

"They broke him into pieces," Ashraf wailed.

"He was already in pieces," I reminded Ashraf.

Saida hovered over the box, uttering little moans of distress. In an effort to console her, I said, "They seem to have packed him quite carefully—cotton wool all around, nice sturdy boxes."

Feisal rushed at the other boxes. Two legs, half a torso, the other half, arms. He was all there. Or rather, all of him was there, except for the hand that had been sent to Ashraf. Feet and the second hand occupied a separate container. While the others unpacked Tut, John stood to one side, nursing his arm and looking superior. Schmidt settled down in the director's chair and began feeding the cat chicken from one of the lunch boxes he had brought. His mustache was twitching. Either he was deep in thought or he was trying not to laugh. Laughter was inapropos, but the situation did have an insane touch of black humor. I felt as if I were at a wake, there was so much groaning and gnashing of teeth.

Ashraf was the first to get his wits together. Unlike Feisal and Saida, he was less concerned with poor old Tut than with saving his reputation. He snatched the box containing the head. "We've got to put him back. Right now, before word leaks out. Feisal, start loading those boxes into the car."

Schmidt looked up. "Now, in broad daylight, with tourists and guards in the Valley watching every move you make?"

"No, we can't do that," Feisal exclaimed. He snatched the box back from Ashraf. "Damn it, be careful. Don't joggle him."

"He won't mind," I said. "He's dead."

Feisal gave me a hateful look. Ashraf stroked his freshly shaven chin. "We must think," he muttered. "Think before we act. To-night, after the Valley is closed . . ."

"I'm afraid it's not that simple," John drawled. "Take your own advice, Ashraf, and think this through. Aren't you even slightly in-terested in the identity of the mastermind? You ought to hold a personal grudge; he was the one who bashed you on the head the other night."

"We know who it was. Your assistant—I forget his name—"

"As I keep telling you, it's not that simple. There's no hurry. Why don't you make yourselves comfortable and let me explain?"

"Not another lecture," I said.

"At the end of which," said John, nostrils flaring with annoy-ance, "I will produce the real instigator of this affair. Please sit down, ladies and gentlemen."

Grudgingly and grumbling, the rest of us took our places around the table. The head of Tutankhamon, placed tenderly on the table by Feisal, lent a macabre note to the proceedings. The solemnity of the meeting was somewhat marred by Schmidt's passing round the box of chicken legs. (The cat had eaten the breasts.)

"If I may," said Schmidt, "I would like to say a few words."

"By all means," said John, with a gracious inclination of his head.

"Thank you," said Schmidt, graciously inclining *his* head. "Referring, John, to your deductions of last night: It seems to me that you left certain matters unexplained. The unfortunate Alan may have been able to locate the group you mentioned by getting access to your private files, but if he wanted money, why devise such a bizarre, complex scheme? Why Tutankhamon instead of an artifact he could sell on the illicit antiquities market?"

"I'm glad you asked," John said. They nodded at each other again. Clearly they had set this charade up, the two of them. Just for the fun of infuriating Ashraf, or for some other reason? John kept sneaking surreptitious glances at his watch.

"Why Tutankhamon, indeed? The only logical answer was that Alan was working with someone else—someone whose primary motive was not financial. We won't be able to question Alan for a long time, if ever. But I think this is how it came about.

"Alan was approached by an individual who had conceived the idea of embarrassing the SCA by making off with one of its most conspicuous treasures. At the outset he believed he was dealing with me. Alan convinced him that he, Alan, had taken over that aspect of the business. Alan also pointed out that the group of people who carried out the actual theft would expect to be paid, and paid handsomely. There was no way of raising that amount of money except by holding the mummy for ransom."

"So it was the other guy who proposed stealing Tut," I said. "But that means . . . That means he . . . Who, damn it?"

"Can't you guess?" John's smile was maddeningly superior.

I looked at Ashraf, who was looking at Feisal, who was looking at Saida, who was watching John, her lips slightly parted.

John looked at his watch.

Schmidt couldn't stand it any longer. He sprang to his feet, pointing at the doorway. "Perlmutter! Jan Perlmutter. Who else!"

The doorway remained unhelpfully empty of Jan Perlmutter.

"Don't be silly, Schmidt," I said. "You just want him to be the villain because you're still mad at him."

"Schmidt is, as always, correct," John said resignedly.

Ashraf sat up with a start. "Perlmutter? From the Altes Museum in Berlin? He's behind this? Why? How?"

"You were driving him crazy," John said simply. "During our interview with him in Berlin, Perlmutter was practically frothing at the mouth when he talked about preserving antiquities. It was as though he had a God-given right to defend them from the barbarians—as defined by him. He is, to put it simply, over the edge. Most of you archaeological types are somewhat demented, you know. Look at the way you and Feisal have been carrying on about the bloody mummy. A sane person wouldn't give a damn what happened to it."

"But Herr Doktor Perlmutter cared," Saida said.

"You prove my point," John said. He looked again at his watch, glanced at the door, and scowled.

"He planned to return it, unhurt," Saida insisted. "We must give him credit for that."

"Credit be damned," Ashraf said furiously. "I will see that he suffers for this, and for his violence against me. I will catch a plane to Berlin tomorrow, after we have returned Tutankhamon to his tomb."

"Forgive me for mentioning," John said, "that you have still to work out how to accomplish the latter. As for Berlin, there is no need. Here he is, in person. Finally," he added in exasperation. "I told him to be here at ten."

All eyes focused on the doorway. "I was detained," Jan said.

He had ruined John's meticulously plotted scenario by failing to appear on cue. The cue being, I presumed, John's smarmy question, "Can't you guess?"

For a criminal who has just been unmasked, Jan looked unnerv-ingly pleased with himself. Silver-gilt curls shining, he moved to-ward a chair. "I could not help overhearing the last part of your conversation," he said coolly. "Your wild accusations are pure fan-tasy, of course."

Ashraf pushed his chair back and surged to his feet, fists clenched. "Coward! You struck me down, from behind. You will pay."

Jan smiled. One could almost hear what he was thinking: These excitable Arabs, they are too emotional to look after their treasures. I wanted to kick Ashraf to shut him up, but I was too far away from him. Schmidt and John were just getting started. How much real evidence they had against Jan I didn't know, but I had a feeling it was flimsy. He would have to be tricked into making a damaging admission. Skilled interrogators know violence is counterproductive in inducing confessions; punching Jan in the chops would only make him mad and reinforce his sense of superiority.

It was good ol' boy Schmidt who took the necessary steps. His shout made the rafters ring.

"Sit down and be quiet!"

Schmidt doesn't exert his authority often, but when he does he is formidable. Ashraf sat down as suddenly as if he had been pushed. If I hadn't already been seated, my knees would have buckled.

"You too," Schmidt went on, glowering at Jan. "Speak only when you are spoken to. I am taking charge of this inquiry and I will brook no interruptions. Yes. That is better. Now, John, proceed with your deductions."

John was still not used to the new Schmidt. Visibly awestruck, he cleared his throat. "As I was saying . . . What was I saying?"

"That all archaeologists are slightly mad," Schmidt prompted.

"Right. Um. Stealing the mummy of Tutankhamon was the sort

of idea that would only have occurred to a monomaniac, someone who placed inordinate value on it and believed that other monomaniacs would share his estimate of its importance. In other words, a psychotic Egyptologist or authority on ancient remains. That ruled out Alan and the gangs of professional thieves. It also indicated that the motive was personal and abnormal rather than financial or political. We had proposed that as one possibility among others, but we had never actually followed through on the idea. I wasted a certain amount of time speculating about a grudge against a specific individual—Ashraf, or Feisal, or me. However, all of us had led blameless lives—"

That was too much for Jan, who had been increasingly maddened by John's use of insulting adjectives. He burst out, "Blameless, you say? You, one of the most notorious . . ."

"Ah," John said. "You knew about me, did you? Make a note of that, Vicky."

"What with?" I asked, looking round for pen and paper.

"I will do it, I will do it," Saida cried. She whipped out her notebook and began scribbling.

"I did know," Jan said. His hands, gripping the arms of the chair, were white-knuckled, but he wasn't ready to concede defeat yet. "During the Trojan Gold affair I spoke with Herr Müller about a mysterious individual who had been an active party in the proceedings and a friend of Vicky's. I had—er—certain government sources available to me, and through them I was able to identify the individual and keep track of his activities. I did so as a precaution, you understand. A criminal of his sort might prove a danger to the museum in future."

"Not a bad recovery," John said judicially. "However, we have now established the fact that you were aware of my former connections.

You made another slip during our conversation at the museum in Berlin. You claimed to be unaware of the existence of the Amarna head, yet according to Alan, he had notified the major museums of its existence."

"His word against mine," Jan said.

"How long have you been in Egypt?"

After John's long-winded exposition, Schmidt's brusque question made Jan start. He took his time about answering. "Two—three days."

"Which?" It was John's turn.

Jan's head turned in his direction. "None of your business."

"It was, in fact, five days ago," Schmidt said. "This has been confirmed by my old friend Wolfgang of the German Institute."

"You had learned from Alan that he was prepared to hand over the mummy in return for the ransom," John said. "You had never intended to do that. You were determined to prevent it at any cost. We know you were at Karnak that night."

Jan's head swiveled back and forth like that of a spectator at a tennis match. The deadly duo didn't give him a chance to reply, just kept hitting him with one accusation after another.

"It wasn't until after you arrived in Egypt that you found out about the murder of Ali and, later, that of the young woman." John took up the tale. Back and forth, back and forth; we were all doing it now. I had a crick in my neck. The only exception was Saida, whose head was bent over her writing. Jan's glance swerved aside, focusing briefly on her before returning to John.

"An honest man, a man of courage and integrity, would have gone immediately to the police. You caved in. You and Alan came to an agreement. He could keep the money, all of it, if he left the mummy to you. You had enough scholarly integrity left to want it kept safe. As you see, your plans for it have been foiled." With a theatrical wave of his hand, John indicated the box that contained the head of Tutankhamon.

Someone laughed. I wasn't the only one who gaped at the box in startled horror. But it wasn't Tut. It was Jan. He had been temporarily shaken by the performance of John and Schmidt but he still had a card up his sleeve, and it was an ace.

"Wrong," he said, leaning back and folding his hands. "My plans, as you choose to call them, are unfolding according to schedule. I presume you were planning to return the mummy secretly to its tomb? It is too late. Last night the press of the world was notified by an anonymous but reliable source that the Supreme Council had allowed Tutankhamon's mummy to be stolen by a gang of common thieves. Representatives of the major news media will shortly arrive in Luxor."

He didn't have to elaborate. I could see it now—the tomb surrounded by clamoring hordes of reporters and cameramen. They couldn't be kept out of the Valley unless it was closed to all visitors, and that move would only increase speculation. And certain people, such as Feisal's jealous subordinate, would be only too happy to talk with the press.

Saida dropped her pen. Ashraf bounded up from his chair. Feisal had turned pale; his lips moved soundlessly.

"So you admit," Schmidt said, in a desperate last-ditch effort, "that you planned the theft of the mummy in order to embarrass the Supreme Council?"

"I admit nothing," Jan said, chin outthrust. "I learned of the theft only recently and felt it my duty to report it. You can prove nothing. And if you attempt to detain me"—he pushed his chair back and stood up—"you will regret it."

Ashraf charged around the table toward Jan. I yelled at him to stop and so did Saida, but he was too infuriated to hear us. Jan snatched up the knife John had placed on the table and scuttled backward.

"Don't touch me," he cried hysterically. "Don't try to stop me."

Ashraf tripped over John's outthrust foot and fell flat.

"You're welcome," John said to Jan. "Go or stay, it's all the same to me."

Eyes bulging, Jan backed toward the door. John twisted a hand in Ashraf's collar, pulled him upright, and slapped him smartly across the cheek.

The slap may not have been necessary; having one's breath cut off has a tendency to decrease belligerence. Ashraf clawed at his collar and John chanted, "'Vicious attack on critic by head of Supreme Council.' Is that what you want to see in tomorrow's newspapers, Ashraf?"

Jan turned and ran. He didn't even stop long enough to brush the dust off his jacket.

"Let him go," John said, keeping a firm grip on Ashraf.

"We're doomed," Feisal said hollowly. "Damn you, Johnny, you expected this."

"Didn't you?" John allowed a touch of exasperation to enter his voice. "Weren't you listening to me? This is what Perlmutter wanted—publicity. He wouldn't have dared walk in here today unless he had already taken steps to achieve it."

"Then why the charade?" Feisal demanded. "Why did you and Schmidt waste all that time interrogating him when you knew he had already won?"

John lowered his eyes. His long lashes—one of his best features, as he knows—caught the light in a golden shimmer. "It was fun," he said.

Schmidt chuckled. "We had him worried for a while."

"He's not worried now," Feisal muttered. He hid his face in his hands. "We're doomed."

"Not necessarily," John said.

The light of hope dawned, touchingly, on several faces. Ashraf's was not one of them.

"What can we do?" he demanded, his tie askew and his hair ruffled. "The bastard is right, we can't drive into the Valley and unload the pieces of Tutankhamon under the very noses of the press. Even if we could barricade the approach to the tomb and keep reporters at bay, someone would see what we were doing . . . Some enterprising pressman would bribe a guard to let him pass . . . One photograph would be enough."

"You're thinking," John said approvingly. "Good. However, you are on the wrong track. It seems to me that there is only one way out of your little dilemma."

There was room in the limo for all of us, though we had to squeeze up a bit because the seventh passenger occupied so much space. Ashraf had insisted on putting the boxes in proper order, in a single layer, so that we could keep them from being joggled. John sat on one side of them and Feisal on the other. I'd seen too many pictures of the naked mummy; it didn't require much stretch of the imagination to picture it side by side with John and Feisal, like those grisly royal effigies at Saint Denis—you know the ones I mean, the king robed and crowned in worldly splendor lying next to a naked rotting corpse. "What I am now so you shall be."

Ashraf's first reaction to John's idea had been a shout of incredulous, outraged laughter. Unperturbed, John went on.

"It's about six hundred miles to Cairo. That limo of yours should be able to make it before dawn if we start right away."

Half convinced, half aghast, Ashraf said, "And then what?"

"If you haven't the authority to get into the museum before hours, no one has. Once he's there, who is going to confess he hasn't been there all along? And who would have the audacity to call you a liar if you say he has been?"

Feisal started to his feet and began pacing. "That's right," he said excitedly. "It would explain everything. The van was an official vehicle, sent by you—"

"To rescue the king from his insalubrious surroundings," Schmidt broke in.

"As I demanded," Saida added, her eyes sparkling.

"And as Ashraf had already decided was right and proper," John said smoothly. "He intended it to be a delightful surprise for critics past and potential—and a nice little publicity stunt. Perlmutter has played right into your hands with his pathetic accusations. Let them burgeon and bloom. When you put Tut on public display, you'll have every media outlet in the world begging for an interview, and Perlmutter will look like a jealous, spiteful fool."

Ashraf's face took on the dreamy expression of an unwilling dieter being presented with a large, thickly iced chocolate cake. "But how . . . Do you know how much those climate-controlled cases in the royal mummy room cost—how long it takes to construct one? We haven't any extras. I can't display Tutankhamon in a crude wooden box."

"Move one of the other kings temporarily," I suggested. "Thutmose the Third, maybe. He looks like a man with a sense of humor."

My little touch of levity was ignored as it deserved to be. "It could work," Feisal said.

"It is brilliant," Saida declared. "It must work!"

We were under way in less than two hours. Ashraf dismissed his driver with plane fare back to Cairo. It wouldn't be the first time he had taken a notion to drive himself. We collected our luggage from the hotel and Schmidt loaded the car with food and drink and a few other comforts I didn't notice until I got in the vehicle. I don't know how he smuggled blankets and pillows out without being seen, but I feel sure he left money to pay for them—probably more than they were worth. Infected by the general hubbub, I trotted back and forth without accomplishing very much; at one point I found myself heading for the lift carrying one shopping bag that contained my galabiya—an item which I sincerely hoped I wouldn't need. The only person who didn't join in the flurry of activity was, of course, John. Leaning against the limo, he made an occasional suggestion.

Ashraf settled himself behind the wheel, pulled on a pair of expensive leather driving gloves, and drew himself up like a ship's captain on the poop deck, or wherever it is captains stand. Schmidt was in the front seat next to him, Saida and I in the tonneau with the boys, living and dead.

"Fasten your seat belts," Ashraf intoned.

I added mentally, "We are about to take off." Hastily I complied. Knowing Ashraf as I had come to, I figured we were in for a rough ride.

As we pulled away from the hotel, another vehicle swung in ahead of us—a dark unmarked car that, despite its lack of official markings, had the unmistakable look of an official vehicle. "What's that?" I demanded, leaning forward. "I thought we wanted to avoid being conspicuous."

"Ashraf always travels with an escort," Feisal muttered.

"We need to get through the checkpoints without being delayed," John said. "I presume you've called ahead?"

"Yes, yes," said Schmidt, already on his cell phone. "They know we are coming."

Everybody knew we were coming. The escorting vehicle began sounding its horn. Cops stopped traffic at intersections. Cars and carriages tried to pull to the side. Sometimes they succeeded, sometimes they didn't. Our caravan swerved around them. At least I think it did. I didn't hear any screams. I could hear Schmidt babbling away on his phone, and Ashraf commenting unfavorably on the skills of other drivers. I tried to close my eyes, but they wouldn't stay shut. The columns of Luxor Temple were far behind us. Karnak's pylons came into view and vanished. The approach to the Nile bridge whizzed by. Then we were out of Luxor and on the road northward.

Ten hours. Assuming nothing happened, like a flat tire or running out of gas or hitting a camel. I should probably explain to those who have never driven in Egypt that camels weren't the only local hazard. The road from Luxor to Cairo is two lanes most of the way, and it isn't well maintained. Potholes and ruts abound, trucks and buses do not yield the right of way. Possibly the greatest hazard is the Egyptian driver himself. If he wants to pass he does, even when there is another car coming straight at him. Usually there's enough room on either side for the vehicles legitimately occupying their respective lanes to edge over far enough to let him through. Usually.

It was all coming back to me. I wished it hadn't.

"Fond memories?" John inquired softly. He is only too adept at reading my mind.

"Not so fond."

"Quite. Look on the bright side. Instead of occupying an antique vehicle held together by wire and prayer, you are traveling in style and comfort. Instead of taking desperate measures to avoid checkpoints and hotly pursuing antagonists, we're on a straight shot to Cairo. Instead of Feisal driving, we have—" He broke off with a grunt as Ashraf pulled suddenly onto the shoulder to avoid an oncoming truck which was in our lane passing a taxi. "Well, perhaps Ashraf isn't that much of an improvement."

"I resent that," said Feisal, from the other side of Tut. He sounded fairly cheerful, however, perhaps because he and Saida were snuggled close together.

"Pleasantly cramped quarters, aren't they?" John inquired. "Have a pillow."

"Or a little hay," I murmured. "It's very good when you're feeling faint."

I tried to follow his advice and concentrate on the bright side, but those grisly memories kept recurring. Just John and me and Feisal that time, John barely functioning after the rough handling he had endured, Feisal jittery as a nervous virgin, Schmidt's whereabouts unknown and a source of nagging worry.

This was definitely better.

It was still daylight when we reached Nag Hammadi and crossed the river to the West Bank. I remembered Nag Hammadi from that first trip. We had never made it across the river, but had had to take off on a mad ride along the East Bank road and through the desert wadis.

"We'll fill up with petrol here," Ashraf announced. "Make use of the facilities, ladies, if you like, but don't linger to paint your faces."

"How are you doing?" Saida asked, linking her arm in mine.

I thought about the question, while we made use. "I don't know," I said honestly. "Everything has happened so fast. This is crazy, you know."

"It's exciting," Saida said happily. "Your John is an amazing man. Is he always this imaginative?"

"That's one word for it."

"Feisal is not." Saida peered into a smeary mirror and took out her lipstick. "But I love him anyhow."

She didn't appear to be in a hurry, so I leaned against the wall and watched her carefully apply fresh makeup. Painting my face was the least of my concerns at the moment.

"I hope you didn't take John's remarks about demented archaeologists personally," I said. "He was just baiting Perlmutter."

"No, he meant it," Saida said coolly. "He lacks the scientific mind. It is very important that Tutankhamon's body survive. Without it the king cannot attain immortality."

"I was under the impression that a statue or painting or even a name could substitute for the physical body. If that's so, Tut—excuse me, Tutankhamon—has a better chance of survival than anyone in history. There must be thousands of images of his mummy and tens of thousands of reproductions of his coffins, his mask, and his statues scattered around the world."

"That is so," Saida admitted. She put her lipstick away and took out an eyebrow pencil. "But I am not certain that they count."

While I was considering this remark and wondering whether she was serious, a fist pounded on the door and Feisal yelled, "Come out of there. We're ready to go."

Saida winked at me. "He enjoys being masterful. It does no harm to let men believe that they are in control, so long as we decide the important matters."

We piled back into the car and rearranged Tut. The last of the light was fading as we headed north. Schmidt began opening containers of various foodstuffs which were, of course, in the front with him. He passed back pieces of chicken, eggs, oranges, and other items.

"I'm not hungry," I said wanly. I remembered, only too well, what it was like driving in Egypt after dark. People don't use their headlights except when they are approaching another car. That sudden burst of brilliance out of the dark is very unnerving until you get used to it—which I never had.

"Eat," Schmidt insisted. "You will need your strength."

"I hope not."

The swollen crimson orb of the sun descended with slow dignity; crimson and purple streamers spread out across the west. The first stars twinkled shyly in the darkening sky. We were going at a good clip, passing buses and trucks. Ashraf was eating a chicken leg and talking on his cell phone.

That left, if my arithmetic was correct, no hands for the wheel.

Knowing it was in vain, I called out, "Ashraf, why don't you let Schmidt make the calls for you?"

"I am telephoning my subordinates," Ashraf said stiffly. "Ordering them to meet me at the museum. Even the great Herr Doktor Professor Schmidt cannot do that."

John let out a breath of laughter that tickled my ear. "A-to-Z Schmidt, the greatest swordsman in Europe. It will take Ashraf a while to get over that."

We slid through another checkpoint, slowing down just long enough for Ashraf to stick his head out the window and bark at the guards, then picked up speed again. Schmidt offered me an orange. Darkness was complete and Ashraf was driving like a NASCAR racer, weaving in and out of semi-visible traffic and singing one of those Arabic songs that wavers up and down the scale. I dropped the orange peel onto the floor. I am going to mess up Ashraf's beautiful car, I thought, and when we get to Cairo I am going to kill him.

I woke up when we stopped for gas.

"Where are we?" I asked, blinking at the lights.

"Minya," Feisal said. "We're making good time."

"Last stop before Cairo," Saida said. She untangled herself from Feisal and hopped lithely out of the car. I followed, not lithely. When we got to Cairo I was going to kill her too. I was as stiff as—well, as a mummy.

The stop was brief. The interminable ride continued. I couldn't stay awake, but I couldn't really sleep either. Bursts of light from approaching cars turned onto oncoming freight trains and dragons shooting flame. Somebody was laughing. Not the dragons, not dead kings. I recognized Schmidt's guffaws. He must be telling jokes. He always laughs louder at his own jokes than anyone else does.

I came to full awareness when a different kind of light impinged on my eyelids. My head was on John's shoulder and his arm was around me. When I stirred he said, "My arm's gone numb."

"All of me has gone numb. Especially my derriere. Remove your damned arm, then."

"As soon, my darling, as you remove your lovely head."

I struggled upright and stared out the window. "We're here. We're in Cairo!"

"Ah," said Schmidt, turning his head around as far as it would go. "You are awake."

"We're here. We made it!"

Great cities never sleep. The lights along the corniche blazed bright, and although the traffic wasn't as heavy as it was during the day, there were people abroad, going home after a night of merriment or heading for work, even at that ungodly hour. The facade of the Cairo Museum shone like raspberry ice. Ashraf headed straight for the heavy wrought-iron gates. They parted and swung slowly back.

The moment the car stopped, one of the doors of the building opened. Several men hurried out and converged on Ashraf. They began talking excitedly. They spoke Arabic but the gist of their remarks was clear. "What the hell is going on?"

Whatever Ashraf said, it was said with enough force to send them scurrying back into the museum. "Get him out and inside," Ashraf ordered, turning to us. He took the lead, picking up one of the boxes. (Half a torso, I think.) Feisal and Schmidt followed suit and so did Saida, cradling the box that held Tut's head tenderly in her arms. Ashraf indicated the last two boxes and barked, "Take his legs."

"Aren't you coming?" John asked me.

I swung my own legs up onto the seat. "I'm going to take a real nap. Wake me when it's over."

It felt wonderful to stretch out. I kicked off my shoes and wriggled my toes luxuriously. Instead of dozing off, I lay there staring dreamily at the facade of the museum. I had been involved in a lot of peculiar situations, but this one was in a class by itself. What was I doing here? I asked myself. In front of the Cairo Museum at four o'clock in the morning, aiding and abetting a trio of demented Egyptologists who were piecing together a dead, dismembered king. What was Tutankhamon to me, or I to him, that I should care about him? I did care, though. Witness the pronouns: I had come to think of that withered mummy as "him," instead of "it."

Some good had come of the adventure. John was in the clear, and we were rid forever of Suzi. Schmidt had turned his back on her when she offered her hand and an apology. Feisal and Saida were headed for the altar. Jan Perlmutter was going to get a well-deserved comeuppance. He might even be blackmailed into sending Nefertiti home. I pictured him stuffed and stuck up on a plinth in his own museum, with a sign saying, "The man who lost Nefertiti."

The sky began to lighten. The sunrise wasn't spectacular; Cairo smog is too thick. A head appeared at the window, and a voice said, "Wake up, Vicky. You must see this."

"I wasn't asleep," I croaked. "What time is it?"

"Seven A.M." Saida opened the door. "Come quickly, it is a sight you will never forget. You will be among the first to see it."

The royal mummy room was softly lit except for a spotlight focused on one of the glass cases. Men in white lab coats with surgical masks covering their mouths hovered over it, making the final adjustments. The masks seemed extraneous, considering what Tutankhamon had been through, but they looked professional. Schmidt and John and Feisal stood to one side looking on.

"Did you have a good sleep?" John asked, putting his arm around me.

"I wasn't asleep."

Thutmose III was still grinning. They must have removed one of the lesser royals in order to accommodate Tut.

The technicians stepped back and there he was. He looked quite peaceful. Like the other mummies, he was decently covered, from chin to ankles. The fabric was brownish and old; Saida had told us that the museum authorities had used ancient linen. Folds of the fabric concealed the fact that his head wasn't attached to his body.

"That's it," one of the technicians said, on a long breath. He spoke English, out of deference to the ignoramuses in the room, and the conversation continued in that language.

Ashraf stepped up to the case and stared into it. "Satisfactory," he said. "Now listen, and listen carefully. I have called a press conference, to be held here in the museum at ten A.M. I will announce that the king's mummy has been here for more than a week, in the laboratory, while we prepared a place for him. After he has rested in the museum for a time, he will return to his tomb in a properly constructed, scientifically designed case like this one. You will avoid reporters at all costs. If you should be questioned, you will repeat the story I have just told. I need not explain what the consequences will be should you deviate from it. Is that understood?"

Nods and sycophantish murmurs of agreement acknowledged understanding. Ashraf had expected no less. With a regal wave of his hand he dismissed the technicians.

"So," he said, rubbing his hands together. "All is in order."

"Except for Tut's other hand," I said, suppressing a yawn.

"It will be restored when convenient. Is there anything else?"

What he meant was, had he overlooked anything important? He looked inquiringly at Schmidt.

"I think not" was the judicious reply.

I gave Tut one last fond look, and we straggled out of the museum, leaving several of the guards—who had been, I assumed, promised the same fate as the technicians if they were tempted to spill the beans—to close the place up. Ashraf was kind enough to offer us a ride to our hotel.

"Have we got a room?" I asked, more in hope than in expectation.

"Aber natürlich," said Schmidt. "I telephoned last night."

"Any news from the Valley of the Kings?" John inquired.

Ashraf laughed fiendishly. "The journalists were informed last night that I would be giving a press conference today. Some won't be able to reach Cairo in time. They will be scooped, as the saying goes, by others."

Schmidt's room was waiting for him, but—the manager informed us, cringing—ours would not be ready until noon. "It does not matter," Schmidt said. "None of us wishes to sleep."

"Speak for yourself," I said.

"But we must attend the press conference."

"Not me. I've seen enough of Tutankhamon to last the rest of my life."

Leaving the others congratulating themselves and drinking coffee, I threw myself down on Schmidt's big soft king-size bed and fell asleep. When I woke up, sunlight brightened the room and Jan Perlmutter was standing in the open doorway.

Fifteen

He hadn't shaved. His clothes were wrinkled and his face was that of an old man. His tie was twisted and the top button of his shirt undone, as if he couldn't get enough air.

"Where is he?" he demanded. Even his voice was unrecognizable, hoarse and broken.

"Who?"

It was the best I could come up with on short notice. I looked from the knife in Jan's hand to the telephone on the bedside table.

"Don't try it," he said. "Where is Schmidt?"

I gave up the idea of trying to reach the phone. My brain was in overdrive, all remnants of sleep dispersed. There's nothing like terror to promote quick thinking. Unfortunately I couldn't think of anything heroic, or even useful.

"Why are you mad at Schmidt?" I asked, stalling for time.

"He hates me," Jan said.

"No, no," I said soothingly. "He doesn't hate you. Nobody hates you. Why don't you sit down and—"

"They all hate me. They have made me look like a fool. Schmidt is the worst. He has held a grudge since the Trojan Gold affair."

I sneaked a quick look at the clock on the bedside table. Almost noon. Where was everybody? They ought to be back by now. Why had they left me alone with a homicidal lunatic?

Jan went on ranting. All he had ever wanted was to rescue the world's treasures. And this was his reward—to be humiliated and abused and threatened.

He was the one doing the threatening, but I decided not to mention that. Nor did I point out that to the best of my knowledge he hadn't been named as the source of the rumors about the theft of Tut. We had discussed exposing him and decided, regretfully, that proving the accusation would be time-consuming if not impossible. He would suffer enough, said Schmidt, from knowing he had been foiled and defeated.

"How did you find out?" I asked. "You clever man," I added.

Jan blinked and stared at me as if he had forgotten I was there. "Find out . . . Oh." He passed his hand over his mouth. When he replied, he sounded almost rational. "I flew to Cairo last night. The news of the press conference was on the radio and television this morning. They were speculating, some of the announcers, about the return of Tutankhamon."

So somebody had been unable to resist spreading the news. It was only to be expected.

"I couldn't believe it," Jan said in an aggrieved voice. "So I telephoned at once to Luxor, to the German Institute, to Wolfgang Muhlendorfer. He informed me that most of the journalists had left the Valley and that Dr. Khifaya's limousine had been observed leaving Luxor in haste and with many people in the vehicle. Even then

I did not believe it, not until I saw the press conference itself, and heard Khifaya boasting, telling a pack of lies . . . And Schmidt, in the background, smiling and stroking his absurd mustache . . ."

His voice had soared into the high pitch of hysteria.

"Ashraf picketed the museum too," I said, hoping to distract Jan from Schmidt. No good.

"Khifaya behaved with dignity. But Schmidt! Prancing up and down with that appalling banner, shouting rude slogans, handing out wurst to the spectators, like a circus clown . . . It was all on the television, and me, hiding behind a column like a frightened rabbit. He made me a laughing stock."

"I was there too," I said.

"*Aber natürlich.* You would obey your superior."

And I was a lowly woman. It was insulting but reassuring to hear Jan dismiss me so cavalierly. I didn't think he would attack me unless I did something drastic. My body didn't believe it. My mouth was dry and my heart was racing.

"Why isn't he here?" Jan demanded. "The press conference ended an hour ago."

"I expect he's on his way." I had to think of something quick, before Schmidt walked in. "Tell you what, Jan. Why don't you hide in the bathroom. Then, when they get here, you can jump out and surprise everybody!"

Degrees of mania are hard to calculate. Like Hamlet, Jan was only mad north-northwest; he knew a hawk from a handsaw, or, in this case, a helpful suggestion from a really stupid idea.

"And what would you be doing?" His eyes narrowed. "But perhaps if I tied you up and gagged you . . ."

He'd have to put the knife down in order to do that. I had learned a few dirty tricks from John, and Jan had gotten flabby, but he was crazy and I was scared and what if he decided to knock me unconscious or use the knife in ways I didn't want to think about before he . . . The alternative was worse, though. Schmidt, with that knife in his chest.

"Okay," I said.

"You agree too readily," Jan said. "Wait. I have a better idea. I will lock you in the bathroom and conceal myself behind the door."

"Okay."

I slid off the bed and stood up. I felt a little braver now that I was on my feet. I wondered if I could trick him into the bathroom and slam the door. No, that wouldn't work, there was no lock on the outside.

Jan stood back and waved me through the bedroom door as I walked slowly toward him. Maybe I could make it to the door of the suite before he . . . No, that wouldn't work either. He was so close behind me that I could feel his breath on the back of my neck. Let him shut me in the bathroom, lock the door, and start yelling? No good. He'd be on Schmidt the second the outer door opened, before anyone heard my screams or understood what they meant.

The decision was taken out of my hands. There was no warning, not even the sound of voices. The door swung open. As I had expected, Schmidt was the first to enter. Make way for Schmidt, the greatest swordsman in Europe! He stopped in the doorway, petrified and gaping. John and Feisal were behind him.

Jan shoved me aside and started for Schmidt. John tried to push Schmidt out of the way, but the solid shape of Schmidt only swayed a little. I was past thinking, I just planted my feet and grabbed hold of Jan's arm. He swung around.

Something hard, like a fist, hit me in the side. It knocked the breath out of me for a second or two, and then I saw that Jan was on the floor, arms and legs thrashing, as Feisal tried to subdue him.

John, who didn't believe in hand-to-hand combat, put an end to it by kicking Jan in the head.

Schmidt was still on his feet, but he was very pale. I tried to ask him if he was okay, but my voice didn't seem to be functioning. They were all staring at me. John came toward me, stepping as delicately as a cat in a puddle, his hands reaching. His face had gone as white as Schmidt's.

"Easy," he said. "Don't move. Let me . . ."

Three words. That was all I needed, three little words. I tried to say them. Then the lights went out.

I came to in a strange room. I lay still, wondering why I felt so peculiar and trying to figure out where I was. Out of the corner of my eye I saw a window. It was dark outside. The room was dimly lit. There was a funny smell. Several funny smells, actually. Not disgusting smells, just . . . funny.

I turned my head. The first thing I saw was a chair next to the bed, and someone sitting in it. Someone familiar. He looked very uncomfortable, slumped over, arms dangling, head bowed.

The name came back to me. "John?" somebody said. The voice didn't sound like mine.

John sat up with a start. "You're awake."

"No, I'm not. I'm not even here. I don't know where I am."

"Shh." He slid from the chair, onto his knees beside the bed. "You're going to be all right."

"I want a drink."

"No drink, not even water for a while. Have a bit of ice."

He slipped a sliver into my dry mouth. It dissolved like the nectar of Paradise.

"I'm in a hospital," I said. "More ice. You look terrible."

"So do you. Here, open your mouth."

A door opened and somebody came in. I deduced that she was a nurse, on account of her wearing a nurse's uniform. She did nurse's things, smiled a professional nurse's smile, and went away.

"How do you feel?" John asked. He grimaced. "Why do people ask imbecile questions like that, I wonder."

"I feel like hell. What happened?"

"You're supposed to rest."

"I've been resting. Why don't you sit in that chair?"

"I'm not sure I can stand up. My knees feel like Schmidt's."

"Have you been here since . . . Since when?"

"Since they brought you in. A little after midday."

"What time is it now?"

"Night," John said briefly.

"I want to know what happened."

I hadn't fully realized how drawn his face was until he smiled. "You sound almost yourself again. In a nutshell, Jan Perlmutter is locked up in a psychiatric ward, under guard, and Schmidt is fine. You probably saved his life—and lost your spleen in the process."

"Is that an organ I can do without?"

"Generally speaking, yes. Anything else you want to know? You are supposed to be resting."

"I want to know lots of things."

He reacted to that harmless statement as if I had told a bad joke. Covering his face with his hands, he sat back onto his heels. His shoulders shook.

"Are you laughing?" I demanded.

"No," John said in a muffled voice.

"Oh."

After a few moments he took his hands away from his face. His eyes were wet.

I had never seen him cry. I didn't think he could. I didn't know what to say.

He took hold of my hand. "Schmidt and Feisal and Saida are in the waiting room. I'm supposed to tell them when you wake up."

"Send 'em in," I said grandly. "We'll have a party."

"You're doped up to your eyeballs," John said, shaking his head. "No party, not yet."

"Stop squeezing my hand, it hurts. Can't you just enclose it tenderly in your long, strong fingers, like heroes in books?"

His face lit up. "You *are* going to be all right. You sound like your normal, rude self. Do you know what you said, just before you keeled over?"

"Three little words," I murmured.

"Three little words, yes. Words you fought a deadly injury to utter. Could they have been 'I love you'?"

"I don't think so."

"You said," John snapped, " 'Elizabeth of Austria.' Why did you say 'Elizabeth of Austria'?"

"I remember now," I said drowsily. The shot the nurse had given me was beginning to take effect. "You remember her, the empress of Austria back in 1890 something . . . She got stabbed by an anarchist, he'd probably be called a terrorist these days, and then she went on walking for, gee, I forget how long, before she collapsed, because she thought he had just punched her in the side, and that was what it felt like, and I thought I should tell you that that was what it felt like, in case you didn't notice—"

"A knife sticking out of your side? I noticed."

"I love you."

He leaned closer. "What was that?"

"I said . . . I don't remember."

319

"Coward. I love you too. Go to sleep." He enclosed my hand tenderly in his long, strong fingers.

Six weeks later. Munich.

John came down the stairs, with Clara draped over his shoulder. Caesar, lying beside the couch on which I reclined, jumped up with a howl and dashed toward them.

"Stop that, you idiot dog," I said. "You saw him ten minutes ago, before he went upstairs."

Caesar stopped and thought it over. Then he came back and lay down again.

"Schmidt is on his way here," John reported. "He's bringing dinner."

"He's brought dinner almost every day. I'm getting fat."

"Maybe you ought to get more exercise."

"I don't feel up to it yet." I leaned back against the cushions and tried to look like Camille.

John wasn't looking too healthy himself. His Egyptian tan had faded and he had lost weight. As soon as I was able to travel, we had returned to Munich. John had made a couple of flying trips to London, leaving at dawn and getting back by midnight, leaving Schmidt to fuss over me. The shop was closed until he found a replacement for Alan. I knew he was losing business, not to mention money. Jen had been driving him up the wall, demanding to know what he was doing and why he wasn't in London. When he explained I had had a serious accident and he was looking after me, she had offered to come and play nurse—an offer that almost brought on a relapse.

I was being unfair and selfish. The truth was that I liked having him around, bringing me things, walking the dog, doing the washing up. We argued all the time and fought some of the time. I liked that, too.

Alan had died without recovering consciousness. Schmidt had wallowed in self-reproach when he heard, but taking care of me cheered him up, and the news from Egypt was balm to his wounded soul. The news from Berlin was even balmier. Jan Perlmutter had resigned from his position. The museum tried to hush up the details, but Schmidt's gossips had told him that Jan was locked up in a maximum-security psychiatric institution. He kept telling the attendants he was King Tutankhamon and demanding that they kneel when they addressed him. I failed to feel sorry for him. The people I felt sorry for were innocent victims like Ali and his grieving mother. We would never know whether Ali had gone to the expedition house as part of his normal custodial duties, or whether he had had a sudden inspiration. It didn't matter, not to him. He was dead because he had tried to do his duty. His family would be taken care of, at any rate. Schmidt had seen to that.

Tutankhamon's triumphant appearance at the Cairo Museum had been featured in the media for days. Ashraf had wrung every ounce of publicity out of it. Privately he had apologized for being unable to give us rewards, medals, and universal acclaim; but that, as he pointed out, would have necessitated making the whole embarrassing affair public.

"That seems to be the story of my life," John had remarked caustically. "The next time I become involved in a case like this I shall demand to be paid in advance."

It had had its moments, though.

"Why didn't you ever tell me you were related to the world's most famous family of archaeologists?" I asked. "Professor Emerson and his wife dominated Egyptology for over half a century!"

Hands in his pockets, shoulders hunched, John stood looking

out the window. He didn't turn around. "I and about eighty other people."

"Surely not that many."

"Look it up. They had only one child, but he had three, and their descendants bred like rabbits. I'm not even in the direct line; I'm descended from their younger granddaughter. That and two pounds ten, as the saying goes, is good for a cup of coffee at any Starbucks."

"Be blasé if you want to. I'm impressed. Amelia P. Emerson is one of my heroines. It was their house we were in, their things we saw. Her legendary parasol, his knife—"

"According to tradition, the knife and the swords belonged to their son."

"But he was a scholar, not a soldier. Degrees from all sorts of places, dozens of books to his credit."

"There are a lot of stories about Ramses Emerson, as he was called," John said. "Some almost certainly apocryphal . . . Never mind my damned ancestors, Vicky, I have to talk to you about something important."

"Okay."

He turned around, opened his mouth, closed it, coughed, and then said, "Would you like a drink?"

"No, thanks."

"I think I will, if you don't mind."

"Go right ahead."

He took his time about mixing it. Here it comes, I thought. Anytime John needed liquor to strengthen his nerve, the news was going to be bad.

He sat down in a chair next to the couch and cleared his throat. Suzi had managed to get the goods on him after all? He was dead broke and had decided to go back into his old business? Jen was on her way to Munich? When he came out with it, I was caught completely off guard.

"You want to have a child."

"I do?"

"I saw it in your face, when you were working on that pathetic baby cap."

"You did?"

"I lack the qualifications for being a proper father."

"You do?"

"That being the case," John said, taking a deep breath, "the only decent thing is for me to get out of your life so you can get on with it."

I sat up straight, yelped, and clutched at my side. "Are you dumping me, you rat?"

John's face turned red. The color contrasted nicely with his cornflower-blue eyes. "Bloody hell," he shouted, "it is impossible to carry on a reasonable conversation with you."

"You weren't being reasonable, you were being noble," I growled. "It doesn't become you. Be yourself."

"Be myself." The angry color faded from his face. His mouth twitched. "I'm over my ears in debt. My business is failing. Another situation like the last one may arise at any moment, without the slightest warning."

"Go on," I said encouragingly.

"Isn't that enough? Oh, all right. My mother is a consummate nuisance. She will never love you. After four weeks in your company I have lost my command of proper English syntax. Do you want to get married, or what?"

"Are you proposing, or what?" My face opened in a big, silly grin.

"According to family tradition, it's the woman who does the proposing."

"The tradition ends here."

"Oh, hell." He dropped to one knee next to the couch and clasped his hands over his heart. "Will you marry me?"

Mouth open, tongue lolling, Caesar looked adoringly at him.

"Not you," John told him. "Vicky?"

It might not be the high point of my life, but it came close.

"I'll think about it," I said.